... a pseudonym before
... ume using her own name.

As a committed Christian and passionate animal-lover
Rita has a full and busy life, but her writing continues
to be a consuming pleasure that she never tires of. In
any spare moments she loves reading, walking her
beloved, elderly dog, eating out and visiting the cinema
and theatre, as well as being involved in her local church
and animal welfare.

Rita Bradshaw's earlier sagas, *Alone Beneath the Heaven,
Reach for Tomorrow, Ragamuffin Angel, The Stony Path, The
Urchin's Song, Candles in the Storm, The Most Precious
Thing* and *Always I'll Remember*, are also available from
Headline.

THE RAINBOW YEARS

Rita Bradshaw

First published in 2006
by HEADLINE BOOK PUBLIS

First published in paperback in
by HEADLINE BOOK PUBLIS

headline

naw

as the Author of rdance with the t 1988.

HING

2006
HING

0 7553 2711 X (ISBN-10)
978 0 7553 2711 9 (ISBN-13)

Typeset in Bembo by Palimpsest Book Production Limited, Polmont, Stirlingshire

Printed and bound in Great Britain by Mackays of Chatham plc, Chatham, Kent

Headline's policy is to use papers that are natural, renewable and recyclable products and made from wood grown in sustainable forests. The logging and manufacturing processes are expected to conform to the environmental regulations of the country of origin.

HEADLINE BOOK PUBLISHING
A division of Hodder Headline
338 Euston Road
London NW1 3BH

www.headline.co.uk
www.hodderheadline.com

This book is for my darling husband who has shared all the clouds of grey as well as the rainbows with me, and who never tells me to pull myself together when my emotional side goes into hyperdrive. A rare quality in a man!

Acknowledgements

Many thanks to my dear mum and late dad for all their memories of the hard but strangely warming years of the Second World War, when everyone pulled together in a way we only catch a glimpse of now and again these days. Research material is invaluable when writing a story of this nature, which spans nearly four decades of radical change. It would be impossible to list all my resources but those below have been of special help.

Memories of Sunderland, True North Books
Life in Britain Between the Wars, L.C.B. Seaman
Our Wartime Days: The WAAF in World War II, Squadron Leader Beryl E. Escott
Bader's Tangmere Spitfires, Dilip Sarker
Fighter Pilots of the RAF 1939–45, Chaz Bowyer
History of the RAF, Chaz Bowyer
Shot Down in Flames, Geoffrey Page DSO, OBE, DFC, BAR
Sunderland's Blitz, Kevin Brady

Author's Note

The districts where the air raids occurred in Sunderland have not been strictly adhered to.

Contents

Covet not the choicest blessings,
A life of sunshine and blue skies,
Nor yet the road that others take
Which beckons by and by.
But look to see the rainbow
Behind the clouds of grey,
Desire to find the wisdom
That enriches on life's way,
And when the storms are over
And new dawns begin to break,
The rainbows of tomorrow
Will find you in their wake.

Anonymous

PART ONE

1916 A Fine Dividing Line

Chapter 1

'You all right, Bess?'

'Aye.'

'You don't look it. Is . . . is it bad news, lass?'

'Aye.' There was a long pause and then Bess Shawe forced herself to say, 'Christopher's dead. Bought it the first day of the Somme.' Nearly two months and she hadn't known, hadn't felt it.

'Oh, Bess.' Kitty Price wanted to put her arms round her friend but they didn't do things like that. Awkwardly now she sucked in her thin lips, rubbing at her snub of a nose before she said, 'My da says the old generals want stringing up by their boots for the mess they're making of the war. Slaughter of the innocent, he calls it.' Then realising she was being less than tactful, she added, 'But you know what my da's like. Opinion about everything from clarts to carlings, he's got, whether he knows owt about it or not. Drives Mam mad.'

Bess closed her eyes for a moment, shutting out the face

of her friend – the friend who was more like a sister, the pair of them having lived next door to each other all their lives. He was dead. Christopher was dead. But more than that, he had a wife and child he had never let on about.

She crumpled the letter in her fingers. Opening her eyes she saw Kitty's anxious expression and after exhaling slowly, she said, 'Don't worry, I'm all right. Look, thank your Elsie for letting me use her address for the letters and tell her there won't be any more. I'm going for a walk, I want to be on my own for a bit.'

'You sure you don't want me to come, lass?'

Bess nodded, not trusting herself to speak. Kitty's concern was warming but weakening; another moment or so and she would be blubbing out the fix she was in and she couldn't do that. No one must know, no one. Her da would kill her if he found out. Oh, Christopher, Christopher, you can't be dead. You can't. You mustn't leave me like this. And then her stomach swirled and she tasted the acidic burning of bile on her tongue. She swallowed, telling herself she couldn't be sick, not here, not now. She had to get herself away somewhere quiet, somewhere where she could sit and *think*.

The two girls were standing on the doorstep of a terraced house and now Bess inclined her head, saying, 'You go back in, Kitty. I'll see you later.' Without waiting for a reply she turned and began to walk swiftly, the letter still clutched in a ball between her fingers.

On leaving Burleigh Street she stepped out into the main thoroughfare of High Street East, narrowly avoiding some foul rotting mess strewn over the pavement. She hated the East End. Her head was spinning and her nose wrinkled with distaste. The smell and dirt tainted everything; the narrow streets with their notorious public houses bordering the docks seemed menacing even in the light of day. How Elsie could bear to live here she didn't know.

And then she caught the thought, biting her lip. Who was she to turn her nose up? Kitty's sister was a respectable married woman with a husband and two bairns; she'd swap places with Elsie tomorrow if she could. In fact she'd be content to live in the worst street in Sunderland, the worst house, *anything*, if only she could turn the clock back to before she'd met Christopher Lyndon.

By the time she turned off the main street into John Street in the heart of Bishopwearmouth, Bess was out of breath. The stitch in her side which had begun some minutes before was excruciating but her rapid steps didn't falter.

The late August afternoon was a hot one and beads of perspiration were on her brow and upper lip under her big straw hat, but now the destination she had in mind, Mowbray Park, was just a minute or two away.

When she entered the park she was barely aware of bairns scampering and mothers pushing perambulators on the path close to the fountain, she just wanted to sit down. Finding a vacant bench she sank down, shutting her eyes for a few moments. Gradually the pain in her side receded and her heart stopped its mad racing. She opened her eyes, still sitting absolutely still as the sights and sounds of a Sunday afternoon registered on her senses.

What was she going to do? She glanced down at the screwed-up letter in her hand and then carefully began to smooth it out on her lap. The black scrawl was authoritative, the contents of the letter more so. Trembling, she read it again.

Dear Miss Shawe,

Your recent communication to Captain Christopher Lyndon has been passed to me by his wife, Mrs Angeline Lyndon, for the courtesy of a reply. My sister-in-law would inform you that her husband was killed on the first day of the Somme. Your letter evidently arrived after this as it was still unopened when returned with his effects. The content of your communication suggests an intimacy with my brother which is totally inappropriate and this has added to the burden of Mrs Lyndon's grief. On top of losing her husband of eight years and the father of her child, she now has to bear the knowledge of his dalliance with a person such as yourself. For my own part I would warn you that if you make any effort to contact Mrs Lyndon in the future, I will place the matter in the hands of the family solicitor. I trust I make myself clear.

It was signed Maurice Lyndon and the last few letters of the signature had driven deep into the paper, as though the writer was possessed of a fury he was finding difficult to restrain.

Christopher married and a father? She gave a little moan and then glanced about quickly in case anyone had heard. But he'd told her he loved her, that she was beautiful and desirable and that when the war was over he'd brave the wrath of his father and marry her. She had understood that for someone of his class to marry someone of hers would be frowned upon, but he'd said that once they could be together all the time and he could be there to protect her

6

from any hostility from his family, he'd make her his wife. And she had believed him.

She bit down hard on the back of her fist to prevent herself moaning out loud again. Now she understood why he'd been so cagey about her meeting any of his friends or writing to his home address. And it had been at his suggestion that she'd arranged for Kitty's sister to receive his letters. He had said that until he could meet her parents and formally ask for her hand it was better to keep things secret in case his father caused a fuss and her parents were offended. In reality, he had been worried that if her da tried to contact him to find out what his intentions were, the truth might have come to light. With the benefit of hindsight it was all suddenly perfectly clear.

Oh Holy Mother, help me in my hour of need. I have sinned, I know I have sinned, but be merciful. Don't let this thing happen to me. And then she stopped the silent gabbling as it dawned on her what she was asking for. Why would the Holy Mother grant a petition to end the life of this baby growing inside her when it was innocent of all wrong? She was the guilty one and she would have to suffer the consequences of her sin.

Three times Christopher had taken her, only three times, but then once was enough, she knew that. Look at Gladys Blackett. Her Shane had had to leave for the front straight after their wedding night and had been blown to smithereens within the week, but nine months later Gladys had produced a bouncing baby boy. A gift from God to comfort her in her loss, all the neighbours had said, and wasn't the bairn the very image of his da? Those selfsame women in the streets here around would brand her a scarlet woman and her baby a flyblow, and they would be watching it as it grew, to seize on any likeness they could pin on some poor man or other they had no liking for.

She couldn't have it. She glanced about her wildly as though the beautiful summer afternoon would produce a solution. She'd have to do something, take something. She'd heard the talk amongst some of the women in the munitions factory who were no better than they should be. But how could she confide in any of them? A quiver passed over her face. She'd have to, there was nothing else for it. They might be a bit rough round the edges but they were kind enough on the whole. Her da wouldn't have her bringing the shame of a bastard into the family, he'd kill her first.

She shut her eyes again, seeing Christopher's handsome face and deep blue eyes under a shock of rich brown hair on the screen of her mind. It had been six months ago, on the eve of her eighteenth birthday, when she had first seen Captain Christopher Lyndon. She and Kitty had recently started work at the munitions factory and the one pound seventeen and six a week they were earning was four times as much as the wage they'd had as parlourmaids since leaving school. So to celebrate her impending birthday they'd decided to treat themselves to a cream tea at Binns. In the doorway she had collided with a tall, handsome man in uniform and dropped the packages she'd been carrying.

He had insisted on buying them tea and cakes in reparation, and then walking them most of the way home to Deptford Road bordering the Wear Glass Works where her father worked. And she had known straight off it was her he was interested in, not Kitty. Something had happened to her that afternoon when he had first smiled at her and she hadn't

8

been the same since. She'd been head over heels, crazily in love. And that was her only excuse, she told herself bitterly. She had been crazy, mad to let him do what he'd done. He'd been her first lad, though, and she hadn't known what it was all about the first time till it was over. And then she'd cried and he'd held her close and told her it was all right and he loved her like she'd never be loved again . . .

After each time, her conscience had seared her like a branding iron but in spite of her shame she hadn't dared to go to confession. She knew the priest was supposed to forget the secrets he was told the minute he stepped out of the dark box, but somehow she wasn't sure she quite believed it. And the thought of remaining unclean wasn't as terrifying as the possibility her da might find out what she'd done. In spite of what her da was like, he was on good terms with Father Fraser; butter wouldn't melt in his mouth when the Father called round the house.

She continued to sit in the sunshine for a long, long time, her head bowed and her eyes staring unseeing at the paper on her lap. Eventually she stirred, and then it was to slowly rip the letter into tiny pieces.

She had given Christopher her heart and soul and mind and body, and he'd just been playing with her, leading her on. She couldn't bear it, she wished she could die.

Enough. The word was loud in her mind and she responded to it, straightening her back and raising her head to gaze about her almost defiantly. It had happened and there was no going back. The only question now was how she was going to get rid of the evidence of her foolishness. And that was how she had to think about it. This thing inside her wasn't a baby, not yet, not till it was born and took breath.

She'd missed three monthlies but apart from the odd feeling of queasiness and a consuming tiredness come nightfall there was no physical sign of what had happened to her. Her stomach was as flat as it had ever been. But that wouldn't continue for much longer.

Bess stood up, letting the fragments of paper shower to the ground like confetti on a wedding day.

But there would be no wedding for her, she thought, beginning to walk along the neatly trimmed path leading out of the park. There never would have been with Christopher and she'd been stupid to believe otherwise. Men like him, privately educated gentlemen who had wealth and influence and ancestry behind them, didn't *marry* working-class girls. Oh, they might toy with them, amuse themselves with such trifles, *dally* with them – her mouth tightened as the word seared her mind – but marriage was kept for the fine ladies of their own class who were used to soft kid slippers and furs.

She wasn't going to cry for him. She passed the museum and library as she left the park but didn't glance at the imposing building, lost as she was in her thoughts. She wasn't going to think about him falling on foreign soil because he had a wife who would do all that, who had the right to do it. From this point on, she was going to think only of herself. It didn't do to be trusting and soft, not in this world. And God didn't care. Half the world was fighting and killing the other half and He did nothing to stop it. And she didn't believe the priests were one step down from the Almighty either.

She stopped, looking up into a high blue sky, the colour as hard and flat as a painting. The thought had come like a revelation but now Bess realised she'd been considering this matter for a long time in the depths of her mind. Her da was cruel and mean and yet Father Fraser thought the sun shone out of his backside. She didn't know if her da was fooling the priest or whether the Father turned a blind eye because her da always stumped up with a good offering, but either way it reduced the priest to a mere man in her eyes. And that's all he was, a man like any other.

Even yesterday such a thought would have immediately made her cross herself and ask for forgiveness but today it was different. *She* was different. Maybe the process of change had begun when she'd met Christopher and listened to his views on everything from religion to politics – most of which she admitted she hadn't understood – but she couldn't blindly accept everything the Church said any more. And when the war ended she wouldn't let her da force her to go back to being a parlourmaid. He'd said a skivvy was all she was good for but she'd show him. She'd make something of herself, do something, become someone.

She began walking again, part of her fearful at her temerity but the other part rearing up against the unfairness of life and the position she found herself in.

But before she could do anything, she had to deal with what needed to be dealt with. For a moment her hand hovered over her stomach, touching the creased linen of her summer coat. And then she brought it sharply to her side, her eyes narrowing. She could do this. She had to do it, she had no option. And she had to do it quickly.

'Ee, lass, what were you thinkin' of to get caught out like that? An' what about your lad? Can't he do the decent thing an' marry you quick afore it shows?'

Bess stared into the yellow face of Martha Todd. When she had first started work at the munitions factory she hadn't understood why the women who filled shells were called canaries, but at her first tea break it had been Martha and one of her pals who had explained that repeated exposure to TNT had turned their faces yellow. Martha and her cronies had thought it a great joke but Bess had been horrified, mainly because she dreaded a jaundiced pallor developing in her own skin. By the time she had worked there a few months and seen two women lose fingers and another blinded in the accidents that were commonplace, she'd realised yellow skin was the least of her worries.

'He . . . he's dead. Killed in action,' she said now, her voice weak, not because of her condition but because they were standing in the section of the factory toilets which had been divided off for use by female employees, and the stench drifting over from the men's side was overpowering. She felt hot and sick but the toilets were the only place she could have a quiet word with Martha. 'Do you know anyone who might help me?' she asked again.

'Lass, there's plenty who'd help Old Nick himself for the right price.' Martha's voice was soft. She had drawn her own conclusions about Bess's father from listening to Kitty and Bess talk, and she pitied the pretty young girl in front of her.

'How much would they want?' said Bess, a little anxiously. She didn't have a great deal in the old toffee tin on the top of her wardrobe at home. When she had been set on at the factory her father had made sure her mother doled back one shilling out of her wage packet, thruppence more than when she'd been working as a parlourmaid. It was only her mother slipping her an extra half-crown on the sly each week that had enabled her to save anything at all after she had bought her toiletries and paid for any extras, such as having her boots soled or new woollen stockings. Before she had managed her stolen evenings with Christopher her only treat had been a seat at the Avenue or Palace or one of the other picture houses with Kitty on a Saturday night.

'Don't worry about that.' Martha's voice was softer still. 'I'm known for bein' as good as me word an' if I say you're all right that'll be enough to get it done, but you'll have to pay after at so much a week. You could do that, couldn't you?'

'Aye, yes.' Bess nodded. 'I could do that.' She gulped and then said, 'How soon could they see me?'

'I dunno, lass, but I'll find out. The thing is, you don't want to go to just anyone for somethin' like this; some of the old wives don't care what they do as long as they get paid. The woman I've got in mind might be as rough an' ready as old Harry's backside but she's a good 'un an' she knows what's what. She'll make a clean job of it, will old Maggie.'

Bess felt she was going to faint or be sick or both. She stared at the other woman from eyes so huge they seemed to fill her face.

'You told your mam you're in a pickle?' Martha asked.

'No, no one knows, not even Kitty. I can't risk me da finding out.' A little shiver passed over Bess's face which said more to Martha than any words could have done. 'You wouldn't tell anyone?'

'Not me, lass. Silent as the grave, I can be.' And when Bess didn't look reassured, Martha added, 'Don't worry, I won't say nowt. I know what it's like when you're livin' with someone like your da. Me own was a swine an' all.' She smiled grimly. 'Put me on the game when I was nowt but eight or nine, he did.'

'Oh, Martha.' Up until now Bess had been both slightly afraid and contemptuous of this woman whose reputation was well known, but never once had she asked herself how a woman might come to be working the streets most of her life. Shame made her voice husky when she said, 'How could you stand it when you were so young?'

Martha shrugged beefy shoulders. 'You bear what has to be borne, lass, that's what I've learned in life. Mind, I'd have liked to have got wed, had bairns an' that, but what decent man would have looked the side I was on?' For a moment Martha's eyes were unfocused, as though she was looking at something Bess couldn't see, and then with a seeming effort she smiled, flapping her hand as she said, 'Anyway, don't you worry, lass, I'll see what I can do. A day or two an' it'll all be over. I'll tip you the wink when I've set it up.'

'Thank you.' Bess tried to smile back but it was beyond her. And then as Martha made to leave, Bess caught hold of her arm. Her voice low and urgent, she said, 'I have to do it, you see, there's no other way. It's not as if it's really a baby yet, is it? It's not going to feel anything. It's not really living.'

The silence that fell on them had no movement in it, even the clatter beyond the confines of the toilets seeming dulled. For endless moments the two women stared at each other, one pair of eyes beseeching and the other pitying. Then Martha murmured, 'Like I said, lass, a day or two an' it'll be over.' Then she turned on her heel and hurried away.

Chapter 2

As things turned out, Martha Todd couldn't fix up the necessary visit to the old midwife she knew in the East End as quickly as she had promised. The very afternoon of the day Bess confided in her, Martha was involved in an accident at the factory which laid her off work for a while. It was over three weeks later – three weeks in which Bess had nearly gone mad with worry – before the older woman sidled up to Bess on her return to the factory. 'Saturday afternoon all right for you, lass?' she whispered out of the side of her mouth. 'She can do it then. You meet me outside the Boar's Head in High Street East at two o'clock an' we'll go along to Maggie's.'

Bess had been about to climb the rope up to the cab of the crane she controlled, one of many which moved shells back and forth across the factory floor. She froze, staring at Martha but unable to speak for the relief flooding her. She had been frightened Martha would forget about her. It was only when Martha said, 'Well, what do you say? You still want it done, don't you?' that Bess managed to pull herself together.

'Aye, aye I do.' She glanced about her and then up at Kitty who was in the next crane. Lowering her face to Martha's, she whispered, 'Will it take long?'

'Aye, long enough. Good few hours. You'll have to rest after for a while.'

'But I see Kitty Saturdays and we go to the pictures in the evening. What'll I tell her? She'll have to cover for me.'

Martha shrugged. 'That's up to you, lass. Just be there for two. An' Maggie wants thirty bob for her trouble. Can you manage that?' She didn't add that normally the price was a good deal higher but that she had called in a favour.

Bess nodded. 'Thanks, Martha,' she said softly.

Martha inclined her head and walked away, and Bess began to climb the rope. The action emphasised the changes in her body which had occurred since she'd last spoken to Martha. The thickening round her stomach and the tingling and fullness in her small breasts was only slight as yet, but she felt her body was reminding her all the time of what was happening. The week for her fourth monthly had come and gone now and, ridiculous though she knew it was, she had prayed like she'd never prayed before that she would see a flow of blood. But of course there'd been nothing.

'What did she want?' As Bess reached the cage of the crane, Kitty leaned out of hers. 'I didn't know you had any truck with Martha Todd.'

Kitty's voice revealed she was disgruntled, but Bess knew it wasn't really because she'd spoken to Martha. The last few weeks she had been so taken up with fear of what would happen if Martha didn't help her, she knew she'd been a bit short with Kitty. She stared into the plain little face of her friend, envying Kitty with all her heart. Kitty's chief problem was the spots which assailed her face. 'I'll tell you later,' she said quietly. And then, when Kitty frowned and flounced back into the crane, she added, 'I'm sorry I haven't been meself lately, lass, but there is a reason. What say we take our bait outside when the whistle blows and have a talk?'

'Aye, all right.' Kitty was instantly mollified. 'You feeling bad, Bess? You've been looking peaky since you had that gyppy belly.'

'Aye, I don't feel too good.' The senna and salts she had taken after Martha had had her accident had scoured her to the point where she'd thought she'd lose all her insides, but still nothing had happened. She had heated the water to near boiling point for her weekly scrub in the old tin bath in front of the kitchen range at home when her parents went for their Friday visit to her brother's house in Monkwearmouth, swigging the half bottle of gin she had surreptitiously bought on the way home before she'd lowered herself into the scalding water. The gin had made her sick and when she had finally climbed out of the bath she had fainted clean away on the clippy mat in front of the fire, but still she hadn't had so much as a show.

'I thought you was still bad. You ought to go and see the doctor, lass.'

'Aye, maybe. We'll talk later anyway.'

It was a round-eyed and blatantly horrified Kitty who sat looking at Bess in a corner of the factory compound at lunchtime. They had found a quiet corner near a stack of pallets close to the gates and Bess had told Kitty everything, leaving her friend too stunned to move or speak. Eventually

Kitty whispered, 'The rotten so-an'-so. To do that, to take you down when he was already married. I can't believe it. He seemed so nice, didn't he?'

Bess didn't reply to this. Instead she said, 'Will you make out I'm with you Saturday as usual? I thought we could say we want to listen to the band in Mowbray Park in the afternoon and that we'd get a pie and chitterlings somewhere before we go to the pictures. That way Mam wouldn't expect me home for tea. Martha . . . Martha said it could take a while.'

'Oh, lass.' Kitty seemed to be on the verge of crying.

With September's coming, the weather had changed. The fierce heatwave in August had broken on the very last day of the month, and September had been heralded with thunderstorms and lashing rain before settling into a cold windy month. Bess shivered and pulled her old coat tighter round her neck, her face white and pinched. 'We'd better go in, it's too cold out here,' she said, making no effort to move.

'Don't worry, lass.' Kitty leaned forward and took Bess's hands. 'I'm coming with you Saturday and if we're late back I'll say you were took bad in the pictures or something. It'll work out.'

Bess felt as though she wanted to sag at the gentleness of Kitty's tone but the tight rein she had kept on herself since the moment she had read Christopher's brother's letter prevented it. She dropped her head before saying, 'You don't have to come. You could go to your Elsie's if you want and I'll call for you there.'

'I'm coming.' And then, her tone uncertain, Kitty added, 'If you want me to, that is.'

'Course I want you to.' Bess's head rose and she regarded

Kitty steadily. 'But it might be . . .' She couldn't find a word to express what she wanted to say. 'You're squeamish, you know you are,' she said quietly. 'You can't stand the sight of blood. Look how you passed out when Nora Gibson lost an eye.'

'That was different, that was an accident.'

'But I don't know what this Maggie woman is going to do or how I'll feel after.'

'All the more reason for me to come with you, surely?' And then Kitty settled the matter when she said, 'You'd do the same for me, lass, now then, so don't argue. I'm coming and that's that.' She squeezed Bess's hands hard before rising to her feet and brushing the crumbs of the sandwiches she'd eaten off her coat. 'And I won't faint,' she said matter-of-factly. 'I'll keep me mam's smelling salts handy. They're awful, like cat's pee.'

Kitty was a staunch Catholic like most of the folk in their street but she hadn't said that what Bess was going to do was a mortal sin or attempted to talk her out of it. As Bess followed her friend back into the noisy, stinking factory building, the acrid odour of explosives thick in the air, she was aware of a deep feeling of gratitude. But then Kitty knew exactly what her da was like . . .

Muriel Shawe's somewhat flat face was deadpan as she placed a large plateful of fried bread and bacon in front of her husband, but as ever her mind was working furiously. All over the country people were enduring 'meatless' days and cutting down on the consumption of bread due to the soaring cost of flour, but was Wilbur prepared to do his bit? Was he heck.

She returned to the kitchen range, took the big black

kettle off the fire and filled the brown teapot with its two spoonfuls of tea. Once the tea had mashed she poured a large mugful for her husband, adding two heaped teaspoons of sugar and stirring it before she put the pint-size mug in front of his plate.

Wilbur did not acknowledge or thank her – and Muriel did not expect him to – he merely continued to devour his breakfast.

For a moment as Muriel stared down at the bent head, at the rich brown curly hair which was as thick as it had been on the first day she had met him some twenty-five years before, she felt a repugnance so fierce her lips pulled back from her teeth with the force of it. But almost immediately she schooled her face into its habitual blankness. As much as Wilbur filled her with loathing, the fear he inspired was stronger.

She returned to the range and fished out the two remaining rashers of bacon from the massive frying pan, placing them on two plates which already held a slice of bread and butter each, cut thin. She put these on the table and then walked to the kitchen door which was ajar, looking up the stairs as she called, 'Bess, lass, it's on the table.'

'Leave her.' Wilbur didn't pause in shovelling food into his mouth, morsels dropping onto his plate as he spoke. 'She knows what time breakfast is; if she can't be bothered to come and eat, she can go without.' He picked up his mug of tea, took a mouthful and then growled, 'Like dishwater, this is.'

Muriel didn't answer him. Rationing was beginning to bite and he was fully aware of this but he still had to have his gripe every morning. She sat down at the table but didn't begin to eat until he shot her a glance, saying, 'Well? What are you waiting for? I've told you, if she's not down in a couple of minutes the table'll be cleared.'

Why had she ever married him? It was not a new thought and as ever the answer was because he had been big and handsome and he had asked for her.

She had been working sixteen hours a day as a kitchen-maid at a big house Whitburn way, and had met Wilbur on one of her half-days off a month. She and one of the parlour-maids had taken a walk down to Holey Rock on Roker beach, and Wilbur had been watching a group of lads play football. She had barely known him when they had wed – one half-day a month was not conducive to any form of closeness. He had seemed a quiet, withdrawn sort of man but this hadn't worried her at the time. Not until after her wedding had she learned that his solitariness hid a brutish unnatural streak which had made her wedding night, and all the nights following it, a time of terror.

At first she'd tried to tell herself that being orphaned at an early age and brought up in the workhouse, he'd never known what tenderness or affection was. He had no family, no friends – she would be everything to him and show him nothing but care and consideration. This thinking had lasted a few months until, after a night of such degradation and bestiality she hadn't thought she'd survive it, she had run home to her mother in Monkwearmouth. She hadn't been able to bring herself to tell her mother exactly what was wrong and Wilbur had come for her within the hour anyway. They had left with her mother's admonition that she was a married woman now and under her husband's authority ringing in her ears. Then had come a respite because within the month she'd discovered she was expecting a child and he hadn't come near her for the whole nine months she had carried their son. After that she had prayed every day she would get pregnant again soon, but it had been eight years before she had fallen for Bess.

As though the thought of her daughter had summoned Bess down, Muriel heard measured footsteps on the stairs. The slow gait brought the worry she had been feeling for weeks to the forefront of her mind again. The time was, and not so long ago either, the lass would have been down those stairs like a dose of salts even knowing Wilbur hadn't yet left for work. There was something wrong with Bess. She'd lost her sparkle, the liveliness which had characterised her from a little bairn, but every time she tried to find out what was wrong, Bess would have none of it.

'Hello, hinny.' Muriel's voice was soft as her daughter walked into the kitchen. 'Come an' have a bite before we start on the range.' Every Saturday morning they cleaned and blackleaded the kitchen range together, larking on like a couple of bairns on occasion. But there had been none of that lately. Her voice softer still, Muriel said, 'Shall I pour you a sup, lass?'

'For crying out loud!' There was a harsh scraping as Wilbur pushed his chair back on the flagstones and stood up. 'She can do it herself, can't she? Getting above herself, she is, and you're to blame. You,' he spoke directly to Bess now, 'your back stick to the bed, did it? And look at me when I'm speaking to you.'

'I'm sorry.' Bess had gone a shade paler.

'You will be if you don't move your backside sharper.' He glared at her, his gaze moving to his wife's wooden

22

countenance a moment later. When neither of them responded by so much as a flicker of an eyelash, he made a sound deep in his throat which could have meant anything. He followed this with the sort of foul obscenity which could be heard down at the docks, snatched up his cap and bait tin from the table and left the kitchen, slamming the scullery door behind him.

The air left Muriel's body in a long sigh of relief but Bess continued to sit straight and still. Muriel looked at her daughter. 'Eat somethin', lass. You're gettin' as thin as a lath.'

Bess's big brown eyes stared into her mother's anxious face. For as long as she could remember she had known her mother was frightened of her father. From a small child she had been vaguely aware of strange noises coming from their room across the landing some nights. Muffled whimpers and sobbing, moans, even the odd cry which had been instantly cut short. She hadn't known what all this meant but it had terrified her nonetheless. It hadn't bothered her brother, Ronald; he had always slept like a log in his curtained-off half of their bedroom before he left to get married five years ago.

Since she had known Christopher she had come to understand the significance of the nocturnal sounds and it sickened her. Disgust had been added to her deep dislike and fear of her father. Before she had known she was expecting Christopher's child, she had harboured the wild idea of renting a room somewhere for her mother and herself, a sanctuary where they could live until the end of the war when Christopher would come and marry her.

Her mouth hardened, and she said, 'I hate Da.' Her hands clenched into fists on the oil tablecloth. 'I've always hated him and I shall tell him one day.'

'No, hinny.' There was a note of panic in Muriel's voice. 'He'd go stark starin' mad. Please, lass, promise me you'd never do that. You're young an' bonny, you'll get married sooner or later an' then you'll be free of him.'

'What about you?' Taking her mother's hand in hers, Bess looked down at the wrinkled skin. 'Would you come with me?'

'Oh, lass.' Muriel was smiling but her voice held the catch of tears. 'What a start to married life that'd be. You'd frighten any poor lad to death if you asked him to take your mam an' all. But thanks for sayin' it. The thing is, I married your da for better or worse an' that's that. An' I've got you an' our Ronald an' his bairns to count me blessings for. I'm happy enough. Now come on, hinny. Eat your breakfast an' then we'll see to the range afore you go out with Kitty later.'

The warm homeliness of the kitchen, the glow from the range and the love in her mother's face were creating in Bess a desire to confide her secret. She'd felt this way more and more lately and now, to combat the dangerous weakness, she rose abruptly to her feet. 'I need the privy. I won't be a minute.'

'Aye, all right, lass. I'll make a fresh brew for when you come back.'

Bess walked out of the kitchen without replying and through into the tiny scullery which was just big enough to hold the deep stone sink on one side and several rows of shelves on the other. She opened the door into the back-yard. The September morning was chilly but dry as she made her way across the yard and into the privy. This was not an unpleasant place. Unlike some of the women in the street of two-up, two-down terraced houses, her mother kept their lavatory sweet-smelling with daily scrubbing and fresh ashes. Inside the brick box, Bess shot the bolt on the door and then sank down on the white wooden seat which extended right across the breadth of the lavatory.

She shut her eyes tightly. Today was the day. Her heart began to pound so violently she put her hand to her chest. By tonight it would all be over and she could get on with her life once more. Her mother had talked of her getting married but she would never get wed, she knew that now. Men were men the world over and she would never trust one again; she did not want to risk tying herself into the sort of misery her mother endured.

She swallowed hard, the well of emotion she had kept banked down since reading the letter threatening to spill over. She mustn't cry, she told herself, not yet. Not till it was over. And even then it would have to be in the privacy of her bed so no one would know.

She sat a moment more, willing herself to rise and go back into the house and laugh and joke with her mother as though it was a normal Saturday morning. And then she felt it. An unmistakable flutter deep inside the faint swell of her belly. She froze, her mouth a little O of surprise and her eyes wide.

No, no. The shout was deafening in her head. It wasn't the baby, she was imagining this. Instinctively her hand went to her stomach over her clothes. Then she hoisted her skirt and petticoat up, pushed down her drawers and placed her hand on the warm, soft skin of her belly. When the strange little flickers came again, a quiver passed over her face. It *was* the baby. It was alive, it was letting her know it was alive.

She didn't become aware she was crying until she felt a

drop of moisture fall on the hand still placed over her stomach. Once started, she couldn't stop. How long she sat there before she heard her mother's footsteps in the yard she didn't know, but still she couldn't pull herself together, not even when her mother became distraught and began banging on the door.

Eventually she managed to say, 'Wait . . . wait a minute, Mam.' She fumbled with her clothing, fished her handkerchief out of the sleeve of her blouse and wiped her face with it before she opened the lavatory door.

'Landsakes, hinny, whatever's wrong?' As Bess almost fell into her mother's arms, Muriel's voice held real fear. 'I knew there was somethin', I've bin askin' you for weeks, now haven't I? What is it?'

'I'll tell you inside.' Bess's voice was low. Kitty's parents were lovely, salt of the earth, and she liked every one of her friend's brothers and sisters but they all had cuddy's ears. And Mr and Mrs Griffiths, the old couple who lived next door the other way, were worse.

Once they were in the scullery, Bess slipped the bolt on the back door before she followed her mother into the kitchen. They stood facing each other and as Bess looked into her mother's anxious eyes she didn't know how to start. In the event she didn't have to.

'It's not that, lass, is it?' Muriel's voice was faint and tremulous. 'You're not in the family way?'

'Oh, Mam.'

Bess's tone was answer enough and Muriel sat down abruptly on one of the hard-backed chairs, all the colour draining from her face. Her mouth opened a few times before she was able to say, 'How far gone are you?'

Bess gulped hard. 'About nineteen weeks now.'

'Nineteen?'

'I'm sorry, Mam, I'm sorry. Oh, Mam . . .' Bess's face was as stricken as her voice and when she flung herself on her knees at her mother's feet, her head buried in her mother's lap as her arms went round her waist, Muriel only hesitated for a second before she began to stroke the dark head.

'Why didn't you tell me, hinny? Why didn't you say somethin' afore now?' Her voice cracked. 'Nineteen weeks. Saints alive.'

'I . . . I was going to see someone. One of the women at work knows this woman in the East End—'

'You've told 'em at work?'

'No, no. Just this woman. And . . . and Kitty. That's all. No one else knows.'

'An' the father?' Muriel asked heavily. 'You told him?'

'He's dead.' It was stark and flat.

'Dead? Oh, lass.'

'He was killed in the war, the Somme. But,' Bess took a deep breath, 'he was married. I didn't know,' she said quickly as she felt the hand on her head make an involuntary movement. She raised her face to look into her mother's and what she saw there made her protest, 'I swear, Mam. I didn't know. He's not from round these parts, he . . . he was a gentleman.'

Muriel rubbed her hand across her face and it was shaking. It was a few moments before she said painfully, 'So there'll be no help from that quarter then?' And when Bess slowly shook her head, the two of them stared at each other.

'I felt it move, this morning in the privy.' Bess's lips quivered. 'I was going to see this woman later, she lives in the East End and . . .' She couldn't finish. 'But now I've felt it move it's different.'

'You can't do away with it.' There was a note of horror in Muriel's voice and she sat up straighter, motioning for Bess to rise. She patted the chair beside her. 'Come and sit down, hinny, and let's have no more talk like that 'cos it don't help no one. It's a mortal sin to even think such a thing.'

A mortal sin. Bess felt years older than her mother and it was a strange feeling. Here was her mam talking about mortal sin when there was her father to be faced. Whatever was going to happen in the hereafter couldn't be as bad as the here and now. 'I'm not going to do away with it, Mam. I couldn't, not now. But . . .' She stopped abruptly. She had been about to say her change of mind was nothing to do with the Church or Father Fraser but this would just cause her mother further distress. 'But there's Da,' she said instead.

Her mother said nothing to this, she didn't have to. They both knew what it would mean.

'If there was somewhere I could go until it's born, I'd do it,' Bess said in a low voice. 'But there's not. Nowhere except the workhouse, that is.'

'You're not going there, hinny. Not while I've breath in me body.'

'But I can't stay here, Mam. Not with him.'

Muriel's face was as white as a sheet as she endeavoured to stay calm. She stood up and cleared away the crockery. She placed the contents of Bess's plate and that of her own into a bowl which she carried to the pantry, slipping it on the cold slab beneath the newspaper-covered shelves. Even in this crisis the old adage of 'waste not, want not' held firm.

She returned to the table and poured herself a cup of warm, stewed tea. Bess declined one with a shake of her head. It was only after Muriel had drunk her tea straight down that she said, 'Father Fraser will have to be here when you tell him.'

'No, Mam.' It was short and sharp.

The fire in the range made a little spit and crackle in the silence that had fallen. It was a minute or two before Muriel leaned towards her daughter, her voice firmer than it had been throughout when she said, 'He won't do anythin' if the Father is here, you know how he likes to keep in his good books. The priests are your da's gate to heaven, that's the way he sees it.'

'I don't want Father Fraser knowing.'

'Lass, everyone's goin' to know afore long,' Muriel said very quietly.

Bess dropped her head, her shame deeper than it had ever been when confronted with her mother's lack of condemnation. If her mam had denounced her and heaped reproach on her head she could have stood it better than this gentle acceptance. But that was her mam all over, so loving, so kind. It had probably been those very qualities that had made her father single her out when they were young; he'd known he could bully and frighten her.

'I'll put me coat on later an' nip an' have a word,' said Muriel resolutely. 'He knows it's your da's half-day on a Saturday; mebbe he'll come back with me an' we can break the news afore your da goes to the football.'

Bess looked at her mother's wrinkled face and tired eyes. Her mam had had a rough deal in life and here she was adding to her troubles a hundredfold. Any further protest about the priest being brought in died on her lips.

*　*　*

When Father Fraser entered the house by the front door, Muriel following respectfully on his heels, he walked straight down the hall and into the kitchen without pausing. Bess stood at his entrance, their eyes meeting for a moment before she dropped her head.

The priest did not speak immediately. He took the chair Muriel fussily pulled out for him and nodded to her offer of a cup of tea. He did not ask Bess to be seated and she did not presume to do so without his permission.

'So, Bess?' The thick fleshy lips in the fat face paused. When Bess didn't raise her head or attempt to reply, the priest allowed some ten seconds to tick by before he said, 'Sit down, girl. We have some talking to do.'

Her colour high, Bess sat, and Muriel — beside herself with agitation — said, 'Would you have a couple of girdle cakes with your tea, Father? Freshly made this mornin'.'

'Thank you, Mrs Shawe.' The priest did not take his gaze from Bess's face which, now the flush of colour had subsided, was as white as lint. His small beady eyes examined the young girl in front of him with a coldness which was habitual. These young lasses! Father Fraser settled his ample buttocks more comfortably on the hard wooden seat, lacing his podgy fingers over the mound of his belly. This was what came from giving slips of girls a man's wage. It never ought to be. He cleared his throat before saying sententiously, 'When were you last at confession, Bess?'

Her head rose and big brown eyes met his. 'Over two months ago, Father.'

'And before that?'

'I . . . I don't remember.'

Muriel placed a steaming cup of tea and the sugar bowl

in front of Father Fraser. Her voice held the obsequious note it always did when addressing the priest as she said, 'Do help yourself, Father.'

'Thank you, Mrs Shawe, but I have resolved to do without sugar in my tea until this terrible war is over. We all need to do our bit, don't we?' He reached for the plate of scones which had followed the tea, finishing one in two bites and sliding another onto the side of his saucer before he said, 'This is a sad state of affairs, Bess. A grievous state of affairs. God's holy order of things will not be mocked. You are aware of this, aren't you? Aware of how greatly you have sinned?' The second scone went the way of the first.

'She is, Father.' When Bess didn't immediately answer Muriel's voice was rushed. 'You are, aren't you, lass?' she added, not waiting for a reply. 'She's heart sorry, Father, but . . . but like I said, she was led on, fooled by this man. He—'

'I think Bess can speak for herself, Mrs Shawe.'

Bess's chin had fallen again, her eyes on her hands in her lap, but now her head shot up at the icy tone. Her cheeks flaming once more, she said, 'All sin is equally grievous to God surely, Father? Isn't that what the Bible says?'

The priest sat up straighter, his eyes narrowing. The heavy silence which now fell on the kitchen was broken only by the sound of Muriel clasping and unclasping her hands in the background, and it was this which made Bess say, 'I'm sorry, Father.'

'This man, this . . . gentleman. I take it he wasn't from these parts?'

'No, Father.'

'But he was of the faith?'

Bess looked steadily at the priest. 'He was married, Father. With a child.'

'That isn't what I asked. Was he of the true religion?'

Bess swallowed hard but didn't lower her gaze. 'He had no religion, Father. He was an atheist.'

This time the silence stretched and lengthened until Muriel, unable to bear it a moment longer, gabbled, 'Won't you have another girdle cake, Father? An' there's more tea in the pot.'

Father Fraser motioned away the offer with an abrupt movement of his hand. His eyes hard on Bess, he said, 'I think it is as well I shall be here when your father arrives home. As big a shock as your condition will be to him, his greater sorrow will be in knowing you have scorned the Church's teaching on consorting with those whose eyes are blinded.'

Did he really believe that? Bess stared at the priest. And then they heard the back door open and footsteps in the scullery. Wilbur walked into the kitchen. She saw his eyes flash round the room before they came to rest on the face of Father Fraser, and as ever a pious note crept into his voice when he said, 'Father, I didn't know you were paying us a visit the day.'

'For once it is a visit which gives me no pleasure, Wilbur.'

'Oh aye?'

'Sit down, my son.'

It was a moment or two before her father obeyed the command; he had sensed something serious was afoot. Just the fact that Father Fraser was sitting in the kitchen would have alerted him to the severity of the crisis. The priest was usually ushered into the hallowed front room on his visits to the house, the fire which lay dormant between such occasions being lit immediately in the colder months.

'Now,' Father Fraser sat up straighter, bringing his hands onto his knees, 'prepare yourself as best you can for a great shock, Wilbur.'

He was enjoying this. Bess found she was quite incapable of movement; she had been from the moment her father had returned home, but her mind was more than making up for the stillness of her body. It told her Father Fraser was experiencing a covert but deep satisfaction at her downfall. She had been an irritating thorn in the priest's side for some time, what with missing Mass and so on, and more than once he had spoken scathingly from the pulpit about the new ideas which were being bandied about and how the war was going to be the ruination of many a young girl. He must be relishing the knowledge he'd been proved right in her case.

Wilbur remained immobile as Father Fraser talked on but his face became a mottled red and his whole body seemed to swell. Muriel was standing by the range, her hand across her mouth. She could have been carved in stone.

When the eruption came it took the priest by surprise, so much so he nearly fell off his chair. Wilbur leaped to his feet with a cry which sounded almost inhuman. Not so Bess. She had been waiting for her father to react. As Wilbur lunged at her, she took sanctuary behind the bulky figure of Father Fraser, knowing her safety depended on it.

Pandemonium followed. Muriel's shrill shrieks and Bess's screams mingled with Wilbur's curses and the priest's remonstrations as he bodily held Wilbur off his daughter. If it had been anyone but Father Fraser, there was no doubt Wilbur would have knocked him to the floor, the rage he was in, but the deeply superstitious streak which made up the main part of Wilbur's belief held firm. To strike a priest was inviting the fires of hell to consume you.

It was only a minute or two before Wilbur came to his senses, but beads of sweat were standing out on Father Fraser's brow, his face as red as a beetroot.

'I'm sorry, Father. I'm sorry,' muttered Wilbur.

Father Fraser was panting heavily and he still stood with his arms stretched wide, Bess cowering behind him, for a few seconds more. Then his hands slowly dropped to his sides and he took the seat he'd vacated, bending forward and touching Wilbur's arm as he said, 'I understand your outrage and disappointment, my son. For a child to be born out of wedlock is a grievous sin to be sure, but when the father is godless, a heathen.' He shook his head. 'You've been given much to bear.'

Wilbur raised his head. He didn't give a damn what religion the father was, not in these circumstances, but his voice did not betray this when he said, 'Just so, Father.'

'But now you must rise above this tribulation with God's strength and direction, Wilbur. The wayward soul needs to be chastised and corrected. Didn't the good Lord Himself extend the hand of compassion to the harlot at Jacob's Well when she truly repented of her sin? Your duty is to see to it that the wicked forsakes her way and sins no more.'

Behind the priest, Bess stiffened. Did Father Fraser understand what he was saying to her da? Did he know he was giving him carte blanche to treat her however he wanted? And she wasn't a harlot. She had loved Christopher, she'd loved him with all her heart and believed they were going to live the rest of their lives together once the war was over.

34

She must have made some involuntary sound or movement although she wasn't aware of it, because in the next moment Father Fraser turned to look at her and her father said, 'You. Get upstairs if you know what's good for you.'

'I . . . I'm sorry, Da.' She knew better than to go anywhere near him but she lifted her hands pleadingly. 'I didn't mean it. I thought we were going to be married, I didn't know . . .' Her lips trembling and her voice low she said again, 'I'm sorry.'

'Not yet you aren't but you will be. Oh aye, m'girl, take it from me, you will be. Because of you I won't be able to hold me head up once this gets around. Now get up them stairs like I told you.'

The priest's grim expression didn't change and Bess knew she had received the only help she was going to get from that quarter. She glanced at her mother, and in the second or two that their gaze held she read the same panic and fear she knew must be reflected in her own eyes. Her life wasn't going to be worth living from this point on. And then the flutter deep inside her belly came again. Bess straightened her back and stretched her neck and it was with her head held high that she left the room.

Chapter 3

'She's a bonny bairn, Ronald, now isn't she? An' as good as gold the day long. She's never bin a moment's trouble.' Muriel's voice held a pleading note as, together with her son, she watched Bess's daughter play with a wooden spoon and an old saucepan lid on the clippy mat in front of the kitchen range.

Ronald Shawe didn't answer for a moment. Then he said, his voice flat, 'Aye, she's bonny, Mam.'

Muriel glanced at his face and then said quickly, 'Ee, lad, you've finished your tea. Have another cup afore it goes cold an' the last of that jam roll. You must be able to smell it 'cos you never fail to turn up when I've just baked one.'

Ronald smiled now, patting his mother's hand as he said softly, 'No one makes a jam roll like you, Mam, but don't tell May I said that or she'll have me guts for garters.'

'Oh, our Ronald.' Muriel, pink with pleasure, placed the last of the roll on his plate. 'Your May's a canny little cook an' well you know it. You don't look as if you're fading away to me, that's for sure.'

'Aye, she keeps me fed.' Ronald's voice was cheery but he didn't feel cheery inside, he never did when he called at his parents' house and was confronted by the evidence of the shame his sister had brought on them all. He wished he could feel differently, wished he could take to the bairn like his mam had but he was with his father on this. Every time he set eyes on Bess's daughter his stomach twisted. But his mam loved her and he loved his mam, so for her sake he held his tongue and pretended to play the fond uncle. But his mam knew. He'd never been able to pull the wool over her eyes about anything. And she had never once suggested she bring the baby over to their house in the twenty or so months since she had been born, which spoke for itself.

'An' you're all keepin' well in spite of this Spanish flu then?' Muriel said now, pouring him a second cup of tea and adding a spoonful of sugar to it.

Ronald nodded, his mouth full of jam roll. His mother tried to keep her voice casual but he knew she was worried. The beginning of 1918 had seen a virulent strain of influenza sweep across the globe and take millions of lives. It was said to hit the old and very young and those with a weakness hardest, so the heart murmur which had prevented him being called up might now prove to be a mixed blessing. September had been a bad month, with people dropping like flies, but they were saying October would be worse. He swallowed before saying reassuringly, 'I'm fine, Mam, never felt better. All right? And they're saying the war will be over by Christmas so that's something to be thankful for.'

'Huh.' Muriel sniffed her disbelief. 'I'll believe it when it happens an' not a minute before.'

'Gamma?'

They had been unaware of the child tottering towards them but now small dimpled hands caught at Muriel's skirt. Muriel bent and lifted her granddaughter into her arms, saying, 'Aye, me bairn? What do you want?' She brushed a wisp of golden-brown hair from the small forehead.

Bright blue laughing eyes under a crown of thick loose curls stared back at her, and when small arms went round her neck in a stranglehold, Muriel hugged the child tight. She had loved both her children from the day they were born but the emotion she felt for this flesh of her flesh was something beyond. Maybe it was a result of the nightmare she and Bess had endured at the hands of Wilbur in the months leading up to Amy's birth when she'd feared the baby would be stillborn. Or perhaps it was the fever Bess had had following the delivery, which had necessitated her taking over the care of her granddaughter from day one, that had created the bond between them. Certainly by the time Bess went back to work when the baby was a few weeks old, she had known the child was a blessing the like of which only happens once in a lifetime, and then if you're lucky. Which was strange considering the circumstances of the bairn's begetting.

The child settled on her lap and Muriel turned to her son again, ignoring the hurt she always felt at his lack of contact with his niece. He had a plateful to deal with at home, that's what it was, she told herself. May kept a clean house and certainly with their eldest being just four and the youngest twelve months, and a two-and-a-half between, she did her duty as a wife. Their fourth was due in a couple of months an' all. Aye, they were good Catholics right enough, but she wasn't daft and she knew things weren't right between her Ronald and his wife. There were times when he seemed as

38

miserable as sin and didn't speak May's name for several visits. Mind, she knew what the root problem was. Just from the odd word Ronald let slip now and again, she knew May's da had too much say in their going-on.

Course, they'd all been grateful when Terence O'Leary had set Ronald on at the Monwearmouth Iron and Steel Works where he was manager when her lad began courting May. Jobs hadn't been so plentiful before the war and it had been a godsend, but sometimes she thought Mr O'Leary had all but bought their Ronald, mind, soul and body. And she herself had heard May remind Ronald that they were where they were today because of her da, which no man would like. He should give her what for but he was too soft.

Attacked by the feeling of disloyalty which always accompanied such thoughts, Muriel now said, 'Thanks for poppin' in, lad.'

'I only come for the jam roll,' said Ronald, the squeeze of his hand on his mother's shoulder belying his words. He got to his feet. 'I'd best make tracks now, Mam. I've got to—'

What he had to do Muriel never found out because the back door opening cut off his voice. The next moment Bess stood in the doorway from the scullery. There was a pause during which brother and sister stared at each other. Ronald hadn't seen his sibling since the day Wilbur had gone to Monkwearmouth to inform his son of Bess's fall from grace, as a result of which Ronald had declared his sister wasn't welcome at his home any more. Bess had received this news in silence and hadn't mentioned Ronald's name since.

'Hello, Bess.' Ronald's voice was flat but his heart was pounding against his ribs. He barely recognised the pretty, sparkling-eyed lass he had grown up with in the gaunt, sickly-looking woman in front of him, and the conscience which had pricked him more than once over the last two years was making itself felt.

Bess inclined her head but it was to Muriel she spoke, saying, 'They've sent me home from work, they reckon I've got the flu and they don't want it spreading any more than they can help. Half the girls are off as it is.' And to Amy, who had struggled off Muriel's lap at the sight of her mother and was now demanding to be picked up, she added, 'Not now, hinny. Mam's feeling poorly.'

'Oh, lass.' Depositing Amy back onto the clippy mat with her saucepan lid and spoon, Muriel took her daughter's arm. 'I told you you shouldn't go in this mornin', you looked middlin' then.'

'And have Da ranting and raving that I was swinging the lead?' It was bitter. And then, as Bess swayed slightly and Ronald made a move towards her, she said grimly, 'Don't touch me. You don't want to get contaminated, do you?' And all three knew she wasn't talking about the flu.

Ronald, his face the colour of beetroot, watched silently as his mother helped Bess to the table where she sank down on one of the hard-backed chairs. He was utterly at a loss to know what to say.

Muriel took pity on him. 'You get off, lad,' she said quietly. 'If this is the flu you don't want to catch it, now then, not with the bairns, an' May in her condition.' She didn't mention Ronald's heart problem; he was a mite touchy about being reminded of what he saw as a weakness.

'Aye, I'd better.' But still he didn't move. He licked his lips. 'Bess?'

For a moment it looked as though Bess was going to ignore him but then she lifted her head. 'What?'

His tongue passed over his lower lip again. 'I . . . I hope it's not the flu.' Say it, he told himself. Tell her you're sorry for how you've been. Tell her she's welcome to call any time, the bairn too. But he couldn't. The words were sticking in his throat and choking him.

Bess looked at her brother for a few seconds, her cheek-bones standing out under her pasty skin which held the faintest tinge of yellow. 'I'll cope,' she said shortly. 'Same as I always do. Anyway, Mam and I are a good team, aren't we, Mam?' She smiled at her mother before resting her head on her arms again. 'I'm cold, Mam. Can I take the stone bottle up with me?'

'Course, lass, I'll fill it now.' Muriel flapped her hand at her son as she bustled over to the big black kettle standing on the range. 'You go, lad,' she said again. 'There's nowt you can do here and doubtless she'll be as right as rain in a week or two.'

Ronald cast a last glance at his sister before his gaze moved to little Amy who was happily engrossed in banging the saucepan lid. The child *was* bonny, there was no doubt about that, and where had those deep blue eyes come from? Had to be the father. For the first time since Amy had been born, he thought, Poor little mite. What a start in life she's going to have. He walked over to his mother, touching the wrinkled cheek with his lips before he said, 'Bye, Mam. I'll see you on Friday then.'

'All bein' well, lad.' Muriel inclined her head towards Bess. 'We'll see how things are.' Once Bess was home from work on a Friday, she and Wilbur went to Ronald's for a spot of dinner and a cup of tea most weeks. 'I'll let you know, shall I?'

Ronald hesitated before walking into the scullery and through to the backyard. Here he stood still, gnawing at his bottom lip before thrusting his cap on his head and pulling his muffler tighter round his neck. It was only the first week of October but already they'd had a couple of white frosts and the air today was raw.

Should he go back in there and make his peace with Bess? It was the perfect opportunity without his father about. He lifted his eyes to the sky which was low and heavy with dark clouds and seemed to be resting on the rooftops. His father wouldn't thank him for it if he did; neither would May's, for that matter. And May would take her cue from her da, same as she did on everything. Mr O'Leary had made it plain that a bastard in the family reflected on everyone, even the in-laws, and that he felt he ought to distance himself from his sister. But seeing Bess today, his heart had gone out to her.

A gust of wind carrying raindrops in its wake settled the matter. He'd best get off home before he got caught in the storm which was forecast; he could always call in and see Bess in a week or two when she was feeling better. Likely she'd be more inclined to accept the olive branch he intended to extend then anyway. Aye, that's what he'd do, he reaffirmed as he strode off down the lane. And if May and her da didn't like it, they'd have to lump it.

By the middle of October most of the schools in Britain had closed because of the influenza epidemic which was taking over two thousand lives a week in the capital alone. The disease was ruthless in its culling of a population already drained by years of war, and although there were now definite signs that the war would be over in a few weeks, no one was rejoicing, least of all Muriel. She stood now in Bess's bedroom listening to her child's laboured breathing. Dr Boyce was examining her for the third time in as many days and although he made a little joke which elicited a wan smile from Bess as he gently pulled the covers up over her chest, Muriel knew he was worried.

Dr Boyce signalled for Muriel to follow him out of the room and down the stairs, and as she did so she was aware that the dull pounding ache in her head she had woken up with was getting worse, along with the leaden feeling in her limbs.

Dr Boyce turned to face her in the hall. 'Normally I'd want Bess taken into hospital the way this bronchitis has taken hold but with the wards overflowing and half the medical staff laid up with the flu she's probably better off where she is. If you can cope, that is.'

'Cope?' Muriel gazed at him, bleary-eyed. 'Oh aye, Doctor. I can cope.'

'Are you feeling all right, Mrs Shawe?' Dr Boyce's tired eyes narrowed. In spite of having been on his feet for nearly forty-eight hours, he still recognised the onset of sickness when he saw it.

'Just a bit weary, Doctor.'

'On second thoughts it might be better if I arrange for Bess to be admitted to the infirmary.'

Muriel's head came up with a jerk of protest. 'No, no, Doctor,' she said hastily. 'You said yourself she's better off here. I'm all right. It's just that the bairn's been up the last night or two. Teethin', she is.' And then, in something of a rush, she added, 'But she's a good bairn, Doctor, an' I don't say that just because she's our own. Happy as the day's long, she is, an' when I think of the time when our Bess was carryin', that's a miracle in itself. If ever a bairn shouldn't have been born, this one shouldn't, with all her mam had to put up with.'

The doctor's voice was gentle when he said, 'There is a fine dividing line between life and death, Mrs Shawe, and I'm convinced it's more to do with the spirit than it is with the body.'

'Aye, I reckon you're right there.' Muriel nodded. 'Our Bess has always been strong in herself – a fighter, you know?'

The good doctor didn't say what he was thinking, namely that however strong Bess might have been, Amy's difficult delivery followed by the gruelling work in the munitions factory and her father's continuing ill treatment had all taken their toll, body, soul and spirit. Instead he smiled and patted Muriel's arm. 'Like mother, like daughter.'

'Oh, I'm not a strong person, Doctor.' Pink with embarrassment, Muriel fiddled with her pinny. 'Not like our Bess. She'll rally round from this flu in a bit an' be as right as rain, you mark my words.'

'I hope you're right, Mrs Shawe, but I shall pop in tomorrow about this time and have a look at her.' Dr Boyce made his way to the front door, stepping down into the street beyond before saying, 'Rest as much as you can, won't you?'

'Oh, I'm all right, Doctor, an' thank you.' Muriel did the curious little movement which was somewhere between a bob and genuflection, and which she kept for the priest and doctor alone, before shutting the front door. When she turned to face the stairs, everything swam for a moment and she put

44

out a hand to the wall to steady herself. Ee, she'd better have something to eat. She'd skipped breakfast this morning because she hadn't felt too good; likely that was the reason she felt a bit funny now. Whatever, she couldn't be sick. Who'd look after Bess and the bairn if she was sick?

When Dr Boyce returned to the house in Deptford Road the next morning, which was a Saturday, it was Kitty who opened the door to him, Amy in her arms. She explained how she'd called round to see Bess a little while before and found Muriel all but collapsed in the kitchen. 'I've sent her to bed, Doctor,' Kitty said earnestly. 'I can take care of things over the weekend, and me mam'll have Amy during the day come Monday when I'm at work. Just till Bess is on her feet again.'

'How is Bess?' the doctor asked, glancing up the stairs as he took off his coat.

'Well . . .' Kitty hesitated for a second before saying, her voice low, 'She seems right poorly to me, Doctor.'

A swift examination confirmed that further complications had set in, pneumonia being the biggest threat. And when Bess made only a token protest at being sent to the Sunderland infirmary, Dr Boyce knew she was aware of just how ill she was.

Muriel was hot and feverish and barely coherent when he walked into the second bedroom, but on hearing he was proposing to send Bess to hospital, she struggled out of bed to prove how much better she was feeling, with the result that she fainted clean away in Dr Boyce's arms.

By the time Wilbur came home at midday, the house was very quiet. He stopped dead on the threshold to the kitchen, eyeing Kitty who was stirring something in a pan on the stove.

'Hello, Mr Shawe.' Kitty was terrified of Bess's father and it showed as she gabbled, 'The doctor's been and Bess is in hospital and Mrs Shawe is in bed. Amy's with me mam and she's said she'll keep her until things sort out with Bess. I've stripped Bess's bed and Mam's soaking all the stuff in our poss tub ready for Monday's wash so there's nowt for you to do. Do . . . do you want to go up and see Mrs Shawe?'

Wilbur kept her waiting for some ten seconds before he nodded at the pan, raising his eyebrows.

'Oh, it's some of me mam's rabbit stew,' Kitty said in answer to the silent enquiry. 'I tried to get Mrs Shawe to have a little but she couldn't. Mam's put in a good few dumplings for you . . .' Her voice dwindled away.

Wilbur was enjoying himself. Kitty's fear amused him. He had always considered her the runt of that litter next door and her friendship with his daughter irritated him.

Still without speaking he seated himself at the kitchen table, breaking a piece of bread off the fresh loaf Kitty had placed there and chewing it as he watched her tip the contents of the pan into a large white bowl. Her hands were trembling as she set the stew before him and for a second he was tempted to move suddenly and make her jump, just for the hell of it. Instead he picked up his spoon and began to eat.

Kitty walked across to the range where a pot of tea was mashing on the steel shelf to one side of the fire. She brought it to the table and placed it beside the sugar bowl. 'I've got to go for me dinner,' she said weakly. 'I'll come back later and see if Mrs Shawe wants anything, shall I?'

Wilbur raised his head, staring at her unblinkingly. 'Aye,' he said slowly. 'I'm going to the football.'

Kitty nodded. Her mam had said he would. Her mam couldn't stand Bess's da any more than she could.

Wilbur watched her collect the dirty pan from the stove and scurry across the room. He let her get right to the back door before he called, 'You! Kitty!'

Her eyes were like saucers as she came back to the kitchen threshold and his pleasure increased. He chewed long and hard on a piece of meat, prolonging the moment, before he said, 'Thank your mam for the stew.' He didn't smile.

'Oh aye, aye, I will, Mr Shawe.' And then she fled as though the devil himself was on her heels.

'I told you he'd still go to the footie, now didn't I, Abe?' Kitty's mother plonked her husband's dinner in front of him as though the situation next door was his fault. 'And there's you saying don't be hasty, give the man a chance. Chance my backside.' She glared at the serene-looking man now stolidly eating his meal, her glance encompassing the remaining five of her nine children still living at home before coming to rest on Amy who was seated on Kitty's lap. 'Poor little lass,' she said to no one in particular.

After dishing up her children's food, Sally Price took Amy off Kitty and began to feed the toddler herself. 'You sure you told him we'll keep her till Bess is back?' she asked Kitty after Amy had taken a few mouthfuls.

Kitty nodded. There wasn't room to swing a cat in the house with her three elder brothers in one bedroom, herself and her older sister in the other and her parents sleeping in the front room, but she'd known her mam would take

Amy. Her mam was like that. And she thought a bit of Bess's mam.

'And he didn't say anything?'

'No.'

'Ignorant so-an'-so. Still, now he knows he's got no excuse to ship the bairn off to the workhouse.'

'Sally.' Abe's voice held mild reproach. 'Who says he was thinking of that?'

'I do,' Sally snapped, 'and you'd see it yourself if you didn't always think the best of everyone. The way he's been with this bairn is a crying shame, and her so bonny. You going to see Bess later?' she added to Kitty.

Kitty shook her head. 'Dr Boyce said best to leave it to the morrer 'cos she'll be tired out, what with the move and all.'

'Well, when you visit you tell her from me the bairn'll be all right with us for as long as it takes for her to get better. I'll pop round and see Muriel later and tell her the same. Put her mind at rest.' Sally looked down at the little girl nestled on her lap, the rosebud mouth wide open for the next spoonful of food. 'Good as gold, aren't you, hinny,' she crooned in a softer voice than she'd used thus far. 'And Mam'll be home soon, never you fear. She's in the right place to make her better.'

But Bess wasn't better when Kitty arrived at the hospital the next day. She was in a little side ward and curtains had been drawn round the bed.

'Are you a relation?' the prim-looking nurse on duty asked. 'Sister says only close relations can visit Miss Shawe and then just for a minute or two. She's very poorly.'

Kitty thought quickly. 'I'm her sister.'

The nurse said nothing but raised disbelieving eyebrows.

Kitty flushed and then threw caution to the wind. 'She'll want to see me,' she said in a low but urgent voice. 'Really she will. We're like sisters, we always have been and me mam's looking after Bess's – Miss Shawe's – bairn and we're seeing to her mam. I need to tell her everything's all right, put her mind at rest. *Please*, Nurse.'

The muscles in the stiff face relaxed slightly. There was a pause and then the nurse said, 'You're her sister, right? With a message from her mam about the bairn.'

'Right.' Kitty nodded in perfect understanding.

'Come on then but you can only stay for a minute.' The nurse led her to the curtains which she drew carefully aside to let Kitty through before following herself. Bending over the bed and smoothing the already smooth coverlet, she repeated, 'Just a minute and then you'll have to go. I'll come and get you.'

Kitty couldn't say anything, she was too shocked by the change in Bess since the day before. Her friend had looked very ill then, now she looked . . . She swallowed hard. She drew up the chair by the side of the bed and sat down as the nurse disappeared, pulling the curtains shut behind her.

'Hello, lass,' she said softly as the sunken eyes in the grey face opened. 'How are you feeling?'

'Kitty.' Bess feebly reached out her hand, her eyes filling with tears.

'Don't fret, lass.' Kitty grasped Bess's cold fingers in her own warm ones. 'Everything's going to be fine.'

'Amy?'

'Me mam's got her and we're keeping her till you're home.

49

She's being spoiled rotten by me da and the lads and everyone. Your mam's got the flu and she's not too good but she sends her love.'

'Kitty.' Bess had to take a gasping breath to continue and Kitty winced at the painfulness of it. 'Don't let him have her.'

'Your da? No, no, he hasn't got her, lass. She's with us.'

'I mean . . .' Another breath. 'When I'm gone. He'll put her away, I know he will.' Bess's lips were scarcely moving.

Kitty's voice was trembling when she said, 'You're not going anywhere except home to Amy once you're better.'

Bess's head moved from side to side on the pillow in silent denial. 'I . . . know, Kitty, and I'm not frightened.' Her mouth opened and shut twice before she could continue. 'Since I've been in here I've made my peace with God.'

'Oh, lass.'

'He's not the God Father Fraser goes on about. He's good, forgiving.' The fight for breath was harder now and when Kitty, panic-stricken, went to rise to call the nurse, Bess gasped, 'No, don't go. Promise me, lass. Promise me you won't let me da put her away, 'cos he will. Mam . . . Mam's no match for him, she never has been.'

'I promise. Course I promise. Me mam loves her, we all do.'

'You . . . promised.' The glimmer of a smile touched Bess's colourless lips. 'Tell her I loved her, that I wanted her. Tell her that when she grows up, that she was precious to me.'

Kitty could barely see Bess's face now for the tears coursing down her cheeks, and when she felt a tap on her shoulder and the nurse's voice saying, 'You'll have to go now, I'm afraid,' she had the mad notion to gather Bess in her arms and run out of the hospital with her. She didn't want her to die here, alone, surrounded by stiff, starchy strangers and the smell of antiseptic.

'I'm sorry.' The nurse was brisk. 'I really must insist you let her rest now.'

'Bye, bye, lass.' Kitty smoothed a lock of hair from Bess's forehead and then bent and kissed where her hand had touched. 'I'll come the morrer and don't worry, your da won't have her.' And as Bess closed her eyes, Kitty gently slid her hand from the limp fingers and blindly made her way out of the room, her heart breaking.

Bess died just as the dawn chorus began the following morning. That same afternoon Muriel suffered a stroke when Father Fraser, against medical advice, took it upon himself to inform the sick woman of her child's demise. By nightfall the mother was a resident in the same hospital that housed the daughter in its mortuary.

Ronald went to see his mother the next day. He didn't tell her that Wilbur was already making plans to send their granddaughter to the workhouse orphanage. Nor did he divulge that his father had thoroughly upset the Price family by riding roughshod over their offer to keep the little girl indefinitely, even going so far as to warn them he would set the law on the family if they didn't hand Amy over to the guardians.

What Ronald did do was to sit on the narrow hard bed for the whole of his visit, holding his mother in his arms. Muriel could not speak, the stroke had taken all one side, but Ronald knew she understood his murmured whispers because the look of abject pleading faded from her eyes as he talked on.

On leaving the sterile confines of the infirmary he went straight to Deptford Road but not to his parents' house. Half an hour later he exited the Price household with his niece in his arms and a bag of her clothes over one arm.

During the tram ride into Monkwearmouth while the child slept cuddled up on his lap, he prepared himself for the furore which would erupt when he walked in with Bess's little girl. Things were already difficult between him and May and it seemed as if they were arguing about everything and nothing these days; Amy's presence in the house would only add fuel to May's ever-glowing fire. His in-laws would create and so would his father. Wilbur had been determined to see the infant shipped off to the workhouse and out of their lives. But he could handle his da the same as the rest of them if he was strong enough, and he would be strong over this. Mostly for his mother's sake, he had to admit; she'd go mad with grief if the baby was put away, but also to make some sort of reparation to Bess, late though it was. And then there was Amy herself.

He glanced down at the tot on his lap who was sleeping with her thumb in her mouth, her other hand clasping the front of his jacket. She had been sitting on Mrs Price's lap finishing her supper when he had walked in the house, and when she had caught sight of him she had smiled and held out her arms. She had never done that before. Of course it was probably because she associated him with her grandma, he knew that, but nevertheless it had touched something inside him, melting the hardness. When all was said and done, you couldn't blame the bairn for her beginnings. If anyone was the innocent in all of this, she was.

As the tram jolted and creaked its way along, he looked

out of the window, his mouth grim. There was going to be all hell to pay because of this wee scrap of a bairn in his arms, and it wouldn't end tonight. He knew that. But he was glad he had taken her, whatever May and his in-laws and his da might throw at him. If nothing else, he might be able to sleep again at night now.

PART TWO

1931 That Girl

Chapter 4

'Mam says your precious Aunt Kitty is going to die an old maid, so there.' Eva Shawe's spotty chin was thrust forward as she spoke and behind her her sister Harriet sniggered.

Amy stared at her cousins. She knew exactly what Eva was trying to do. Amy's deep blue eyes with their thick spiky lashes held the other girl's for a moment more and then she shrugged slender shoulders, turned her back on them and continued to scour the black-encrusted pan in the deep stone sink in the scullery.

There was silence for a moment and then Eva's taunting voice came again. 'Plain as a pikestaff, Mam says she is, and with as much chance of ever catching a husband. One look at her face and even the wind changes direction.'

Amy didn't care that she was playing right into Eva's hands by answering her cousin back; she wasn't going to have them laughing at her Aunt Kitty like this. Not without saying something. She braced herself and turned round, her clear creamy skin flushed a deep pink. 'Sure your mam wasn't talking about you?' she said coldly.

Eva's olive complexion turned brick red. Harriet gave a long drawn out 'Ooooh' of admonition although her equally plain face was alight with anticipation of what Amy's remark would mean.

'I'm telling Mam of you,' said Eva, her gratification in what she'd accomplished diminished by the home truth. 'Think you're everybody, you do.'

'No, I know who I am.' Amy knew better than to turn her back on them again. After a battle of words like this, Eva liked nothing more than to catch her unawares with a sly kick or punch, after which she would run like the wind to her mother's side to tell tales, most of them grossly exaggerated.

'Aye, and so do we, don't we, Harriet?'

Eva bounced her head conspiratorially at her sister but Harriet said nothing. She never did. She just liked to stand back and watch the fun.

'Your mam wasn't married when you were born,' Eva went on. 'Everyone knows that. Went with anyone, she did. And so that makes you a . . .'

Eva stopped short of saying the word but it hovered in the air between them. Bastard. She'd flung it in Amy's face some months before when she had first realised the significance of what it meant, but after the ensuing fight with Amy, when her brothers had told their mother what she had said, Eva had received the first and only spanking of her life. Her mother had warned her then that if she ever heard her say the word again she wouldn't be able to sit down for a week.

It was after the pandemonium and upset of that day that Ronald's four older children had realised how different Amy was. There was deep shame attached to their cousin, a shame which encroached on the family name as a whole, and for this reason Amy's beginnings must never be mentioned. Not even by them.

Amy was now ramrod straight but she didn't give in to the desire to slap the sneering smile off Eva's face as she had done when she was younger. She didn't want to give her cousin the satisfaction, besides which Eva was a dirty fighter and always won. Her voice shaking in spite of all her efforts to hide how upset she was, she said, 'You're a truly nasty, ugly person, Eva, inside where it really counts. And even if your outside changes, that won't.'

The back door opened as she spoke. Amy turned her head, expecting to see her Aunt May back from shopping and mentally steeling herself for what would follow. But it was her eldest cousin, Perce, who stood stamping the snow off his boots. He had been taken on at the Iron and Steel Works by his grandfather on leaving school at fourteen two years before, and eighteen months later Bruce had joined his father and brother. The family had swelled to eight children – Betsy and Ruth, the twins, at eight years old, Thomas who was five and little eighteen-month-old Milly had followed the four older children – but with three wage packets coming in, the Depression hadn't affected them as much as some folk.

Perce immediately sensed the atmosphere in the scullery. 'What's going on?' His dark eyes flashed over Amy's face to rest on Eva's. 'What have you been saying?' he asked roughly.

'Oh, that's right, take her side as usual.' Eva began to cry. 'She called me ugly, didn't she, Harriet? She said I was ugly and that she'd be May Queen this year and she wouldn't choose me to attend her.'

'I didn't.' Amy's voice was quiet in contrast to Eva's gabble.

In spite of the fact that she knew Eva was right and that Perce would take her side, she wished it had been her aunt who had come in. The last few months she had admitted to herself she was frightened of Perce and yet she couldn't say why. He was always nice to her, like Bruce. As nice as Eva was nasty. Both lads had been that way since she could remember. But whereas Bruce was easy-going and gentle and made her laugh, Perce was . . . different. The way he looked at her, the number of times he seemed to accidentally brush against her made her all on edge when he was around. It was silly, she knew, but sometimes she felt as though his gaze seemed to go through her clothes to her bare skin.

Amy took a deep breath and spoke across Eva who had begun to embroider her story even more. 'Eva was saying nasty things about my mam and Aunt Kitty. I told her she was ugly inside and she is, but I never mentioned being May Queen or anything like that.'

'You!' Eva rounded on her. 'You're a dirty little liar. I never started it, did I, Harriet?'

Harriet stood gnawing on her thumbnail. Amy knew she didn't want to get on the wrong side of either of her siblings; they both had a way of making life unpleasant for anyone who crossed them. She wasn't surprised when Harriet dropped her head and took refuge in the tears she could turn on and off like a tap when it suited her.

Perce had taken off his cap and jacket and hung them on one of the pegs in the scullery. He raked back his thick brown hair, his voice a growl when he said to his sisters, 'Get up them stairs, the pair of you. I'm sick of your carrying on. It's about time you started to grow up a bit.'

'Oh you, our Perce!' Eva stood her ground. She was the

only one of Perce's brothers and sisters who wasn't a little afraid of him. This was partly due to the fact that she knew she was her mother's favourite and could count on her protection, but also because she was wily and cunning and knew how to get the upper hand. She tossed her head at him now, her lank plaits bobbing. 'Just 'cos you want to show off in front of Amy.'

Perce's neck turned a dull red, the colour creeping upwards into his cheeks. 'Shut your face.'

Amy stared at them both. She sensed undercurrents of a nature which puzzled her, the more so when Eva said, 'You still courting Cissy Owen then?'

'None of your business.'

''Cos her brother says she's been crying every night for a week. He told me at school she's sure you've got your eye on someone else.'

'She doesn't know what she's on about.'

'I think she does.' Eva put her hands on her dumpy hips, her brown eyes tight on her brother's dark countenance. 'And you're barmy if you think Mam would stand for it.'

'I said she doesn't know what she's on about.'

Amy was listening now with a mixture of amazement and relief, although she wouldn't have been able to explain the latter emotion, even to herself. Perce had a lass? He had never said or brought her to the house. Amy's gaze left Eva and fastened on Perce. He was tall and hefty and looked a lot older than sixteen and she noticed for the first time that he was quite handsome. She felt silly. Of course Perce would have found himself a lass, he'd left school well over two years ago and was earning steady money, thanks to his grandad. He'd be a catch for the lasses round about.

The arrival of Aunt May cut short any further taunting. Amy waited for Eva's normal tittle-tattle to her mother to begin and returned to her scouring. The others followed their mother through to the kitchen. To Amy's surprise, Eva made no mention of their altercation to her mother. From what she could hear, the two girls were setting the places for the Saturday fry-up they always had when Uncle Ronald and the lads finished work for the week, and Perce was explaining to his mother he was home a little earlier than his father and brother because his grandad had asked him to run an errand to one of their customers.

The heavy pan clean at last, Amy stood for a moment looking out of the tiny slit of the scullery window. She hoped the thick snow wouldn't stop her Aunt Kitty's regular Saturday visit. Aunt Kitty always took her to see her Grandma Shawe while her grandfather was at the football, but today she'd promised they would go and have tea at Binns too, as an extra birthday present. Amy's hands, red and chapped from the scouring and cleaning she had been doing all morning since her breakfast at seven o'clock, touched the tiny silver cross at her throat. Her Aunt Kitty had given it to her the Saturday before for her fourteenth birthday which had fallen on a weekday. As usual it had been a quiet sort of birthday. Her Aunt May did not like her birthday being celebrated in the house. She didn't bake her a cake, which she always did for a family birthday, or give her good wishes. This birthday hadn't passed totally unnoticed in the Shawe household, however. Bruce had wished her a happy birthday and given her a box of chocolates.

'What are you standing there for?' When her aunt appeared in the doorway, her voice was sharp. 'Daydreaming again, girl?'

Amy stared at the thin, unprepossessing woman in front of her. She couldn't remember when it had first dawned on her that her aunt didn't like her, but along with the knowledge had come the realisation that she rarely called her anything but girl. And when her aunt thought she was out of earshot she referred to her in that way to Uncle Ronald too. That girl.

'I've just finished seeing to the pans.' Amy motioned with her hand towards the pile at the side of the stone sink. They had taken well over an hour to clean. 'They were the last job.'

May nodded, her pale blue eyes assessing the result. 'Good. Bring them through then and hang them up,' she said briskly. She didn't offer any thanks for what had been a full morning's work and Amy did not expect any. Although the other children who were still at school all had little chores to do, none of them were expected to work like she did. But they were Aunt May and Uncle Ronald's own bairns, whereas she had been taken in when otherwise she would have been placed in the workhouse orphanage. Again Amy couldn't have said when she had come by this knowledge, it was as though she had always known it. But it was only in the last few months after the fight with Eva that she had ceased striving to win her aunt's affections.

'Aunt Kitty said she was going to take me to tea at Binns this week.' Amy picked up two of the heavy pans. 'Can I wear my Sunday frock, Aunt May?'

There was a pause and Amy knew her aunt wanted to refuse.

'Aye, if you're careful,' May said at last.

Amy had just put the pans away when the sound of crying

filtered through from upstairs. It was Milly, woken from her morning nap. Amy went to fetch the child without being asked; this was one of her many unspoken duties.

She picked the baby out of the cot, which was placed next to her aunt and uncle's bed, and stood for a moment gazing round the room. It was comfortable and nicely furnished, as was the whole house. But she knew her uncle hadn't provided the money for it. Mr O'Leary, Aunt May's da, had seen to it all.

Rocking the baby in her arms, Amy's mind went back to the time when they knew they were going to move to Fulwell. She had only been six or seven but she could remember the rows which had ensued for weeks before her Uncle Ronald had told them they were leaving Monkwearmouth. She especially remembered sitting on the stairs one night with Perce and Bruce, the three of them listening to Mr O'Leary in the kitchen below with Aunt May and Uncle Ronald. He'd declared that with the arrival of the twins there was no way his only child was going to be stuck in this rabbit hutch of a house where there wasn't room to swing a cat. He'd found a nice property, he boomed. A three-bed terrace, with the fourth having been converted into a bathroom housing an indoor privy, bath and basin. And downstairs a front room, sitting room, kitchen and scullery would mean the family weren't on top of each other all the time like they were now.

She and the boys had clutched each other, their eyes wide at the thought of an indoor privy, but Uncle Ronald had spoken and said just as loudly as Mr O'Leary that they were staying put in Monkwearmouth and that was that. Only it hadn't been. Her Aunt May had cried and cried and the rows had begun and then Aunt May had taken to her bed and the doctor had said she was suffering with her nerves. Shortly after this they had moved to Fulwell.

Amy left the room and walked downstairs, collecting the twins and Thomas from the sitting room where they'd been playing with their colouring books and crayons. By the time Ronald and Bruce walked in five minutes later, the little ones had washed their hands under Amy's supervision and everyone was seated at the kitchen table.

Bruce smiled at Amy and she smiled back. Whatever the situation she always felt happier when Bruce was around. He was one of those people who always seemed to carry the sun wherever he went. She found it strange that with only eighteen months separating him and Perce, the two brothers were so different. In nature, that was. They looked very similar.

Her eyes followed her thoughts and she glanced at her eldest cousin and found Perce's gaze hard on her. She stared at him for a second, taken aback by the look on his face. If she didn't know better she would have said he was angry with her but she hadn't upset him in any way, had she? No, she was sure she hadn't. She blinked and the look was gone. But it had unnerved her.

Kitty arrived just as they were finishing their meal. When the knock came at the back door, May answered it although Eva and Bruce were nearer the scullery. They heard her voice, stilted and cool, inviting Kitty in. As though it was some great honour, Amy thought darkly. Her Aunt May did it to make Kitty uncomfortable, she was sure of it, but it never worked because Kitty just ignored the tone and was as cheerful and talkative as she always was.

'Hello, lass.' Kitty's eyes went straight to Amy as she entered the kitchen. 'Ready for the off?'

'I just have to change my frock,' said Amy, jumping up from her chair and rushing upstairs.

An uncomfortable silence followed her departure, which was broken by Ronald saying, 'Busy at work, Kitty?'

'Aye, fair rushed off our feet but with two million unemployed I'm not complaining. Mind, it bears out what me mam said when I got set on at the laundry after the war. She said the need for munitions might wane but laundries will always do a good trade.'

Ronald nodded but did not pursue the conversation, realising too late he'd probably put his foot in it with May by mentioning Kitty's job. Her promotion to manageress at the laundry had been a sore point with his wife since she'd heard the news. But then May had never liked Bess's friend or the interest she took in Amy. He couldn't understand why. Kitty was a grand little lass and always cheerful, whatever might ail her. May could do worse than take a leaf out of Kitty's book, in his opinion. He smiled at Kitty and she smiled back at him, her plain face with its slightly pock-marked skin lighting up as it always did when she smiled.

Amy reappeared in the next moment and Ronald reflected for the hundredth time how bonny his niece was. His daughters had inherited May's sallow skin and straight, thin hair, with the added encumbrance of the O'Leary large nose, whereas his lads had all taken after his own da and had thick curly hair and attractive features, but Amy was in a class of her own.

Amy's eyes were shining as she fetched her hat and coat from the scullery and quickly pulled them on while Kitty, pleasant as ever in spite of May's sour face, made her goodbyes. Only Ronald answered her, the others merely inclining their heads and the younger children squabbling over the last piece of fried bread.

Ronald left his seat and followed his niece and Kitty into the backyard, pressing a shilling into Amy's gloved hand after he had glanced over his shoulder to make sure May hadn't followed him. 'Late birthday present,' he said gruffly as Amy stared at him in surprise. 'Our little secret, lass. All right?'

Dear oh dear. If ever a man was henpecked, thought Kitty, this one was. And it was a shame because Ronald was so nice. More than nice. Kitty kept her thoughts to herself, smiling at Ronald before saying briskly to Amy who had just thanked her uncle, 'Come on then, hinny, your grandma is on tenterhooks to see you. We might be a little late back the night, Ron, what with going to Binns and all. That won't upset the apple cart, will it?'

Kitty's meaning was clear and Ronald shook his head, his voice low as he said, 'No, no, that'll be all right. I'll explain to May. You two have a nice time and give my love to Gran, Amy.'

Out in the narrow back lane which ran between terraced backyards, they slipped and slithered their way along frozen ridged snow, giggling when one or the other of them nearly went full length. This part of Fulwell housed quite a few solicitors, bank managers and the like and was almost middle-class. There were no overflowing lavatory hatches with their accompanying smell as most of the large terraced houses had had similar conversions to that of Ronald and May's home, and some of the backyards had even been laid to grass.

If Amy's life had been different, thought Kitty, if the bairn had had even a little affection shown her by her Aunt May, she'd have landed on her feet. As it was, she was nowt but a skivvy and an unpaid one at that. But at least Bess's da hadn't had his way. Kitty rammed her hat further on her head as a gust of icy wind nearly took it. Ronald had stood up to him and the others once in his life at least.

'My mam wants to see you,' she said to Amy once they'd exited the back lane and begun the walk to the tram stop. 'She's got something for you for your birthday.'

'Really?' Amy gave a little skip and a hop, curbing the impulse to pivot round two or three times as she was wont to do when the peculiar joy of living filled her. Anything could cause these brief explosions of sheer happiness – a beautiful sunset, the blackbird singing his heart out at twilight on the brick wall at the end of the yard, even the sight of newly fallen snow when it glittered like diamond dust – but since the incident with Eva in the summer she hadn't felt the inexpressible emotion welling up until it filled every part of her. Until now. She caught hold of Kitty's hand, her voice shy as she said, 'I love you, Aunt Kitty.'

'And I love you, hinny.'

'I wish . . .'

'What?'

'Oh, nothing.' How could she say she wished Aunt Kitty was her real aunty and that she lived with her and Mr and Mrs Price in their little house in Deptford Road? Kitty might tell Mrs Price and she might let on to Gran and then her gran would be upset. Her gran thought the world of Uncle Ronald. But when she was with Kitty and her mam and da she felt . . . normal. They liked her. Just as she was they liked her. 'I just wish it could be Saturday every day of the week, that's all.'

They stood with arms linked until the tram came. The

journey was just a few minutes and when they alighted, Kitty said, 'We'll go in and see your gran first, shall we? And then Mam before we go to Binns.'

Amy nodded. Much as she liked Kitty's mother, she couldn't wait to see her grandma. Every Saturday when she had to leave her for another week she had a physical ache in her chest that didn't go away all the rest of the evening.

Muriel's eyes were fixed on the door when Amy and Kitty entered the front room. The four walls had enclosed her world since the stroke twelve years before. Although she had recovered her speech after a while, her heart had been severely affected. From the time she had left the infirmary she had remained virtually bedridden, moving only from the single bed which had been brought downstairs from Bess's room to the large leather-covered commode which also served as a chair for any visitors. She knew her neighbours and friends pitied her and she could understand it — most folk in her condition would find life a trial. What they could never understand because she could never tell them was that the last twelve years had been the happiest of her life in some ways. Of course she still grieved for Bess, there wasn't a day went by when she didn't have a little tear, but each day since she'd come home from the hospital had been an extension of the two nine-month periods when Wilbur hadn't touched her. Then it had been because she was carrying a child, now it was the fact that he found any sort of illness repulsive. If only she could have had Amy living with her she would have been the happiest woman alive, but it was a comfort to know her Ronald was bringing up the lass with his bairns. Young folk needed other young folk.

'Hello, me bairn.' Muriel held out her arms and Amy ran to the bed and kissed her grandmother before perching beside her while Kitty seated herself in the leather chair.

'Has he gone?' Kitty asked quietly.

'Oh aye, over twenty minutes ago.' Muriel smiled at them both. 'It's just the three of us.'

Amy wriggled her contentment. When she was with her grandma like this she often wished she could stay nestled into her side for ever. 'Look what Aunt Kitty gave me.' She had been pulling off her coat and scarf as she spoke and now lifted up the little cross which was lying in the hollow of her throat. And then, because she knew it would please her grandmother, she added, 'And Uncle Ronald gave me a whole shilling for my birthday to spend however I like.'

'Fancy.' Muriel smiled at the light of her life. 'Well, I've got somethin' for you an' all now you're all grown up an' about to leave school.' She didn't dwell on this. She knew the lass had wanted to go to the secondary school, bright as a button Amy was, but she could understand Ronald and May's reasoning that if their lads had had to leave at fourteen and work, it was only right that Amy should. Mind, Ronald's bairns didn't have as much up top as Amy did from what she could make out. Not that she saw much of any of them. Still, she shouldn't complain. At least Ronald came once a week to see her.

'Go across to the fire,' she said to Amy, and when Amy slid off the bed and did as she was told, she added, 'Now pull the rug back a bit.'

Amy turned with a questioning look on her face but Muriel, enjoying herself, said, 'Go on, go on, it won't bite you, lass.'

The shop-bought rug was a leftover from the days when the room had been Muriel's pride and joy, a mausoleum for only the most honoured visitors. It covered half the bare floorboards which once had been polished to perfection.

Amy knelt and pulled the thin fringed material to one side. 'There's nothing here, Gran.'

'That's what folk are supposed to think. See that floor-board with the little chip out of it? Put your finger in there an' lever it up. That's right, go on. There's summat wrapped in a bit of old sacking an' a little bag beside it. Bring 'em here, hinny.'

Beside herself with excitement, Amy brought the square package and little dusty pouch to her grandmother, laying them on the eiderdown. Muriel leaned back on her pillows for a moment or two, her gnarled, veined hands resting on the sacking as she caught her breath.

Kitty hadn't said a word during the proceedings but when Amy glanced at her she raised her eyebrows, expressing curiosity and surprise.

'Now you're not goin' to be able to tell anyone about this in case it gets back to your granda, all right?'

Amy nodded, and when Muriel turned her gaze on Kitty the younger woman said quietly, 'You know me, Mrs Shawe. I won't say nowt.'

'I know that, Kitty. By, I do. You're a good lass and no mistake. What I would have done without you an' your mam the last few years since I've been in this bed I don't know.' The two women smiled at each other before Muriel lifted the item wrapped in the sacking and said to Amy, 'Take a look at this, hinny. You're goin' to have to hide it for the time being' – she didn't say until she had passed on but that was

71

what she meant — "cos the roof nearly went off this house when your mam gave it to me for me birthday. She was sixteen when she had it took.'

'Oh, Gran.' Amy stared down at the photograph of her mother, a shiver of sheer wonder vying with the lump in her throat. This was her mam, her *mam*. Her grandma and Kitty had described her mother to her but it wasn't the same as seeing her. Before now there had only been the picture of her mam as a little baby lying on a sheepskin rug, the same as her grandma had had taken of Uncle Ronald when he was a bairn. These were on her grandma's mantelpiece — her eyes flashed briefly to them — but they just looked the same as any baby to her. This was different. She gazed into the large dark eyes in the photograph. They looked dreamy, soft, and the bow-shaped mouth was half smiling. This was her mam when she was only two years older than she was now, before she met the man who had hurt her so badly. Amy never referred to him as her father, not even in her mind. Suddenly she burst into tears.

'Ee, come on, me bairn.' Muriel's voice was gentle but it held a gratified note. 'I knew you'd like to see her proper. I was goin' to keep the picture till you got wed or somethin' but . . .' Her voice trailed away. She couldn't say that there were more and more days lately when she doubted she'd still be alive to see that occasion; she didn't want to upset the lass by speaking of her death. 'But I thought you were old enough now not to let on to your granda,' she went on. 'He said it was a waste of money, your mam havin' it done for me. Said she'd got ideas above her station, her goin' to a fancy photographer in town an' all. On an' on he went till I put it away for safe keepin'.'

'She's beautiful, isn't she, Gran?' Amy's eyes, luminous with tears, met her grandmother's.

Muriel stared into the great blue pools. Her Bess had been bonny, she had taken after Wilbur in her colouring and thick curly hair and had turned heads from the minute she'd been born. But bonny as Bess had been, she wasn't a patch on Amy. There was something about her granddaughter's face, a delicacy, a fragility – oh, she didn't have the learning to know the words to describe it. And the bairn's eyes, she had seen blue eyes before but never the vivid violet shade looking at her so tenderly now.

Men would want her. Panic brought her hand fluttering to her throat, her heart undergoing a number of rapid palpitations.

'You're goin' to be leavin' school soon, hinny.' Muriel leaned forward and touched Amy's arm, bringing her granddaughter's gaze from the photograph. 'An' not everyone out there in the world is what they seem on the surface. You'll have to be careful, you understand me? You know what happened to your mam an' she wasn't bad, far from it, but she was gullible. An' some men see a bonny lass an' have to have them, right or wrong.'

Gran was talking about *him*. Amy stared at her grandmother, her face growing pink. She blinked. 'Don't worry, Gran.'

'But I do, hinny.' Muriel's breathing was laboured. 'Your mam was a sweet trustin' soul an' look where that got her.'

Amy didn't know what to say. Her grandmother had never spoken like this before. In all their conversations about her mother she had only related incidents from Bess's childhood or things her mam had said and done which illustrated how

73

loving and considerate she'd been. It had been Kitty who had told her about Christopher Lyndon. She was glad he was dead. It was not a new thought. After what he'd done to her mam, he hadn't deserved to live and be happy.

Amy laid the photograph carefully on the bed before placing her hands on her grandmother's, which had been pulling agitatedly at the eiderdown. 'I'm not like Mam in the trusting people sense, Gran,' she said quietly. 'All right?'

She could see her grandmother was surprised but Amy couldn't find the right words to explain further. She just knew she would never let a lad take her down without their being wed. The way her Aunt May and Mr O'Leary and especially her granda looked at her sometimes wouldn't let her for one thing. Her mam hadn't been bad and neither was she and one day she would show the lot of them. Quite what she'd show them she wasn't sure, but she'd make it happen. And it would be for her mam as well as for her.

'You've got a level head on your shoulders, hinny, that's for sure,' said Muriel, somewhat reassured. 'Just you make certain some canny lad with the gift of the gab doesn't turn it, that's all I'm sayin'. Silver-tongued, some of 'em are. Isn't that right, Kitty?'

Kitty smiled, a smile which was rueful but without rancour. 'To be truthful I haven't had too many spinning me a line, Mrs Shawe, but rest assured if one tries he'll be up the aisle and standing in front of the priest with me clothed in white afore he can blink.'

Muriel and Amy laughed, as Kitty had meant them to, but as Amy looked at her mother's best friend, she thought, The lads hereabout must be mad not to see what a lovely person she is; she'd make anyone a wonderful wife. The echo of Eva's spiteful remarks about Kitty came to mind and impulsively Amy said, 'Whoever gets you will be the luckiest lad in town, Aunt Kitty.'

Kitty's lids blinked rapidly; she swallowed and moistened her lips before she said, 'Thanks, lass, but I'm not holding me breath. Happen I'll carry on as I am and that doesn't seem a bad thing on a Sunday afternoon when all our lot come for tea with their bairns. Bedlam it is.'

She didn't mean it. There was something in Kitty's eyes which pained Amy and she turned from it, saying quickly, 'What's in the little bag, Gran?'

'What? Oh aye. Here, take a look.' Muriel thrust the velvet pouch at her granddaughter.

Amy loosened the drawstrings and peered inside before tipping the contents on the bed. Three pound notes fluttered onto the eiderdown.

'This was goin' to be for a bit of a do when your mam got wed,' Muriel said softly. 'I started savin' the odd penny or two from me housekeepin' on the sly from when she was born until I ended up in this bed twelve years ago. Me own weddin' was a pauper's affair an' I wanted me lass to have a nice dress an' a knees-up. I knew your granda wouldn't agree but I'd got in mind for Bess to say to the young man, whoever he was, that it had come from his pocket. I'd got it all worked out.' She smiled a watery smile, her lips trembling. 'Course sometimes there were weeks when I couldn't put anythin' away. Your granda's always had to know the ins an' outs of old Meg's backside an' I swear he could add up what I'd spent down to the last farthin'. Mean as muck, Wilbur was, unless it came to tickets for the footie or money spent on his baccy and beer.'

'But I can't take this, Gran.' Amy was staring in awe at the notes.

'You can an' you will, hinny. Put it away in one of them post office accounts or summat an' no one will be any the wiser. Kitty'll go with you to set it up, won't you, lass?'

'Aye, yes. We could go this afternoon,' said Kitty.

'There you are then, it's settled. It'll be a weight off me mind to know you've got it an' your mam's picture, bless her heart.'

'Oh, Gran.' Amy suddenly laid her face against her grandmother's, and when Muriel hugged her close with a strength which belied her frail frame the two of them clung to each other for long moments.

Chapter 5

By the time Amy and Kitty left the warmth of Binns later that day after a delicious tea of wafer-thin sandwiches and cream cakes, it was quite dark outside. Fawcett Street was still thronged with Saturday shoppers despite the snow which had begun to fall thickly again, but the bright lights from the shops and the hustle and bustle all added to the magic of a perfect afternoon.

On leaving her grandmother's house they had gone next door to Mrs Price. Kitty's mother had presented 'the birthday girl' with a beautifully knitted scarf and gloves in bright red wool, along with two lace handkerchiefs in a little box.

After talking the matter over with Kitty and Mrs Price, Amy had decided to leave her precious photograph safely tucked up in Kitty's bedroom until there came a time when she could have it herself. Sharing a bedroom with Eva, Harriet and the twins meant nothing was private at home. For the same reason she had left the little passbook which the post office had given her after she had deposited the three pounds with them in Kitty's care too.

'Well, lass, it's been an unusual sort of afternoon.' Kitty grinned at her as they made their way to the tram stop, the snow already coating their hats and shoulders. 'Fancy your gran having that money hidden away all them years.'

Amy smiled back but said nothing. To be truthful, the contents of the little pouch hadn't thrilled her a tenth as much as the photograph of her mother. She had stared and stared at it all the time she was in Kitty's house and it had been hard to part with it when they had left. But it was for the best to leave it where it was. She gave mental confirmation to the thought. Not only would her grandma be in trouble with her granda if it was discovered at home but for years now any little items she possessed had a tendency to go missing or get spoiled. The mother-of-pearl hairbrush her Aunt Kitty had bought her for her eleventh birthday had lasted a week before she'd found it smashed at the bottom of the stairs; items of clothing tended to get snagged or torn, hair ribbons went missing, the Bible she'd been presented with at Sunday School had deep grooves in its cover and several of its pages were loose. The list was endless.

'I have to say you could have knocked me over with a feather when I saw what your gran had got. I didn't—' Kitty stopped abruptly, clutching hold of Amy's arm as she said in some surprise, 'Isn't that Perce standing at the tram stop? It is, I'm sure of it.'

At that moment the tall broad youth turned to face them, a smile spreading across his face and his voice jolly as he called, 'Well, well, well! What are you two doing in this neck of the woods?'

'Just been to tea at Binns, no less.' Kitty's voice was equally gay as she replied, the small pause when she had waited for Amy to speak swallowed up as she went on, 'And you? I thought football was the order of the day on a Saturday afternoon for you and the rest of Sunderland's male population?'

Perce laughed. He waited for them to reach him before he said, tapping his finger against the side of his nose, 'I had to see a pal in town about a spot of business he'd got going down. I left Da and the others at the match, they'll tell me what happened and the score.'

All this time Perce hadn't once looked at Amy, he had kept his eyes fixed on the woman at her side. Now his gaze turned to his cousin. 'You on your way home?' he asked easily.

He had known she was finishing the afternoon with Aunt Kitty by having tea at Binns. He had probably heard her tell his mam earlier or something but he *had* known. She had never been more sure of anything in her life. There had been no pal, no business. She felt suddenly weak and sick, all her half-formed fears and misgivings of the last months coming together to tell her Perce liked her – in *that* way. The way a lad likes a lass. She forced herself to nod. 'Yes, I'm going home.'

'Me too.' His eyes left her and returned to Kitty. 'Seems daft you coming all the way to ours only to come all the way back when I'm on hand to see she don't get lost in the snow,' he said jovially.

Kitty looked at him uncertainly. Put like that it did sound daft but she always saw Amy home. 'Amy?'

Amy drew in a deep silent breath. If she said she wanted Aunt Kitty to accompany her on the journey, Perce would know she was frightened of him. 'It's coming down thicker than ever,' she said, marvelling that her voice sounded so normal. 'You don't want to have to walk back if they stop the trams, Aunt Kitty.'

'No, I suppose not.' Kitty sounded relieved. She turned to Perce. 'It *is* a night and a half,' she said gratefully, 'and if you're going straight home . . .'

'Wouldn't be going anywhere else in this weather.'

'All right then.' Kitty turned to Amy. 'I'll see you next week then, lass. Here, have the tram fare.'

'No need.' Perce reached out and placed a large meaty hand on Kitty's arm as she began to open her bag. 'I've got it. Look, here's the tram now. Bye, Kitty.'

'Bye. Bye, lass.' Kitty suddenly sounded unsure but as they stepped onto the tram she didn't follow them, merely waving somewhat forlornly as the tram creaked away.

Amy felt very small and insignificant as she sat down on one of the wooden seats. Perce sat down beside her, his big brawny torso dwarfing her. 'Had a nice time?' he asked.

'Yes, lovely.'

'Called in to see Gran as normal, I suppose?'

She was aware of his eyes burning into the side of her face but she kept her gaze trained straight ahead as she nodded. 'She looks forward to it. It can't be much fun being stuck in that bed all the time.'

'Suppose not.' He didn't sound interested.

Despite the butterflies in her stomach it riled her enough to look at him. 'It wouldn't hurt the rest of you to call in more often.'

His eyes narrowed and then opened again. 'I will if that's what you want,' he said softly. 'I'll go for you.'

She'd known it, hadn't she known he'd planned this? 'It's not what *I* want,' she said sharply. 'You should *want* to go, she's your grandma.'

He didn't reply to this. What he did say was, and in a tone that made her embarrassed, 'I'll go and see her every day if you want me to. I'll do anything for you, Amy. You must know that.'

'Don't be silly.' She knew her face was burning but she couldn't do anything about the hot colour; she had never felt so uncomfortable. She glanced nervously around, hoping no one could hear them.

'I'm not being silly and don't pretend you don't know how I feel about you. I've watched you, you know all right. Look,' his tone, which had turned slightly angry, returned to its former soft persuasive whisper, 'I want you to be my lass one day, that's all I'm saying. You'll be leaving school soon and lots of lasses take up with a lad then.'

She stared at him. 'I'm only fourteen, I can't have a lad.'

'I don't mind waiting a bit. Not for you.'

She wouldn't have him as her lad even if she had to spend the rest of her life as an old maid. She couldn't quite put her finger on it but Perce had always reminded her strongly of her Granda Shawe. 'We live in the same house,' she prevaricated quickly. 'It wouldn't be right. You're like my brother.'

'Like your brother, am I?' He emitted a hard laugh that was more like a bark. 'And Bruce, is he like your brother too?'

'Bruce?'

'Don't come the innocent, I've seen you two billing and cooing.'

Amy reared up in her seat, her voice louder than she intended as she said, 'We have not!'

'Anyone would have thought he'd given you a box of gold nuggets rather than a box of cheap chocolates.' Then his voice changed again. 'Look, I don't want to argue with you, Amy, and I bought you something for your birthday but I wanted to give it to you when we were by ourselves.'

He had been reaching into his jacket pocket as he spoke and when he drew out a small package she stared at it, making no move to take it.

'Go on.' He shoved it into her lap. 'I told you, it's for you.'

Her hands shaking slightly, Amy undid the string holding the brown paper together. It unfolded to display an item of clothing, a silk and lace petticoat with ribboned shoulder straps. She knew instinctively this was not the sort of gift a lad should give a girl. She looked at it in the same manner in which a rabbit would view the snake about to bite it, her hands falling limply by her side and the petticoat lying across her lap.

'Don't you like it?'

'I can't take this. You know I can't take it.'

'I know nothing of the sort.'

'It's not . . . proper.'

'Not proper?' He laughed but again it wasn't a real laugh. 'For crying out loud, girl, it's nineteen thirty-one not eighteen thirty-one.'

'I can't. I don't want it.' With her hand she tipped the paper and petticoat onto his lap and he had to make a quick movement to prevent the lot sliding onto the mucky floor of the tram.

For a moment there was silence and then he said quietly, 'If you think I'll let Bruce or any other lad have you, you're wrong, Amy. You're mine. Get that through your head because it'll save a lot of trouble in the long run. I'll give you time to get used to the idea, I'm in no rush, but you so much as look at another lad and you'll live to regret it.'

She couldn't believe he was saying these things. 'I told you, I'm too young to have a lad.' She raised defiant eyes to his. 'But even if I wasn't, I wouldn't go with you, Perce Shawe. And you can't tell me what to do, so think on. I'll tell Aunt May what you've said.'

Perce was staring into her flushed face. As she held his gaze she didn't know what to expect next, but it wasn't the sudden relaxing of his countenance. 'That's one of the things I like about you,' he said very softly. 'You've got more spirit than plenty of lads I know. Firebrand, aren't you, under that cool butter-wouldn't-melt-in-my-mouth front. You'll suit me. Oh aye, you'll suit me very well.'

She turned from the hot light in his eyes, pretending to take an interest in the view outside the tram window. After a moment or two she heard the rustle of paper and then Perce moved slightly as he stuffed the petticoat back into his jacket pocket. Even the brief contact of his body against hers made her feel sick. It was in that second Amy admitted to herself she was terrified of the walk home once they had left the relative safety of the tram.

Contrary to what she'd expected, Perce made no effort to take her arm or touch her once they had alighted into the snow-filled night. It could be because they were still in the main thoroughfare, though. What would happen when they had to turn off into the back lane which led to their house? Could she insist they entered by the front door? But none of the family ever used it, everyone would think it strange. Her heart pounding, Amy told herself she didn't care what

Uncle Ronald or Aunt May or her cousins thought. She'd tell them why she hadn't wanted to walk down the back lane with Perce, she'd tell them what he had said.

As though he had read her mind, Perce said quietly, 'You try telling that lot indoors about tonight and I'll deny it, you know that, don't you? And guess who they'll believe? Blood's thicker than water, they'll say. She's like her mam but she's started even earlier.'

'Don't you dare talk that way about my mam.'

They had reached the entrance to the back lane. Her heart pounding, Amy stopped in her tracks but to her mingled fright and surprise she found herself held in a grip she was powerless to fight against and manhandled the first few feet down the cut. As she struggled, Perce muttered, 'Give over, I'm not going to hurt you. I told you, I want you to be my lass, all above board and done right. And for the record I don't care about what your mam did.'

Jerking herself free, Amy nearly went headlong but for his hand coming out to save her, but again she shook it off. For the first time she was truly aware of the power in the male body in front of her; she'd felt like a rag doll in his grasp. The frozen snow beneath her feet with its deceptive covering of fresh flakes was lethal and she was finding it difficult to stay on her feet but she was too panic-stricken to pick her way. How she got to their backyard without breaking her neck she didn't know, especially with the dark night and whirling snow pressing down on her, but as her gloved fingers fumbled with the latch to the gate, Perce's hand came down on hers.

'Remember what I said,' he said quietly, bending down so his mouth was close to her face. 'I'll behave meself for the present and be patient but don't you think you can mess me about.'

She remained quite still but the moment his hand lifted she was through the gate and into the backyard. Then she was opening the back door and stepping into the relative warmth of the small scullery. Instead of taking off her outdoor clothes and making sure her boots were clean as every member of the family had been drilled to do by May, she almost pushed open the kitchen door. It was the sound of her grandfather's voice that checked her. Of course, it was a Saturday night. The panic of the last few minutes had taken it out of her head. Her granda always came back with Ronald and the lads and Mr O'Leary for a bite after football on a Saturday afternoon.

Perce was in the scullery now too, and with feverish haste Amy pulled off her gloves and stuffed them in the pockets of her coat before divesting herself of her coat, hat and scarf and hanging them on a peg. Perce was busy scraping the snow off his boots on the cord mat just inside the back door but she was aware he was looking at her all the time he did so.

Amy glanced at him in spite of herself.

'I'm sorry,' he said immediately. 'I didn't want to frighten you, just to make you understand. I can't stand you looking at other lads, that's the way I feel. It . . . it does something to me.'

His voice was low but the look in his eyes brought panic bubbling again. 'You're like a brother,' she said again, willing him to understand. 'It would be wrong.'

'We're cousins, just cousins, and it wouldn't be wrong. Even if it was, I wouldn't care, the way I feel about you, but it wouldn't anyway. And I've said I'll wait till you're ready. I can't say fairer than that. Don't . . . don't be mad at me.'

This was worse than him manhandling her. She looked away from the puppy-dog pleading in his eyes and swallowed hard. But she couldn't pretend. 'I couldn't like you in that way so it's no use you waiting,' she said, and opened the door of the kitchen before he could stop her.

Mr O'Leary, her granda, Aunt May, Uncle Ronald and Bruce were still sitting at the remains of the evening meal, the younger children having gone through to the sitting room, judging from the sounds emanating from that direction. Her uncle smiled at her but it was only Bruce who said hello. She saw his eyes narrow as Perce followed her into the kitchen and he said, 'I thought you weren't going to be home till late? Business with Stan, wasn't it?'

'Turned out it wasn't worth missing the second half for.' Perce pushed past Amy, clapping both his grandfathers on their backs as he said, 'All right then?' before adding casually to his mother, 'Kitty and Amy were at the tram stop and Kitty asked if I'd bring Amy home to save her the journey in this weather.'

'Frank Kirby says the law was nosing about asking questions about Stan recently.' Bruce hadn't taken his eyes off his brother.

'Frank Kirby's nowt but a gossipy old woman.'

'And Stan's a villain and you know it.'

Wilbur cut across what was fast becoming an argument between his grandsons, his cold eyes on Amy. 'Some folk take advantage of any kindness they're shown. Fine state of affairs when your aunt has to struggle to dish up by herself 'cos you're off gallivanting. Don't you think so, Terence?'

'Aye, I do an' all, Wilbur.'

Normally Amy would have let the remark go unchallenged. She was used to both men's censure. But tonight with her nerves as taut as piano wire, the unfair criticism caught her on the raw. She stared into the two men's faces, one handsome and the other anything but, but both alike in their dislike of her. 'Eva and Harriet were here, weren't they?' she said sharply. 'As far as I know they haven't lost the use of their hands.'

There was a moment of stunned silence followed by several condemning voices.

'Why, you cheeky little madam!' This was from her aunt.

'How dare you!' A boom from Mr O'Leary.

'This is what comes of letting her fraternise with that rabble next door to me.' Wilbur had actually risen from his seat, his face thunderous. Ronald and Bruce stood too, the former uncertainly as though he wasn't sure what to do next but Bruce moved swiftly to stand in front of Amy, shielding her from their grandfather. Bruce wasn't as heavily built as Perce, his height had a leanness to it, but Amy was glad of her cousin's protection when Wilbur said, 'She needs the belt, Ronald, same as her mother. It's the only thing some females understand. If you can't bring yourself to do it, I can.'

Even May looked askance at this. 'I don't think so, Da,' she said, 'but she'll be punished, rest assured of that. Getting a mite too big for our boots, aren't we, madam?' she added directly to Amy. 'I think someone needs taking down a peg or two.'

'I think it might be a good idea for you to have a word with that Kitty, Wilbur, and tell her Amy won't be going out on a Saturday for a month or two, not till she can control her tongue.' Terence O'Leary didn't take his eyes off Amy as he spoke.

Amy stared at May's father. Not seeing Kitty would mean not seeing her grandma and she couldn't bear that, and she knew her grandma looked forward to the time they spent together all week. She was always saying so. 'That's not fair,' she burst out.

'You to talk of fairness, you ungrateful mongrel.' Wilbur was fairly spitting out the words. 'Your aunt and uncle have provided a roof over your head for the last umpteen years and this is all the thanks they get. I knew it'd end up like this. You're your mother all over, m'girl. That's the trouble.'

Terence O'Leary nodded slowly. 'You're right, Wilbur.'

'I'm glad he's right.' Amy's voice was very loud but shaky. 'I want to be like my mam, so there.'

'Glad, are you?' Wilbur snorted contemptuously. 'Well, there you have it, straight out of the horse's mouth, Terence.'

'Hang on a minute, you two.' Ronald had gone white; they were all shaken by the scene which had erupted with such suddenness, all except the two older men. 'She's only a bairn, it's natural she'd stick up for her mam. And our Bess shouldn't have done what she did, none of us would say different, but the fella was more to blame than her in my book. Taking down a bit lass when he had a wife and family tucked away was a dirty trick. It'd have been bad enough if the girl was a rum 'un, but our Bess – pure, untouched.'

'You're sure about that, are you? That she was pure?'

'*Da.*'

'Oh, all right, all right.' Wilbur flapped his hand. It was clear he and Terence had been surprised by Ronald's championing of first Amy and then Bess. Surprised and somewhat annoyed. 'I don't want to fall out with you, Ronald, but I just hope you and May don't live to regret taking her in, that's all. You've heard the old adage about biting the hand that feeds you.'

'Da.' The admonition was weary now.

'Aye, well, I've had my say.' Wilbur glanced at May. 'I'll have me coat and cap, lass, if it's not too much trouble.'

'Me an' all,' said Terence with a sour look at Ronald.

'You're not both going?' May protested. 'Not yet.'

Their sullen nods sent May to fetch the jackets and caps from their pegs in the scullery after a scathing glance at Amy.

Amy's cheeks were burning and her stomach was churning, and when the two men left without another word to anyone and by the front door – not the back which was customary for them to use – the seriousness of the row was magnified tenfold.

May saw them out and after a few mumbled words in the hall the front door opened and closed and then she was back in the kitchen. 'I hope you're satisfied with all the trouble you've caused,' she snapped at Amy. 'Upsetting everyone like this.'

'Hey, steady on, Mam.' Bruce's voice was mild. 'It wasn't really Amy's fault. They're always going for her for no reason.' Usually he kept out of any altercations but today Bruce found he was feeling sorry for his cousin. Amy had looked so unhappy when she'd walked in, so fed up, and it was true what he'd said about his grandas. Eva and Harriet could get away with murder but Amy only had to breathe for the two men to be down on her like a ton of bricks. He wondered why it had never really registered on him before what a rough deal she had all round. He looked his mother full in the face as he added, 'And you know how she likes to see Gran Shawe and Gran likes to see Amy.'

'Oh, I see. I'm to blame then, am I?' May glared at her son. 'Nice Saturday this is.' She stalked out of the room, her footsteps going up the stairs. Bruce stared helplessly at his father who shrugged his shoulders in irritation at his wife before going after her, muttering under his breath as he did so.

Bruce rubbed his hand across his face before glancing at his cousin. She was standing still and looked very white, her lips trembling, and the feeling of pity intensified. She was just a bairn and yet his grandas talked to her as though she was muck under their boots most of the time. It wasn't right and it had gone on long enough. No doubt he and his da would get it in the neck from his mam but that didn't matter. He put his arm round Amy's shoulders. 'I meant what I said, lass. This wasn't your fault. They always have to start over something, that's the way they are.' His voice gruff, he added, 'Don't let the old miseries get to you, lass. That's what they want. I know I shouldn't say it but they're bullies, the pair of them. Come on, Amy, dry your eyes and forget about them. They're not worth it.'

As Bruce handed her his handkerchief Amy raised her head and pulled away a little to dab her face. She happened to glance at Perce who was still standing on the other side of the kitchen table and who hadn't said a word throughout. The look in his eyes froze her for a moment, but then she dragged her gaze away from the fixed stare and handed the handkerchief back to Bruce. 'Thank you,' she said shakily, taking a step backwards. 'I'm all right now.' She waved her hand at the laden table. 'I'll clear the dinner things and wash up.'

'There's no rush. Why don't you sit down a minute and I'll pour you a cup of tea? Mam had only just made a fresh pot when you walked in,' Bruce said gently.

'No, no.' She backed away still further from the kindness in his face and the tender quality to his voice, even as she silently upbraided herself. She was doing exactly what Perce wanted by reacting like this. She ought to let him see he couldn't frighten her or make her behave differently with Bruce. But the dark fury in his eyes *had* frightened her. Somehow he didn't seem like a lad of sixteen; in some ways he was more a full-grown man.

Just three weeks later Bruce was set upon when he was returning from a night out with some pals. It wasn't late, only half past ten, and the last of his friends lived a couple of streets before theirs which meant he'd only had a five-minute walk alone. He had come by their back lane, which was dark and unlit. It was something all the householders did without thinking twice about it.

The two neighbours who carried a bleeding and semi-conscious Bruce into the kitchen were full of indignation at the attack. Bunch of ne'er-do-wells by all accounts, they told a stricken May and Ronald. Being a Friday night they likely thought the lad had still got his wage packet on him. If it hadn't been for old Mr Newton coming into his backyard to check his racing pigeons – a fox had been skulking about – they might have done for him, the way Mr Newton said they were hammering the lad. The old man had yelled his head off and the gang had scarpered when they and others had come running out, but it was a fine state of affairs if folk couldn't use their back ways come nightfall without this sort of thing happening. Course, the Depression was a lot to blame. What with riots in the streets and the unemployed getting more and more desperate, law and order were breaking down.

May insisted on the local constable being called, but although he was appropriately grave-faced and concerned, he admitted there was little chance of finding the culprits. The lad had been hit from behind at the beginning of the attack by his own account, and then he'd only been aware of hands going through his pockets before they had started to use their boots on him while he lay on the ground. With no descriptions and no clues as to why they should have picked on Bruce, the constable said, he doubted the law would make much headway with this one. But it might be wiser for the time being to use the front door after dark, just to be on the safe side.

They had all been upset about what had happened but Perce in particular seemed to take the attack on his brother as a personal affront. He had tramped the back lanes in the vicinity for a few nights until May, half mad with worry, had persuaded him to give up for her sake. After this he informed them during dinner one night that he had asked Stan to make discreet enquiries among some of the more question-able types he knew. But nothing had come of that either.

In view of all this Amy felt awful about her initial suspicions when Bruce had first been brought home. How could she have imagined for one moment Perce was at the bottom of the attack on Bruce? she asked herself for the umpteenth time two Fridays after the incident. She glanced out of the corner of her eye at her two cousins. Bruce and Perce were sitting with their father toasting their toes in front of the sitting-room fire, the three of them enjoying the beer and chitterlings Perce had brought in for their supper. It was May's evening for visiting her parents and she had taken Eva and Harriet with her, Ronald pleading a gyppy tummy at the last minute.

Amy watched her uncle tucking into the chitterlings. His stomach didn't seem too bad now, she thought wryly; nine times out of ten he would make some excuse not to accompany Aunt May to his in-laws. She didn't seem to mind, she always appeared on edge anyway when Uncle Ronald and Mr O'Leary were together.

For once the house had a nice feeling to it. With Aunt May and Eva and Harriet out, and the younger children fast asleep in bed, Amy could have felt comfortable and relaxed as she sat with a pile of mending in one of the easy chairs. But ever since the night Perce had told her how he felt she had been tense. All the time he seemed to be looking at her, even when he wasn't, which sounded daft but that was how she felt. And even with the bathroom door locked she hurried through her ablutions each morning, hating the fact he was still in the house when she didn't have any clothes on.

In just three weeks' time though, at Easter, she would be finished with school for good and starting work. She would be grown up and everything would be different. True, Aunt May had made it clear that most of her wage would be taken for her board, but for the first time in her life she would have a small amount of money which would be her very own. It was some recompense for not being able to go to the secondary school as her teacher had recommended.

Amy did not count the three pounds hidden away in the post office. In view of how the money had come to her, it would remain untouchable for the foreseeable future and it therefore barely hinged on her consciousness, except as a warm reminder of her grandmother's love for her.

'You seem in a world of your own the night, lass.' She glanced up to see her uncle's eyes on her. 'Not still brooding about your Aunt May getting you the job with Mrs Tollett, are you? It'll work out all right in the end. With things as they are at present, a housemaid's job, any job, isn't to be sneezed at, and you said the housekeeper there seemed pleasant enough.'

Amy nodded. 'Yes, she was.' Everyone had been pleasant when her aunt had taken her for the interview with the housekeeper who virtually ran the guest house on Roker's promenade, but the truth was that she didn't want to go into service.

'Just see how you get on, eh? Something else will turn up sooner or later.'

Her uncle was trying to be kind and for a second Amy was tempted to tell him what she was going to do the next day but she held her tongue. If her Aunt May got wind of it she would stop her and it would be Mrs Tollett's for sure.

'I think I'm for bed.' Bruce stretched his legs as he spoke, wincing slightly as he stood up. He had returned to the iron and steel works a week after the attack, but his face still bore evidence of the beating he'd endured and Amy knew he was often in pain although he never complained. It made her feel quite odd at times to think what might have happened if Mr Newton hadn't been worried about his pigeons. 'Night, all,' Bruce added. 'Don't let the bed bugs bite.'

Bruce smiled at her as he looked her way and Amy smiled back but immediately lowered her head to the torn shirt in her hands in case he engaged her in conversation. It was silly perhaps but these days she felt it was better if she kept Bruce more at arm's length. Not that she thought his affection for her was anything other than that of a brother for a sister, but with the two brothers getting on so well since the night Bruce had been attacked it was just . . . better. She didn't want to search her feelings more than this.

When her uncle made no move to leave the room but settled himself more comfortably with the evening paper, Amy relaxed a little. She had been careful to avoid being alone with Perce since he had declared how he felt but sometimes it was difficult and added to the jumpiness that played on her nerves. She would have felt better if she could have told her Aunt Kitty what he had said but somehow she couldn't bring herself to mention it. This was partly because the whole incident had been so disagreeable but also because Perce had made her feel that she had encouraged him in some way, even tried to play him off against Bruce. And although she knew she hadn't, she didn't want Aunt Kitty to get the wrong idea.

Amy let her thoughts drift back to the exciting but scary event she had lined up for the next afternoon as her uncle read his paper and Perce dozed. It had all started the previous Saturday when she and Kitty had been window shopping in High Street West after they had left her grandmother's house. She had spotted a notice in the window of a newly opened establishment which had read, 'Waitresses wanted. Only those with good deportment, attractive hands and a cheerful disposition need apply. A good head for figures and a sharp memory an advantage. Excellent remuneration for the right candidates.'

She had looked at the notice and then at Aunty Kitty, and

Aunt Kitty had smiled at her before saying, 'If you're thinking what I think you're thinking, have a go, lass. They can only say no.'

She'd protested she didn't dare but then a feeling of recklessness had come over her and she'd found herself pushing open the door and walking in, Aunt Kitty at her heels. The upshot of this was that she had an interview tomorrow afternoon at four o'clock. And Aunt Kitty had promised she would help her put her hair up before she went. Amy's hand drifted to the thick plait at the back of her neck. She would have loved to have had it cut into a fashionable bob ages ago but Aunt May wouldn't hear of it. Oh, she did *so* want to work in the hustle and bustle of the town instead of being shut away changing beds and cleaning other people's mess in Roker.

For a second the thought that she might not be offered the job was unbearable. Surely the restaurant would pay more than the eight shillings a week Mrs Tollett was offering. If it didn't, she was scuppered, even if she managed to pass the interview and be offered the job.

Her stomach turned over and she pricked herself badly with the sharp needle, drawing droplets of blood. She sucked her finger, gazing desperately at the material in her hands. She knew she wouldn't sleep a wink tonight.

At five to four the next afternoon Amy walked through the imposing doors of the restaurant, outwardly confident and inwardly scared to death. Kitty had filled her in with some background information about the place while she had put her hair up. Apparently the new style of restaurant had caused quite a stir in the town. It was unashamedly modelled along

the lines of the Lyons' Corner Houses which had been operating in London for a couple of decades, and their motto
was cheap, cheerful and fast.

'Enid who works for me at the laundry, well, her sister
got took on a week ago,' Kitty said, her fingers coiling and
fastening Amy's thick curls on top of her head as she spoke.
'And Hilda is a looker, like you. That's important. Lyons' call
their waitresses Nippies and they're all bonny lasses so that's
what the owner of Callendars wants. And it's not just one
restaurant but three in one, Hilda says. The top floor is a
proper restaurant and they have a band playing in the evenings,
but downstairs there's a café on one side and then a sort of
tea shop on the other that only sells tea and coffee and cream
cakes. But all the waitresses, along with the waiters that work
upstairs, have to wear black and white uniforms. Hilda says
they're lovely, though, nice dresses and starched frilly aprons
and little hats that stand up like coronets. You'd look a picture,
lass. You're sure to get the job.'

'Did Hilda say how many girls have applied?' Amy asked,
not really wanting to know the answer.

Kitty shrugged and Amy knew it was a lot. 'Quite a few,'
Kitty admitted, 'but that doesn't mean you won't get offered
a job. It's worth a try anyway, you've got nothing to lose.'

Nothing to lose. But she *had*. Amy's mind was buzzing as
she walked through what she now realised was the café part
of the establishment. It was immaculate, huge rubber plants
and waving palms bordering a sea of tables with lovely white
cloths and shining cutlery. All the tables had a small vase with
a flower in it. If this was the café, what was the restaurant
like upstairs?

'Can I help you?'

The girl who spoke to her was fresh-faced and pretty, her bobbed hair and spotless apron reflecting everything Kitty had said about the staff. Amy tried to smile but her face felt frozen. 'I've come about a job,' she said quickly. 'They told me to be here at four o'clock for an interview.'

'Oh aye, that'll be with Mr Callendar, he sees everyone personally, but the manager, Mr Mallard, will take you along to his office,' the girl said brightly. She pointed to a quiet spot between two rubber plants. 'Wait there and I'll tell him you're here.'

'Thank you.'

Her tone must have reflected how she was feeling because to Amy's surprise the girl suddenly leaned forward, touching her arm as she whispered, 'You'll be all right, lass. Don't worry. Just remember to speak up and don't mumble. He can't abide mumblers, Mr Callendar. And smile. He's always going on about us smiling and being cheerful for the customers.'

Amy nodded, her smile of thanks more natural now. 'I'll remember.'

It was only a moment or two before the girl reappeared with a tall, well-dressed man in a beautifully cut suit. Amy saw the girl mouth, 'Good luck,' before she went off to deal with some customers, and again the little touch of friendliness was warming.

'Miss Shawe?' The manager was middle-aged with a smart little moustache. 'Please come this way.'

Amy felt very small and very young as she followed Mr Mallard through a door which led into a narrow passageway. Some yards ahead was another door to which Mr Mallard gestured as he said briefly, 'Kitchens,' before branching off to the left, where a flight of stairs rose sharply upwards. At the top of these the manager pointed to a door which was slightly to the right. 'Main restaurant. And this,' he nodded to their left before knocking twice on the door, 'is Mr Callendar's office.'

A voice called from within and the next moment Mr Mallard stood aside for her to precede him into the office. Amy found herself in a large, luxurious room furnished with a sofa and long low table in one corner, a row of filing cabinets in another and several grand paintings on the coffee-coloured walls. The thick green carpet stretched from wall to wall and the curtains at the two sets of windows were floor length. All this she took in with one swift glance before her attention focused on the man sitting behind the large dark desk at the far end of the room, positioned so that the light from one window streamed over his shoulders.

'Miss Shawe, sir,' said the manager in a slightly bored tone. Amy supposed he must be tired of presenting applicants to Mr Callendar. 'And the chef would like a word when it is convenient.'

'Problems, Robin?'

His voice was pleasant, cultured, and without the slightest trace of an accent, but the way the light was falling prevented her from seeing his face clearly.

'He isn't satisfied with the quality of the latest delivery of vegetables, sir.'

'Is that all? Well, deal with it yourself. Pander to him. Get someone to go and buy some more if necessary. Whatever. I want him tickety-boo for that big party from the Gentlemen's Club tonight. Word of mouth, Robin. Word of mouth. We can't afford any disasters at this stage.'

'Quite so, sir.'

For a moment after the door shut behind her Amy wasn't sure what was expected of her, and then the deep pleasant voice said, 'Come and sit down, Miss Shawe.'

It made everything stranger to be addressed as Miss Shawe. Amy all but scuttled to the straight hard-backed chair set in front of the desk. It didn't help that as she approached Mr Callendar, she felt more flummoxed than ever. She had imagined he would be about the same age as the manager or older, but the dark-eyed, dark-haired man sitting in the big leather chair was young, she could now see. Well, youngish. And there was something about him that reminded her of that film star everyone liked, Gary Cooper. And then she blushed scarlet for thinking such a thing.

'So you would like to work here, Miss Shawe. Why is that?'

Amy stared at him, completely nonplussed. She should probably have expected such a basic question, she realised now, but her previous interview for the position of house-maid at Mrs Tollett's guest house hadn't prepared her for anything like this. The housekeeper there had directed all her conversation to Aunt May for a start, merely smiling at her now and again, and the woman had only been interested in when she was due to leave school and whether she could work without constant supervision, things like that.

Amy cleared her throat. 'I think it would be interesting meeting people all the time,' she managed at last.

The dark eyes stared at her for a moment. She wanted to look away but instinct told her not to.

'I have your name and address here but no other details,' Mr Callendar said after what seemed like a lifetime to her overwrought nerves. 'Perhaps you'd like to tell me a little about yourself. Where you're working now, for example.'

Amy drew in a quick breath. He clearly thought she was older than she was so the new hairstyle had worked, but would he think her too young for the position once he knew the truth? But she couldn't lie, he'd be bound to find out.

'I'm not working,' she said. 'I mean not yet. I leave school at Easter.'

'You leave school . . .' His voice trailed away and his eyes widened. 'How old are you, Miss Shawe?'

'Fourteen.'

'Fourteen?' He leaned back in his chair and gave a chuckling laugh. Amy had the nasty feeling he was laughing at her. 'Good grief, I thought you were at least sixteen or seventeen,' he said ruefully. 'Girls these days . . .'

Amy found she didn't like his tone, quite why she didn't know. She straightened in the chair, her voice crisper as she said, 'If I look older it's probably because I put my hair up for the first time today. I thought it would be expected if I was to serve food.' This wasn't really true because it had only just occurred to her but in the circumstances she felt it was justified. 'And I do have the offer of another job but I don't want to take it unless I have to.'

He moved his head backwards as though to see her better. After a moment or two he said, 'Can I ask what this other job entails?'

Her chin rose. 'It's working as a housemaid in a guest house.'

His eyes moved over the gold-tinted brown curls and heart-shaped face. 'Why did you apply for it if you didn't really want it?'

In for a penny, in for a pound. This wasn't going at all as she'd hoped. 'My aunt insisted,' she said briefly. And then when the dark eyebrows rose in silent enquiry, she added, 'I live with my aunt and uncle and they feel I should get a job rather than go to secondary school. The housemaid's post was the only thing available, with jobs being so scarce at the moment, but I don't want to go into service.'

'Some would say waitressing is along the same lines.'

From the stories she'd heard from several girls she knew who were in service, this was plain ridiculous.

'I don't think so,' she said firmly.

He straightened in his chair, bringing his hands palm down on the desk. She waited for him to tell her she could leave now. Instead he said, 'You live with your aunt and uncle, you say. Where are your parents?'

She blinked. 'They're dead.'

'I'm sorry. Was this recent?'

She thought quickly. 'My mother died when I was nearly two years old. My . . .' she had to force herself to say the word, 'father died before I was born, in the war.' Which was true enough. 'My uncle, my mother's brother, took me into his home.'

'No brothers or sisters?'

She shook her head. 'Just eight cousins,' she said flatly.

'I see.' What he saw, Amy wasn't sure. Then he said, 'Perhaps that explains the air you have, an air that's older than your years.'

His tone now suggested he was trying to be nice and so she said, 'Perhaps,' and then waited.

'You don't smile much,' he said suddenly.

Again she blinked, remembering what the kind waitress

downstairs in the café had said. But she wasn't a clown who had to smile to order. The spirit of rebellion that had sprung up more than once lately – usually to her cost – flared. 'I smile when there's something to smile about,' she said quietly.

'Do you indeed.'

A silence fell between them and he sat looking at her, a half smile bringing the corners of his mouth upwards as if he were amused. 'Would my offering you the job be sufficient cause?' he asked after long moments.

Did he mean it? She stared at him uncertainly. 'Is that what you're doing?' she asked hesitantly.

He nodded. 'If you can bring that elusive smile into play with my customers, that is.'

She beamed at him. 'Oh, I will, of course I will. Thank you, Mr Callendar.'

'My manager, Mr Mallard, will tell you the conditions of employment and so on. Remuneration will be in accordance with age and experience, of course. Do you understand?'

Amy nodded. 'Thank you,' she said again, although now she was thinking she should have asked what that would mean for her, considering she was on the very bottom rung of the ladder in every way.

After turning and pressing a bell push set in the wall behind him, Mr Callendar stood and Amy rose too, taking the hand he proffered. His handshake was cool and firm and then, as though he had read her mind, he asked, 'What wage do housemaids get these days?'

'Eight shillings. At least that's what I was going to be paid.'

He smiled. 'We can do better than that.'

'Oh good!' And then she blushed as he grinned. 'I mean

thank you,' she added hastily. 'My aunt wouldn't have let me accept if it was below eight shillings.'

'Is she waiting for you downstairs?'

'My aunt? No, she doesn't know I'm here. I've come with a friend, my mother's friend,' she qualified because it sounded better. 'She's doing some shopping and I'm meeting her later.'

'Ah.' There was a polite knock on the door to the office and Mr Callendar called, 'Just a moment, Robin,' before he said, 'So do I take it I've been party to a spot of mutiny, albeit unintentionally?'

He didn't sound as if he minded and his eyes were lovely, all sort of twinkling. Amy gave her first totally natural smile since she had walked in the room. 'I'm afraid so, Mr Callendar.'

'Good. I've always been something of a rebel myself.' He moved from behind the desk and walked across the room with her. He opened the door and said to the manager, 'Come in a moment, Robin. I want a brief word,' before turning to her to add, 'If you'd like to wait downstairs, Miss Shawe, Mr Mallard will be down shortly.'

'Oh aye, right, thank you.' Flustered now, Amy almost forgot to add, 'Mr Callendar,' before she hurried past Mr Mallard and made her way back to the café. As she returned to her post between the rubber plants, the waitress who had spoken to her before passed, spinning on her heel when she noticed her.

'How did you get on, lass?'

'I've been offered a job.' Amy knew she was grinning from ear to ear but she couldn't help it.

'I thought you would be with your looks. What do you think to our Mr Callendar then? Bit of all right, isn't he?'

A little taken aback, Amy nodded.

'Word has it he came up north because his young wife died and he wanted to get right away from all the memories.' There followed a deep sigh. 'Isn't that romantic? Look, I've got to get on but I'll see you when you start. When is that?'

'What? Oh, I don't know. At Easter, I suppose. I leave school then.'

'You still at school?' Wide brown eyes expressed their surprise. 'I'd never have guessed.' And then as the door at the rear opened and the manager walked through, the girl said, 'I'm Verity, by the way. Bye for now,' and she scurried away.

By the time Amy met Kitty outside the Palace Theatre, she could hardly contain herself. 'Ten shillings,' she said jubilantly after she'd told Kitty she'd got the job. 'Ten shillings plus any tips, although Mr Mallard says they aren't much where I'll be working in the café and tea room.' She hadn't cared for the manager. He was from the south the same as Mr Callendar, but unlike the owner he had seemed snooty and abrupt as he'd explained her duties. And if anyone should have been like that, surely it was Mr Callendar, him being rich and owning the place. She'd gained a distinct impression that Mr Mallard didn't like the north or its people, especially when he had spoken of the meanness with the tips. It had been on the tip of her tongue to say that however bad things were down south, everyone knew the north was suffering more in the Depression.

'Oh lass, that's grand.' Kitty smiled broadly at her. 'I'll say it now although I wouldn't have done before, but your mam would have hated to see you go into service. She'll be smiling down the day, sure enough. Pleased as punch, she'll be. You know that, don't you?'

What Amy said was, 'Oh, Aunt Kitty,' and her voice was soft and full of deep affection. Whenever she was with her mother's friend she felt as though her mam was nearer somehow.

They gazed at each other for a moment and then Kitty cleared her throat and said fondly, 'Pity you've got to get back, lass. I'd have loved to have treated you to a seat in here,' she waved her hand at the cinema, 'to celebrate. Remember when they brought in the talkies last year and we went to the first showing of *Their Own Desire*? Your Aunt May was pea green that one of me lasses at the laundry had a sister working as an usherette who helped with the tickets. Came down off her high horse enough to ask me for a favour then, didn't she!'

Amy nodded. Aunt Kitty was smiling about it but she could still recall the anger she'd felt when Aunt May had barely expressed her thanks once the tickets were in her hand. Her voice a little subdued now, she said, 'I'd better get off home, Aunt Kitty, or I'll be late for my dinner.'

The interview and then the talk with Mr Mallard had taken longer than she had expected, and she was loath to give Mr O'Leary and her granda any excuse to go for her again. They'd taken the tack of ignoring her existence since the previous episode and she found she preferred it that way.

'Aye, all right, lass, we'll talk on the way and you can tell me everything that happened so's I can tell your grandma. She likes to know all the ins and outs where you're concerned. I'll nip in quick before your granda gets home.'

Amy nodded. 'Thanks, Aunt Kitty, but tell Gran I haven't told them at home yet so I don't know if Aunt May will agree to me going.'

'Oh, she will, hinny. The extra money will speak for itself and the place is perfectly respectable, after all. Mind, Father Fraser would find fault with it, no doubt. The last time he called on me mam he was going on about the waitresses' hemlines at the Grand being too short. The Grand, of all places. But your Father Lee is all right, isn't he?'

The last carried a note of wistfulness. Amy knew Kitty had had several run-ins with her priest lately; he didn't hold with women being employed in positions of authority when men were out of work. He had made Kitty feel so uncomfortable about her promotion at the laundry that she hadn't been to Mass in weeks. Amy inclined her head again. 'Father Lee is lovely,' she agreed. 'Uncle Ronald often says him and Father Fraser are like chalk and cheese.'

'I can think of a better word than chalk to describe the old misery.' Kitty grinned but Amy had to force a smile. She'd feel better once she'd faced them all at home.

Chapter 6

'You've done *what*?' May's voice was shrill.

'Got another job,' repeated Amy, adding hastily, 'and it pays two shillings more at least than Mrs Tollett's.'

She had arrived home just in time to help her aunt dish up the evening meal and everyone was now tucking in. It had been Perce and not her granda this time who had turned to her a few moments before and said, 'Cutting it a bit fine, weren't you? What delayed you?' And she had answered, matching her tone to his, 'I've got another job, I had the interview this afternoon.'

'What do you mean, *at least* two shillings more?'

She might have known her aunt would pick up on that. Amy put down her knife and fork. 'It isn't a housemaid's job,' she said, aware everyone except the three youngest children and little Milly in her high chair had stopped eating to stare at her. 'It's at Callendars in High Street West and it's wait-ressing. I get ten shillings but then sometimes there's tips on top of that.'

'Ten shillings?' Perce chipped in and again his tone caught Amy on the raw. 'They're having you on. Who'd pay ten shillings plus extras to a bit lass still at school?'

She had known Perce wouldn't like her working at Callendars. It would suit him to think she was stuck away in Roker in that quiet guest house cleaning and making beds and the like, not seeing a soul. The realisation hit in the same moment that she acknowledged she'd also been aware Bruce would react as he was now doing when he said, 'I've heard talk of this new place and it pays well although they're particular who they take. Amy's done all right for herself if she's got in there.'

'Aye, I've heard talk an' all.' Wilbur's lip curled. 'Some bloke with more money than sense from the south thinking he can set up here with fancy ideas and not much else. There's not many who can afford to waste money on a meal out, and if they can, they want good honest plain food, none of your highfalutin rubbish. He won't last the year. She's better at Tollett's.'

Amy didn't move, and the expression on her face did not alter. Quietly she said, 'The manager explained to me today that they are serving a variety of food for different pockets and tastes and keeping the prices down. The café is for fried fish and soups and that sort of thing, and the tea shop is for morning coffee and afternoon tea.' She ignored her grandfather's snort of contempt. 'The main restaurant caters for business functions and wedding receptions and that sort of thing, as well as for respectable people who just want to have a square meal and a pleasant evening out. The nearest place that's anywhere similar is in Newcastle, so Mr Mallard is convinced they've got lots of scope.'

'Lots of scope my backside!' Perce glanced round the table. 'I'm with Granda on this. You know where you are with working as a housemaid. It's steady money for a steady job.'

Amy stared at her cousin. She hadn't realised until this moment just how much she disliked him. 'At Mrs Tollett's I'd be working from seven in the morning until seven at night six days a week, and the housekeeper acted as though she was doing me a favour in allowing an hour off for my dinner.'

'So?' Mr O'Leary came in with his two pennyworth. 'A bit of hard work never killed anyone.'

'It didn't do my mam much good.' The minute the words were out she regretted rising to his provocation. She had promised herself she would keep calm whatever was said, and here she was biting back in the first minute or two. She looked away from the florid face with its big pockmarked nose as she said, 'The whole point is it's more money at Callendars right from the start and if everything goes well as they expect it to, it would be good to be in right from the start.' Kitty had told her to mention that. 'If it doesn't,' she shrugged her shoulders, 'there's always something like Mrs Tollett's.'

'You think you can just pick something like Mrs Tollett's up whenever you want to?' Wilbur asked scornfully.

Amy faced him. 'Aye, I do.'

Her answer seemed to floor him for a moment but he managed a 'Huh!' in reply.

May entered the fray again. 'When would they want you to start?'

'The day after I leave school.'

May nodded and then turned to Ronald who had said nothing thus far. 'What do you think?'

Ronald didn't answer his wife directly. Instead he looked at Amy and said, 'Do I take it the two shillings would be extra board to your aunt?'

He was throwing her a line and Amy took it. She nodded. 'Of course,' she said quickly. 'If it's all right with you, Aunt May,' she glanced at her aunt, 'I'd keep any tips and use them for my tram fare, along with the shilling we agreed I'd have when I was going to work for Mrs Tollett, but I would give you nine shillings for board.'

'Then I'd say with the slump worsening she'd be as well to take the job,' Ronald said mildly. 'To my mind there's no guarantee she would be kept on somewhere like Mrs Tollett's any more than at Callendars the way things are going round here.'

May didn't look at her father or her father-in-law when she brought her eyes away from her husband's face. She smoothed her apron and said, 'That's settled then but I don't know what Mrs Tollett will say. I think I'll write and tell her. She's got a couple of weeks to get someone else so it's not as if we're leaving her in the lurch.'

Wilbur made a sound in his throat which was some-where between a growl and a sigh but did no more to break the silence which followed as everyone began eating again. Amy wasn't tasting her food. *She'd done it.* Her legs felt trembly with reaction. And without anything like the scene she'd imagined on the way home, thanks to her Uncle Ronald.

Exactly a week later, on Saturday morning, Amy received a letter from Mr Callendar asking her to call in and see him 'on an urgent matter of some importance'. The letter burned a hole in the pocket of her skirt all morning as she black-leaded the range, scoured the kitchen flagstones with soda, whitened the front doorstep and bleached the pavement and went about the hundred and one jobs her aunt had lined up for her.

She waited until she and Kitty were seated on the tram into Bishopwearmouth later in the day before she showed her the letter. 'Do you mind if I go there first before we go to Gran's?' she asked when Kitty's eyes had scanned the couple of lines of writing.

'Aye, you go, lass.' Kitty tried to hide her disquiet. 'Mam's asked me to pick up a pound of scrag ends and some rabbit pieces from that butcher she likes in Crowtree Road. She's got it in her head some of the others aren't above trying to pass off the odd dead cat and worse, and she might be right at that. You don't see as many moggies round here as you used to. Anyway, I'll be thereabouts when you're done or waiting outside. And don't worry, I'm sure it's something and nothing.'

Amy nodded but she felt there was something ominous about the letter and she sensed Aunt Kitty thought so too.

There was a small group of men on the other side of the road opposite Central Station when they alighted from the tram, some leaning against the wall, some with their hands in their pockets. Amy knew without looking that they were out of work. There were men at most corners these days, caps and mufflers on and boots patched and shined. They all had the same dead look in their eyes. She always found it painful to see them but today, with the letter in her pocket, it was worse. She didn't know what she'd do if something had happened to stop her working at Callendars, and Aunt

May had already written an apologetic note to Mrs Tollett.

The café seemed busy when she pushed open the door although the tea shop was only half full from what she could see. She was about to approach one of the waitresses when Mr Callendar himself walked through the far door at the back of the café. She watched him hesitate as he caught sight of her and then he was walking towards her, a smile on his face. 'Miss Shawe.' He extended his hand and shook hers, saying as he did so, 'Thank you for responding so promptly.'

'You said it was urgent, Mr Callendar.'

'In a manner of speaking.' He let go of her hand, glancing around him. 'Let's go to my office, it's quieter there.'

He was embarrassed. As Amy followed him across the café, the butterflies which had been fluttering in her stomach since she had first read the letter were now doing a fandango. Was he going to sack her before she had even started the job? What had she done wrong?

Mr Callendar opened the door into the corridor and then stood aside for her to precede him, before leading the way up the stairs to his room on the first floor of the building.

'Please be seated, Miss Shawe.' He gestured to the chair in front of his desk and only sat down once she had. Then it seemed as though he didn't know how to begin. He stared at her before reaching into one of the drawers in the desk and bringing out an envelope. 'Before I show you this I would like to assure you that no one else but myself has read it.'

His words were meant to reassure Amy but they had the opposite effect. 'What is it?'

In reply he pushed the envelope across the desk. 'This must have been slid under the door sometime on Tuesday night because I found it when I arrived Wednesday morning.

Fortunately I'd come in very early to clear some paperwork so no one else knows of its existence.' The name and address on the envelope had been put together using pasted letters cut from a newspaper, as had the message on the single piece of paper inside.

Dear Mr Callendar,

I understand you have recently taken a Miss Amy Shawe into your employ as a waitress. I wonder if she told you the truth about her background, namely that her mam was nothing more than a common prostitute who wasn't married to Miss Shawe's father. Correct me if I'm wrong, but is this really the type of person you want working for you? I would have thought your customers have the right to expect better. Because you are not from these parts I wasn't sure if you knew the facts, but believe me, everyone else does. It wouldn't reflect well on your establishment if the news got around that it was being used for immoral purposes, and I have reason to believe that Miss Shawe is certainly her mother's daughter in this respect.

It was signed simply, 'A wellwisher'.

Amy's mouth had fallen open slightly as she read the poison. She could hardly take it in for a second and then her head snapped up, her breathing sharp. 'This isn't true,' she declared hotly. 'My mam wasn't a – what this letter says. She wasn't. It wasn't like that.'

'Please don't upset yourself.'

'She wasn't married when she had me but that wasn't her

fault. He, the man, strung her along and . . . and . . .' No, she couldn't cry. Please, please, don't let me cry. She swallowed against the massive lump in her throat. 'He did die in the war like I told you,' she said, her face burning, 'and it was only then my mam found out he was married. But she never went with anyone else. That's all lies.'

'Miss Shawe, I never expected anything else. A letter of this type,' he nodded to the paper which Amy had dropped as though it was burning her, 'is always the same. A tissue of lies with just the merest touch of truth to give it some credence. However, I felt you should be informed of it if only to warn you that someone . . .' a slight hesitation, 'someone doesn't seem to like you very much. Have you any idea who could have written this?'

One name sprang to mind even as her whole being cried out, no, no, he wouldn't do that to her, not Perce. They had grown up together, he said he wanted her to be his lass. Surely he wouldn't do something as horrible as this. But who else was there? And he had been furious she was going to work here.

'Miss Shawe?'

'I . . . I don't know.'

Charles Callendar stared at the arrestingly lovely face in front of him. This little episode had the stamp of jealousy all over it. Probably one of her pals who knew about her beginnings had tried for a position as waitress here and had been turned down. Women, girls, could be the very devil when their noses were put out of joint. But to suggest that this poor girl who was little more than a child was in any way corrupt would have been laughable if it wasn't so dreadful. She had innocence written all over her. Gently he said, 'Have any of your friends applied for a job here that you know of?'

Amy shook her head. Her hair was in its normal thick plait at the back of her neck today, and she was unaware of how young and defenceless she appeared. 'I don't know of any,' she said.

'Would you like me to take this matter further?'

'Further?' The colour had come and gone in Amy's face several times throughout their conversation and now she looked ill.

'It's not unusual in matters of this nature to inform the police.'

The police? Her heart was pounding against her ribs. She glanced at the piece of paper lying curled on the desk so the pasted letters were obscured, but she could still see every mean little word in her mind's eye. She had never felt so alone or ashamed in her life. And for this man to know, this handsome nice man who spoke so posh and everything . . . She kept her eyes on the letter and he had to lean forward to hear her when she said under her breath, 'I don't want anyone else to read it.'

'They are very discreet in such matters.'

It was the sympathy and kindness in his voice that enabled her to raise her head and meet the deep brown eyes. 'I don't want to,' she said again. 'You . . . you don't know what they're like round here.' How could he, coming from where he'd come from and being one of the upper class and all? How could he understand about the gossip which spread from backyard to backyard like wildfire? And there didn't need to be any truth in it, that was the thing. There was always some old wife who would justify the backbiting by nodding her head and saying, 'There's no smoke without fire, now is there?

You answer me that.' And they would agree and continue with their sport.

Why, just a few weeks ago the new priest who had taken over from Father Lee on his retirement had stopped doing home visits, and she had heard Aunt May whispering to Uncle Ronald that it was because some of the lasses who were no better than they should be were always hanging around him. The fact that the new priest was young and good-looking had made the bishop worried for him because of the 'talk'. And her uncle had shaken his head and said grimly it was coming to something when a man of God couldn't go about his business without them getting their fangs into him.

If they were like that with a priest, what would they say about her?

'Well, it's up to you, of course.' Charles Callendar admitted to a feeling of relief. It wouldn't have been the most auspicious of starts to the business to have to call in the local bobby but he would have done so if the girl had wanted it. 'Perhaps it's better to treat such rubbish as just that – rubbish, eh?'

Amy nodded.

'You're sure?'

Again she nodded.

'Then we'll dispose of it accordingly.' He reached into his pocket and brought out a box of matches. He put the letter into a large heavy ashtray at the side of the desk and said, 'Here goes.' The sheet of paper blackened at the edge and caught fire, and within moments it was nothing but ash. 'There.' He smiled at her, his eyes crinkling at the corners. 'Don't give it another thought.'

Amy thought that was a silly thing to say. Her face must

have given her away because the next moment he shook his head. 'I know, easier said than done,' he said ruefully. 'But try anyway. Now,' his tone became brisker, 'I mustn't keep you any longer. It's not as if you work here yet, is it?' he added with an attempt at lightness as he rose to his feet.

He was saying she could still have the job? As Amy followed him across the room she wanted to ask to make sure but she didn't know how to put it. They went down the stairs and he opened the door into the café for her.

'We'll see you in a couple of weeks then, Miss Shawe,' he said, 'and please don't let this unfortunate incident dwell on your mind. Good afternoon.'

'Good afternoon and th-thank you, Mr Callendar.' Suddenly she felt painfully shy.

He had been about to say 'My pleasure,' but realising this wasn't exactly appropriate in the circumstances, he changed it to, 'Not at all.' He shook her hand and remained in the doorway as Amy made her way out of the building.

When he re-entered his office he didn't immediately apply himself to the list of urgent matters requiring his attention. Instead he sat down at his desk, his fingers idly toying with the thick glass ashtray as he stared at its contents. Damnable thing, this. His finely sculpted lips pursed as he leaned back in the chair. Left a nasty taste in the mouth. A lovely girl like that and someone wanted to do her harm. He didn't understand the sort of mentality that could lend itself to doing something as low as that letter.

He reached into the bottom drawer of his desk and drew out a half-full bottle of whisky and a small glass tumbler. He poured himself a generous measure and swallowed it in one gulp before pouring another and putting the bottle back. He emptied the ash from the ashtray into the waste-paper basket and then ripped the envelope into small pieces and disposed of that too, finishing the second tumbler of whisky. The neat alcohol burned a path down his throat and into his stomach, creating warmth where there had been emptiness.

There was something about Amy Shawe that reminded him of Priscilla although he couldn't put his finger on what it was. He shut his eyes against the pain which always accompanied thoughts of his late wife, even now, some two years after her death. If only he could picture Priscilla other than how she had looked that last night, lying in an ocean of blood with the tiny still body of their newborn son beside her. He opened his eyes and stared round the room. But he couldn't. He could stare at their wedding picture for hours on end but that other image was superimposed on their smiling faces. Would she have rallied round in spite of the haemorrhaging if the child hadn't been stillborn? No one could give him an answer to that.

He raked a shaking hand through his thick hair before rising abruptly and beginning to pace the room. He needed another drink. Hell, how he needed another drink. But he knew that the way he was feeling, it wouldn't stop at one. Better to wait until he got home — if you could call that miserable box of a flat he was renting home. Still, it was somewhere to lay his head and prepare himself for the struggle of getting through the next twenty-four hours. And then the next twenty-four and the next.

He walked over to the window and looked down into the busy street below but he didn't see the crowded pavements and Saturday bustle. 'A day at a time,' he murmured to himself.

That was what the doctor he'd consulted a few months ago – when he'd finally admitted he couldn't sleep since Priscilla's death – had said. Take it a day at a time, Mr Callendar. Don't try to look ahead.

He swung round, flinging himself back into the chair and dropping his head in his hands. Work can be an excellent panacea against brooding too much. That had been another of the doctor's little gems. Charles's mouth twisted. Maybe a new venture or something of that nature would help. The man had been full of platitudes, and all the time the gold-framed photograph of the good doctor's plump wife and four smiling children had looked down at them from the wall of his office.

But something had come from the meeting, although it had been a few days before he acknowledged that the germ of an idea had taken hold. In the following weeks he had sold his portion in the family engineering businesses to his elder brother, much to his mother's dismay. She had insisted his late father would have wanted the two brothers to run his small empire together. He had cashed in some bonds his grand-mother had left him, along with what remained of his stocks and shares after the Wall Street crash two years ago. With the over-valued pound, trade recession and world Depression, his overall lump sum hadn't been as much as he had expected, and he had lost more money when he had sold the house he had bought with Priscilla shortly before their marriage. But this had not concerned him; he'd just wanted to get right away from the south and do something new.

A knock on his office door brought him out of his reverie. He put the tumbler away with the bottle of whisky before he called, 'Yes?'

'Is everything all right, Mr Callendar?' Robin Mallard poked his head round the door. 'I thought I saw the young lady who came for an interview last week back here again. I didn't think she was starting with us until Easter week.'

'She isn't.' Charles Callendar found he didn't want to say anything more. He had told the girl no one but he knew about the contents of the letter, and this was true. To mention it now in any connection whatsoever would be a betrayal. He didn't know why he hadn't mentioned its existence to his manager. He had certainly been about to more than once in the last day or two, but then the recollection of a young, beautiful but strangely lonely face had stopped him. He looked the other man straight in the eye as he said smoothly, 'I think she must have been a little overcome last week and she couldn't remember one or two points you discussed with her. She called in to see you and clarify these and I happened to catch sight of her so I took care of it.'

'I see.' Robin Mallard's stiffness expressed his disapproval that his employer had so far forgotten his position as to concern himself with one of the least of his staff.

Charles was aware of the nature of the man's thoughts and he found he was amused rather than annoyed. He was such a stuffed shirt, Robin, but damn good at his job which was all that mattered in the long run. If the business was going to sink or swim on what he himself knew about running a restaurant, they would soon be in the red, that was for sure. That was why he was paying Robin double what he'd get elsewhere, even in London. To humour him, he said, 'I know how busy you are on a Saturday, Robin, so I thought I'd help out. I trust that's all right?'

'Of course, sir.' The manager unbent a little. 'It's just that the restaurant world is such an enclosed community. It wouldn't do for Chef or one of the senior waiters to get the idea a waitress had your ear.'

Quaint turn of phrase. Charles kept a straight face with some difficulty. 'The pecking order, you mean?' he asked gravely, dismissing the mental picture of Amy Shawe holding his severed ear aloft.

'Quite so, Mr Callendar.'

'I think people are protective of their position in all walks of life, Robin.'

'Maybe so.' The manager cleared his throat. 'But the young lady is quite fetching, as are all our waitresses, of course, which can be a two-edged sword in my experience. Now if you'll excuse me I'll just see how things are shaping up for the dinner dance later.'

Charles blinked as the door shut. Cheeky hound! Was Robin suggesting people might think he had designs on the girl? Damn it, she was a child, fourteen years old, and he was a grown man of twenty-six who had buried his wife and baby two years ago. For a moment or two he was inclined to call his manager back and tear him off a strip. 'Damn cheek,' he muttered out loud, shaking his head with some bewilderment before he reached for the pile of papers on his desk and tried to clear his mind of everything except the accountant's report in front of him.

But the desire for another drink had left him for the present.

PART THREE

1932 Suitors

Chapter 7

Amy stood quietly in front of Mr Mallard, her hands folded behind her back, her eyes downcast and her feet together as each waitress had been drilled to do if she was ever summoned into the holy of holies – the girls' nickname for the manager's office. Since Mr Mallard had called for her a few minutes before, she'd been racking her brains to think what she might have done wrong, but thus far nothing had presented itself. She hoped it wasn't too awful. She loved her job, she had never been so happy in all her life and she would just die if she got the sack as one or two other girls had done who hadn't measured up to Mr Mallard's high standards. But he was always fair, she had to give him that.

'Ah, Miss Shawe.' Mr Mallard looked up at last from the papers on his desk. He always kept the junior staff waiting a minute or so before he deigned to speak to them, and although Amy was used to this strategy it still unnerved her. 'A full twelve months since you joined us. I hope you have enjoyed your time here.'

'Very much, sir.' Her stomach was turning over.

Mr Mallard nodded. 'Good, good,' he said. He gestured to the chair to the side of her. 'Please be seated.'

Amy's eyes widened as she did as she was told. In the last year she had been in this office several times but she had never been asked to sit down before.

'You have become a very good waitress, Miss Shawe, mainly because you listen to those more experienced than yourself and put what they say into practice.' Mr Mallard smiled at her and she was so surprised she didn't even smile back. 'For that reason I am going to give you the chance of working upstairs for a period of three months to see how you get on. If in that time you show yourself to be worthy of my confidence in you, the position will become permanent. If not, you will return to the café and tea shop. Do you understand?'

'Yes, Mr Mallard.' Amy's eyes were shining. 'Thank you, sir. Thank you.' The restaurant! Where the waiters and only a select few of the waitresses worked, and where the tips were said to be amazingly generous on occasion. And it was so grand in there. Chandeliers hanging from the ceiling, great big mirrors and glittering glass cabinets everywhere, and the tables covered with the most exquisite linen cloths and napkins.

'Your hours will remain the same in number but will obviously have to meet the requirements of the restaurant so a substantial part of your time here will be in the evening. Might this be a problem?'

It might but she wasn't going to admit to it. 'No, Mr Mallard.' She'd cross the bridge of how she was going to get home late at night when she came to it.

'Mr Duckworth will show you how things are run in the restaurant later and once you are working there you will report directly to him.'

Amy nodded. She liked Mr Duckworth, the head waiter, all the staff did, although she had come to like Mr Mallard too since she had been working at Callendars, deciding her first impression of the manager hadn't been fair. He was just a bit unapproachable.

'Now as I've explained, you will be on probation for three months starting from next week. You will receive an increase in pay of two shillings per week forthwith. If at the end of this time you are considered suitable to continue working upstairs, your pay will be reviewed again. I think that's all for now, Miss Shawe.'

Again Mr Mallard smiled, and this time Amy smiled back before saying again, 'Thank you, Mr Mallard. I'll do my very best not to let you down.'

'If I doubted that you wouldn't be sitting here right now. Hard work and trustworthiness are rewarded at Callendars.'

'Yes, sir.' Amy rose to her feet and all but floated out of the office. The restaurant! This was her first step up the ladder and she would make sure it wasn't her last. And a two shilling rise, with more at the end of three months. That would persuade Aunt May to agree to the late hours, especially now that both Perce and Bruce were on short time. Mind, they'd probably have lost their jobs altogether if it wasn't for their granda manoeuvring things – as Aunt May reminded Uncle Ronald at every opportunity.

The light in Amy's eyes dimmed a little as the situation at home swept over her, but then she shrugged it aside and stepped into the bustle of the café. Immediately Verity was there. 'Well?' The other girl caught hold of her arm, drawing her to one side. 'What did old Mincing Mallard want?'

Amy kept her voice low as she said, 'He's offered me a chance to work in the restaurant for three months to see how I get on up there.'

'You? But I've been here longer than you, so've Ellen and Hilda.' Verity didn't actually add, 'It's not fair,' but she might as well have.

Amy stared at her friend. 'I'm sorry,' she said awkwardly.

'Oh, it's not your fault.' Verity's tone was grudging. 'It's him, Mincing Mallard. He's never liked me much, nor any of us who don't suck up to him and think he's the next thing down from God Almighty.'

Amy didn't know what to say. There was no truth in the veiled accusation. She didn't suck up to the manager but neither was she prone to coming in late now and again like Hilda or dropping things like Ellen. And Verity, although good at her job, usually made sure she was out of the door on the dot at six o'clock and would wriggle out of the more mundane duties like cleaning the tables and sweeping the floor if she could. And Mr Mallard noticed such things even if he didn't always mention them.

'When do you start upstairs?' Verity asked after a short, tense silence.

'Monday,' said Amy flatly, all her joy in the wonderful opportunity gone, even as she told herself she should have expected this. She liked Verity, she liked her very much but she wasn't blind to her friend's nature. Verity was funny and bright with a wicked sense of humour that had them all in fits of laughter most of the time, but as an only child whose doting parents had given up on ever having their own baby by the time she arrived, she was used to having her own way.

'I suppose it's more money too.' Verity was allowed to keep most of her wage for herself but money seemed to slip through her fingers like sand.

Amy nodded. 'Which will come in handy with the lads on short time and Eva not leaving school till the summer. I don't suppose she'll earn much in service even then.'

The two girls looked at each other for a moment and then Verity's gaze dropped away. 'I'd better see to my customer,' she muttered shortly.

'Verity, don't be like this.' Amy caught at her friend's arm as she turned but it was jerked away.

Verity's voice was sharp as she said, 'Be like what? I'm doing my job, that's all. Isn't that what we're here for? To wait on people?' And she hurried away.

Amy stood looking after her. Should she tell Mr Mallard she had changed her mind about the job in the restaurant? Not that he'd necessarily offer it to Verity, of course. He could even advertise for someone from outside to replace the waitress who was leaving. And they did so need the extra money at home. The huge row between her aunt and uncle over dinner last night had boiled down to things being so tight.

She bit hard on her lip as she started to clear the table nearest to her. Aunt May had begun the argument by saying that her da had offered to help out with new shoes for all the bairns. Uncle Ronald had forbidden it, as Aunt May must have known he would, and then the mother and father of an argument had ensued which had culminated in her uncle storming out of the kitchen, shouting he was master in the house, not Mr O'Leary.

Amy frowned. Her Aunt May and Verity were quite similar

in some ways if she thought about it, although it had never struck her until now. Both thought they could always have exactly what they wanted. But she couldn't see Verity ending up as bitter and disgruntled with her lot as Aunt May was, and she didn't want to lose Verity's friendship.

She carried the tray piled high with dirty dishes out to the kitchen before returning with fresh cutlery and a clean cloth.

She had never had a real friend of her own age before, she reflected. Her aunt hadn't allowed any of them to bring other children into the house or even the backyard, and because she'd been kept busy with household chores in the evenings and at weekends she hadn't played out in the street with neighbours' bairns like her cousins had.

She'd talk to Verity in their lunch break and sort something out then. The two of them got on so well, after all.

The lunch break for the waitresses who worked in the café and tea shop was staggered so that none of them were away from Callendars at the busiest time of the day, namely from twelve o'clock until two. Ellen and Hilda took an early slot from eleven o'clock to midday, Amy and Verity left at two and returned at three o'clock and the two most recent girls had the short straw of waiting until three before they could eat. After gulping down their sandwiches in the little room off the kitchen designated for staff use, Amy and Verity would always wander round the surrounding shops together, so when Amy reached the room to find it empty she stood for a moment blinking uncertainly. She was sure she'd seen Verity leave the café dead on two but because she herself had been tied up with a customer she hadn't been able to follow straightaway. Just to make sure, Amy popped her head round the door leading into the café and peered around.

'Looking for Verity?' Ellen stopped on her way to the kitchens with a tray of dirty dishes. 'She's already gone and I might as well tell you she's got her bloomers in a twist about you having the job upstairs.'

'Oh, Ellen.'

'Aw, don't look like that.' Ellen's tone softened. 'I can understand her in a way. I suppose me an' Hilda felt a bit miffed when she told us earlier but I don't hold with falling out over it. When all's said and done, it's not us who decide such things.'

'She thinks I've tried to get on Mr Mallard's good side but I promise you I've only done my job as I saw it, Ellen.'

'Aye, well, it's not Mr Mallard—' Ellen stopped abruptly and to Amy's surprise turned pink. Her voice was flustered as she mumbled, 'I'd better get this tray to the kitchen.'

'What's not Mr Mallard?'

'Nothing. Look, don't let Verity upset you.'

'What's not Mr Mallard, Ellen?' Amy repeated quietly.

Ellen stared at her helplessly for a moment or two before she said, 'It's not Mr Mallard who decides which one of us goes upstairs, is it?'

'Isn't it?' Amy was genuinely surprised.

Ellen shifted from one foot to the other. 'It's Mr Callendar. This is his place, after all. That's what Hilda says anyway.'

Something in the other girl's face made Amy say, 'What else does Hilda say?'

'Aw, come on, lass. You know he likes you. I'm not saying you've ever done anything . . .' The expression on Amy's face caused Ellen to pause a second before she rushed on, 'But he likes you, everyone knows that.'

Amy was flabbergasted. 'You think . . .' She couldn't go on for a moment. 'You're all saying I've been carrying on with Mr Callendar?' She couldn't believe this was happening. Mr Callendar had always been kind to her since the episode with the letter shortly before she had started work here, and she knew it was because he didn't want her to think he believed the lies which had been written about her, but that was all it was. How could they think for one moment she had been . . .

'Does everyone think this?' she asked fiercely.

Ellen's chin came up and her tone if not the words she used said quite clearly, Don't take that tack with me. 'Well, it's not surprising, is it? He doesn't stop and have a chat with the rest of us like he does you, and you're always the one who takes his tea tray up and sometimes it's five or ten minutes before you come down.'

Amy didn't say, But we're only talking. He asks me about my life at home and how things are, and I tell him about little happenings here and at home, things to make him laugh because he's lonely. Lonely and sad. Can't you see that? Instead she said, 'Mr Mallard asks me to take the tray.' But her voice carried no conviction because for the first time it dawned on her that Mr Callendar had probably told the manager to arrange it that way.

Ellen gnawed at her lower lip, aware she had said too much and this might rebound on her badly. 'It's none of my business anyway. I'm just saying what the others think.'

Amy stared at her, her mind in turmoil.

'You won't say anything, will you? To him, Mr Callendar?' Ellen's voice was urgent. 'You know how things are at home with me da and the lads on the dole. Me mam would go barmy if I lost this job. Da came in last night soaked to the skin after trying to get work round the doors all day, gardening and such. But there's nowt going. You won't drop me in it, will you, Amy?'

'No, I won't drop you in it.'

'Oh ta, thanks, lass, I knew you wouldn't.' Ellen stood a moment more and then bustled away, wishing she hadn't opened her mouth in the first place. She had always thought the same as the others but now she wasn't so sure. And Hilda would kill her if she found out she'd quoted her.

Amy went back into the small staffroom and stood staring sightlessly at the row of coats hanging on pegs all down one wall. She sat down on one of the two benches the room held, her legs trembling. They all believed she was carrying on with Mr Callendar; they'd probably been gossiping about her for weeks, *months*. It was utterly devoid of truth but that wouldn't make any difference. *Was* that the reason she had been given the job in the restaurant, because Mr Callendar had told Mr Mallard it had to be her? Not because of merit?

She shut her eyes tightly, running her hand over her fore-head before opening them again. If so, it would have been due to his kindness again, nothing else. Nothing else except perhaps pity? As the thought struck, she physically reared up against it, jumping to her feet. Why hadn't she ever consid-ered before that Mr Callendar might be feeling sorry for her? That it was a kind of charity which had prompted him to talk to her? If she had been given the job in the restaurant out of pity she couldn't accept it.

Her pride, always tender because of the manner of her birth, was smarting. She glanced round the room wildly, wondering what to do. She was still pacing about some ten minutes or so later when Jinny, one of the restaurant waitresses, walked in. Unless there was a special function of some kind the restaurant opened to the public at five o'clock, an hour before the café and tea shop closed, but the restaurant staff came on duty at half past two in the afternoon and worked until eleven or later, depending on how busy they were.

Jinny's entrance reminded Amy that the room would soon be full of the upstairs staff taking off their coats and changing their outdoor shoes for the black leather ones Callendars provided as part of the uniform. After saying hello to Jinny – a nice motherly kind of woman whom Amy had always liked but who now, she felt, might be thinking all sorts of things about her – Amy left the room and walked along the corridor towards the back stairs which led to Mr Callendar's office on the first floor. Sometime during the last ten minutes her mind had been made up, she realised, and she had to deal with this immediately if Mr Callendar was in. Before she lost her nerve. Before she let the prospect of the new job and better money persuade her to say nothing and just avoid the restaurant owner in future. That was the easy way out and she couldn't do it. She had to know the truth. But she wouldn't drop Ellen or any of the others in it. She'd promised Ellen that and she wouldn't break her promise.

Her heart was beating a racing tattoo as she made her way upstairs, praying she wouldn't meet Mr Mallard who would be bound to ask her what she was doing. She wouldn't know how to answer him. She didn't know how she was going to broach the matter with Mr Callendar either, but once she was actually face to face with him she'd take it from there.

She didn't hesitate before she knocked on the door of

the office and when his voice called, 'Come in,' she opened it immediately. She saw him glance up from the papers strewn on the desk in front of him and then his eyes widened slightly in surprise. 'Amy?' He had long since dropped the 'Miss Shawe' when he spoke to her in private but she was always careful to address him as Mr Callendar or sir. She didn't want him to think she was taking liberties. 'Is anything the matter?'

She supposed her face had already given her away and after closing the door behind her she walked across to stand in front of the desk. He waved at the chair she usually sat in while he drank his tea or coffee and they had their little chats but today she remained standing. 'I need to ask you something, sir,' she said evenly.

'Yes? What is it?'

'Did you tell Mr Mallard to give me the job in the restaurant?' She was watching him closely but the only reaction was a wrinkling of his brow.

'I'm sorry, Amy, I don't quite understand.' He leaned back in the big chair, resting his elbows on the upholstered arms. 'Mr Mallard has offered you a position in the restaurant?'

She nodded. 'Yes, sir.'

'And why would you think I had asked him to do that?'

She knew her face was red because she could feel the hot colour burning her skin. 'I didn't, not at first, but then . . .' She didn't know how to go on. She took a deep breath. 'People seem to think it was because you had singled me out for the position. They think it was favouritism.'

'People?'

'I . . . I can't say who, sir. I'm sorry. I promised, you see, and I wouldn't want to get anyone into trouble.'

'That's not good enough. If there is talk of this nature it needs to be stopped. I insist on knowing, Amy.'

She hadn't heard him speak in such a hard voice before and now a sense of panic was uppermost. He was going to be awkward and she couldn't blame him but she hadn't been prepared for this. She threw caution to the wind. 'The thing is . . .'

'Yes, what is the thing?' he asked when she stopped in confusion.

'The thing is most of the people employed here have families who are out of work. I know the slump is bad in the south where you come from, Mr Callendar, but it's worse here. The shipbuilding and the mines are on short time and shifts are being cut, everyone's scared to death of the workhouse.' She stopped, he wasn't interested in all this. 'I really can't say who told me,' she said flatly. 'I'm sorry, sir.'

'I see.' Charles waved at the chair again. 'Well, sit down at least.'

Nothing more was said until she sat down. A good ten seconds ticked by and then Amy said again, 'I'm sorry.'

'Stop apologising, for crying out loud. You've got nothing to be sorry for.'

The bark in his voice brought her stiff and tense but to her horror she felt the pricking of tears at the back of her eyes. She couldn't cry, not in front of Mr Callendar, she told herself, fighting the tears.

Then he said in a much quieter voice, 'I'm the one who is sorry, Amy, for snapping at you, but this sort of thing makes me so mad. Look, I had absolutely nothing to do with Mr Mallard offering you the job, all right? Mr Mallard is my manager and he makes those sort of decisions with the staff who work here. I still like to have the final say in any new staff we take on but once people are working here, any promotions are left to Mr Mallard. Like the old Chinese proverb goes, why keep a dog and bark yourself?'

He was trying to make a little joke but for the life of her she couldn't respond by smiling. But his voice had carried the ring of truth and she didn't doubt him.

'If Mr Mallard thinks you're good enough to work in the restaurant it's because you are and that's all.' He paused. 'I should imagine the extra money will come in very handy at home so just look forward to the new opportunity and forget all this. I'm afraid when you get a bunch of women working together there are always petty jealousies and friction if one person does particularly well.' He grimaced. 'Oh dear, did that sound bigoted? Emmeline Pankhurst would be turning in her grave, no doubt. Thirteen years after the vote for women and I make a statement like that. I suppose you're a champion of women's rights like most girls these days.'

Was she? She didn't really know enough about all that or lots of other things if it came to it but that was another thing she could look up at the library when she got the chance. Mr Callendar often set her mind thinking by the odd little remark he made, and since her chats with him she had realised how ignorant she was.

She smiled, eager to promote the lightness which had come into their conversation. 'If by that you mean me telling my aunt I wasn't going to be chief cook and bottle-washer at home any more now I was working, then yes.'

He nodded. 'Good grief, yes, I'd forgotten about that. It caused ructions for days, didn't it? But you were wise to start as you meant to carry on.'

'That's what Kitty said.' There followed a silence during which their eyes met and held. Suddenly Amy felt flustered. She was finding Ellen's words had changed the way she looked at Mr Callendar somehow. She'd always regarded him as her employer, and during their talks she had often felt sad for him when he had revealed what his family were like, but now she was seeing him as a man. A very attractive, engaging man. And she realised just how much she would miss their private talks if they stopped.

She stood up hastily. 'I had better get back to the café.'

'Of course. And please don't concern yourself about this.' He stood up with the politeness which was habitual with him and she inclined her head before turning and walking over to the door. She left the room without glancing backwards.

Dear gussy! Alone again, Charles plumped down in his seat with enough force to make the chair creak in protest. Well, he had known it would happen one day, hadn't he? Ironic it had come about by something he'd had no hand in whatsoever, though. But of course all these months of having her bring his morning coffee and afternoon tea had set the tongues wagging, and he *had* arranged that. But the need to talk to her, to find out more about this child woman had been overwhelming in the beginning, and then the more he'd discovered, the more fascinated he'd become. And she *was* fascinating, Miss Amy Shawe.

He swivelled round in the chair to face the window. But she was still a complete innocent, even if her outward form had matured dramatically in the last year. It had seemed quite incredible to him at first, the fact that she had come from the tangle of mean streets in this dockside town and yet was as she was. Damn it, he'd been an arrogant so-and-so when he had first arrived here. A grim smile touched his mouth. Thinking that only the upper classes could have finer feelings. He had since learned that working-class respectability was fiercer and more unforgiving than anything he had known in his hitherto sheltered life.

He half turned, reaching into the drawer for the whisky bottle and glass. He would have to stop drinking so much. It was something he told himself several times a day, every day. The neat alcohol warmed him and the bottle had gone down an inch or two by the time he replaced it in its hideyhole.

He shouldn't have put Amy in the position where she could become a focus of common gossip. He'd had his warning from Robin even before the girl had started working for him. He sighed, shaking his head. But he had found he was selfish where Amy was concerned, selfish and weak. The only thing to his credit was that he hadn't told her how he felt, nor would he until she was some months older, perhaps approaching sixteen or just after. Of course he had no idea how she'd view his attentions or whether she would think he was too old for her. She liked him, but liking wasn't loving.

He sat for some minutes more, lost in thought, his eyes cloudy, and this time when he reached into the drawer he did not reproach himself.

Chapter 8

Bruce glanced round the table as Amy told them her news. His family's reactions varied but none was a surprise to him. His father was genuinely pleased for her, his mother was thinking only of the extra housekeeping coming her way, Eva was as jealous as blazes and Harriet, as ever, was taking her cue from Eva. Betsy and Ruth and the youngest two were interested only in their dinner. These responses, if not all favourable, were relatively normal. And then there was his brother. Bruce turned his head and looked directly at Perce who was stolidly eating, his eyes on his plate, but his brother's impassive stance didn't fool him.

When had it first dawned on him that Perce liked Amy, and moreover that his cousin was aware of Perce's feelings and did not welcome them? He wasn't sure. It could only be a matter of weeks ago. He was probably as thick as two short planks not to have noticed earlier.

Bruce speared a piece of mutton with his fork and began to chew, his thoughts centred on Perce. He had hero-worshipped his brother at one time. Perce had always been broader and bulkier than him and had made sure the school bullies left him alone when they were younger. Lately, though, since Perce had got mixed up with Stan and his cronies, his brother had changed. Or perhaps he'd always had a bit of a nasty streak, like their Granda Shawe, and he'd never noticed. Whatever, since they had been on short time he had the feeling Perce was sailing close to the wind more and more, involving himself in shady deals with the motley crew from the East End he was so pally with. Not that his mam minded, not with Perce slipping her extra housekeeping often as not. Perce wasn't mean, he'd say that for him.

Thomas, sitting at the side of him, spluttered over a piece of the mutton stew he was eating, half choking, and Bruce's mind returned to concrete things for a moment. 'Steady on, you.' He patted the small boy on the back, half laughing, and Thomas's bright eyes laughed back at him. It was no co-incidence the child was sitting next to him. Thomas looked up to him in the same way he himself had looked up to Perce in years gone by, and the pair of them had a bond which didn't exist with his other siblings.

He took his eyes from the child and glanced at his father who was congratulating Amy on her move to the restaurant.

Ronald's gaze met his in the next instant and as though he knew Bruce was the only member of the family who would give the right response, he said, 'Doing all right for herself, isn't she? Twelve months and she's already on her way up.'

Bruce smiled at his father but spoke directly to his cousin when he said, 'More than all right. You'll be manageress of that place before you're finished, lass.'

Amy's reply was lost in the harsh scraping of Perce's chair as he stood up. 'I'm off. Business in town.'

'Business?' Ronald's voice was sharp, and not for the first time Bruce felt his father was as suspicious of Perce's activities as he was. 'What business are you doing at this time of night?'

Perce turned at the kitchen door and looked at them all, his handsome face unsmiling. He shrugged. 'Probably nowt,' he said offhandedly. 'A pal of mine mentioned a boat brought in some damaged goods they were going to sell off cheap but there might be nowt in it.'

More likely goods that fell off the back of a lorry. Bruce stared at his brother. But if Perce wanted to risk a spell inside, that was up to him. He was sick of challenging him about it. And he was glad Perce was going out; he wanted to ask Amy if Perce had tried it on at all but there always seemed to be someone or other about. Perhaps tonight he'd be able to have a quiet word with her. He had thought more than once lately about striking out down south, especially since he had been on short time, but he didn't like the idea of Amy being left without any protection if Perce had his eye on her. Not that he thought that Perce would try to make her do anything she didn't want to. Did he?

As Perce left the house, Bruce was forced to recognise he really wasn't sure.

An hour later Bruce had his opportunity to ask Amy about Perce. Eva and Harriet and the twins were playing outside, the two younger children were in bed and Ronald and May were arguing heatedly in the kitchen, a not uncommon occurrence. Amy had taken a pile of mending through to the sitting room and was tackling a torn shirt sleeve when Bruce walked in.

'They're at it again, tearing strips off each other.' He shook his head wearily. 'Why can't they give it a rest now and again?'

There was no reply to be made to this. Instead she tried to lighten his uncharacteristically melancholy mood. 'Is this one of your shirts and, if so, what on earth have you been doing to tear it so badly? The sleeve's hanging on by a thread.'

He glanced at the offending article. 'It's Perce's.'

He sensed rather than saw her recoil, and when she quietly put the shirt back in the basket and brought out one of Thomas's little vests, he sat up straighter on the hard horse-hair sofa and said without any preamble, 'Has Perce been bothering you?'

'What?' The small vest fell out of her fingers.

'He has, hasn't he? What's he said? What's he done?'

There were a few moments of silence in which he imagined all sorts of things before she said, 'He hasn't done anything.'

'But he's said something? Something that's frightened you?'

Again the hesitation before she said, 'No. No, he hasn't.'

He didn't believe her but he couldn't very well drag the truth out of her. 'If he does anything, I want you to tell me, all right? Do you understand what I'm saying?'

Whether she understood him or not he never got to find out because his father stomped into the room in the next moment, his face as black as thunder. 'You coming for a jar?'

Bruce stared at his father. Unlike quite a few of the men they worked with, his father rarely frequented public houses, even on pay day. He would sometimes have a bottle of beer at home but that was normally when he or Perce had brought a couple in, and this had happened less and less since they had been on short time. His father's only indulgence was his baccy.

'Now?' Bruce asked, looking up into his father's furious face.

'Aye, now.'

Bruce got to his feet. The row was probably a continuation of the one the night before; his mam never let anything drop.

Amy watched them go. She was aware of her aunt banging about in the kitchen but she didn't go in to her, her mind preoccupied with her conversation with Bruce. She was glad her uncle had come in when he had. She didn't lie very well but she couldn't tell Bruce the truth. If he started on Perce, there was no knowing where things would end. And it wasn't as if Perce had done anything since the time he'd told her she was going to be his lass. He might well have forgotten all about it; he had girlfriends, after all. This thought carried no conviction. She only had to catch Perce's eye now and again to know he still wanted her. The expression on his face at these moments had the power to make her flesh creep.

She began to apply neat stitches to the little vest, her thoughts causing her to frown as she worked. If it wasn't for the knowledge of how much it would upset her grandma, she would ask Aunt Kitty if she could move in with her and Mr and Mrs Price. They would be happy to have her, she knew they would, but her gran wouldn't understand why she wanted to leave Uncle Ronald's and she couldn't very well tell her about Perce. If her gran then told her granda he'd twist it round so it was all her fault somehow, and Perce would probably deny everything anyway. A huge family row would ensue and it would be her gran who would be the most upset. No, she had to stick it here, Perce or no Perce, but if he came out in the open and said anything else she would make it plain she hadn't changed her mind and never would.

She sighed, breaking the thread to the vest with her teeth and then reaching into the basket for another garment.

It was some time later when the front door knocker banged. Once upon a time she would have jumped up and answered the door herself, now she waited for her aunt to do it. She wasn't going to go back to being at everyone's beck and call and it was little things like this that set the tone, she'd found. She still did plenty to help round the house – she glanced at the basket of mending – but these days it wasn't taken for granted and her aunt actually thanked her now and again.

She heard voices and then the sound of someone being shown into the front room. Her aunt popped her head round the sitting-room door in the next moment and the look on her face brought Amy to her feet. 'It's the Father,' May whispered as Amy hurried over to her. Father Lee had come partly out of retirement the year before when the situation with the young priest had become sensitive, and now it was the elderly priest who made any necessary house calls. 'Father Fraser rang him and asked him to come round.'

'Is it Gran?' Amy's hand clutched at her throat and all the colour left her face.

'No, no, it's your granda. He was took bad at work apparently. Can you go and fetch your uncle from the Blue Bell? It would be the one night he's out drinking. I don't know what the Father will think.'

Amy, her eyes wide and questioning now, began to say, 'What's happened to—' but her aunt cut her off with an urgent flap of her hand.

'Get your hat and coat and go now. And be sure to tell him the Father's waiting to talk to him. And tell Eva and the others to come in while you're about it, I didn't realise it was so late. Your uncle at the pub and the bairns out playing in the dark, the Father will think we're as bad as the McHaffies in Newcastle Road.'

The McHaffies were a family notorious for their insobriety and neglect of their numerous dirty-nosed offspring, and knowing that whatever had befallen her grandfather, the priest catching them on the hop would upset her aunt more, Amy said, 'No, no he won't, he knows you and Uncle Ronald too well for that.' She brushed past her aunt as she spoke and hurried into the kitchen and through to the scullery where her outdoor clothes were hanging on their peg.

As she was buttoning her coat, her aunt appeared in the doorway. 'Go the front way, it's quicker,' she muttered, taking Amy's arm and leading her back into the hall as though Amy didn't know where the front door was. Her aunt opened the door and virtually pushed Amy out into the street, stuffing a couple of peppermints into the pocket of her coat. 'Tell Bruce and your uncle to suck these on the way back,' she muttered. 'I don't want them breathing all over Father Lee stinking of beer.'

Amy fairly flew down the road. The pavements were shining with the drizzling rain that had begun to fall, and when she came to the corner where a group of children, her cousins among them, were playing some game or other, she called over her shoulder, 'Eva! Your mam wants you all in and look lively, Father Lee's called round,' knowing that would move them quicker than anything.

The street lamps were making pools of muted light on the wet ground as she turned in the direction of Fulwell Road and the Blue Bell Inn, and she had almost reached the public house when her arm was caught from behind and she was swung round with such force she ended bang up against Perce's broad chest. 'Where're you off to?' he said thickly, the smell on his breath and slurred voice suggesting it wasn't only Bruce and her uncle who had been drinking. 'Who are you meeting this time of night and in the dark?'

'Let go, you're hurting.' She pulled away from him, her voice fierce. 'Your mam's sent me for your da, Granda's been took bad.'

'Oh aye?' He didn't seem to care and this was confirmed when he said, 'I don't want you working in that restaurant at night, you hear me? It's bad enough you're in the café in the day with lads ogling you and the like, and you in that dress an' apron like a French maid in a promenade peepshow.'

'What?' She didn't understand the reference to the French maid but she knew it wasn't very nice because peepshows were mucky.

'You heard me. And don't pretend you don't know what they want. Well, I'm not having it. You're not taking that job.'

'I am.' He was blocking her way and when she tried to move round him, he didn't let her. Her heart was pounding but she was angry as well as frightened, and her voice was loud when she said, 'Let me pass, I need to get Uncle Ronald. The Father is waiting at home for him.'

'Let him wait.' Suddenly he reached out and Amy found

herself manhandled into the shadows, one beefy arm round her waist lifting her off her feet and his other hand across her mouth, stifling the scream that rose in her. 'I said I'd give you time to get used to the idea you're going to be my lass and I have, I've played it straight, haven't I? But I won't be messed about. You try playing fast and loose with me and see what you get,' he said over her head.

She struggled violently, her arms and legs flailing, but he was big and solid and could have been a brick wall for all the effect she had on him.

'Aw, Amy, Amy.' She found the trembling softness in his tone now more terrifying than his threats. He had her pinned in a shop doorway across the road from the Blue Bell Inn, and although the outside of the public house was lit well enough, they were standing in almost total blackness. He kept his hand across her mouth as he turned her round to face him, holding her captive by pressing his lower body against her. 'Be nice to me, that's all I'm asking. There's plenty who wouldn't have waited as long as I have. Them other lasses, they mean nowt, you know that, but a man has needs. That's all I go with them for. But you, if you're nice to me, I wouldn't look the side another lass was on. I swear it. And we'll do the courtin' however you want it. I'll tell me mam if that's what you want.'

When his hand moved she tried to scream but his mouth had already covered hers, wet and cavernous. His tongue forced her lips apart and his spittle made her want to retch. She bit down hard, causing him to swear as he jerked his head back, but again his hand covered her lower face. Wedging her with his legs, his other hand was now inside her coat, pulling at the buttons of her blouse. They gave way, accompanied by the sound of tearing and then his hand was on the small full mound of her breast, squeezing hard.

Nearly mad with fear, she continued to fight, trying to twist and turn but she was like a rag doll in his grasp. His hand left her body to fumble with his trousers and then something hard was pressing against her belly. 'You wouldn't have it nice, would you?' He was trying to yank her skirt up as he spoke, his breath hot on her face. 'I wanted to do it proper but you wouldn't have any of it. You've made me do this.'

As he released the hold on her lower body with his legs just long enough to hoist her skirt up round her waist, she acted. From somewhere she found the strength to bring her knee up into his groin. He emitted a shrill sound, something between a scream and an animal yelp, before crumpling at her knees, his hands going between his legs.

It had been instinct that had guided her actions and it was the same sense of self-preservation that made her kick out at him and send him sprawling so that she could jump over him. She felt him try to clutch at her but he was doubled up and groaning and in no state to chase her. For a moment her legs seemed too weak to hold her as she stumbled out of the doorway onto the pavement, but terror enabled her to run blindly across the road into the light. Her hand was actually on the door of the public house when she realised the state of her clothing. She turned to look back but the doorway was in blackness and she couldn't see if Perce was still there or not. Certainly he wasn't coming for her and that was the only thing that mattered.

Feverishly she straightened her skirt and pulled her gaping blouse together over her torn petticoat. Two or three buttons were still hanging on and her stiff fingers made hard work of slipping them through the buttonholes but eventually it was done. As she fastened her coat and pulled the belt tight she saw a shape emerge from the doorway, still half doubled up. Her eyes wide, she stood poised to dash into the Blue Bell but he didn't attempt to come towards her; he stood still for a minute before stumbling away in the opposite direction. The relief was so overwhelming she felt faint.

She stood for a few moments more until she was sure he had gone, her teeth chattering and her head beginning to clear as the raw panic diminished. Her hat. As her hair wafted about her face she realised her hat had to be in the shop doorway where it must have fallen some time during the struggle. She couldn't go back over there. Everything in her rebelled at the thought. But if she went home without her hat her aunt would be bound to ask where it was.

In that moment Amy acknowledged she wasn't going to tell anyone about Perce attacking her. It was too shameful, too horrible. Everyone would look at her differently, and if Perce denied it they would believe him and not her. Everyone would be thinking about her mother and what had happened. The words Perce had thrown at her the year before still burned vividly in her mind: 'I'll deny it and guess who they'll believe? Blood's thicker than water, they'll say. She's like her mam but she's started even earlier.'

Would Mr Callendar think like that? She rubbed her hand across her face as she admitted to herself it was his opinion of her that was important. She wouldn't be able to bear it if he did. She leaned against the wall of the pub, only vaguely conscious of the drone of conversation from within and the odd laugh.

She had to get away from Perce, she couldn't live at Uncle Ronald's after this. She'd ask Kitty if she could live with her, it was the only solution. If her grandma got upset, she'd have to get upset. Amy shivered convulsively. There'd be ructions all round and hell to pay but it couldn't be helped. Nothing would make her stay at home now, not after this.

Walking across the road and retrieving her hat was the hardest thing she'd ever done, but once it was in her hand and she had dashed back to the Blue Bell, the panic subsided. She brushed the felt down before putting the hat on, and, taking a deep breath, opened the door of the public house and stepped inside.

The next day Amy learned that there was something which had the power to persuade her to stay at Ronald and May's house. Wilbur Shawe died shortly after Ronald arrived at the house in Deptford Road and Ronald had proposed that Muriel come to live with them.

'She can have the front room,' he suggested to an outraged May who had sat waiting up for him, along with Bruce and Amy. The six younger children were asleep. Perce had come in late and after a cursory word with his mother in the kitchen had gone straight to bed. Amy had been in the sitting room at the time and although the sound of his voice had made her tremble inside she hadn't had to set eyes on him, for which she was thankful. 'We still have the sitting room and no one ever goes into the front room unless it's when the Father calls.'

'I won't have it.' May was white with fury. 'Do you hear me, Ronald? I won't have it. You know how I've got every-thing just right in there and all my best bits in the china cabinet Da bought us. There's no room for a bed.'

Ronald didn't shout or protest. He simply stared at his wife for a moment before saying quietly, 'Have you thought what everyone will say if her only son doesn't offer her a home? There are hundreds of families with ten and more in two rooms in this town and they take in their old 'uns without a word of complaint. How do you think the Father and the rest of them round these doors will view us if they hear we couldn't make room for my mother here? You chew on that, May.'

May did chew on it and it nearly choked her, but the upshot was the next morning it had been decided that the frail old woman would be brought by taxi to Fulwell at the weekend to take up residence in May's hallowed front room.

Amy was on tenterhooks all day at work, Verity's coldness barely registering on her, and as soon as she could she left the building in the evening and made her way to Deptford Road. Her uncle had said the night before that the Prices had offered to take care of her grandma until the weekend when she could be moved.

At some point during the day Amy had accepted that her plan to move to Kitty's house was over. If she did that, it would most likely mean that she wouldn't be able to see her grandmother again because her Aunt May would be furious at her going or, more accurately, she thought grimly, at the prospect of the money she brought in suddenly stopping. Either way, one thing would be certain, she wouldn't be welcome at her aunt's house any more.

The front-room door was open when she entered her grandmother's house by the back door and went through the kitchen into the hall, and she heard Mrs Price saying, 'Now get that out of your head, Muriel, do you hear me? Landsakes, woman, no one knows what you've had to put up with from that man. It's relief you're feeling and no wonder. I don't hold with this notion where immediately folk die they become saints. Father Fraser might say Wilbur was a good man but he didn't live with him, did he? And when all's said and done, his passing is God's will, lass.'

Amy had paused in the hall, uncertain whether to make herself known, but then she pushed the door wider and stepped into the front room. As two pairs of eyes turned towards her, Mrs Price said immediately, and with some relief, 'Amy, lass. I thought you'd come the night. I said to you, Muriel, didn't I, she'd come as soon as she could. Now you sit with your grandma, hinny, and I'll get a sup for you both. She's a bit upset,' she muttered to Amy as she passed her. 'Talk to her, lass.'

Amy went and sat on the edge of the bed and she could see at once her grandmother had been crying. She asked a question that most people would have found strange in the circumstances but she knew how things had been between her grandparents. 'What's the matter, Gran?' she said softly as she took her grandmother's hand.

Muriel's sunken eyes swam with tears again and for a moment she couldn't answer. Then she said, 'The Father called round earlier.'

'Aye?'

'I . . . I was havin' a cup of tea an' a bite of sly cake Sally had brought in an' we were laughin' about somethin' she was sayin', I can't remember what now. He . . . When Sally had gone he said I ought to ask God's forgiveness for not showin' proper respect an' that marriage was holy an' I was mockin'

God's order of things. Wicked, he called it.' Muriel couldn't go on.

Amy put her arm round the bony shoulders. 'It's all right, Gran. It's all right.'

'He said he'd pray for my immortal soul as though . . .' Muriel gulped hard. 'As though he thought I wouldn't get into heaven. An' the thing is, hinny, I can't put me hand on me heart an' say I'm sorry your granda's gone. He was a devil of a man.'

'I know he was, Gran.'

'He sent your poor mam to the grave as sure as if he'd stuck a knife in her.'

The door opened and Sally Price was back with a tray holding two cups of tea and a plate of teacakes. Her voice loud, she said, 'I've told your gran she has to take all he said with a pinch of salt. There's priests and priests, in my book, and I'm not afraid to say,' she crossed herself, 'Father Fraser is one on his own. Now Father Bell at St Jude's or Father Skelton are different again. Grand, they are.' She handed Amy her cup and then leaned over to give Muriel hers, patting the old woman's veined hand as she did so. 'He only sees what he wants to see, Father Fraser. Now haven't I said that before, Muriel? So don't fret. When our Patrick was a bairn he had nightmares for weeks after the Father caught him reading a comic and put the fear of God in him.'

'Sally, lass, he's a priest.' As far as Muriel was concerned that said it all.

'I know, I know, but all I'm saying is don't let him scare the wits out of you. Look, you'll soon be with your Ronald. Have a word with Father Lee.' She straightened. 'I'd best get back and see to me dinner. I'll be bringing yours in a bit later. There's plenty for you if you want a bite, lass,' she added to Amy.

'Thank you, Mrs Price, but I can't stay too long.'

'Oh, lass, don't rush off.' Muriel clutched at her granddaughter's hand. 'They know you're comin' here, don't they?'

Amy nodded. The look on her grandmother's face was heart-rending and for a moment she had the weird feeling that their positions had been reversed, and that she was dealing with a distraught child who was scared of the bogeyman. If confirmation had been needed that she couldn't leave home, it was there in her grandma's eyes. 'I'll stay,' she said softly, a weight compounded of love and compassion and obligation settling on her shoulders.

Somehow she would deal with Perce. Somehow.

PART FOUR

1933 The Proposal

Chapter 9

Muriel lay staring into the deep glow of the fire which May had recently banked down for the night with wet tea leaves. The household was asleep but she had been dozing on and off all day, something she was prone to do these days, and now she was wide awake.

It was the first anniversary of Wilbur's passing but not a soul had mentioned it. It might be out of respect for her feelings but she didn't think so. She was sure they'd all simply forgotten. Wilbur would be turning in his grave but she didn't think anyone missed him or would wish him back, not even Ronald. As for her, the last twelve months had made her appreciate what a prisoner let out of jail unexpectedly must feel like. She shifted her position against the pile of pillows behind her back which kept her upright day and night and enabled her to breathe more easily.

Her eyes moved to the put-you-up positioned a few feet away. She could just make out the shape of Amy's head on the pillow in the dim light. From the first night she'd taken up residence in her son's house her granddaughter had insisted she wanted to be close at hand once she was home from work, and although she'd protested Amy shouldn't be a nursemaid to an old woman like herself, she had to admit it had been heaven on earth to have the bairn close. They had some right good cracks together but then they always had. She smiled to herself in the darkness. Ray of sunshine, Amy was. The only ray of sunshine in this house.

Her smile faded as her mind returned to the worry which occupied most of her waking hours. She hoped she was wrong, oh, how she hoped she was wrong but the suspicion that Ronald was seeing another woman just wouldn't leave her. He'd been different the last little while, happier in a — she searched her mind for a word to describe her son's demeanour — secret way. That was it, secret. Not quiet as such or calm, like folk become when they've made peace with themselves and their lot and gain a measure of joy from life because of it. It wasn't like that. Mind, could anyone be joyful married to May? Or May and her da more like because if ever there were three in a marriage, there were in Ronald's. Terence O'Leary had a lot to answer for in her book.

Muriel moved restlessly, her chest getting tighter as she got more agitated. Forcing herself to breathe evenly and slowly, she tried to relax. It wouldn't help no one if she was took bad with one of her turns.

Course, things had got worse between May and Ronald when Perce had upped and skedaddled just after she had arrived here last year. Right do that had been, she thought grimly. Throwing in his job and declaring he could do better joining forces with some of those pals of his who were no better than they should be. Bruce had reported only last week he'd seen Perce about town in a smart new suit and driving a motor car. He was dancing with the devil, that one. But the loss of his wage had hit the family hard and even when Eva had been taken into service, they'd still been hard pushed. Useless to say to May they weren't as bad off as some, she didn't want to hear it, but it was the truth nonetheless. Look at Sally and Abe, reduced to the Means Test with Abe having caught TB, and Kitty not able to accept a shilling rise without it being deducted from the family dole. Criminal, it was. Even the few pence bairns earned on a paper round was treated the same.

Muriel brooded on the cruel effect the Means Test was having for a minute or two and then her mind returned to her son once more. Should she come straight out and ask him? But what good would that do? Whether he was or he wasn't, he'd deny it. Her brow wrinkled and her bony fingers plucked nervously at the satin eiderdown as they were wont to do if she was anxious. Who could it be? To her knowledge the only women he knew were the neighbours, apart from the couple of lasses in the office at his works, but he wouldn't start anything with them, not under the nose of his father-in-law. And what woman in her right mind would dally with a married man with umpteen bairns anyway? They did, though, that was the thing. Her fingers reached for the glass of water on the little table by the head of the bed but in the dark her hand fumbled and the glass went flying.

'You all right, Gran?' Amy was up like a shot, her hair a black tousled halo in the dim light from the street lamp outside the window. Muriel always had the curtains slightly open, she didn't like to sleep in pitch blackness.

'Aye, aye, hinny, it's only me water.'

'I'll get a towel.'

Amy felt her way into the kitchen; one of the economies May insisted on these days was no gas mantles being lit after they had retired for the night, except in a dire emergency. When Amy had mopped up the water on the table and floor she fetched her grandmother a fresh glass and plonked herself down on the edge of Muriel's bed. 'Do you want one of your pills, Gran?'

'Aye, I might do, lass, if it's not too much trouble. I'm sorry I woke you.'

'You didn't.' Amy handed her grandmother one of the tiny white pills as she spoke. 'I hadn't gone to sleep.'

'No? That's not like you. You're normally gone as soon as your head touches the pillow an' I'm not surprised at it, workin' all them hours on your feet. Mind, I know your uncle's grateful for what you bring in to the house, lass, an' it was right good of you to give 'em the tips an' all after Perce was gone an' they was strugglin'. I can't believe what some of them folk give you, though. Your granda used to say it's nature's law that the rich get richer an' the poor get poorer an' though he weren't right about much, he was about that.' When there was no response, Muriel said quietly, 'You got anythin' on your mind, hinny?'

'No. Yes. Oh, I don't know.' Amy hesitated and then said, 'It's nothing, Gran, not really.'

'It's enough to keep you awake, lass.'

'But I don't know if I'm imagining it.'

Muriel reached out her hand and patted Amy's arm. 'You're not much given to fancies so let's hear it.'

'It's . . . Mr Callendar.'

'Oh aye?'

'Well, you know we talk sometimes an' all that but he seems different lately.'

Muriel's pulse quickened. 'In what way, lass?'

'It's not so much what he says, although he's told me all sorts of things about him and his family and they seem a bunch of cold fish, Gran. Not like him. But . . . well, I'm not sure but I think he likes me, you know, in *that* way. But like I said, I could be imagining it.'

Muriel didn't think so. Listening to her lass's chatter over the last twelve months and the way the owner of Callendars always singled her out and wanted to talk to her, she'd felt in her bones the man had his eye on Amy. If this Charles Callendar was above board, Amy would be in clover. If he wasn't . . . But he hadn't put a foot wrong thus far, or tried to take advantage of the lass. And Amy was bonny enough to capture any man's heart, and she was blossoming more every day. Amy was too good for the lads hereabouts, that was for sure. She didn't want her lass working her fingers to the bone and ending up with a couple of bairns hanging on her skirts before she was twenty. But how did Amy feel about this new development?

Trying to keep all trace of excitement out of her voice, Muriel said, 'If he *does* like you, would that be a bad thing, hinny? Could you like him?'

There was a pause and then Amy said shyly, 'He's nice, Gran, and although he knows ever so much, he never makes me feel silly. He's read so many books and he knows about everything. He loves music, proper music, I mean. He's got a gramophone in his office now and sometimes when I take his dinner in to him at night he'll talk about Liszt or Strauss or Wagner, whatever's playing. He had *Vienna Blood* on tonight, Gran, and it was beautiful. Just beautiful.'

'That's nice, pet.' Muriel wasn't interested in *Vienna Blood*. 'And you say he looks a bit like Gary Cooper?' She had remembered Amy had said that in the early days and, looking back, that was probably when she first pricked up her ears about Amy's employer.

There was a longer pause and Muriel wished she could see her granddaughter's face clearly.

'Aye, he does, he's . . . very handsome,' Amy said at last. 'All the girls think so, so . . .'

'So what?' Muriel asked when the silence lengthened.

'So he can take his pick. You know, of female companions.'

Muriel decided on a little plain speaking. 'That's all very well but didn't you tell me he wouldn't have anyone but you bring his dinner at night? Even after he knew folk were gossipin'?'

'But that was because they *were* gossiping and he doesn't think you should give in to that sort of talk. But he comes from a different world. His people would expect . . .' Her voice trailed away and there was a different note in it when she said, 'Anyway, he hasn't said anything so I don't know why I'm talking about it.' She slid off the bed as she spoke and returned to her put-you-up which creaked in protest as she lay down. 'Night, Gran,' she said softly.

'Goodnight, me bairn. Don't let the bed bugs bite.'

It wasn't too long before Amy's regular deep breathing told Muriel her granddaughter was asleep. She felt tired herself now; any conversation, however brief, had that effect on her, but from the moment Amy had laid down she had begun to pray. Not the jumbled kind of praying she did in her head all the time, praying that took in everything from Wilbur's sojourn in purgatory to the ache in her big toe which had been giving her gyp lately, but concentrated, strong, focused prayer. Let everything come right with this Mr Callendar, God. Let him make himself plain, and soon. Oh, Mary, Mother of God, I can tell she likes him, I could hear it in her voice. She don't dare believe he feels the same way, that's the thing. Her poor mam had a rough deal all round and I want better for Amy, a life of comfort and ease, of being cherished and cared for. That's not wrong, is it? To wish someone is loved? Please, Holy Mother, let me see the bairn settled before I go.

At just after half past six the following evening Muriel's prayers were answered. Amy had just placed Charles Callendar's tray in front of him, saying as she did so, 'The soup is fish and vegetable tonight, followed by stuffed shoulder of lamb.' She lifted the silver lid covering the main dish. 'Looks lovely, doesn't it?'

'Yes, it does.' He didn't even glance at the food but kept his gaze locked on her.

Amy had been smiling but now her face straightened. He watched the colour flood into her cheeks and she appeared flustered. 'I'd better get back,' she said quickly. 'We're short staffed tonight and—'

'Please sit down for a moment, Amy. I need to talk to you.' He rose from his seat, walked across to the gramophone and lifted the stylus off the record which had been playing. He came to sit on the side of his desk in front of her. She didn't raise her eyes to his. 'I want to ask you something and I would like you to speak frankly, as one friend to another. Do I appear a little ancient to you, over the hill, as it were?'

'What?'

As she raised her eyes to his in astonishment, he had to smile at the expression on her face in spite of the fact he was all knotted up inside. Whatever she'd been expecting him to say, it clearly wasn't this.

'No, of course not.' She smiled as though it was ridiculous to even consider such a notion.

It was a start. His heart was beating like a drum and for the hundredth time since he had first set eyes on her he asked himself why she had such a profound effect on him. It wasn't just her beauty, although with her maturing she was getting lovelier and lovelier, but Priscilla had been beautiful and he knew other women who were just as attractive. But even with Priscilla he hadn't felt like this. Amy was staring at him and he cleared his throat. 'Second question,' he said in as light a tone as he could muster. 'Do you think you could ever see me as more than just a friend and employer?'

She blinked.

'I've asked you so many times to call me Charles when we are talking like this but you never do. You're always so correct.' He smiled, acutely aware he didn't want to frighten her but that he had to *know*. He'd waited until her sixteenth birthday but every day since it had been more torturous and he couldn't wait a moment longer. 'I just wondered if this is because you want to keep a distance between us because anything beyond friendship is impossible, or whether it's because you feel it's a suitable way to behave.'

His voice was normal but as Amy gazed into his face she felt a trembling start deep inside at the look in his eyes. She had thought she'd glimpsed it once or twice before but then it had been veiled and unclear. Now it was there for her to see and it was thrilling. She tried to be circumspect but it was hard. 'I suppose the latter. I didn't want you to think I was taking advantage of your kindness.'

'Kindness?' He shook his head. 'I haven't been kind, Amy. I've been selfish, very selfish. I've put you in a position where you have been talked about and I shouldn't have done. I knew this, there's no excuse, but frankly,' he leaned forward, taking both of her hands in his and she realised she wasn't the only one who was trembling, 'I couldn't help myself. I love you, Amy. I think I loved you almost from the first moment I saw you. I know I'm older than you by some twelve years but I don't feel that when we're together. In fact, sometimes I feel I'm the sixteen year old. You're so wise.'

'Wise? I'm not wise. You know so much about everything, music, politics . . .'

'That's nothing, just information.' He slid off the desk and stood up, drawing her out of her chair. 'I'm talking about something you can't be taught, something you either have or you haven't and very few people have. And you're strong, too, and pure and good. Oh, Amy,' he pulled her closer into the circle of his arms, 'do you think you could love me? Tell me, put me out of my misery. Could you?'

Since Perce's assault she had wondered how she would feel if something like this happened, but she'd known if it was with Mr Callendar she wouldn't panic. The delicious fragrance she'd noticed before when she'd been close to him was stronger now, mixing with the faint smell of cigar smoke on the fine twill jacket he was wearing. A little shiver spiralled up through her body but it was of excitement, not fear. She nodded shyly. 'Yes,' she whispered.

'Oh, my love.'

When his mouth descended and she found herself being

held tighter than ever, she stiffened just for a moment, but then his warm firm lips moved from her mouth to her eyes, her ears, her chin, and she felt borne away on a dizzy enchantment. She had dreamed of being kissed like this, she told herself in wonder. Before Perce had spoiled everything, she had dreamed it could be like this. Her eyes closed and now when his mouth found hers again she was ready for his kiss, no longer merely compliant but beginning to kiss him back.

She felt him shudder, his voice thick when he said, 'I love you, Amy, more than I have ever loved anyone. I'd promised myself I'd give you time to get used to the idea of being with me after I had declared my feelings, but frankly I don't think I can. I care for you too deeply. I know you so well and you know all there is to know about me. I just have to ask you now, will you marry me?' As her eyes widened in shock, he lifted one hand from her waist to tenderly stroke a wispy curl from her forehead. 'I know I'm going about this like a bull in a china shop,' he added ruefully, skimming her lips with the lightest of kisses. 'Doing what I shouldn't and rushing you.'

She stared at him. She was having trouble taking in that she was actually in his arms like this, perhaps because she had imagined it so many times in the last months before berating herself that she was being silly and that he didn't like her in *that* way at all. She felt heady, exhilarated that a man like him, a cultured, handsome, *wonderful* man, wanted her. Loved her. She wanted to say yes a hundred times before he changed his mind and the magic bubble burst. Instead she found herself saying in a small voice, 'What about your family? Your mam and brother and everyone?'

'What about them?'

'Do they know about me?'

'Does it matter?' He smiled. 'I know about you.'

'You know what I mean,' she said very seriously. 'Would they approve of you marrying someone from . . .' she had been about to say the working class but changed it to, 'the north?'

He shrugged. 'If you want the truth I doubt whether they would be particularly interested one way or the other.' Her expression showed a mixture of surprise and disbelief. 'Amy,' he went on, 'my experience of family life is very different to yours. As far as my parents were concerned, children are something you have to continue the family name. When my mother had provided two boys for this purpose she felt she had fulfilled her obligations. We, my brother and I, were brought up by servants, as both my parents had been brought up by servants. They didn't consider this unkind or unfair, it was the natural way of things to them.'

'It sounds very cold-blooded,' she said quietly.

'It was.' He shrugged again. 'My brother didn't mind. I did. Anyway,' he flexed his shoulders as though throwing something off, 'say my name, Amy. I shan't believe this is real until you call me Charles. It will seal the pact somehow.'

Many times in their talks together he had said something that seemed inordinately boyish, even naive, and it was in these moments she had found herself falling for him. She looked into his face and the trembling inside grew stronger. She loved him, she knew she loved him and she had done for a long time even though she'd told herself she didn't because she had never imagined he would want her enough to ask her to be with him, to marry him, not with all the ladies who came in the restaurant and gave him the eye more often than not. She had resigned herself to the fact they would just continue to be friends. And yet she hadn't really, she contradicted herself immediately. She had hoped. Oh yes, she had hoped. 'I love you,' she said softly. 'I think I have for a long time.'

'Charles,' he prompted, his eyes glittering.

'Charles.' She giggled nervously.

'And you'll marry me? Soon?'

'Yes, I'll marry you.'

She couldn't say anything more because he swept her right off her feet, cutting off her breath with the force of his kisses as he swung her round until they were both giddy.

'I'm going to make you so happy, Amy. You've had a rotten deal of it one way and another, but all that will change now. And no more of these.' He whipped off her little cap and apron despite her laughing protests. 'From now on you're going to be too busy preparing for the wedding and furnishing our home to think of anything else. But don't worry, until we're married and you leave your uncle's place, your aunt will get her pound of flesh by way of your wage packet each Friday. We don't want to upset the apple cart, do we!'

It was going to be upset anyway. Aunt May would be spitting bricks at her good fortune and Eva would be pea-green once she heard the news, but Amy wasn't going to think of them now. Now she was going to be kissed again and that was all that mattered.

Charles insisted on taking her home in his car once they came up for air. He first called Mr Mallard into his office and told the manager Amy had done him the great honour of agreeing to become his wife, an announcement Mr Mallard took calmly in his stride, despite the fact he was already one waiter and waitress down in the restaurant. Indeed, he seemed to have been expecting it.

'May I offer you both my warmest congratulations,' he said with something of a wry smile, 'and best wishes for the future.'

'You may, Robin, you may,' Charles said boyishly. 'We're going to see Amy's family now and I shan't be back tonight. Hold the fort, would you? And tell Chef I'll discuss those new menus he has in mind tomorrow morning, and make some excuse to Mr Preston's party for me. They're bridge club friends and will expect me to put in an appearance at some point.'

'Don't worry about a thing, sir. You just go.' Mr Mallard ushered them out of the office as though he was a father sending two children to a party.

As they walked downstairs Amy's head was spinning. She had to resist the impulse to pinch herself to see if she was dreaming. She glanced down at the attractive but practical frock that was part of her uniform. When she had changed into this just a few hours ago she'd been Amy Shawe, waitress, with nothing more exciting in front of her than wondering if the chef was going to throw another of his paddies before the evening was finished. Now ... She breathed in deeply, finding it difficult to stand still when what she really wanted to do was to dance and twirl and use up some of the adrenalin pumping round her body. Now her whole life had changed in one fell swoop. She was going to be Charles's wife, his *wife*. He was everything and more any girl could possibly want.

It felt terribly strange to be helped into the opulent Rover a few minutes later after she had quickly changed into her own clothes. She had never ridden in an automobile before and as she glanced round the shining interior that smelled of leather and cigars, her heart, which had only just started to beat in a regular fashion, speeded up again.

'I've dreamed of you sitting beside me like this.'

The quality of his voice caused hot colour to flood her face and she found she didn't know what to say. 'It's . . . it's a beautiful car.'

'I want to surround you with beautiful things. You know the house I've just bought near Ryhope, well, I bought it with you in mind. That's why I haven't moved in yet or furnished it. The first time I sleep there will be when I carry you over the threshold as Mrs Callendar.'

Mrs Callendar. Her heart pounded more violently and she felt a moment's brief panic at the speed with which things were moving.

Whether he sensed this or not she didn't know, but instead of starting the engine he leaned across to her, taking her hand. 'I love you, Amy.' His voice was tender and he cupped her chin with his other hand, drawing her gaze to his. 'You believe that, don't you? And I feel we've gone through the first stage of our relationship in the last two years. I've never talked to anyone like I've talked to you, you know me better than I know myself, and I like that. It's a good start to a marriage to be best friends. But I am a man and wanting you for so long, needing you—' He stopped abruptly, shaking his head. 'It's nearly crucified me at times. I don't want a long engagement, Amy. In fact I'd like us to be married as soon as it can be arranged.'

He kissed her again and although she knew no one could

see them, parked as the car was at the back of the restaurant, she felt as embarrassed as if half the diners were watching. But the smell and feel of him combined with his experience in a realm she had no knowledge of proved intoxicating. She had only really been kissed by her granny before, and then usually on the cheek. Now she was finding this closeness to another human being brought forth all sorts of emotions she was barely aware of. But she liked it. She liked it very much.

'And I want to take you out of that house, show you what it is like to be really loved.'

'My granny loves me.'

'Sensible lady.' His brown eyes were looking into hers and they were dark pools, warm and deep. She felt she could drown in his eyes. 'You don't want a long engagement when there is nothing stopping us being together, do you?' he murmured. 'I know I haven't been to church since I came up here but I'll go and do my penance this very Sunday and arrange a meeting with the priest. He'll be full of admiration for you, bringing a lapsed Catholic back into the fold. I need you, Amy.' His voice was now so low and husky she could barely hear him. 'I'm lonely, every moment I'm not with you I'm heart lonely. I've lived for the times you've walked into the office; the rest of the time I've just been existing. I want to know you're mine, be able to reach out and touch you, wake up with you, go to sleep with you . . .'

The catch in his voice brought such a swell of tenderness into her breast it wasn't hard to say, 'I want it too, I do.' She wanted to make him happy again. He'd been through such a lot, she couldn't imagine what he must have felt when Priscilla and the baby died. For the first time in their acquaintance it was she who touched him, putting her hand to the side of his face where he caught it and kissed her fingers.

When Charles Callendar knocked on the front door of Ronald's house, the Rover parked in the narrow road outside and his arm very firmly round Amy's waist, it could be said the shock waves reverberated clear to Newcastle. In spite of the superior air of the district which proclaimed many of the householders had an indoor privy, the good wives weren't above twitching their starched lace curtains and observing the goings-on of their neighbours, the same as common folk.

It was Eva who opened the door, and so surprised was she that she promptly shut it in their faces before she ran to get her mother. By the time May opened the door again, Amy was wondering what on earth Charles thought of them all. She knew her grandmother would have a bird's-eye view of Charles from her bed next to the window but thankfully the curtains in their front room, if not in the houses either side, did not flutter.

May ushered them into the sitting room where Ronald was hastily doing up the top button of his shirt and Eva and Harriet were standing goggle-eyed to one side of the hearth. There was no fire burning in the grate, nor had there been for some time. These days any fuel was needed for the range in the kitchen and to keep the small fire going in Muriel's room.

Introductions were made, and then Charles turned to Ronald and without any prevarication said, 'You must be wondering why I am here, Mr Shawe, and why I have brought Amy home this evening. I wonder if I might have a word with you in private?'

Ronald looked at the handsome, well-dressed man in front of him and then at Amy's shining face. Without further ado he peered over Charles's shoulder at his wife. 'Perhaps you'd take Eva and Harriet and see if Mam's all right,' he said calmly.

For a moment Amy thought her aunt was going to protest but then she swept from the room with Eva and Harriet in her wake, Amy bringing up the rear. In Muriel's room May hardly waited until Amy had shut the door before she said, 'Well, girl?'

She would be so glad not to hear that every day of her life. Amy didn't reply to her aunt immediately. Instead she walked across to the bed holding the frail old woman who was looking at her so intently, and there she said softly, 'Mr Callendar has asked me to marry him, Gran.'

Muriel stared at her granddaughter a moment more and then all the air seemed to leave her body in a long deep sigh. She sank back on the pillows, her rheumy eyes smiling. 'I'm glad, lass.'

'You? He's asked you?' Eva looked from Amy to her mother. 'Has he, Mam?'

May opened her mouth but no words came out. She made an almost imperceptible motion with her head which could have meant anything before turning and leaving the room, still without saying a word. A moment later they heard her footsteps mounting the stairs.

Mouth agape, Eva looked at Harriet but her sister was staring at Amy with unconcealed fascination and envy. 'Can I be a bridesmaid?' she asked hopefully.

By the time Charles left the house some time later it had been agreed the wedding would take place as soon as all the necessary arrangements were in place. He was grinning as he drove away, he couldn't seem to stop and even when he drew up outside the building in which his top-floor flat was housed his spirits weren't dampened.

Another couple of months and he would be out of this dismal place, he thought as he opened the front door of the flat. He would be living in the bright, new, clean house he had bought near Ryhope, with Amy as his wife. His *wife*. His heart leaped and thudded as it had been doing all evening.

Although he hadn't had a bite since lunchtime he didn't bother to make himself a sandwich but walked straight into the sitting room, the window of which overlooked Lampton Drops. It had been the view of the river and its central location that had persuaded him to take the flat when he had first moved up to Sunderland. It had nothing else going for it, in his opinion.

He walked straight over to the cocktail cabinet which had been one of the few items of furniture he'd brought with him from the sale of his house in the south. Nestling inside were a host of unopened bottles of whisky and brandy. He poured himself a measure of brandy and drank it down in one. He refilled the glass to the top and then carried it and the bottle over to the big comfortable chair in front of the small grate. He didn't bother to try to light a fire; he'd always had a housemaid to do this when he had lived with his parents and again once he was married, and when he had moved to Sunderland he'd never got the hang of it.

He had done it. He grinned again, drinking half the glass of brandy before leaning back in the chair and stretching his legs. After all the agonising of whether she would or she wouldn't, he had finally done it and it had gone better than ever he had hoped. And the uncle hadn't seemed too bad a sort, not when he had been on his own at least. After the wife had rejoined them, the man had seemed to shut up like a clam, barely speaking except to say he was fully in favour of the marriage and that they had his blessing. The sour-faced witch hadn't thought much to that if her face had been anything to go by although she had said all the right things in a fashion.

He finished the brandy and poured another glass before shutting his eyes and letting the familiar, warm glow the alcohol always gave him take over his senses. Many a night now he went to sleep like this, waking in the morning with a thumping head which only cleared after he had washed and shaved and had another shot to steady his trembling hands. But all that would change after he married Amy. All the loneliness of his life, a loneliness which had been with him long before Priscilla's death, in fact since he had been sent away from home at the age of seven to boarding school, would vanish when Amy was his wife. They would be happy, so happy. He smiled a befuddled smile.

The bottle was completely empty by the time Charles fell asleep, one arm draped over the side of the chair and the other still clutching the glass in which a few drops of brandy remained.

It had not occurred to him in all his musings of the last hour or two that he had been wrong when he had stated Amy knew all there was to know about him. But the empty bottle at the side of him, and all the other ones stacked in one corner, were sufficient proof that she did not.

Chapter 10

'Hey, man, isn't that your Perce? Honouring us with his presence, is he?'

Bruce glanced across the yard towards the gates of the iron and steel works. Aye, it was Perce all right and got up like a dog's dinner in that suit he'd seen him in before. Had he come to offer another chance of some quick money, no questions asked?

Perce was smiling when Bruce reached him and he clapped his younger brother on the back. As men streamed past them, one or two called out a greeting to Perce who responded with a wave of his hand, his eyes on Bruce. 'How goes it?' he said as though they'd last spoken just that morning instead of weeks ago. 'You still on short time?'

Bruce stared at him. Perce knew the answer to that or he wouldn't be here at this time of the day. Only those on short time left at one o'clock. Twenty-five hours a week and there had been talk it might be down to twenty before long. They'd be eating bread and dripping for dinner at this rate once

Amy's money stopped. He nodded. 'Aye, it don't get any better.'

Perce shrugged. 'Talk is it won't, man. The backbone of the country's just about broken but you don't have to work here. I told you I'd see you all right if you came to work for me and it wouldn't be peanuts either. You'd be earning real money.'

Bruce shook his head. 'And risk having my collar felt by the long arm of the law? I don't think so.'

'If you want to get on in life you have to take the odd risk.'

'Aye, well, it seems to me you're taking enough for the both of us so let's just leave it like that, shall we?'

'There's more and more being laid off, you know that. The shipyards are as bad as the mines now and the government doesn't give a damn. If you go on the dole they don't recognise the first week and then there's three days lying on, that's if you can get a brass farthing out of them at the end of it.'

'I don't intend to go on the dole.'

'There's plenty who said that who are now standing cap in hand.'

Bruce shrugged. He had come to realise over the last year or two that he and Perce would never see eye to eye on a lot of things. He would have liked it different but he wasn't a bairn and he had to face facts. From being close as boys they had grown into two very different individuals.

There was silence for a moment and then Perce said, 'Fancy a beer?'

'Aye, all right.' His throat was as dry as sandpaper and he'd sweated like a pig all morning, besides which he missed going for a pint with Perce now and again like they'd once done.

The pub Perce chose was one of the less salubrious in the vicinity. Neither of them spoke until they were at the bar. Perce ordered two pints. After handing one to Bruce he gestured to a table in the corner by the window. 'Let's sit down.'

They sat facing each other amid the wreaths of smoke made by the pipes of several old men at the bar. A couple of mangy-looking fox terriers slept at the feet of one individual. After a moment or two Perce said, 'A little bird's told me Amy is getting wed to that ponce from the south.'

Bruce's antennae pricked up. He didn't like Perce's tone. 'She's marrying Charles Callendar, aye,' he said.

'And you're happy about that?'

Bruce's brow wrinkled. 'It's nowt to do with me, man, who she marries.'

He was aware Perce was staring at him very intently as though trying to work something out. After a moment or two, his brother said, 'You're really not bothered?'

'About Callendar? Of course not. Mind, if it'd been some wrong 'un she'd got herself mixed up with that would have been different. But she's done well for herself with him. She won't want for nowt, that's for sure.'

Perce settled back in his seat and took a long pull at his beer. He wiped his mouth with the back of his hand. 'I'd got it wrong then. I always thought you were sweet on our little cousin.'

'Me?' Bruce's eyes narrowed. 'The boot's on the other foot, isn't it?'

Perce looked at him. 'Been talking to you, has she?'

'She didn't need to. I've got eyes, haven't I?'

Perce said nothing to this. After some seconds he lifted his glass and drained the contents. 'Want another?' he offered.

'I'm having one.' Bruce reached into his pocket. 'Don't be daft, man,' Perce said as he rose to his feet. 'I can buy me own brother a drink or two, can't I?'

Once they had two fresh pints in front of them, Perce said, 'In the family way, is she?'

Bruce choked on a mouthful of beer. '*What?*'

'Well, it's all a bit quick, isn't it? Come on, she talks to you, she always has done.'

And you have never liked that. Bruce stared at him. Why hadn't he clicked on to that before? Perce was jealous of how well he and Amy got on. Bruce put his glass on the table. 'If you don't know by now that Amy's not that sort, you'll never know,' he said coldly.

'Oh, you.' It was said with contempt. 'Never have been able to see the nose in front of your face, you haven't. She played us off against each other for years, can't you see that? And all right,' he raised a hand as Bruce went to speak, 'I know now you didn't think of her in that way but I didn't then. She's laughed up her sleeve at me, kept me dangling on a bit of string and used you to keep me fired up.'

Bruce couldn't believe what he was hearing. He was truly astounded. 'You're barmy,' he said at last.

'Aye, barmy I might be, but you tell me why she's getting wed in such haste then if her belly's not full? It's the oldest trick in the book to catch a lad. But he's no lad, this Callendar, is he? He's rolling in it and that's why she's given him what she wouldn't give me.' Perce's face had gone red and the veins either side of his nose had swelled but he wasn't shouting. In fact his voice was low. Bruce genuinely didn't know what to say to convince his brother he was wrong on all counts.

'Well, she's caught her toe, she's took the wrong fella for a ride. She's not wed yet, is she, and she'll find that walk to get up the aisle is longer than she thinks. I'm not going to be made a monkey of. She made me feel like the lowest thing on two legs and all the time she was whoring for Callendar. I expected you to see it. I thought you'd be as riled up as me.' Perce paused for breath and looked at his brother. Bruce's expression disconcerted him. It dawned on him that he'd said too much.

He swilled the second pint of beer down his throat, slapped the glass down on the table and rose to his feet. 'I'm off,' he said shortly.

'What did you mean, she'll find the walk up the aisle longer than she thinks?' Bruce had risen too, barring Perce's way. 'What are you planning?'

'Nowt.'

'It didn't sound like nowt to me.'

'Get out of my way, Bruce.'

'You hurt a hair of her head and you'll pay for it, brother or no brother. Do you hear me?'

'Oh aye, I hear you.' Perce's eyes bored into Bruce's. 'And I'm shivering in me boots. Now get out of my way, I shan't ask again.'

He *was* barmy. He'd obviously been brooding about all of this so long it had addled his brain. But he was all wind and water; he wouldn't do anything to hurt Amy, not Perce. Would he? The last year or two he'd turned into a dodgy kettle of fish, that was for sure, but this was something different.

Bruce stood aside and watched Perce walk out of the pub.

He felt so churned up inside he didn't know what to do with himself.

On leaving the pub he caught a glimpse of Perce turning the corner into Wreath Quay Road, and without really knowing why he began to walk that way too. When he saw his brother turn left into Hay Street, Bruce found himself running the last few yards to the head of the road. To the right was a grid of terraced streets but Perce was walking on the left-hand side which consisted of warehouses and a goods yard and sheds.

With no very clear idea of what he was going to do beyond trying to reason with Perce again now that he might have cooled down a little, Bruce walked on. Before Perce reached the goods yard he turned off into one of the warehouses and didn't come out.

Still with no plan of action, Bruce made his way to the spot where Perce had disappeared. Apart from a group of snotty-nosed bairns playing some game or other, the eldest of them in charge of a squalling baby in a dilapidated perambulator, there was no one about. As he reached the warehouse he heard voices within. There were two doors but only one was ajar and it was to this he was drawn, treading as lightly as his hobnailed boots would allow. He recognised Perce's voice straightaway and it was clear he was still agitated because he was letting off steam to someone.

'. . . try to pull the wool over my eyes. He's sweet on her, I'd bet me last farthing on it whatever he says now, but he hasn't the gumption to admit it.'

'Aye, well, let's hope you're right 'cos it'd be a shame if you paid out that tidy sum to have him worked over for nowt.'

'Well, this other one will get more than being worked over, trust me. And this time I'll tell 'em to make sure it's not in a back lane where they can get interrupted. His own mother won't recognise Charles Callendar by the time he's dumped in the river.'

'All right, Perce, all right, calm down, man. Look, we've business to do the day so let's get on with it. I want this latest lot cleared out of here by tomorrow morning, I've got a buyer in mind.'

'Aye, aye, but first I need a drink. I've got a bottle of that whisky you like upstairs in the flat. How about we wet our whistle before we get started, Stan?'

'Sure you haven't had enough already?'

'Aye, I'm sure.'

This last from Perce was a growl and it appeared Stan wasn't going to argue. Bruce looked about him for somewhere to hide but it seemed that Perce's flat could be reached from within the warehouse because in the next moments their voices became more distant and then faded away altogether.

The numb feeling that had overtaken Bruce when he had first heard his brother speaking lasted until he was safely back on the main road. Then he found he was shaking so much he had to lean against the wall of a house.

Perce seriously intended to do Charles Callendar harm; more than that, it had been his brother who had been behind the beating he had received that time in the back lane, and the police had said then that if the assailants hadn't been interrupted they could have done for him.

Bruce ran his hand over his face which was damp with perspiration in spite of the cold spring day and bitter north wind. He turned to face the wall, his hands above his shoulders and pressed against the bricks as he stared at the ground. It was unbelievable, but he had just heard it with his own ears. He stood there for some time, all the warmth and sentiment of childhood memories turning to ashes. His brother had done that to him, his own brother, the same brother who had fought off more than one bully at school for him and got his nose bloodied in the process.

He had to stop Perce. He straightened. He owed him no loyalty, not now, this was too serious. But how to go about it?

He turned abruptly, beginning to walk towards North Bridge Street and the Wearmouth Bridge, his mind racing as a possible solution presented itself. If he followed this through, it was better to do it in the main town away from Monkwearmouth.

The wind bit harder as he crossed the bridge and he stood for a few minutes looking down into the river where tugboats, colliers, salvage ships and other big craft jostled with the smaller vessels. Some six years before, when work on this bridge had begun around the old one in an effort to keep the traffic moving, he and his father and Perce had come to stand and watch. He had been eleven years old then and Perce nearly thirteen, and he remembered it as a good day. They had brought sandwiches and some of his mam's homemade lemonade and had eaten their lunch in the sunshine, marvelling at the construction taking place. One of the Italian ice-cream sellers had passed them pushing his cart, and Perce had treated them all to a cornet from the money he'd had in his pocket from his paper round.

The memory caused Bruce to screw up his face for a

second like a child with the stomachache before he told himself that that had been then and this was now. Things had changed. He and Perce had changed, and the roads they had taken since that time were diametrically opposed. He could see very little of the brother he had fought and cried and laughed with as a bairn in the hard, aggressive individual he had spoken to today. And Perce was planning to do serious harm to an innocent man and ruin Amy's life. That was what he had to remember here.

His mouth hardening, he turned from the river and made his way into Bishopwearmouth and the main post office. He had never used a telephone before, and he stood quietly watching how it was done for some time before he looked up the telephone number of the local police station in the much-thumbed directory.

This had to be done today, before Perce and his cronies moved whatever it was they had stolen and the necessary evidence was gone. He couldn't prevaricate or rethink this. Anyway, there was nothing to rethink. It was as simple as that.

The scandal of one of their number being involved in handling stolen goods and all sorts of rum goings-on was a nine-day wonder in Fulwell. The impact on the Shawe family was not what it would normally have been, however. Thomas was ill, very ill, and the doctor was increasingly worried.

Betsy and Ruth had caught the measles from a schoolfriend and passed it on to their two younger siblings, but whereas little Milly and the twins were poorly for a couple of weeks and then started to recover, their brother went steadily downhill. On the day the *Echo* reported that Percival Ronald Shawe and a Mr Stanley Irvin had both been sentenced to seven years' imprisonment, Thomas was rushed into an isolation ward at the infirmary. May, whose fear of hospitals and all things medical bordered on the phobic, announced she couldn't bear to visit him, and as Ronald didn't get home from work in the evening until nearly six o'clock and visiting time on the ward was between three and four o'clock in the afternoon, it was Amy and Bruce who sat at the little boy's side each day.

It was on the third day, when Thomas was sleeping, that they began to talk about Perce and it was then that Amy revealed how he had first badgered her and then later attacked her and what he had said. Now he was safely locked away, it had released something in her. With Charles's engagement ring on her finger and the knowledge Perce was unable to hurt anyone, she found she needed to share her secret with someone. No, not someone. With Bruce. She felt he was the only one who would truly understand.

Bruce did not speak immediately she finished; he was finding it impossible to utter a word, so great was his anger towards his brother. But if ever he had needed confirmation that he had done the right thing in seeing Perce was put away, he had it now. 'Why didn't you tell me this before?' he asked after a few tense moments.

Amy swallowed. 'If I could have told anyone it would have been you but I suppose I was frightened you'd go for him and then he would have it in for you, and he can be so nasty when he wants to be.'

More nasty than, thankfully, she need ever know now, Bruce thought. 'He could have tried it on again at any time, laid in wait for you somewhere,' he said quietly. 'Don't you see that?'

'But he didn't.'

'But he might have. Hell, Amy, you should have told me.'

He was upset and she couldn't really blame him. Amy reached out across the bed and the small occupant lying so still and rested the tips of her fingers on the bedsheet in front of Bruce. 'Friends for fairs?' she whispered softly.

He looked down at her small hand. The old northern saying – friends in earnest – had been a private way of making up after an argument between them as bairns but they hadn't used it in years.

He shook his head at her, reaching out and taking her hand as he said, 'I shouldn't let you talk me round like this, it was plain stupidity not to tell me. But,' he smiled wryly, 'friends for fairs. This time. But don't you dare be so foolish about anything so potentially dangerous again.'

'I won't,' she said, smiling faintly. 'I promise. And I forgive you for shouting at me,' she added, her voice light to let him know she was teasing.

'If we weren't in here I would have shouted all right.'

He let go of her hand, settling back in the chair as the child in the bed stirred and then moaned a little in his sleep. Bruce looked down at his baby brother, his heart going out to him. Thomas was going to need him when he came out of hospital because they'd already warned there was a good chance his vision and hearing would be affected by the disease. There was no way he could go down south now. Not for a long, long time at least.

Much as he wanted to be at his brother's side, Bruce was glad when the nurse came to tell them visiting time was over. It was proving incredibly painful to see the once lively little boy who had been into everything lying so still and white.

They walked home rather than catching a tram, both of them glad to be out in the weak May sunshine after the anti-septic confines of the hospital. Thomas hadn't woken before they'd left and although they were deeply worried about the child's condition, by unspoken mutual agreement they didn't voice their fears. Instead Amy filled the time talking about the house Charles had bought on the edge of Ryhope and their plans for it. When he had first taken her to see the large detached five-bedroomed property which was surrounded by its own grounds, with a separate staff annexe, she had been overawed by it. After two more visits she began to come to terms with the fact that she would be mistress of such a grand residence.

'I wish we didn't have to have a housekeeper and maid, though,' she said as they passed a line of cherry trees in full blossom, the pink petals raining down on their heads like confetti as a gust of wind rustled the branches. 'But Charles says once he's married and in his own house, it will be expected of him. Certain standards to maintain and all that.'

Bruce glanced at her. 'You'll be his wife and it will be your home too,' he said quietly. 'You'll have a say in things.'

She didn't reply to this.

They walked on in silence until they had passed over the Wearmouth Bridge. Then Bruce said, 'Are you sure you aren't tired? We can catch a tram the rest of the way if you want.'

'No, I'd rather walk. Bruce . . .' Amy stopped, looking up at him in a way that made her appear far younger than her sixteen years. 'There's no way Perce would be able to talk or bribe his way out of prison, is there?'

'No way,' he said firmly. Her manner had touched him deeply; normally Amy gave the impression of being a good deal older than her age. 'He's in there for the duration of the sentence, the judge made that very clear. Some of the stolen goods in that warehouse were from a robbery where a man was badly hurt and that was taken into account in the sentencing.'

She nodded, and as they resumed walking said, 'Who do you think tipped the police off about the stuff being in Perce's warehouse and flat? That was what the paper said, wasn't it? That the police had received a tip-off?'

'Aye, that's what it said. Likely some informer or other. The police do have them, you know, criminals who grass on their own.'

'I'm not sorry, Bruce. That sounds awful, doesn't it, because it's caused such a lot of upset and your mam is beside herself about it, but I'm glad he's locked away.'

'Aye, I am an' all.' In that moment the need to confess to someone that he had turned in his own flesh and blood was so strong he could taste it. It had been the right thing, the only thing to do, but he hadn't expected the burden of guilt would be so heavy. But Amy was the only and also the last person he could tell. She would be scared to death to think that Perce had been planning to hurt Charles simply because she was going to marry him.

They said no more as they walked on in the cool sunlit evening, but both their minds had returned to the small figure in the hospital bed and both were praying he would soon be home.

Thomas died at two o'clock in the afternoon three days later. When Bruce arrived at the ward he saw only a neat, newly made bed. He could make no sound to the nurse who came hurriedly to his side, saying, 'Oh, Mr Shawe, someone should have met you. I'm so sorry, we did everything we could and the doctor really thought he was turning a corner but in the end his heart just gave out. Is there any history of heart trouble in the family? A weakness of some kind?'

'My . . . my da. He . . .' He couldn't go on.

'I'm so very sorry, he was a dear little boy. Look, sit down a minute and I'll get you a cup of tea.'

She must have led him out of the ward and into a small waiting area although he wasn't aware of it. And he barely registered her returning and placing a cup of tea beside him. He had never imagined Thomas wouldn't come out of hospital. Poorly still maybe, perhaps disabled in some way, but he would come home. Only last night he had finished whittling a little wooden puppet for him in the shape of a donkey. Thomas's teacher had been reading a bairns' book to the class, *Winnie the Pooh*, before he'd been taken ill, and Thomas had been on and on about the donkey in it. He'd had the puppet in mind even before Thomas was ill but hadn't done anything about it. And now it was too late.

He bowed his head, his heart crying out, I'm sorry, Tom. I'm so sorry. I should have done it for you before. And all the times you wanted to come for a walk with me or play football and I put you off. I wouldn't have done it if I'd known. You know that, don't you? You know I loved you even if I didn't say so? Please, God, let him know. Let him know.

When he heard someone walk into the waiting area he assumed it was the nurse again, but the next moment he felt soft arms go round his neck and Amy was kneeling on the tiles in front of him, her face wet with tears.

'He's gone, Amy.' Bruce gripped her hands as though they were a lifeline. 'And I wasn't there, he was all alone.'

They sat huddled together, her face pressed against his and their tears mingling.

'He adored you, Bruce,' she said, 'and he loved you for coming in specially to see him each day. Even the nurses said so. And they said it was peaceful. He just went to sleep earlier after the doctors had been round and never woke up. He would have known you were coming later and that would have made him happy. You were so good to him, so patient and kind.'

When the tears stopped, it was still a while before Bruce straightened, and it was only then that Amy rose from the floor to sit beside him. 'How am I going to tell Mam and Da?' he muttered. 'They weren't expecting this, none of us were. How am I going to say it?'

'I'll be with you. We'll tell them together.'

He took out his handkerchief and scrubbed at his face with it. Fighting back emotion, he said, 'I didn't think you were going to come to the hospital today. Didn't you say you were going to spend the afternoon with Charles at the house? Isn't some furniture being delivered or something?' He was feeling acutely embarrassed now that Amy had seen him in such a state. Men didn't cry.

'I somehow felt I needed to be here and Charles is very understanding. He didn't mind.' And then her voice changed. 'The doctor's coming.'

They both stood up as the doctor and a solemn-faced nurse entered the room.

They had come to explain why little Thomas had died, and they did it gently and with compassion but it made no difference to the grief-stricken young people in front of them. Thomas had gone and they would never see him again. That was all they could really take in.

Chapter 11

'Darling, I understand about Thomas, really I do, but I don't see why we should put back the wedding.' Charles took Amy's hands in his, shaking them slightly as he said, 'Now the funeral is over, life has to be lived again, don't you see? And forgive me for saying this, my love, and don't think I'm being unfeeling, but it won't help anyone if we postpone getting married.'

They were sitting in the drawing room of what was to be their married home, a fire blazing in the hearth despite the warm May day outside. The weather had finally made up its mind to be kind in the last few days and even the constant north-east wind had changed to a pleasant breeze, perfumed with lilac and wallflowers and the heady scent of hyacinths – in this more select residential area of Ryhope at least. It would take a most resourceful flower indeed to think of blooming in one of the back-to-back terraced streets of the main town.

'We've had the furniture delivered for the rooms that

matter and Mrs Franklin and Lucy are due to move into their quarters at the weekend. Everything is arranged. They will have two weeks to put the house to rights so that once we are married things should run like clockwork. I can appreciate you might prefer to honeymoon later in the year, but to postpone the actual wedding is not sensible.'

'It doesn't seem right, Charles.'

'Darling, I know Ronald and May took you in as a child but when all's said and done Thomas was not your brother. He was your cousin. Everyone understands that and no one would expect us to put the wedding off because of what's happened. I'm more than prepared to forgo the festivities at night and restrict the wedding breakfast to a small party of immediate family, but anything other than that really is not viable. You can see that, can't you, my sweet? You can see that it is only compromise that is needed here?'

Amy lowered her gaze from his and directed her eyes towards the crackling fire. 'You're being very reasonable,' she agreed flatly. How could she explain to him what it had been like – what it was *still* like – at home since Thomas's passing? By his own admission Charles had never really participated in what she considered normal family life. From babies he and his brother had only been brought out of the nursery by their nanny to say goodnight to their parents in the evening before the adults dined. From the age of seven they had moved from one institution to another – an expensive preparatory school, followed by another public boarding school and then university. How could Charles understand the consuming black cloud that hung over the household these days, which even had little Milly refusing to eat and crying all the time? Her uncle had withdrawn into himself, her aunt and her granny were distraught and the whole family was in shock. It was awful, just awful.

'Look, come and see the bedroom suite which was delivered yesterday,' Charles said, drawing her to her feet as he spoke. 'It will take your mind off things. And the new writing desk for the morning room came too.'

Amy allowed herself to be led to the door and when Charles turned in the doorway, his arm round her waist, and said, 'This really is the most beautiful room, isn't it? Imagine an eight- or nine-foot Christmas tree in that far corner by the piano,' she tried to be enthusiastic in her reply.

And the room *was* beautiful, all the rooms in the house were. The ornate high-ceilinged drawing room, elegant morning room, dining room, breakfast room and Charles's book-lined study were tastefully decorated and quite lovely, and the enormous kitchen at the back of the house could have swallowed the ground floor of her Uncle Ronald's house whole. The house boasted not one but two bathrooms, one off the master bedroom and then a family bathroom, and all the bedrooms were large and spacious. When he'd first bought the house Charles had had each room redecorated from top to bottom, with new carpets and curtains throughout, but he had acquired no furniture.

'That was something I had in mind for us to do together,' he'd told her the first time he had shown her over their future home. 'If I could persuade you to say yes to marrying me, of course.' She had laughed with him, declaring he must have known he wouldn't have to use much persuasion and in answer he had lifted her right off her feet and swung her round and round until she was pleading for mercy.

She glanced at him now as they made their way into the oak-panelled hall and over to the winding staircase. He had quite literally swept her off her feet in every way, she reflected. And she loved him, she *did* love him, so why had she felt the tiniest element of relief when she had thought the wedding would have to be postponed?

And then she answered herself: because it had all happened so fast, that was all. There was absolutely no other reason. How could there be? And Charles was probably right. The church was booked and everything was arranged, it would be difficult to reschedule now. If he was happy with a much quieter affair than they had first planned, she couldn't very well argue with that, could she? She was so glad she'd held out against the combined pressure of Harriet and the twins and insisted she wanted no bridesmaids now in view of everything. Apart from the rush to get her own dress and veil, let alone dresses for bridesmaids, she had known if she had one of her cousins she would have to have all of them. And the thought of Eva marching down the aisle behind her as chief bridesmaid wasn't to be borne.

'There. Do you like it now it's in place?' Charles had opened the door to the master bedroom with a flourish and a big grin on his face.

Amy stared at the bedroom suite she had ordered in the happy days before Thomas's death. Charles had favoured a deep mahogany one which she'd thought was cumbersome and dark, and when she had seen this light oak one with a gold trim and ornately carved dressing table she had fallen in love with it. He had immediately deferred to her, declaring that if she liked it then he liked it too. She turned to him now, a catch in her voice as she said, 'It's lovely.' He had given her so much, he was so generous and kind and loving. She was the luckiest lass in the world.

Amy married Charles on the first Saturday in June just as news broke that Charlie Chaplin had secretly married Paulette Goddard two days earlier. 'He can't be as happy as I am,' Charles whispered to his new wife as they sat at the head of a long table, which was in fact several smaller tables placed together in Callendar's glittering restaurant which was closed to the public for the day.

There had been a satisfying number of oohs and aahs when Amy had walked down the aisle of the church on Ronald's arm, her long white dress accentuating her tiny waist and her frothy veil held in place by a wreath of tiny pink and white rosebuds, the same flowers reflected in the posy she was carrying. Her wedding finery had taken every penny of the nest egg in the post office but Charles had played ball and given the impression he had covered the cost when Amy had explained the situation to him, and Muriel had been over-joyed she had provided for her granddaughter.

The service passed in a dream but once they were in the wedding car and Charles kissed her, everything became real. He held her within the tight circle of his arms and told her he was the luckiest man in the world, smothering her face with kisses. Amy hadn't wanted the short journey to the restaurant to end.

She reached for Charles's hand now, replying to his whispered words with a quiet smile and then glancing down the table at the assembled guests. There were twenty-four at the reception. Before Thomas had become ill the number had been over one hundred and fifty, mostly made up of friends and business colleagues of Charles's. On the left side of the table sat Charles's mother and her sister, the latter having moved into the Callendar home when Charles's father had died. Next to the aunt sat Charles's maternal grandmother and two great-aunts. Then came Charles's brother and wife and their two quiet and very well-behaved children. On the right side Amy's uncle and aunt, Bruce and the five girls made up the family party, although Amy had insisted Mr and Mrs Price and Kitty be present, much to May's chagrin. She had been only slightly mollified when, for the sake of family harmony and in view of the grief May was suffering, Amy had included Mr and Mrs O'Leary.

Muriel was too ill to leave her bed but Amy had been closeted in the front room all morning, involving her grandmother in all the preparations. It had been her granny's fumbling gnarled fingers which had slowly fastened the little buttons at the back of her wedding gown and helped her secure her veil in place.

There was no doubt in Amy's mind that their wedding guests were an ill-matched assembly. May and the O'Learys were falling over backwards to ingratiate themselves with Charles's relations, but his family didn't seem in the least bit interested in anyone. Kitty and her parents were as quiet as mice, clearly somewhat overawed, and Ronald seemed to have washed his hands of his wife and was devoting himself to little Milly. Eva and Harriet and the twins spent most of the time whispering behind their hands, but at least Bruce was his normal self, she thought fondly, catching his eye and smiling at him.

Ronald got to his feet as Verity and another waitress began to serve coffee. Six months after Amy had begun to work upstairs, Verity had joined her there, but the two girls had never really got back on their old footing.

Ronald's speech was short, very short. 'I'd like to wish Charles and Amy health and happiness always,' he said formally, 'but most of all gain with contentment. To be content with each other and your lot in life is a true blessing.' He didn't look at his wife during this but Amy did, and May's face was like stone. 'Would you all raise your glasses to the bride and groom.'

In a break with tradition, it was the best man, Charles's brother Edward, who next stood. His speech was even shorter. After glancing at his mother, who was yawning behind her hand, he said quietly, 'I'm not one for speeches but would everyone rise and drink to Charles and Amy on this, their special day. To Charles and Amy.'

Amy took another tentative sip from her glass. She had never tasted champagne before and she wasn't sure if she liked it or not. She caught Kitty's eye and as Kitty winked at her and then pulled a face she got the impression her friend was feeling the same.

Then Charles was on his feet and although his voice was not loud it had a quality to it which commanded attention. Even Eva and Harriet stopped their whispering. 'This is the happiest day of my life and I'm glad you can all share it with my wife and I.' He smiled at Amy, who smiled back, her cheeks growing pink. 'It's not everyone who gets a second chance of happiness and I'm fully aware of how fortunate I am. In Amy I have a wife who is beautiful not only on the outside but on the inside as well, where it really counts.'

His words echoed those that Amy had flung at Eva years before and for a moment the scene in the kitchen was there in front of her. She glanced down the table at her cousin and Eva's eyes met hers, something in their dark depths telling Amy her cousin had neither forgotton nor forgiven what had been said that day.

Charles's face lost its smile and his voice became sombre as he continued, 'The good book tells us we should rejoice with those that rejoice but also weep with those that weep. There has been great sorrow within Amy's family recently and we have indeed wept at little Thomas's passing. We believe he is living life to the full in a better place but it is hard for the loved ones he has left behind. I would like to thank Amy's aunt and uncle and cousins for their bravery and unselfishness in being present with us all today.'

There was a murmur of acknowledgement round the table and May dabbed at her eyes, but Amy was wondering if she had imagined the slight emphasis Charles had placed on her relationship to the family. As though he was distancing her from them.

'Now I would ask you all to rejoice with those that rejoice. Would you please stand and raise your glasses to my precious wife, my beautiful Amy, the new Mrs Callendar.'

He turned to toast her with his glass but also his eyes and Amy smiled up at him, a glow spreading through her at the love in his face. They were going to be the happiest couple in the world, she just knew it.

It was half past seven when Amy and Charles left the restaurant amid a shower of confetti thrown by Kitty and Sally Price. Charles's mother and the rest of his relations had departed for London two hours before, and with their going the constrained atmosphere within the restaurant had lessened, especially after Charles had invited Robin Mallard and the rest of the staff to join them. The drink and chatter had flowed, and at one point Verity had sidled up to Amy when she was standing alone for a moment. Verity pressed a little package into her hand, saying, 'I know everyone clubbed together for the rose bowl for you and Mr Callendar, but I wanted to give you something myself. For old times' sake.'

The small silver teaspoon was ornate and beautifully fashioned. Surprised and touched, Amy hugged Verity.

'I'm sorry I haven't been the best of friends,' Verity said quietly, 'but I can see why Mr Callendar fell for you, Amy. We all can. Even those of us who are pea-green with envy.'

Amy went pink. 'Thank you,' she said, not knowing what else to say.

'Don't forget to call in and see us when you're in town, will you.'

Amy smiled but said nothing. Charles had already made it clear he didn't want her calling in at the restaurant too often. She had protested at first but he had explained he had always liked to keep his private life and business life totally separate before he had met her. 'I want to know you're waiting for me at home,' he had murmured, kissing her until she was breathless. 'That when I walk through the door I'm in a different world, our world.' She hadn't quite understood what that had to do with her not visiting Callendars, but it wasn't important enough to quarrel about.

The evening was sunlit and warm as they emerged onto the pavement, laughing and trying to shake the confetti from their hair and clothes. Some passers-by stopped and watched as Charles helped her into the back of the wedding car he had hired for the day, and when Amy threw her bouquet into the little crowd, a stranger caught it. 'Ee, sorry, lass, I didn't mean to do that,' the big buxom matron dressed in a long black coat and black hat called, before saying to the woman next to her – who happened to be Kitty – 'Here, lass, you have it. You're one of the party, aren't you?'

The car drove off amid much laughter and banter, but when everyone went back into the restaurant to collect their things, Bruce didn't follow them. He wanted a few minutes to himself. He had been terribly conscious all day of one little person who should have been with them and the effort of being bright and cheerful for Amy's sake had taken its toll. He walked across the road to a shop doorway and stood in the shadows. He took a small tin from his pocket and rolled himself a cigarette with the tobacco and papers it contained. Long gone were the days when he could afford to buy a packet ready made, he reflected soberly.

He stood undecided as to whether to go straight home or back into the restaurant but he really didn't want company. His mother appeared with Milly, his grandparents and other sisters behind them. Terence O'Leary must have ordered a taxi because one soon drew up and they all piled in.

A taxi no less. His grandfather was aiming high the day but then he would like to make a show in view of Amy marrying into the Callendar family. He'd bet that had stuck in his granda's craw when he had first heard the news. He wasn't surprised his father hadn't joined the crew in the taxi, though; his granda and father were barely on speaking terms these days. Neither were his mam and his da, if it came to it.

Mr and Mrs Price and Kitty were the next to emerge but as he watched them walk away down the street they all stopped at the corner, then Kitty began to walk back to the building they'd just left. 'You go on,' he heard her shout after her mother had called something. 'I'll catch you up. Put the kettle on if you get home before me, I'm dying for a cuppa.'

He watched the thin figure in the cornflower blue dress and straw hat disappear into the building and after a moment or two he stirred himself to walk across the road. He'd catch the tram home with his da, he decided. Likely his da was feeling a bit put out at his mam up and skedaddling with his grandparents. He had thought his brother's death might bring his mam and da closer together but he'd seen no signs of it to date. Why his mam constantly rubbed his da's nose in it he didn't know, but there was barely a day went by lately when she didn't remind him he was still only employed because of the strings Terence O'Leary pulled to make it so.

His mind preoccupied, he walked into the couple canoodling on the stairs leading up to the restaurant.

His shock at seeing his father and Kitty wrapped in each other's arms was so absolute that for a moment he couldn't move a muscle. They had sprung apart as he'd blundered into them and Kitty gasped, her hand going over her mouth. Then his father drew Kitty against him again, his arm round her waist.

'Hello, lad,' Ronald said steadily. 'I thought you'd gone home.'

'Bruce—' When Kitty reached out to him Bruce recoiled so sharply he nearly fell backwards.

'No, don't. I can't believe it. I can't believe the pair of you would do this.'

'You go on home, lass. Go on, it'll be all right. Me and the lad have got some talking to do.'

His father was talking to Kitty as though he wasn't there, Bruce thought numbly. He wasn't even trying to hide what they had been about. And Kitty, Kitty of all people. She was almost one of the family, she had been Amy's mam's best friend.

He must have said Amy's name because Kitty said quickly, 'She doesn't know, no one knows. And we didn't plan for this to happen, Bruce. I swear it. It took us by surprise, didn't it, Ron? Tell him.'

Ronald gently turned Kitty to face him. 'Lass, don't fret. You go on home and I'll explain everything that needs to be explained. I'll come round later so you'd better get ready to tell your mam and da, but we'll do it together when I arrive. It's time this was out in the open. I'd have done it weeks ago but for our Thomas.'

His father's voice was softer than Bruce had ever heard it when directed at his mother, and it was this more than anything else that brought home the fact the affair was serious. Final.

'Ron, you can't, not with her just losing the bairn.'

'No more ifs and buts, lass. We're doing this my way from now on. I love you and I'm not ashamed of it.'

Bruce could hardly take in that it was his father talking like this. He watched as the pair of them looked at each other, a long look, and then Kitty passed him without saying anything more, Amy's bouquet hanging limply in her hand. When she had disappeared out of the door, Ronald said, 'Right, lad. Are you prepared to listen to my side of it or have you already got me hung, drawn and quartered? I'd like to explain if you'll let me.'

'I'll listen.'

'Come on then, it's a nice evening, we'll walk home.'

In the street Ronald didn't begin talking immediately. They had walked as far as Bridge Street and the Wearmouth Bridge was in front of them before he said, 'This hasn't been going on years if that's what you're thinking. Just a few months, in fact. Since Christmas. I bumped into Kitty in the Old Market when I was looking for a few stocking fillers nice and cheap for Milly and the twins and—' He stopped abruptly.

'And Thomas.'

'Aye, and Thomas.' Ronald rubbed his hand across his mouth. 'Anyway, she was loaded up with bits and pieces and it was a bitter day and she looked perished. I suggested we have a cup of tea somewhere before we went our separate ways. We went to that little café at the end of Coronation Street.'

Bruce made a sound deep in his throat. He didn't care where they had drunk their tea.

Ronald must have understood because he spoke more quickly. 'Amy's mam and Kitty had been best pals since they could walk, I've known her all me life, but that day . . . Well, it was like I was seeing her for the first time. It . . . it happened just like that. I can't explain it.'

He must have expected Bruce to say something because he was silent for a few moments. When they reached the bridge, Ronald stopped and took his son's arm, forcing him to halt too. 'I don't expect you to condone it, lad, because if it was anyone else in my shoes I'd call them all the names under the sun. A married man with bairns, it's not right. I know that. My only defence is that before Kitty and I got together I'd thought about throwing meself off this bridge more than once. Oh aye,' he added as Bruce's eyes shot to his, 'I'm not joking, lad. Just that same afternoon I'd stared down at the water and thought how easy it'd be to just let it take me down. Let the bairns have their Christmas, I thought, and then . . .'

'Da!' Bruce jerked his arm away. 'Flaming hell, Da.'

'I'd had enough. Of your mam, your Granda O'Leary, all of it. Anyone looking at me and your mam would think we got on all right, wouldn't they, eight bairns an' all. But right from the day we was wed she's had me touch her on sufferance.' He swallowed deeply, then went on, 'She wanted bairns but not the making of them if you understand my meaning.'

'You shouldn't be talking to me like this, Da.'

'No, you're right there but I want you to understand. You above anyone else. Not to condone but understand. The priest saying a few words over you and a piece of paper don't make a marriage, lad. Remember that. I'm more married to Kitty right now than I've ever been to your mam, and I'm selfish enough to say to hell with the rest of the world from now on. I want to make Kitty happy. Your granda will take in your mam and the bairns, he's been wanting me out of the hockey for years, let's face it. And me and Kitty will take your gran with us, Kitty's all for that.'

'But . . . but Mam will never allow it. She won't divorce you, you know how she feels about it. The Church—'

'Aye, aye, the Church.' Ronald started walking again and now Bruce had to hurry to keep up with him. 'I don't care about the Church, lad, nor the folk who fill the pews of a Sunday all pious and holy and then murder folk with their tongues come Monday. There's some good 'uns among 'em, I know that, but likely they'll be the ones who remember the bit about casting the first stone. But we'll be far away from here anyway.'

'But won't Kitty want to be married?'

'Aye, she does, but she wants me more. Funny that, ain't it? And in my eyes we will be married. She'll be Mrs Shawe and she'll wear a wedding ring and no one will be any the wiser. But I'm going, lad. You finding us like that was a sign, like her getting that bouquet. If I don't do it soon it'll go wrong somehow. I feel it in my bones. And I couldn't stand losing her. That's it in a nutshell.'

Bruce felt numb. He knew he should plead on his mother's behalf, talk to his da, try to persuade him to see reason. But the years of watching how it had been for his father had frozen his tongue. They were in Monkwearmouth before he said, 'When?'

And his father replied, 'Now, tonight. I'd have done it weeks ago but Kitty didn't want to upset the apple cart with Amy getting wed. And then our Thomas went and she worried about that. I shan't take nowt with me but a few clothes an' such because it's not mine to take. It's your granda's. She's told me that often enough. Kitty will write to her mam and da when we're settled somewhere, and Amy too I shouldn't doubt. I shall say for you to have the address if ever you ask for it. I don't expect anything, lad, but it'll be there if you can see it in your heart to ask for it.'

They didn't speak again the rest of the way home. When they reached Fulwell, Ronald's steps became quicker, as though he couldn't wait to get it over with. They passed Eva and Harriet and the twins with some of their friends in the back lane, and when they entered the house by the scullery, it was quiet. Bruce went straight upstairs and as he reached his room he heard his father begin to talk to his mother in the sitting room.

He sat down on his bed, wringing his hands between his legs. His stomach churned. What a day! What a midden of a day, he thought. It was all very well his da saying his mam and his sisters would go to his granda's, but what if his mam had other ideas and wanted to stay put? His gran too? With his da's going he'd be man of the house and he couldn't just leave them all. His dream of moving away would never happen. He ran his hand through his hair. His da and Kitty. He still couldn't take it in.

He heard something smash as the voices downstairs rose and then he heard his father leaving the sitting room and going in to his granny. A minute or two later there were footsteps on the stairs and then his father pushed open the bedroom door. Ronald was as white as a sheet and he carried a bulging cloth bag in one hand. Drops of blood were oozing from a cut on his temple. 'I'm off, lad. Take care of yourself, all right?'

'What happened to your head?'

'It's nowt, I didn't dodge quick enough.' Neither of them smiled. Ronald mopped at his forehead with a handkerchief. 'I'm sorry, lad, but like I said, it's this or the river and I'm not ready to go now, not after I've found what I've been looking for all me life. Watch out for your gran for me the next few days, there's a good lad. I've told her I'll send for her as soon as we've got a place; it'll only be a day or two. I'll hire a van, something, a lorry maybe, so she can travel in her bed. It'll work out. I've told her it'll work out all right. Just keep her spirits up till I come for her. All right, lad?'

They stared at each other but for the life of him Bruce

couldn't move. He stood, tense and unthinking, the numbness on him again. He didn't want his father to go like this, he didn't want him to go at all. Beyond that he couldn't think.

'I'll be seeing you then.' Ronald turned as if to make for the stairs but then swung round again and walked into the room. He dropped the bag and took his son into his arms in a way he hadn't done since Bruce was a little boy. He hugged him hard and Bruce's arms went round his father, holding him so tight it didn't seem as if he would ever let him go. When finally they drew away from each other, both their faces were wet.

Then Ronald picked up the bag at his feet and walked out of the room without looking back. Moments later the front door banged and almost immediately Bruce heard his mother running up the stairs. She appeared in the doorway and said immediately, 'Did you know? About him and that little madam?'

'Course I didn't know. Not till tonight.'

'Kitty Price. Kitty Price of all people. I'll be a laughing stock when word gets out it's Kitty Price he's gone off with.'

Bruce stared at his mother. She wasn't bothered about his da going, not really, he thought with some amazement. It was more the fact he had gone off with another woman and Kitty in particular that was getting to her.

'How long has it been going on? Do you know?' May began to pace the room. 'It doesn't take two minutes for folk to get wind of something like this. When I think of how I've slaved to keep a decent home, he's never come back to muck and grime like some I could name. Hot meal on the table and his shirts ironed every day.'

'Mam, sit down, please. Look, come downstairs and I'll make you a cup of tea.' Bruce put his arm round his mother and as he did so, May's lip quivered.

'First Perce disgracing us and now your da, and all I've ever asked for is respectability. That's not too much, is it?'

'Come on, Mam.' Bruce led her out of the room.

As they reached the kitchen, May said, 'Your granda's been proved right as he always is. He said from the start I could do a sight better than Ronald Shawe and that we'd need to keep a tight rein on him or suffer the consequences.'

Bruce stared into his mother's tight face and for the first time in his life he fully understood just what his father had had to put up with over the years. He suddenly found he wouldn't have wished his da to stay another minute. And he was glad Amy was out of all this too because one thing was for sure, life wouldn't be worth living for the next little while.

On the other side of Sunderland, Amy was lying next to her new husband. Charles was fast asleep, one arm flung across her waist. She liked the closeness of his body next to hers, she thought drowsily. In fact she liked everything about being married up to then. Even 'that' hadn't been what she'd expected from the odd comment she had heard from the married women at the restaurant, most of whom seemed to bewail the frequency of their husbands' attentions. According to what she'd gathered listening to them, the first time was invariably painful and pleasureless, followed by a routine of lovemaking – how often seemed to depend on the individual man but was always too much for the woman concerned – which was only endured by lying back and thinking of other things.

True, Jinny had disagreed with the others, declaring she looked forward to her husband's lovemaking and had never thought of the price of bread once in the fifteen years they had been married, but she had been the exception. All the others seemed to plan the family's meals for the week, what shopping they needed to do, anything to forget what was happening to them.

Amy smiled to herself. She rather thought she was another exception too but then that was because Charles had been so patient and gentle with her. He had drawn forth responses and feelings she hadn't thought herself capable of, and after a time of touching and stroking and kissing her in the most intimate places, the actual act itself hadn't been unpleasant. One brief moment of pain and then a sensation of aching tightness which had led to something rather nice in the end.

She blushed in the darkness. Yes, she definitely was going to enjoy being a wife and she would make Charles so happy. She was determined on that.

She had been a bit surprised at the two bottles of champagne he had drunk before he had gone to sleep, though; she would have thought the amount he had consumed throughout the afternoon would have been enough for anyone. But then perhaps champagne wasn't like proper alcohol, like beer and whisky and stuff. It was as fizzy as bairns' lemonade, after all.

She closed her eyes, the unaccustomed comfort of the expensive feather bed and the satisfying warmth of Charles's body tipping her over the brink of drowsiness into sleep.

PART FIVE

1933 New Beginnings

Chapter 12

Amy stood staring out of the drawing-room French windows into the garden beyond, but she wasn't seeing the landscaped grounds stretching out in front of her. Bruce had just left after coming to say goodbye to her. He was moving away, and she knew she was going to miss him. Not that she didn't understand why he was leaving, she told herself. It had been six weeks now since her wedding and four weeks since Terence O'Leary had moved May and the rest of the family into the four-bedroomed house he and his wife occupied. When her grandma had got all upset at the thought of leaving Sunderland and had confessed she'd been homesick for her old neighbourhood and friends, Sally Price had immediately offered her a home with them, which Muriel had accepted with alacrity. This meant Bruce had no responsibilities to tie him to the north and it was his time to make a break, she knew that, but she would still miss him.

She turned from the window and looked across the beautifully furnished room. Marriage wasn't turning out to be quite what she had expected, not that she'd told Bruce that, of course. She had presented a front to him that said all was perfect. But it wasn't perfect. She frowned to herself. She didn't understand why Charles had to drink so much before he could sleep each night. He said it was like a sleeping pill but more pleasant and tried to make a joke of it, but once or twice he'd had a job to climb the stairs to their room. Not that he had been drunk, she told herself hastily. Drunk was like old Mr Reeves in Monkwearmouth who used to wake up the street with his dancing and singing when he came home from the pub, or the McHaffies who would brawl and fight until the police van took them away. No, of course Charles wasn't drunk, but . . .

She shook her head, unable to explain her unease. She sat down on one of the sofas and took up the book she had put down on Bruce's arrival. She wished her grandma had agreed to come and live with them when she had asked her to, immediately she had found out her uncle had gone off with Kitty. But her grandma had been adamant newlyweds needed time on their own. Amy raised her head, staring at the wall opposite. Her uncle and Kitty. It was unbelievable really. She had been flabbergasted when Bruce had come round to tell them. And she couldn't help feeling let down that Kitty hadn't confided in her. It was probably unreasonable but she couldn't help it. Her gran had said that after living with May for years she didn't blame her son for grasping a bit of happiness, and Amy agreed with this in part, but she had the notion that if the woman concerned had been anyone other than Kitty her gran wouldn't have felt quite the same. Thought the world of Kitty, her gran did, and so did she. Kitty was still Kitty whatever she had done.

Amy glanced at the clock. Another three hours before Charles would be home. She so wanted to see him tonight. Bruce coming to tell her he was going away had been upsetting in itself, but it had also stirred up the sense of loss she had felt when she had first realised Kitty wouldn't be there any more. She missed her, even more than she had thought she would.

The afternoon dragged and when six o'clock came and went and Charles still wasn't home, Amy began to worry. At half past seven she was just beginning to wonder if she should tell Mrs Franklin, the housekeeper, to put dinner on hold when she heard his voice in the hall.

When he opened the drawing-room door she bounded into his arms, saying, 'Where have you been? I was worried. Are you all right? Has anything happened?'

'I'm fine, sweetheart.' The slurred tone to his voice and the strong smell of whisky both hit her in the same moment.

She drew back, looking up into his face. 'You have been drinking.'

'Business meeting. Went on a while. Bit of a problem at the restaurant.' He detached himself from her and walked across to the cocktail cabinet where he poured himself a large measure of brandy.

Amy remained standing exactly where she was. 'Don't you think you've had enough already?'

He turned, his eyes narrowing. 'No.' He glanced at his watch. 'And tell Mrs Franklin to hurry up with dinner. I'm damn hungry.'

'It isn't eight yet.'

'I don't care what time it is. I told you, I'm hungry.'

By the time they had eaten the dinner served by a stiff-faced Mrs Franklin, Amy was forced to recognise the truth she had been trying to ignore for the last six weeks. Charles *was* drunk. Maybe not the dancing and falling over or fighting kind of drunk, but drunk nevertheless. This time he had difficulty even rising from his seat, the empty decanter in front of him witness to the fact that his meal had been more of the liquid variety than anything else.

On reaching their bedroom he fell on the bed fully clothed and was immediately asleep, snoring loudly. Amy cried herself to sleep.

The problem with the restaurant continued and with it Charles's increased drinking. No longer did he wait until he got home for his first drink, often he had had several by the time he arrived home. From eagerly awaiting his return as she had done in the first weeks of her marriage, Amy now began to dread it. She never knew from one day to the next if he would be drunk or sober, and whenever she tried to talk to him about it he would either laugh it off or turn cold and distant. In the mornings he would be her Charles again – mostly. Once or twice he awoke with such a thumping head he disappeared into his study before breakfast and Amy suspected it was to have a glass of something or other. She didn't know what to do or who to speak to, not with Kitty and Bruce gone. And although she visited her grandma several times a week, she couldn't confide in her. Her grandma was so happy at the Prices', so bright and cheery that she couldn't spoil things for her.

By the time summer was over and October had been ushered in with hard white frosts, Amy was getting to the end of her tether. Her emotions were in a state of perpetual vacillation. On the occasions when Charles didn't drink so much that he fell asleep immediately he got to bed, she told herself things were improving. They would make love in their big bed and although the smell of drink would be strong on his breath, he was the kind, charming and loving man she had married. They would talk about their plans for the future, about babies and fitting out a nursery and Amy would go to sleep feeling they might have turned a corner. Then the next night or the next he would return home the worse for wear and a different person, surly and uncommunicative.

Then, at the beginning of November, something happened which began to change Amy's feelings for the man she had married so happily only months before. The day had been a bitterly cold one with a savage wind and she hadn't put her nose out of the house, spending the day sorting through the big boxes in the loft which were mostly full of old bits and pieces of bric-a-brac and rubbish the previous owners had left. She and Charles had had a good evening the night before, and when she emerged from the loft for a bath she felt content and hopeful. She had enjoyed doing something constructive; she was discovering she wasn't made to sit about twiddling her thumbs all day receiving this person or that or visiting people Charles thought might be socially advantageous.

She sang to herself in the bath and she dressed in a frock Charles particularly liked, arranging her hair with more care than usual and taking time over her appearance.

At half past seven her stomach was churning. He was late, and usually that meant only one thing. Either he had been sitting drinking in his office or he had called in at the Gentlemen's Club on his way home. Either way it didn't bode well for the evening ahead. But she could be wrong.

Maybe this time he *had* been tied up with business. She stared into the leaping flames of the blazing fire in the drawing room and began to pray like she hadn't done for a long time.

Two or three minutes later she heard his voice in the hall but gone were the days when she would spring into his arms. Now she always waited to gauge his mood. As soon as he opened the door she saw he was three parts to the wind and disappointment and anger made her voice tight as she said, 'You're late again.'

'I have a business to run or hadn't you noticed?' He barely glanced at her as he walked across the room and poured himself a large brandy from the decanter on the side table near the cocktail cabinet.

Amy warned herself to say nothing for the moment. Mrs Franklin would be calling them through to the dining room any moment and she didn't want to quarrel in front of the housekeeper.

They didn't speak while Charles drank his brandy. His gait was unsteady as they entered the dining room a few minutes later and he thumped heavily into his chair. His face was morose as he glanced at the table. 'There's a stain on this tablecloth.' He poked at a tiny pinhead of a mark. 'If I can see it, why can't that useless chit of a maid?'

Her voice steady, Amy said, 'You told Mrs Franklin and Lucy that the laundry bill was too high the last time. I suppose Lucy thought you would prefer the cloth to be used again rather than having a clean one brought out.'

'She thought wrong.'

'I'll have a word with her tomorrow.'

'Make sure you do.'

Oh, she hated him when he was like this. After glaring at

him, Amy reached for her bread roll and broke it in half, buttering a morsel before popping it in her mouth. Mrs Franklin entered with the soup tureen, and Amy knew the housekeeper had assessed Charles's mood because there were none of the smiling pleasantries she sometimes indulged in as she served the soup. Instead she went about the duty silently and efficiently before noiselessly leaving the room.

Charles barely touched his soup but he poured himself a glass of wine, drinking it straight down and then pouring another. 'Want one?' He raised his eyes to her.

'No, thank you.' If she had left it like that it might have been all right but after the night before when he had been so nice, the disappointment was keen. 'I think you drink enough for both of us,' she added tartly.

She saw the muscles in his jaw clench but Mrs Franklin entered the room at that moment, wheeling in a trolley with several dishes on it, Lucy just behind her. Lucy cleared their soup bowls and placed their dinner plates in front of them before leaving the room, and Mrs Franklin lifted the lid off the meat dish and expertly placed two medallions of pork on Amy's plate with the serving tongs. She bent over to do the same for Charles, the tongs with the meat in her hands, when he reached forward abruptly for the wine, knocking the tongs so violently the small pieces of pork fell onto his lap.

'For crying out loud, woman!' He leaped to his feet, brushing at his trousers as though he was covered when in fact the food had barely left a mark. 'What's the matter with you?'

'I'm sorry, sir.' Mrs Franklin stepped back a pace, her face tightening.

'And so you should be. Well, see to it, see to it.' He gestured irritably at the pork lying on the floor. 'Damn it all, I don't know why I'm paying you what I do.' He strode to the window and stood with his back to the room.

Amy said nothing while Mrs Franklin cleared up the meat, served Charles two more portions followed by their vege-tables and then left the room. But the moment the door was closed, she spoke.

'That was totally uncalled for,' she said flatly. 'It was your fault, not Mrs Franklin's, and you shouldn't have spoken to her like that.'

He swung round, staring at her tense face. 'Don't be so ridiculous. The woman's as clumsy as hell.'

'She is not.' Amy found she couldn't leave it. 'She's an excellent housekeeper and you know it. You were totally unfair and you ought to apologise.'

He came to the table and refilled his glass. 'You really don't know what you're talking about. I have no intention of apolo-gising,' he said, his voice noticibly slurred.

'And I have no intention of sitting here and continuing to eat this meal as though everything is all right,' Amy said, rising to her feet and throwing down her napkin.

'Where do you think you're going?' he growled furiously.

'To bed, but first to the kitchen to see if Mrs Franklin is all right.'

'To apologise for me? Is that it? Over my dead body. Sit down and eat.'

'I'm not hungry.'

'Sit down, Amy.' His face was red with temper. He thrust out his arm and tried to press her down into her chair. She resisted and he slapped her across one cheek so hard her head snapped back. She felt as though her neck had cracked.

She didn't have to think about what to do next. Instinct kicked in. She pushed at him with all her might, catching him unawares and sending him sprawling backwards. He made a vain grab at the table but only succeeded in sending the tablecloth and all the dishes cascading to the floor. He hit the ground with crockery and glass smashing around him.

For a second she stood, her breast heaving, and then she turned on her heel and left the room.

She walked swiftly towards the stairs, passing a startled Mrs Franklin and Lucy who had burst from the kitchen saying, 'Madam? What's wrong?'

'Mr Callendar has fallen over.' She didn't stop. 'You will need a dustpan and brush.'

On reaching their room she shut the door and locked it, standing with her back against it as her legs threatened to give way. She stood like this for a full minute, unable to take in the enormity of what had happened so suddenly downstairs. She felt as sickened as when Perce had tried to rape her. Charles's unexpected violence hurt her heart more than her bruised and stinging cheek.

She half expected him to come ranting and raving after her but all was quiet downstairs. After a while she forced herself to move away from the door. She undressed quickly, put on her nightie and brushed her hair as she did every night. Her movements were jerky and mechanical, her eyes stretched wide as though she was staring into the dark.

She was sitting on the edge of the bed when reaction set in and the tears came, and then she sobbed as though she would never stop, wild thoughts milling about in her mind.

She would leave first thing in the morning before he was awake and go to the Prices'. She would tell them everything. Yes, she would do that. Or should she book into a hotel somewhere so he didn't know where to find her? Perhaps even go to Newcastle.

She cried herself to sleep but when she awoke again in the middle of the night the empty side of the bed brought fresh pain and anguish of a different nature. How could something that had been so good go so wrong? she asked herself, curling up into a little ball under the covers, missing Charles's warmth and the comfort of his body. She didn't understand it. He couldn't love her any more, not to behave like this. He was regretting marrying her, that was it. Well, she was regretting it too, she hated him. No, no she didn't, she loved him.

On and on her thoughts tumbled until, her head aching and her pillow damp, she slept again.

She awoke midmorning to a gentle tapping on the bedroom door. 'Amy?' Charles's voice was husky. 'Please, darling, let me in. Please, my love. I have to talk to you. Please.'

'I don't want to talk to you.' She sat up in bed, brushing the hair out of her eyes as she spoke and her stomach began to churn.

'I know and I don't blame you. I wouldn't blame you if you never speak to me again. But please, please, darling, open the door.'

She climbed out of bed, her heart in her mouth, and padded across to the door. She unlocked it and then stood back as he opened it from the other side. He had been crying, she noticed that at once, and he looked dreadful. She stared at him and as he went to reach out to her, she said, 'Don't touch me, Charles.'

'Oh, Amy, Amy, don't look at me like that. I'm not going to hurt you.' His eyes moved to the bruise already showing on one cheek and he groaned. 'I'd rather cut off my right hand than hurt you again. I don't know what came over me. I swear, I swear by all that's holy that I'll never do anything like this again. Forgive me or else I can't go on. I mean it. I can't live without you. I've said I'm sorry to Mrs Franklin.'

This last was said in the manner of a little boy and as Amy felt her heart begin to melt she tried to steel herself against it. The hurt, neglected child in him who had become more apparent the more she had learned of his childhood always had the power to move her.

'Please, Amy, forgive me. I'll do anything you want, anything. I'll get you the moon if you want it.'

She stared at him, her face white except for the blue-red mark where his hand had landed. 'I don't want the moon, Charles. I just want the man I married back again.'

'You have him, I swear it. I swear it, my love. Please, please. I worship you, I adore you. Please don't shut me out.'

She didn't want to shut him out. She needed him every bit as much as he needed her. 'Promise me you won't drink again.'

'I do. I won't.'

'Promise me, Charles. Say it.'

'I promise. I won't drink again. Anything. Just say you forgive me and you still love me.'

'You know I love you.'

As he took her into his arms, Amy shut her eyes, her heart racing. Maybe this had had to happen for him to finally see

225

he couldn't go on the way he had been going. Perhaps it was meant to be. If that was the case, it was worth it. She loved him, she would always love him. She didn't want them to be at odds with each other or living the way her Uncle Ronald and Aunt May had lived, at virtual war within four walls. She would do anything to make this work for them.

Charles managed to abstain for seven weeks but on Christmas Eve, after they had entertained three prominent dignitaries of the Gentlemen's Club and their portly, well-dressed wives, he declared he had a spot of indigestion. He disappeared into his study with the last of the wine from the table and then opened a bottle of brandy. He spent the night snoring in an armchair, explaining his actions the next morning by saying the business was now verging on going into the red.

Thus began a cycle of behaviour which was to sicken Amy. If Charles drank late at night in his study and remained downstairs, things were tolerable. True, she tossed and turned in their bed and cried herself to sleep as often as not, but the abusive behaviour which seemed to flare when he had consumed a certain amount of alcohol was contained.

All too often, however, he drank before he got home and insisted on more with his dinner, by which time he was liable to fly off the handle at the slightest thing. When Amy tried to persuade him to discuss his business worries with her, he flatly refused, often becoming hostile in the process.

Mrs Franklin left their employ in the middle of March and Lucy a week later. Amy couldn't blame them. By July they had lost a second housekeeper and maid, and this pattern was to repeat itself once more before the end of the year.

But still Amy fought for her marriage. She had promised

before God to love, honour and obey, she told herself, even when she had to wear high-necked dresses with long sleeves to hide any telltale bruises. In sickness and in health. And she couldn't help feeling this seemed like a sickness, a sickness in the mind. The man who lashed out at night was not the same individual of daylight hours. The real Charles, the Charles who needed her so badly and relied upon her love and support, had to be helped. She couldn't abandon him.

Kitty wrote to say she and Ronald had secured employment and were living in Manchester, but Amy didn't mention her problems when she wrote back. She continued to visit her grandmother regularly but put on such a good act when she was with the old lady that Muriel never suspected a thing.

Inwardly, though, the strain was taking its toll. For two years she had known Charles as a kind and generous employer whom she had come to see as her friend, then he had been an ardent suitor and finally a gentle and loving husband for the first couple of months of their marriage. In the worst of his drunken bouts Charles would accuse her of all manner of failings, declaring she wasn't a good enough, caring enough, capable enough wife. He invariably backtracked in the morning, and Amy knew in her heart that their present situation wasn't her fault, but in her low moments his words would come to haunt her.

Whatever business concerns ailed him, he ought to be able to share them with his wife, surely? Why did he turn to the bottle instead of her? What could she do differently? She asked herself these questions over and over again in the dark moments before dawn when she couldn't sleep, but she never took into account that she had only seen the man Charles wanted her to see in the time before their marriage. Neither did she fully understand that Charles's addiction had the power to turn the most altruistic of souls into a self-absorbed being with little consideration for anyone else.

Then, at the end of the year, two events occurred which gave Amy hope that all would eventually be well. She did not view the first in this light initially. Charles had communicated with his mother only by telephone since their marriage and the calls had been short, and rather tense at his end. So when he passed a letter over to her at the breakfast table one morning at the beginning of December, saying, 'How do you feel about a couple of guests at Christmas?' she looked at him in surprise before reading the short note. His mother had written that she and her sister would like to spend the Christmas holiday with them this year if this was convenient. That was all. No asking after their health or comments about the weather or any other polite social discourse. Amy raised her head and met her husband's eyes. 'Do you want them to come?'

After a moment or two, he said, 'Yes, I suppose so. We have never been close as you know but when I made the decision to pull out of the firm and move away, I felt a little guilty, I suppose.'

Amy remained silent, her eyes on his face, thinking, I don't know you, not really. Before this morning she would have sworn on oath he wanted nothing further to do with his mother, but she could read in his eyes this was not the case. Although he was trying to hide it he was thrilled she had written, like a little boy overwhelmed by the unexpected approval of a revered adult. She nodded. 'Then of course they must come.'

'You don't mind?'

For answer she said steadily, 'She's your mother.'

He blinked. 'Thank you,' he said softly. And then in one of the gestures which up to recently had always melted her heart however bad things had been the night before, he reached across and stroked a finger across her cheek to her mouth, saying, 'I don't deserve you, do I?'

Amy stared at him. Without animosity she said, 'Promise me something, Charles. Promise me you won't have a drink, both in the time leading up to Christmas and while they are here. Will you do that?'

She didn't know how he would take it but when his face worked she thought for a moment he was going to cry, and his voice was thick when he said, 'Oh my love, I'm sorry. I'm so, so sorry. I don't mean to . . .' He shook his head. 'I only ever mean to have one or two, that's all.'

'But you never do,' she said softly, her tone tinged with sadness rather than rebuke. 'So don't drink at all. You're fine when you don't drink at all.'

'I don't remember.'

'What?' His voice had been a whisper.

'These days when I drink I don't remember what I've done or said. It's . . . frightening.' He reached out to her, holding her hand very tightly. 'But I know I've hurt you sometimes. What am I going to do, Amy?'

It was the first time he had talked like this and the relief was overwhelming. Her eyes became misted. 'We'll fight it together.'

'But you don't know what it's like.' He groaned, resting his forehead on their joined hands. 'I promise myself over and over it won't happen again but I can't help it. Like a dog returning to its vomit.'

His voice trembled on the last words and as she gazed down on his bent head she remembered the incident of two nights ago, when he had become so enraged that she had spent the night in one of the guest bedrooms with the door locked. She had actually taken a poker from the fireplace and placed it near the bed in case he should break the door down, telling herself she would not be manhandled again. The memory of her very real fear that night prevented her from gathering him in her arms now as she was inclined to do. It wouldn't help either of them for her to fuss him and say it was all right, because it was not all right. She had to be strong for both of them. He had to see they couldn't continue to live as they had been doing.

'Charles, look at me.' She waited until he raised his head. Then, her voice soft, she said, 'However badly the business is doing, it's not worth this, can't you see that? I don't care about the house and car and all those things. I'd rather live in a mud hut with you and be happy than have you so . . . different. Will you go and see someone, a doctor?'

He straightened, withdrawing his hand, but his voice was quiet when he said, 'That would be of no use. I know what the problem is and the solution is simple.'

'Please, Charles. For me?'

'I can't, Amy. I'd feel . . . No, I can't. But I won't touch any alcohol again, I promise. Look, I'll clear out the sideboard, all right? Get rid of it all, the wine cellar too. I don't care what people will think when they call. We'll tell them we've gone teetotal. That we've read some book or other which advocates total abstinence for prime health, how about that?'

He was grinning now and she forced herself to smile back.

His last words had reminded her she hadn't been to confession for months. She had gone to the local Catholic church in Ryhope a few times but Charles hadn't wanted to attend and she had felt conspicuous on her own. Now she thought, I'll go every Sunday, God, and in the week too, if You only make this work. And then almost immediately she chided herself for the bargaining quality to her prayer. She would go anyway, she decided, and she would light a candle for Charles. It wasn't as if she didn't have enough time, after all. In the spring and summer she had busied herself in the garden, refusing Charles's offer to get a gardener and doing all the work herself. It had been a joy to work in the open air; in fact she felt it had kept her sane at times, and what with visiting her grandmother several times a week and entertaining, she had been kept busy until the autumn. The last few weeks time had begun to hang heavily on her hands but when she had suggested to Charles they do without a housekeeper and maid, thus saving money as well as giving her more to do, he had been horrified. A baby would be the perfect answer to the increasing vacuum in her life, but with Charles as he was she had been glad as well as sad when each month had proved she was not to be a mother.

Whether it was the inordinate amount of melted candle wax or Charles's resolve in the next weeks, Amy didn't know, but he was true to his word and removed every trace of alcohol from the house, even the housekeeper's cooking sherry. A week of heavy frosts at the beginning of December when the world remained shrouded in white from one day to the next, followed by thick snow and blizzards in the second week, proved a trial for many. Not so Amy. For the first time since the beginning of the year she dared hope everything was going to be all right. She and Charles made a family of snowmen in the garden at the weekend, the current housekeeper and maid looking on from the warmth of the kitchen window and shaking their heads at the madness of their employers. They ate muffins by the roaring fire in the drawing room when they came in with blue frozen hands and red noses, and later, in the snug warmth of their big bed, made love till dawn. Charles told her she was the most precious, beautiful, wonderful woman in the world, and day by day the misery of the last twelve months began to fade.

Even when Christmas Eve dawned and the cab arrived with their guests, Amy took it all in her stride. While Charles paid the cabbie, Amy led Charles's mother and aunt into the house which was bright with Christmas decorations, welcoming them in so warm a manner they couldn't doubt her sincerity. It set the tone for the holiday period and Amy supposed the visit could be called a success, but by Boxing Day she was longing for their guests to leave. Charles's mother had a curious effect on her husband, she found. She felt almost embarrassed to see the way he constantly put himself out to gain his mother's approval, doing things to get her attention in the way a young child would rather than a full-grown man. Mirabelle Callendar was such a self-contained, cold woman, and it didn't go unnoticed by Amy that she never volunteered any affection towards Charles or anyone else for that matter, and on the one or two occasions when Charles tried to kiss his mother, she would turn her face away so his lips barely skimmed her cheek.

Charles's mother and aunt left the day after Boxing Day, having promised to spend the New Year with Charles's brother and his family, and later that morning Charles left for his office. He didn't return home for lunch but it was snowing heavily again and Amy assumed he was finishing what needed to be done so he didn't have to turn out again once he was home. When it began to grow dark she telephoned the restaurant to find out when she could expect him back.

By the time she replaced the receiver she was trembling. She knew she hadn't imagined the note of pity in Robin Mallard's quiet voice when he informed her Mr Callendar had left at noon for the Gentlemen's Club and had not returned.

She began to pace the floor. What should she do? What *could* she do? She had seen the look in his eyes as they had waved his mother off. It must have been the same look he'd had when, as a little boy, his parents had driven away from the boarding school they'd just dumped him at with barely a farewell. *Wretched woman.* She wished now they hadn't come at all.

She glanced at the ornate marble clock on the carved mantelpiece. It was nearly five o'clock. She sat down, only to spring up again. Should she call a cab and go to the Gentlemen's Club to talk to him? She dismissed this idea in the next instant. There would be a terrible scene if she did that. She could only wait.

At eight o'clock she ate dinner alone, sitting at the vast dining table. She had to force each mouthful down but she told herself she must eat. She couldn't go to pieces. At half past nine she retired to their bedroom but did not immediately begin to undress. Instead she stood for some time staring at the big bed. Just this morning she had woken to Charles kissing her lips and murmuring sweet nothings as he stroked the hair from her face. Had it all been an act to keep her happy and playing her part so his mother went away with a good impression?

It would seem so. Oh! She dropped down onto the stool at the dressing table. Let her be wrong. Let there be some other reason for this. Don't let him have spent the afternoon drinking.

Charles didn't return home until the following morning. He arrived just as Amy was having breakfast, and when she heard him talking to the housekeeper she continued with her bacon and eggs. After a minute or two he appeared in the doorway to the breakfast room and although she knew he was there, she didn't raise her head until he said, 'Good morning.'

She stared at him but said nothing, and it was clear her attitude was proving disconcerting because he gave a huh of a laugh. 'I suppose you want to know where I've been.'

He was acting like an overgrown schoolboy caught out in some misdemeanour or other. Whatever his hurt from his childhood, he had to grow up and start acting like a man, she thought with a healthy dose of anger. She had tried to make him talk to her several times over the Christmas period when they had been alone in their room at night, but he was determined not to open up to her. Now he was punishing her for how his mother had treated him; that's what it felt like, right or wrong. She loved him. She had told him she loved him until she was blue in the face and she had showered him with affection the last few days. He couldn't keep throwing it all back in her face.

When she still didn't answer him the sheepish stance disappeared, and it was with a touch of aggressiveness that he said,

'All right, so I had a few last night, satisfied? It isn't a crime, is it?'

'I can see that.' Her eyes moved over his bloated face and rumpled clothes.

'Oh, for goodness' sake, woman! What's the matter with you?'

Woman. It rankled as much as girl had done all through her childhood but she had made herself a promise that she wasn't going to have a shouting match, not in view of what she had to tell him. She had planned to do it over a candlelit dinner the night before but it would have to be here and now.

She placed her napkin by her plate and stood up, her voice even when she said, 'What is the matter with me? I'm going to have a baby, Charles. That's what the matter is.'

And then she walked straight past him without looking at his amazed face and slack jaw, and quietly shut the door behind her.

Chapter 13

Following the news that he was to become a father, Charles once more became a reformed character. Contrary to what she'd expected, Amy did not feel unwell in the early days of her pregnancy, her only ailment being a consuming tiredness but that disappeared in the fourth month. By the sixth, the mound in her stomach was obvious, she'd put on a little weight all over and was, in her husband's words, blooming.

The only shadow over her happiness at being pregnant – besides the faint worry caused by the newspapers in recent months, which were fond of reporting dire warnings that Europe was beginning to beat drums of war in answer to the increased threat from Germany – was the number of business trips Charles made which involved overnight stays away from home. These had begun shortly after she had told him she was expecting a child and happened more frequently as time went on, sometimes as often as twice a week.

Amy tried to tell herself these trips were necessary and that her suspicions as to their legitimacy were unfounded.

Nevertheless, she found herself checking his clothes and smelling his breath for any signs he had been drinking each time he came home. But she couldn't fault him. He also insisted that his problems with the business were over and that the restaurant, café and tea room were doing well, but Amy didn't altogether believe this either. However, with things so harmonious between them and nothing to go on but a gut feeling, she let matters rest, instead dwelling on thoughts of the baby.

She found she delighted in being pregnant. Her changing shape, the first time she felt the flutter that spoke of new life deep inside her, the now strong kicks and movements from the child in her belly that sometimes woke her in the night were all fascinating. This little person would be hers, flesh of her flesh. It would belong to her and she to it, and already her maternal feelings were strong. As her pregnancy progressed, the need to be with her granny increased and now she visited the old lady every afternoon. The two of them would talk of her mother and Muriel would tell her granddaughter how much Bess had loved her. Each time Amy returned home, she'd gaze at the precious photograph of her mother which had pride of place above the mantelpiece in the drawing room. Her poor mam. When she had been expecting, her mam had been the object of shame and scorn and her grandfather had treated her abominably. But although this experience had been very different for them in one way, in another it was just the same. She knew she already loved her baby as much as her mam had loved her.

It was during one of the visits to her granny in the middle of June, when Amy was thirty weeks' pregnant, that Muriel was taken ill. One moment the old lady was laughing at something Sally had said as the three women sat with a cup of tea and a slice of Sally's seed cake, the next she was clutching her chest and gasping for breath. Sally sent Abe galloping for Dr Boyce and Amy held her granny in her arms as Muriel slipped into unconsciousness, her last words, spoken in a faint whisper through blue lips, being, 'I love you, me bairn.'

By the time the doctor arrived ten minutes later there was nothing he could do. Muriel's valiant heart, which had been labouring for years, was still. Amy sat clutching her granny, shocked and numb. She could not believe the indomitable old lady wouldn't suddenly sit up and finish her cake, apologising for giving them all such a scare. Death had removed every sign of pain from the wrinkled old face and Muriel looked as if she was sleeping peacefully.

Abe fetched Charles from the restaurant, and it was not until Amy caught sight of her husband and he took her into his arms that she began to cry. Then she found she could not stop. Dr Boyce gave her a sedative before Charles drove her home and put her to bed, but when he wanted to call their own doctor the next morning she refused.

'All the pills in the world won't bring her back.' Amy touched her husband's arm. 'And I have to face that.'

'But not all at once, dear.'

'Yes, all at once. It's the only way I can cope. I can't shut it out. It's happened. And there is our baby to think of. He or she is the most important thing in all of this. There is a train of thought that suggests medication has an effect on a child in the womb.'

'Oh, sweetheart.' Charles shook his head. 'I'm sure it would be all right for you to have something to help you sleep.'

'I'd rather not.'

'Very well.' His voice was soft. 'I won't try and persuade you if you've made your mind up because I know it will be no use. And don't look at me like that, it wasn't a criticism. One of the things that first caught my attention about you was your independent spirit and strength. Most of the women I had known before I met you were used to being pampered and cosseted, they lived in ivory towers where the more unpleasant things of life couldn't touch them. They would wilt under adversity.'

'I think you were associating with the wrong sort of people then,' she said very seriously.

'And I think you are right.' His arms went about her and he held her gently. They remained quiet for a moment or two, looking at each other. Then he said, 'I wish I had a tenth of your strength, Amy. Do you know that? But you have married a weak man. How weak I wasn't aware of until quite recently. That, perhaps, is my only excuse.'

Although he hadn't said so directly she knew in her bones he was talking about his desire for the bottle, and in that moment she knew she hadn't been wrong about his overnight business trips. She wanted to ask him where he went and how much he drank, but in spite of all his talk about her strength, she just didn't have the energy for it, not with her grandma having gone. Nor could she face bringing up the subject of the business right now. These problems would have to be dealt with, but in a little while. After the funeral. Somehow the time between then and now was her granny's. She leaned against him, saying, 'You can be strong if you wish it, Charles. I know you can.'

He smiled at her but didn't reply. A second or two later he patted her hand and walked to the door of their bedroom.

There he turned and stared at her as she lay against the pillows. 'Stay in bed today at least.'

'I'll see how I feel.' She knew she wasn't going to stay in bed. There was the funeral to arrange, for a start; her granny wasn't going to have a pauper's send-off. She would be buried with respect and then folk could come here for the reception. She had to contact her uncle and Kitty, and let May and her cousins know what had happened. And then there was Bruce. Perce was a different kettle of fish; she would let Aunt May inform her eldest son of his grandmother's passing. There were a hundred things to do and she would feel better if she kept busy.

The six days between Muriel's death and the funeral felt like six months to Amy, but eventually the burial took place on a warm summer's day, the birds singing and the sun resplendent in a blue sky full of fluffy white clouds. Amy remained stiff and controlled throughout the short service and the burial in the churchyard, but her heart felt as though it was being torn out by its very roots. It didn't help matters that Charles had vanished on one of his 'business trips' two nights before, returning the next morning very much the worse for wear. He'd excused his bleary eyes and sickly appearance by saying he had a bad headache and hadn't slept well. Amy, upset and near the end of her tether, hadn't challenged him, afraid she would say more than was prudent.

Charles knew how much she needed him at the moment, she told herself bitterly. How could he leave her just before the funeral? And what would happen when the baby was born if he couldn't even support her now? Would he continue to disappear every so often when the fancy took him? Or, worse, would he take to drinking at home again with all the horror and difficulties that brought with it? She supposed she had been naive and foolish to believe their having a child together could change him, but she had thought so, deep inside. Or perhaps she had just hoped so.

Amy glanced at her husband as he sat, silent and appropriately solemn-faced in the smart funeral carriage beside her. Ronald and Kitty were sitting opposite them. Kitty had declined to accompany Ronald at first but when she'd learned that May had refused to attend, even going so far as to ban the children's presence too, she had travelled up with him and come to the funeral.

The Prices were in the next carriage, quite overcome with the grandeur of the cortège, and Bruce was with them. Many of Muriel's old neighbours and friends were following too.

Charles caught Ronald's eye. 'I'm glad Bruce was able to come,' he said quietly. 'I understand he's working in Sheffield as an apprentice mechanic and you correspond regularly.'

'Aye, that's right.' Ronald ran his finger round the inside of his starched shirt collar which was chafing his neck. He knew his mother had understood his leaving the town but he wished with all his heart he had been able to see her one last time. 'He seems to have landed on his feet.'

Charles nodded. 'He tells me the two of you get on well.'

'Oh aye. Bruce is a good lad, always has been.'

As the two talked on, Amy listened to them with only half her mind. The circumstances had made seeing Bruce and Kitty again bitter-sweet. Her precious, *precious* granny was gone and it was hard to believe she would have to start living the rest of her life without her. She sat quite still in the carriage, her gaze fixed on her hands lying in her lap. What am I going to do without her? she thought. How will I bear it? And then the child in her belly kicked hard and instinctively she covered the place with her hand. She would have her baby and she would get used to the loss of the little woman who had been so much more than a grandmother. Her granny would expect that.

Sally said much the same thing later in the afternoon. Her grandmother's friend was standing with her husband and Ronald and Kitty, and as Amy passed, she caught her arm, drawing her into their circle. 'Your gran would be right pleased with how you're coping, lass. I can tell you that. She was never one to wear her heart on her sleeve, was Muriel, but she thought the world of you. Oh aye, she did that. And with the little one coming she would have wanted you to knuckle down and get on with things.'

Amy nodded. 'Yes, I know, Mrs Price.'

'And she'd have been tickled to death with such a send-off,' Sally added with unconscious dark humour. 'Put great store by a good wake, did your granny, but then you know that, lass. Aye, you've done her proud, right enough.'

Amy nodded but it was an effort. She wished this awful day would end and everyone would go home, but as yet there was no sign of this happening. Everyone was enjoying themselves too much for one thing. Charles had arranged for his kitchen staff at the restaurant to provide a wonderful spread which had been brought to the house, and with a good supply of beer, wine and spirits to augment the copious cups of tea some of the old ladies were drinking, it had turned into quite a party. But Kitty's mother was right, her gran *would* have loved to think her departure from this mortal plain was accomplished with such gusto.

Amy smiled at Kitty and Kitty smiled back, mouthing silently, 'You're doing fine.' It warmed Amy, especially because there had been an awkwardness between the two of them when they had first greeted each other at the church. She wished Kitty well, she really did, but everything was different and she hadn't expected it to be. She had imagined herself perhaps confiding in Kitty and asking her advice about Charles's drinking but now she saw that wasn't possible. Kitty was with her uncle and likely to tell him everything and she didn't want that.

Amy left the group and continued her duties as hostess. She noticed Charles and Bruce deep in conversation, a glass of whisky in their hands. Dear Bruce. Her eyes misted as she looked at her cousin. He was just the same as ever despite the air of affluence the smart suit he was wearing gave him. She had hugged him at the church as though she would never let him go but he didn't seem to mind. She wondered now what he thought of Charles.

Charles had had several whiskies. They were apparent in his flushed countenance and overloud voice. She wished she could take the glass from his hand and order him to drink no more. She knew the signs. Soon he would become irritable and quarrelsome, it happened every time. And he had promised her on his oath that he wouldn't touch any alcohol when he had insisted they couldn't have a 'dry' wake as she'd requested.

She walked over to the two men but it was Bruce she spoke to. 'I'm so glad you could come. Were they all right about you having the time off work?'

'Aye, no problem. Not after I'd explained why.' His voice low, he added, 'My mam wouldn't come then?'

'No, and she wouldn't let any of the girls come either.'

'That's a pity.' He turned his eyes to where his father and Kitty were standing. 'I can understand it though.'

Amy's gaze followed his and she nodded. 'I'm glad you're doing what you're happy at,' she said quietly, 'but it's as well you got out when you did, for more than one reason. You wouldn't have wanted to have to choose between your mam and your da and you're far enough away now to be neutral.'

Bruce's voice was wry when he said, 'Aye, that hadn't escaped me either. Mind, Mam's not unhappy where she is, far from it. I think she actually prefers it with her mam and da although she would never admit to it; she likes to play the wronged woman for all it's worth. But Da drove her mad most of the time as you know. Not that that would persuade her to give him a divorce. He's written to ask her several times, you know.'

Amy shook her head, her face betraying her shock. 'I didn't know.' She hadn't met one Catholic who had ever contemplated a divorce though perhaps she should have expected her uncle and Kitty would want to get married.

'I think he could wait till hell freezes over and Mam will still dig her heels in but that's up to them.'

'Yes, I suppose so.' Amy smiled at him before turning to Charles. She gave him a straight look and then dropped her eyes meaningfully to the glass in his hand. He ignored her but she had expected him to.

It was as the first guests began to leave that Amy found herself alone with Kitty for a few moments. Ronald was deep in conversation with Bruce across the other side of the room and Amy found she felt more comfortable with her old friend without her uncle being present.

Kitty must have realised how she felt because she said straightaway, 'I know it was a bolt from the blue, me and Ronald, but I'd always carried a torch for him. I'd never have let on, not in a million years if he'd been happy with May, but . . .' She shrugged.

Amy didn't know what to say. Eventually she managed, 'He's happy now. You only have to look at him to see that.'

Kitty grinned. 'Oh aye, he's happy all right.' Then, her face straightening, she said, 'And you, lass? Are you happy? Oh, I know this with your granny has knocked you sideways, but I mean with him. With Charles. Is everything all right?'

Amy stared at her, taken aback. She didn't know if Kitty had picked up on something or whether she was enquiring because they hadn't seen each other since the wedding, but suddenly it was natural to say, 'Not completely. He's got business worries and he's drinking too much. Much too much, Kitty.' There was a break in Amy's voice as she said this and Kitty hesitated for a moment before taking Amy in her arms and hugging her.

'I'm sorry, lass. I'm so sorry.'

'You won't mention what I've told you to anyone, not even my uncle? Please, Kitty. I'd hate for him to think the worse of Charles and I'm sure when the business picks up he'll be his old self again.'

There must have been a lack of conviction in her voice because Kitty now said, her voice low, 'Look, lass, if ever you want to get away for a bit there's always our place. It's rough and ready, I don't deny it, and nothing like this, but you would be more than welcome any time. And of course I won't say anything to Ronald if you don't want me to.' Kitty rubbed her little snub nose as she was apt to do when agitated or concerned. 'Promise me you'd come if you needed to?'

Amy nodded. 'Thanks, Kitty.'

'I've missed you, lass.' Kitty's voice was soft. 'We'd have been hung, drawn and quartered if we'd stayed round these parts but I'd have liked to stay near you. Especially now, with the babbie an' all.' They hugged again, both near tears.

It wasn't long after Amy's chat with Kitty that the house began to empty, and not before time. Amy was feeling exhausted. By twilight all the clearing up was finished, the housekeeper and the maid had retired to their quarters for the night and Amy had taken a glass of warm milk up to bed with her. Charles had disappeared into his study with a bottle and Amy hadn't had the energy to challenge him. If the past was anything to go by, he would remain there until morning and the way she was feeling it was the best thing. She felt terribly let down and sad that he had put his desire for a drink before her at such a time.

She drank the milk as she lay fully clothed on the bed, too tired to begin undressing immediately. Eventually she roused herself. She took the pins out of her long hair and let the thick waves and curls hang down her back as she began to undress. The black alpaca dress had a row of tiny ebony buttons all down the front, with stiff little buttonholes, and Amy was halfway through unfastening these when the door to the bedroom suddenly burst open.

'*Charles.*' She jumped, her hand going to her throat as she spun round. 'Whatever is the matter?'

'Thinking of leaving me, are you?'

'What?' She stared at him as he kicked the door shut. 'I don't know what you're talking about.'

'I heard you.' He came towards her with an unsteady gait,

his eyes bloodshot and his tie hanging loose. 'Talking to that little baggage about me. Didn't know I was the other side of the alcove, did you? I heard all of it.'

Amy stood her ground. 'If you heard what I said then you know I didn't mention leaving you,' she said steadily. 'I confided in Kitty because she is the one person I can trust and because I'm at my wits' end. Don't you know how your drinking is affecting me, affecting *us*?'

'Don't give me that.' He made a movement with his hand as though to swipe something away but still she didn't flinch. He was frightening her but she wouldn't give him the satisfaction of showing it. 'I know what you're up to. I saw the way you looked at your dear cousin, and now you're conveniently arranging a visit to your uncle's place. He's in on this, isn't he? What was your cousin going to do, wait till you got there and then "drop" by?'

He was right in front of her now and the full force of his whisky-soaked breath nauseated her. Suddenly she felt angrier than she ever had. She had endured the sort of day she wouldn't have wished on her worst enemy and the least he could have done was to be there at her side supporting her. Instead he had slowly drunk himself into this state and he was now accusing her of having an affair with Bruce, if she had heard him correctly. She glared at him, her eyes flashing as she said, 'I am going to have your child in nine weeks' time, Charles. Have you completely lost your senses? Bruce is like a brother to me and I'm like a sister to him. To suggest anything else is ridiculous.'

For a moment he looked taken aback at her vehemence. Then he recovered himself, growling, 'I heard you, damn it. She invited you to stay with them.'

'And what is wrong with that? Kitty's my friend and Ronald is my uncle. And while we're on the subject, I might just take her up on the offer if only to give you a chance to pull yourself together. In a few weeks there is going to be a baby in this house and I'm not having our child brought up amid such contention. If you won't take hold of your drinking for me or for yourself, then do it for our child.'

'Don't tell me what I can and can't do.' His face had taken on the ugly look she recognised of old.

'Someone has to.' She needed to rest her hand against the wall, she was feeling faint, but she didn't want to show any sign of weakness. 'And don't think you can manhandle me again because I won't stand for it, not now. Those days are gone for good, do you hear me?'

He shook his head slightly as though he was having difficulty following what she was saying, and Amy seized the moment to slip past him, running across the room and wrenching the door open. She had seen what was in his eyes and if he shook her violently or slapped her as he had done in the past it might harm the baby. If she could reach the housekeeper's quarters she would be safe. The fact that the housekeeper and maid would be party to their domestic problems didn't matter. Nothing mattered at this moment except protecting the child in her belly.

She was halfway down the stairs when he caught hold of her, swinging her round to face him with such force that she lost her footing and fell against him. He staggered back and let go of her arm. As he sprawled on the stairs, Amy found herself trying to clutch him to steady herself but then she fell backwards in what was almost a crouching position, her back hitting the stairs first.

She didn't feel anything until she was lying at the bottom of the staircase in a crumpled heap, but even as she lost consciousness, she knew what had happened. The explosion of red-hot pain which began in her womb and then spiralled up through her body told her the baby was coming.

Chapter 14

By the time Amy reached the hospital she was fully conscious and in the grip of such pain she felt she was dying. But she was willing to give up her life, she prayed, as long as God protected her baby. She had bargained with the Almighty all the way in the ambulance, promising Him she wouldn't scream or cry out or make a fuss as long as He allowed her child to live. That was the only thing that mattered now.

When the ambulance men had suggested Charles accompany her to the infirmary, she had become hysterical, so it was the housekeeper, her face ashen, who had ridden with her, but once at the hospital Amy had been whisked away to a side ward. The pain was forcing her knees up and her chin down into her chest constantly but she was determined not to make a sound. She was still praying everything would stop, that somehow Mother Nature would realise it was far too soon for the baby to be born and allow it a few more weeks. Even one or two. Anything.

In her feverish state it seemed to Amy that she had a crowd

of doctors and nurses around her. From the way they were scurrying about, she knew they were concerned. She wanted to tell them to concentrate on the baby and not her, but no sooner had the nightmarish contractions ended than they began again without even a pause, and speech was impossible.

She could hear someone moaning in the background and the sound was so horrible she wondered why the doctors didn't do something to help whoever it was. She didn't realise the sound was coming from herself.

She lost all sense of time as the pain caused her to retch over and over; a huge vice squeezed her belly until she had no breath left. At some point one of the medical staff took hold of her hand and Amy clung on to the solid link with reality with all her might, refusing to let go even when she began to push.

She was vaguely aware of a doctor working on her with forceps as she pushed down. He was squeezing and manipulating and just when she thought she didn't have any more strength to try, the nurse holding her hand said, 'That's it, Mrs Callendar, the head's out. Just one more push.' As she strained down she felt the baby slip from her and then something warm follow. 'My baby . . .' She was shaking uncontrollably as she raised herself the moment after the cord had been cut, and she just had time to catch a glimpse of a sweet little face before the nurse said, 'Lie back, dear, you're bleeding quite heavily. Just keep still now.'

Her baby. It was beautiful, beautiful. But shouldn't it cry? Didn't all babies cry when they were born? She tried to ask but the retching took hold again and for a few minutes the room swam and she felt as though she was going to pass out.

The nurse holding the bowl and stroking Amy's forehead glanced across at the doctor who had cleared the baby's tiny airway. He was now giving artificial respiration to the perfectly formed little boy lying so limply under his hands, but in spite of all his efforts the baby never once took a breath.

And then one of the nurses said, 'Doctor?' and he looked across to where she'd inclined her head and saw the ever-growing red stain soaking the sheet under Amy's body. Gently he wrapped the tiny little body in a snowy white blanket, shaking his head at the nurse who bit down hard on her lip. Walking across the room to Amy he saw she had lost consciousness which was probably the most merciful thing in the circumstances. But if he wasn't to lose the mother as well as the child he had to act fast to stem the bleeding. He was due to go off duty in a few minutes and he hated leaving after something like this. He knew he wouldn't get much sleep tonight.

The team around Amy worked furiously under the doctor's direction for some time, but eventually he said, his voice terse, 'Inform the theatre staff to scrub up and someone call my wife and tell her I shan't be home for hours. Where's the husband? I need to have a word with him.'

'Mrs Callendar was accompanied by her housekeeper, Doctor, who has since returned home. She led us to under-stand the husband was too intoxicated to stand by himself when the ambulance arrived. She telephoned a little while ago to ask for news and said Mr Callendar is still sleeping it off.'

The doctor stared at his nurse for a moment and then looked down at the ashen-faced woman on the bed. 'I hope the so-and-so never wakes up,' he said bitterly, shocking his staff. Then he strode out of the room with a face like thunder.

When Amy next woke it was in the dead of night, and thinking that she had only been asleep for a few minutes, she turned her head on the pillow, her voice a whisper as she said, 'I want to see my baby.'

Immediately the nurse who had been dozing in a chair by her side was awake, her voice soft as she said, 'You're awake, Mrs Callendar. That's good.'

'My baby?' But even as she spoke, Amy's eyes were closing and she slipped back into the deep sleep which had followed the operation to remove her womb but which had been necessary to save her life.

It was daylight when she next surfaced and this time she was aware of deep aching pain but it was a different pain to the one she'd experienced when her baby was being born. There was no nurse by the bed this time but when she went to raise herself on her elbows, one appeared at her side. 'Easy does it,' the matronly woman said cheerfully, assisting Amy into a sitting position and arranging the pillows behind her back as she spoke. 'Now, do you feel like a sip of water?'

Amy's head was spinning but the nausea which had taken hold when she had first sat up was diminishing. She swallowed hard, her lips so dry she felt they were cracking. 'Yes, please.' She could see she was in a large ward with a row of beds either side and a nurse's station right in the middle. After she had taken what amounted to a thimbleful of water, she said, 'Where is my baby?'

The nurse didn't answer this directly. Instead she said, 'You have been very poorly, Mrs Callendar, and the doctor had to perform a little operation. He'll be round shortly to explain everything to you. Now you mustn't try to get out of bed. If you need anything, just call one of the nurses. Will you do that?'

The woman was talking in a tone one would use for a bairn. Amy stared at her, a dread settling on her. She wanted to ask about her baby again but instead she said, 'How long have I been here?'

'In the hospital? I understand you were brought in late Tuesday evening and it is now Thursday morning,' the nurse said brightly. 'Your husband sat at your bedside all through visiting time yesterday afternoon but you were still too heavily sedated to know he was there. No doubt he'll be in later. He was very concerned about you.'

'Has he seen the baby?'

'Let's just leave things until the doctor comes, shall we, Mrs Callendar? He's due,' she glanced at the small watch attached to her crisp white apron, 'in ten minutes. Now, would you like me to wash your hands and face and brush your hair before he comes?'

She couldn't care less about what she looked like. The sense of panic which was taking hold was stronger than the pain she felt at the slightest movement. Nevertheless she nodded her head and submitted to the nurse's ministrations.

Amy was sitting with her hands folded on the coverlet and her eyes on the door when the doctor walked into the ward a few minutes later. She saw his eyes go straight to her bed and then the nurse who had helped her with her toilette spoke to him, her face sombre. The doctor nodded and made his way to her, the nurse accompanying him. As she drew the curtains round the bed, the doctor smiled at her. 'Sitting up already? That's good, that's good.'

No, it wasn't good. Nothing was good. Amy stared at him and she forced herself to speak quietly when she said, 'I want to know what's happened, Doctor, and where my baby is.'

Five minutes later the doctor rose from the chair beside his patient's bed. He had been kind, very kind, and even now Amy could feel his eyes on her almost like a physical touch. She hadn't spoken all through his discourse and when he had finished and asked her gently if she understood all he had said, she had nodded. Yes, she understood. It was simple. Simple and devastating. Everything inside her was screaming but still she sat like stone, the blood thundering in her ears and her soul pierced through.

'Keep the curtains round the bed for the time being, please, Nurse.' The doctor bent and patted Amy's hands and she looked up into the concerned elderly face, wondering why she wasn't crying. He had just told her her little boy was dead and that she would never be a mother. Shouldn't she be crying?

'Can I see him?' she whispered.

'See him?' For a moment the doctor's brow wrinkled and then he said quickly, 'Oh no, my dear, I'm afraid that's not possible. You had a miscarriage. Your baby never breathed by himself, you see.'

'What have you done with him?'

'Now don't agitate yourself, you must keep calm. You have had a major operation and you won't feel yourself for some time.'

'I want to see him.' As she tried to get out of bed, the nurse was there, pushing her down with firm, capable hands.

The next moment she felt something prick her arm but even as she went into unconsciousness she could hear herself saying, 'I want to see him, I *must* see him.'

She continued to ask to see her baby on the second day and the third. By the fourth she didn't ask so often and on the fifth not at all.

She didn't talk to anyone and she refused any visitors, lying most of the time with her eyes shut. That way the picture of a small sweet face was clear on the screen of her mind. It was all she had left of her child and she couldn't bear to think the image might become blurred or fade altogether.

On the seventh day Charles walked into the ward. The matronly nurse was with him, gushing, 'Now here is the young man who has been waiting so patiently to see you.' Amy stared at Charles's face and felt the screaming inside which had never lessened erupt from her mouth. It threw the ward into pandemonium and brought doctors and nurses running, but when Amy next woke from a drug-induced sleep, she found a stillness had settled on her. The screaming had been silenced. In its void was an acceptance that the old Amy was gone and in her place was someone whom she would never have chosen to be and whom she barely understood. This new person was filled with anger and bitterness and a deep hatred. It would change everything, her whole future, her entire life. She couldn't continue being Charles's wife, and she did not want to live in a place where there was any chance she might see him.

Because of him her baby was dead and she had been mutilated and stripped of everything that made her a woman. That's how she felt. She was barren. Wasn't that what they called someone like her in the Bible? A distasteful word, shameful.

She lay in the small single room she had been moved to after the screaming episode, her rational mind telling her she had to do something, make plans to leave. But that would involve talking to people and as yet she couldn't face it. She just wanted to drift into nothingness, to be in a place where she didn't have to think or feel. She didn't term this heaven in her mind, not now. God hadn't listened to her plea for her son. He didn't care and she didn't care about Him. If there was a heaven and hell she was in the latter right now and no amount of incense or candles or sprinkling with holy water could alter that. When she left here she would be on her own, totally on her own, and she would make it on her own too. And still she hadn't cried.

Amy discharged herself from the infirmary three days later, against medical advice. The long wound in her lower stomach wasn't hurting so much now, and only the day before, the kind doctor had informed her it would soon fade into a faint pink and then a silvery colour which would be barely notice-able. She had wondered why he would think she cared about what her stomach looked like, why she would care about anything, but she had quietly thanked him, recognising he was trying to be of some comfort.

She waited until she thought Charles would be at the restaurant and then she dressed once more in the black dress and underclothes she'd worn when she was admitted, and which had been stored neatly in her bedside locker. The frock's full gathers under the bust line mocked her new shape but she didn't dwell on this. She needed all her strength for what she was about to do.

One of the nurses called a cab for her, and she settled

back in the seat and concentrated her mind on her plan of escape, going over each step in her mind. She hadn't considered what she would do if Charles was at home; the very thought of seeing him brought the rage rising.

July had come in on the crest of a heatwave while Amy had been confined in bed but a storm the night before had brought cooler, unsettled weather. As the cab took her to the house she had shared with Charles for over two years, it began to rain. It seemed fitting somehow.

When the cab approached the large iron gates which opened onto the pebbled drive of the house, Amy saw they were open. This meant Charles was not at home and, sure enough, as the vehicle scrunched its way to the front of the house she saw the garage doors were ajar and the Rover was gone. She felt the air leave her mouth in a long whoosh of relief. She hadn't realised until this moment how tense she had been at the thought of seeing him.

After instructing the driver to wait, Amy walked to the front door and rang the bell. It was opened immediately by Cecilia, the current maid. The young girl's mouth dropped open at the sight of her mistress on the doorstep. Mrs Randall appeared as Amy stepped into the hall. The housekeeper's voice was full of consternation as she said, 'Mrs Callendar, whatever are you doing home? We weren't told—'

'No one was told, Mrs Randall. I wanted it that way. I wonder if you would help me with some packing, and perhaps you, Cecilia, would fetch the portrait of my mother which is hanging in the drawing room. I have a cab waiting and a train to catch.'

Mrs Randall stared at her for a moment and then said softly, 'Of course, madam. And after Cecilia has brought the picture, would you like her to prepare sandwiches and a flask of tea for the journey?'

Thank goodness she understood without having it spelled out. Amy nodded. 'That would be very welcome, thank you.'

In the master bedroom Mrs Randall packed a suitcase quickly and efficiently with the clothes Amy pointed out, making sure the portrait of Bess was well protected in the midst of the clothes and adding toiletries and other personal items. Amy changed her dress and shoes, leaving the black dress where it fell. It symbolised everything she was leaving behind. After choosing a summer coat, they went downstairs. In the hall Amy said, 'Would you take my case to the cab, please, and tell him I'll be a minute or two. I have a letter to write.'

Again they stared at each other and then Mrs Randall said worriedly, 'Are you sure you are strong enough for this, madam? For a train journey by yourself, I mean? I have a sister in South Shields who runs a small guest house and she would be more than willing to take care of you for a little while until you are stronger. She is very discreet,' she added quietly.

'Thank you, Mrs Randall, but I have already made arrangements,' Amy lied. South Shields wasn't nearly far enough away. 'I shall be perfectly all right.'

'Excuse me for being so forward, madam, but have you sufficient funds to hand?' Mrs Randall had gone pink at her temerity. 'It's just that I have a little money tucked away for a rainy day under my mattress and you are more than welcome to borrow it. I've never been one for the post office or banks,' she added.

The housekeeper's unexpected kindness touched Amy

deeply. It was dangerous, though; it pierced the iron control and brought the hurt and grief to the forefront of her mind, rather than the anger and hatred which was sustaining her at present. She swallowed helplessly, turning away as she said, 'Thank you very much, Mrs Randall, but I shall manage.' She walked steadily to the morning room, shut the door behind her and then leaned against its solid bulk for a moment as her legs wobbled.

She took several long breaths, willing herself not to break down. It was harder than she had thought, being home again. But this wasn't her home, not any more.

The thought brought her straight and stiff once again and she made her way to the writing desk set in front of the large bay window. She took the key to the desk out of her handbag and unlocked it, taking out the cash box inside. She had been about to settle a number of household bills for the tradesmen who delivered their meat, bread, groceries, coal and other items to the house before she had been taken into hospital so the box held a tidy amount.

Once the contents of the box were in her purse she took a piece of writing paper, picked up her pen and dipped it in the inkwell. She did not hesitate as she wrote; the words had been engraved on her mind for days.

Charles, I am going away and I have no wish to speak to you or to see you again. You may do what you like with regard to the matter of a divorce but I shall not live as your wife again. In the same way I have no child, I have no husband. Once I've engaged a solicitor I shall instruct him to write to yours so that any legal niceties connected with our separation can proceed. I shall not ask for a penny from you, nor would I take one even if it was offered. If you have ever had any feeling for me at all, please do not try and find me. I shall not hold myself responsible for my actions if you do.

Amy.

She read it through once, folded the paper, and slid it into an envelope and sealed it. She did not write Charles's name on the front. She picked up her handbag and coat and left the room. Mrs Randall was standing in the hall waiting for her, Cecilia by her side, and Amy held out the envelope, saying, 'Could you give this to Mr Callendar, please, Mrs Randall? I would prefer that you didn't telephone him but let him have it when he returns home.'

'Yes, madam, I understand.'

'And thank you, both of you. I . . . I don't expect we'll meet again.'

'Oh, madam.' Mrs Randall shook her head. 'I'm so very sorry.'

'Goodbye.' Amy took the cloth bag holding the food and drink from Cecilia and turned away. She couldn't say any more without falling apart.

In the cab Amy did not look back at the house or the woman and young girl standing on the doorstep. She kept her eyes straight in front as the vehicle drew away from the house and made its way out of the drive. She was feeling exhausted now, sick and ill and frighteningly weak, but once she was on the train she could rest. Until then she could not afford to relax the tight rein she was keeping on her mind and body.

When they reached Central Station, the cab driver was very helpful. From the sidelong glances one or two folk gave her, Amy gathered she was looking as ill as she felt, and she was grateful for the man's hand at her elbow as he carried her suitcase to the ticket booth. It wasn't until she was asked her destination that Amy realised she couldn't face going to Kitty's after all. If Charles did try to find her it would be the first place he would look, besides which she didn't want to be with anyone she knew, not even Kitty. She didn't want to have to talk or socialise. She wanted to disappear. 'London, please.' Her voice was little more than a whisper and she had to repeat herself before she was given her ticket. And then the kind cab driver carried her suitcase to the train which, as luck would have it, was just about to leave, and within minutes she was watching the station disappear from the window of the train.

She didn't say goodbye to the town which had been her whole world for eighteen years. As puffs of smoke from the engine passed the window, she shut her eyes and leaned back against the seat. She had done it. She had got away without having to see him again. For now that was enough.

Chapter 15

Amy never could remember much of the journey to London. She could recall the train belching into King's Cross station late at night, and she realised she must have slept for most of the time. After struggling off the train, a porter was on hand to carry her case, and he found her a friendly cabbie who recommended a cheap guest house not too far from the station. There was one single room vacant. It was very small but clean, and she paid the landlady a month's rent in advance and collapsed into bed. There she remained for forty-eight hours. The dam finally broke and she was unable to stop crying.

For two weeks after this she left her room only to eat breakfast at the guest house, and then later in the day dine on soup and a roll at a nearby café. All her waking hours were blanketed in a dull grey bleakness which saw no hope and no future, and at night she would plunge into nightmarish dreams from which she'd wake with her face and pillow wet.

Her rational mind told her she should do something; begin to look for work, find a solicitor as she had said she would, write to Kitty and Ronald and let them know she was safe, but she didn't know how or where to begin and so she did nothing. And all the time, whether she was asleep or awake, her arms ached to hold her baby and she longed for her granny. She seemed to have no control over her grief and it was tearing her apart.

At the beginning of the third week Amy looked at the small amount of money in her purse which was all that remained from the cash box, and she was jolted out of the destructive cycle. She had to find work if she wanted to eat, it was as simple as that, and despite the fact that she had wished herself dead more than once in the worst of her anguish over what had happened, it just wasn't in her nature to sit still and slowly starve. That night she bought a paper. Apart from domestic work, there were few jobs for women advertised. With very nearly two million men currently out of work, it wasn't surprising.

For the next few days Amy applied for every job that didn't have the label 'domestic' on it, but be it in the laundries, factories, canteens or shops, there seemed to be thirty or more women for every vacant post. She knew her bleached, sickly appearance didn't help. The two dresses she had brought with her hung on her like a sack now, although they had fitted perfectly before she had become pregnant.

By the beginning of the fourth week, Amy was becoming resigned to the fact that she would have to take domestic work of some kind. It was poorly paid for very long hours but she had no choice. And she would have to move out of the guest house and find a cheaper room elsewhere in a less salubrious district. She was worried how she would cope with hard physical work; she still felt weak after the operation and completely drained at the end of the day. But needs must.

She bought another paper to look at while she ate her evening meal at the café but felt too dispirited to open it as she sat staring into her bowl of soup. The proprietress, a garrulous little woman with round cheeks like rosy red apples, bustled over to Amy's table. They had taken to passing the time of day recently and Mrs Briggs was aware of Amy's search for work. She was also extremely intrigued by this young woman who kept herself to herself and who had the most arresting, saddest face she had ever seen. It wasn't natural, Mrs Briggs reasoned, for a woman as beautiful as this one to be alone and friendless. There was a mystery here and she had always been partial to solving puzzles.

'No luck then, dearie?' Mrs Briggs gestured to the paper.

Amy glanced up and forced a smile. 'Not yet, no.'

Mrs Briggs nodded sympathetically. Then she pulled out a chair opposite Amy and sat down, leaning forward as she whispered, 'Excuse me asking, dearie, but have you been under the weather lately? You look right poorly. Maybe a spot of rouge would help when you go after something.'

Amy felt herself flush. 'I had an operation,' she said quietly, telling herself Mrs Briggs meant well. 'But I'm better now. Well, nearly.'

'An operation?' Mrs Briggs's voice dropped even lower. 'Well, that'd do it. Make you feel bad for weeks, them hospitals. Never been in one myself but my Reg was took in a year before he died and he was never the same when he came out. Sickly he was, and him a six-footer with a belly on him like a good 'un. Did for my Reg, them hospitals.' And then realising she wasn't being exactly tactful, she added, 'But of course it's different with you, dearie.'

Amy had never thought she would ever want to smile again but now she gave her first natural smile for weeks. She had seen the little woman in action several times over the past days and Mrs Briggs had a talent for putting her foot in it which was truly incredible. 'Yes, it's different with me,' she agreed.

Amy's smile had always lit her face, and Mrs Briggs stared at her. The proprietress considered herself first and foremost a hard businesswoman. She'd had to be, she would tell anyone who would listen, what with her Reg dying when their youngest was still in nappies and the eldest of their six children three years away from working. Through blood, sweat and tears she had built the little café she and her husband had started together just after they had married into a thriving concern, but it hadn't been easy. Seventeen years she'd been on her own, bringing up the family and running the café, and although there was only her Polly at home now she still didn't know what it was to sit with her feet up for more than five minutes. Consequently she never let her heart rule her head. It didn't put cash in her till or pay the mortgage. So it was with some surprise that she heard herself saying, 'Look, dearie, my Polly – you've seen her serving now and again when she isn't helping me out the back – she's getting wed in a few weeks and her intended is adamant he don't want her working.' The sniff with which Mrs Briggs said these words left Amy in no doubt as to how the little woman viewed Polly's fiancé.

'I was going to put a notice in the window in the next

little while for a cook-cum-waitress-cum-bottle-washer, someone who will muck in with me and do what's necessary, you know? I can't pay much, not as much as some, leastways, but Polly's old room'll be going spare and all meals will be thrown in. If you want to give it a try for a couple of weeks to see if you suit, you're welcome. If we get on all right you could move in when our Polly goes.'

Amy stared at the bright face in front of her. She had heard what Mrs Briggs had said but she couldn't take it in. It seemed too good to be true. Aware that the little woman was waiting for a response, she managed to stutter, 'I . . . I don't know how to thank you, Mrs Briggs. I . . . It's wonderful. I'll do anything you want.'

'I shan't ask you to do anything I wouldn't do myself.' Mrs Briggs's voice was brisk now. In truth she was wondering what she had let herself in for. The girl looked as though a breath of wind would blow her away. 'But it's no picnic, I tell you that now. You'll be on your feet all day long and then there's the food to prepare for the next day once we close and have cleaned up. You'll be at it six days a week full gallop.'

'I've worked in a café before.' Amy tried to pull herself together and give the proprietress some confidence in her new employee's capabilities. 'And a restaurant.'

'Have you now? Serving?'

'As a waitress, yes, but we'd help out in the kitchen on occasion. Not often, though. But I'm a quick learner and I like cooking.'

Slightly reassured, Mrs Briggs said, 'Well, you know the sort of food I serve: good, plain and wholesome. None of the fancy rubbish you get up in the West End. Everything's homemade; I bake my own bread, make my own pickle and relishes, everything. Cheap and filling, that's what I've built my reputation on.'

She stood up as she spoke and Amy, anxious to set the seal on the offer, said, 'When would you like me to start, Mrs Briggs?'

'Well, another pair of hands never goes amiss here. How about tomorrow morning? I open at six thirty to catch the factory staff who want a bit of a fry-up afore they start work but you needn't come in till eight. There's always a pile of washing up feet high by then.'

'I'll come at six thirty if you want me to.'

Their eyes met and Mrs Briggs smiled. 'Yes, all right then.' She cocked her head to one side, for all the world like a bright-eyed robin. 'I think you might just do, dearie,' she said approvingly, 'but we'll see how we get on, eh?'

The two of them got on very well. Admittedly for the first little while Amy arrived back at the guest house so exhausted she could barely undress before falling into bed. At five thirty in the morning, when she dragged her protesting body out from under the warm covers, she wondered how she would get through another day without falling asleep on her feet. But after a quick wash she dressed and did her hair and by then she felt more like herself.

She always made a point of arriving at the café a few minutes before half past six, and she didn't depart in the evening until a few minutes after eight o'clock, when it closed. Mrs Briggs had told her she could leave earlier while she was still waiting for Polly's room, but Amy had decided to start as she meant to carry on. Besides which, and she didn't feel she could explain this to her employer even though they were fast becoming friends, she welcomed the fact that she was too tired to think once she got back to her lonely little room. Her sleep was deep and dreamless these days and she was grateful for it.

When Polly married her fiancé in the middle of August, the radio and papers were full of the news that Britain was increasing her defence spending to counter the threat from Hitler and his Nazi party, but the looming prospect of war passed Amy by. She was learning to cope with the present again; the future could take care of itself.

Amy moved into the flat above the café the morning after Winnie Briggs's daughter left. Her room was spacious; it contained a wardrobe, dressing table and three-quarter-size bed along with an armchair. It was light and cheerful, as were the small lounge and Winnie's bedroom, and it boasted a bathroom complete with privy. Downstairs most of the area was taken up by the café, with a relatively small kitchen and scullery tucked away at the back of the building. This was where all the food for both the café and their own needs was prepared and cooked.

From the moment Amy took up residence in the flat and hung her mother's picture on the wall in her bedroom where it was the first thing she saw every morning, she felt settled. The workload was even heavier but being on the premises made all the difference and she enjoyed Winnie's company in the evenings. The small woman was a natural comic who loved an audience, but she was motherly too. She fussed over Amy, making her eat more, and slowly Amy regained the weight she'd lost, the once vivid scar on her stomach beginning to fade to the silvery hue the doctor had mentioned.

The scars in her mind were a different matter; these would stand no probing. For this reason Amy did not allow herself to think of the past at all. If she ever let her guard slip, the feelings of bitterness and anger were as raw as they'd been when she left the north, and then she was all at sea again. Consequently she trained herself to keep the door in her mind permanently closed.

The grief for her baby and the loss of her grandma she couldn't shut out, but these were separate emotions and distinct from the disillusionment and fury she felt over Charles and the devastating circumstances he'd had a hand in.

Deep down in the layers of Amy's mind was the knowledge she would have to contact her husband's solicitors eventually. For the moment she told herself she couldn't afford to engage a solicitor and in this way she put it out of her mind.

One day she would deal with the past. One day she would contact Kitty and Bruce, take up the threads again. One day she would re-examine everything and perhaps it wouldn't hurt so much. One day. But not yet.

PART SIX

1941 Air Force Blue

Chapter 16

'So, you all think you've got what it takes to be part of the Women's Auxiliary Air Force, do you?'

Amy didn't make the mistake of speaking or glancing round the bus at any of the other WAAF recruits as the corporal who had been sitting beside the driver got to her feet. It was obvious the question was rhetorical.

'Myself I doubt it.' A pair of eagle eyes swept over the bus's occupants. 'But time will tell. You might not be aware of it now but when you volunteered it wasn't for a glamorous life of chatting up handsome young airmen. You are coming onto a training camp and be trained you will, like it or not.'

It sounded more like a threat than an encouragement. The young girl sitting beside Amy in the bus which had been waiting for the WAAF rookies at the railway station gulped audibly. Amy didn't dare say anything to try and reassure her, not with the corporal still eyeing them.

'You won't like the food, you won't like your barracks,

you won't like the drill instructors and you sure as eggs won't like your service undies, but I've heard all the gripes before and then some, so save your breath. Do we understand each other?'

A bus full of black, brown, red and blonde heads nodded in unison.

'Good.' The corporal allowed herself a grim smile. 'Welcome to your temporary home in the back of beyond, girls.'

The back of beyond was right. As the corporal carried on speaking, Amy glanced out of the window at the snowy fields stretching either side of the narrow lane down which they were travelling. When she'd volunteered for the WAAFs she had expected to be detailed to one of the camps in or around London for her basic training, not one on the outskirts of Hull. The intensive bombing of recent months and the increasing intake of WAAF recruits had meant volunteers were sent to wherever beds were available, and she had landed up much further north than she would have liked. Not that it really mattered, she told herself in the next moment. She had joined up to do her bit and Britain winning the war against the Germans was the important thing, not personal issues. The last eighteen months had all been leading up to this and even now it seemed incredible how life had changed so drastically.

As the corporal talked on, Amy let her mind drift back to the moment when the reassuringly predictable life she'd led since moving in with Winnie had been shaken. Winnie's Sunday roast had just begun to sizzle in the oven downstairs when they had heard Neville Chamberlain's announcement that Britain was at war with Germany. They had stared at the wireless and then each other, the bright September sunshine outside the flat's window out of keeping with the sombre news.

The first war measure had been the introduction of a blackout which was rigidly enforced by a civilian army of ARP wardens, and Winnie had immediately made an enemy of the warden detailed to their area, referring to him as little Hitler. Amy smiled to herself. Dear Winnie, she was going to miss her and her fights with the warden. Even now she could picture Winnie's gleeful face when a few months after the war had started, the newspapers had reported that more than four thousand people had died in blackout accidents, compared to three members of the British Expeditionary Force being killed in action. Winnie had cut out the article and waved it under the warden's nose every day for a week until the poor man had threatened to get the law on her. Then had followed Dunkirk and the Battle of Britain, and suddenly the inconveniences of the blackout and rationing didn't seem worth complaining about beside the constant fear of invasion or aerial attack.

Amy's eyes were on the bleak snow-swept scene outside the window but she wasn't seeing it. She was back with Winnie on a gorgeous September afternoon the year before. There had been just a few fleecy clouds in the sky and the streets around the café had been full of Londoners enjoying the last of the summer's sunshine, which had been good for business.

The café had been full and she had been humming to herself when she and Winnie, along with their customers, had been drawn out onto the street by the sudden explosion of folk shouting and pointing up into the sky. She would never forget the chill she had felt as she'd stood there with the sun blazing down. A great flotilla in V formation had gradually spread across the blue like a black rash, the scream of bombs following. The Blitz, that's what the newspapers called it. And the planes had come every day from then on, over and over. How she hated them.

The bus jerked over a pothole in the rough road and everyone rose an inch or two before settling in their seats again.

That's why she was here really, Amy thought, as she looked round the bus. That's why she'd decided on the WAAF. She wanted to help Britain's airmen fight the Luftwaffe, annihilate them as they had tried to annihilate everyone in London in those awful raids. The one at the end of December had cemented her decision to join up as soon as Winnie could get someone to help her in the café.

The Luftwaffe had known the Thames was at its lowest ebb tide that Sunday night, and they had purposely sent high-explosive parachute mines to sever the water mains at the beginning of their raid. The thousands of firebombs they'd dropped on the city had turned it into an inferno and even now Amy could hardly bear to think of how many friends and neighbours had been killed. One of Winnie's sons and his wife and three children had been crushed to death as they had hurried to the nearest Underground station. A wall had fallen on them. Polly had been killed when her Anderson shelter had received a direct hit. Her husband had been fire-watching at the time and had come home to no wife and no home.

The bus came to a stop, bringing Amy back to the present. A sea of huts with the odd brick building standing out in the snowy vista beyond the camp's gates was in front of them. The corrugated metal covering of the Nissen huts appeared less than inviting in the freezing conditions.

This thought obviously occurred to the girl at her side because in a small voice she said, 'It looks pretty awful, doesn't it?'

Amy smiled. 'It might not be as bad as it looks. I'm Amy Shawe, by the way.' She'd reverted to her maiden name after arriving in the south and had used it when joining up. She hadn't mentioned her marriage simply because she did not think of herself as a married woman. Her old life was dead and gone; the years before she had moved to London were not something she allowed herself to think about.

'I'm Gertrude Russ but everyone calls me Gertie.' The girl smiled timidly. She was pretty but to Amy's eyes appeared very young; Amy doubted whether she should be here at all. The enlisting age was eighteen but it wasn't unusual for girls to slip in underage as birth certificates weren't required. 'Pleased to meet you.'

'Likewise.' As girls began to pile out of the bus hauling hefty suitcases or bags, Amy added, 'We'd better fall in or fall out or whatever they call it.'

Gertie nodded. She looked to Amy as though she was about to cry, and the girl who had been sitting behind them must have thought this too because she said, 'Don't let 'em see you're scared, lass, or they'll eat you alive.' She thumped Gertie bracingly on the shoulder as she spoke. 'We'll all stick together and you'll be all right. The name's Nell, by the way. I was supposed to come with me pal but she chickened out at the last minute, silly devil. I said to her, they're going to bring National Service in for women sooner or later so you might as well volunteer now and choose where you want to be, and you can't beat Air Force blue.' She grinned at them and Amy, warmed by the northern accent, grinned back and introduced herself and Gertie.

Outside the bus they all stood shivering in the icy air while a service policeman who had been manning the gates checked their papers. Nell, who appeared to be a fount of knowledge, whispered, 'This is one of the war-built camps, you know, so don't expect much. The permanent stations have brick living quarters with central heating and all sorts, but we'll be lucky if we get a tin hut to sleep in with a hole in the ground for the privy.'

Gertie looked so horror-stricken, Amy said, 'There are some brick-built buildings. Perhaps we'll be in one of those.'

Nell shook her head. 'They'll be the education block and gymnasium and parachute store, likely as not.' She put a finger to the side of her nose. 'Me sister joined up a few months ago and she come here. Coo, the stories she told. There was no water laid on when she was here, perhaps there still isn't, and there was a mile or so of unmade road separating the huts from the messes an' such. She said they used to sink up to their knees in the mud and half the girls ended up in hospital with pneumonia, and the other half pretended they'd got it 'cos they wanted to go home.'

'I'm sure your sister exaggerated a bit.' Amy caught Nell's eye and nodded at Gertie, whose face was now as white as the snow banked either side of the road. 'And look, this road's a proper road. I'm sure they've made improvements since your sister was here.'

'Aye, you could be right. She said they were still building parts when she came.' Nell didn't sound convinced. Then she added, a twinkle in her eye, 'Mind, Beryl did say there were compensations. One airwoman to every five airmen was one of 'em.'

'Right, girls, follow me.'

The corporal, who wasn't nearly as tall as she had appeared whilst standing in front of them all on the bus, now strode off down the road, arms swinging, and as everyone hastily gathered up their things and hurried after her, there was no time for further conversation.

The next hours were a blur of activity during which Gertie stuck to Amy's side like glue. After dumping all their bags in the education block, they filed into a room for a lecture about rules and regulations and correct procedures. Amy gathered from the other girls' glassy stares that they had taken in as little as she had. After this they were herded here and there, signing this bit of paper and then that, and received their uniform from the clothes store, for which they had to queue for what seemed like days. Straight after this they were led to the cookhouse armed with their newly acquired irons (knife, fork and spoon), where they enjoyed a filling meal of bangers and mash followed by jam roly poly and custard. Then it was back to the education block where the same little corporal was waiting to lead them on the trek to their sleeping quarters.

They all struggled out into the freezing cold, dark night, weighed down with their bags had clutching their bundle of uniform and bits and pieces, utterly confused and demoralised. It was snowing again, the flakes whirling and cutting through the icy air like little stinging blades, and as half of the girls had arrived in high-heeled fashion shoes, there was plenty of slipping and sliding before they reached the first of the Nissen huts which were to be their sleeping quarters. Amy was just glad that since Nell's sister's time someone had laid decent roads round the camp.

The corporal stopped outside the first hut and read out several names. As the girls concerned stumbled into the hut, everyone else looked longingly after them before hurrying after the corporal who was on the move again. Five girls peeled off at the next hut and then six more at the one beyond that. Gertie was now looking extremely anxious although Amy couldn't see her face very well. The snow gave a little illumination and the corporal was carrying a torch which she clicked on only to read from the list of names in her hand. 'I hope we're together,' Gertie whispered. 'Do you think she'd let me change with someone if we aren't?'

Amy didn't have time to reply to this before they had stopped again and the corporal read out, 'Gertrude Russ, Amy Shawe, Rebecca Stamp, Anne Stewart and Nell Taylor.' It was only then Amy realised they were being billeted in alphabetical order of their surnames. She had been too cold and weary to take it in before.

They filed past the corporal who immediately strode off, the remaining girls following her like chicks after a hen. Amy opened the door and they all stepped inside, lugging their cases after them.

A row of narrow beds, each with a locker beside it, stood either side of a black, pot-bellied stove. Some of the beds, the ones nearest the central stove, Amy noticed wrily, were already occupied. The remaining ones had a neat pile of pillows, blankets, sheets and mattresses on them. The temperature inside the hut wasn't much different to the outside in spite of the cast-iron stove with its long flue.

'Hello there.' One of the girls who was muffled up to the eyebrows in a thick coat, scarf and woolly hat was sitting cross-legged on her bed eating an apple. 'You must be the last few. We all got here this morning. Rum place this, isn't it?'

Amy nodded. Well, it was.

'Grab a bed.' The girl waved her hand apologetically. 'I'm afraid the only ones left are near the door.'

'Aye, so we see.' Nell dumped her things on one of the beds and then zipped open the huge cloth bag she'd brought with her. 'Anyone fancy a wee bevvy before we turn in?' she asked cheerfully, holding up a full bottle of whisky.

'What a good idea!' Another girl with a broad London accent jumped off her bed and made her way over to them. 'Let's have a party. I can't think of anything better on our first night than a housewarming. I've got a box of chocolates I've been saving for my first night away from home in case I needed cheering up. Any of you others got any goodies?'

By the time everyone had contributed to the feast there was a decent pile of food and some bottles on the metal table next to the stove. Winnie had been positively paranoid that Amy was going to waste away in the WAAF, and the enormous rich fruit cake she'd insisted on pressing on Amy – which had practically doubled the weight of her case all by itself – was greeted with awed oohs and aahs by everyone present.

'Blimey, lass!' Nell's mouth was visibly watering. 'That's a bit different to the eggless fruit cakes me mam's been serving up at home. Your mam must have used up her rations for the month with that beauty, and look at the fruit in it. There's more than a month's worth of points there an' all.'

Amy continued cutting chunky slices of cake so she didn't have to look at Nell as she said, 'A friend of mine made it, we've been running a café together for some years, her café. She's a very good cook.'

'You're telling me. Likely to send you the odd food parcel, is she?' Nell added hopefully.

'Probably,' said Amy, laughing.

'Then you're me friend for life, lass. I've had oatmeal buns an' carrot cookies coming out of me ears at our house. Not that me mam don't try, bless her, but she's took all this palaver the Ministry of Food keeps churning out about experimenting with what's available too much to heart. We've had potato fingers and potato floddies and potato carrot pancakes for weeks, and her marrow surprise was a surprise all right. Guess what it was stuffed with?'

'Potato?' someone called out as everyone rocked with laughter.

'Aye, it was an' all. It was the last straw for me da. He said if she didn't give him something with a bit of meat in it he'd give *her* a surprise, and it wouldn't be wrapped with a pink ribbon neither.'

Even Gertie had lost her terrified expression and was doubled up with laughter now, and the evening got merrier as the whisky and a couple of bottles of homemade blackberry wine vanished, along with most of the food. By the time Amy burrowed under the covers in her service striped pyjamas, her greatcoat and a couple of jumpers laid out on top of the thin blankets for extra warmth, she felt things weren't too bad. Nell had told them all her sister had admitted to sobbing her heart out at lights out on her first night but there was none of that in their hut, mainly thanks to Nell,

Amy thought drowsily. The plump, pretty, northern girl was very much like Winnie in personality; a card, as Pamela, the girl from the East End of London, had labelled Nell. But a very nice card. And one anyone would be glad to have in their pack.

The next morning brought hurdles that made Amy very grateful for the settling in and camaraderie of the night before. There was the undressing and washing in front of girls who had been strangers twenty-four hours ago – and the baths were housed in a delapidated shack with thin walls and a roof which allowed the icy wind free rein – and also the dreaded medical inspection. This was called the FFI or Free From Infection test, and poor Gertie turned green when she learned it was a regular part of WAAF life.

Jabs, chest X-rays, doctor's examinations and – the most humiliating of all – checks for head lice and venereal diseases reduced some of the girls to tears. Even Nell lost her sparkle as they passed the morning in various states of undress while being shunted from pillar to post. It didn't help that although the airmen and airwomen were treated in two different surgery rooms with their own waiting areas, every so often some lost airmen would wander into their vicinity, causing a few of the more shy girls to squeal in protest. 'They ought to count themselves lucky,' Nell muttered darkly to Amy. 'My sister says on most stations men and women are treated in the same surgery. Nothing's left to the imagination, according to Beryl.'

It took Pamela to bring a smile to frozen faces. The thin blonde girl strode out of the doctor's office into the waiting area clad in her thick service vest and winter knickers which resembled a product of a hundred years ago, and glanced round at the sombre faces. She grinned. 'They're ready in there for the next poor cow,' she said loudly, 'but I'm sure you'll all be pleased to hear that this particular member of the herd is as clean and healthy as ever the Air Force could wish for. Fur's sleek and shiny, hooves nicely trimmed, teeth perfect.' The nurse who had followed her out looked askance and everybody tittered.

Amy was the next to go into the doctor's room and she was a bundle of nerves. The moment came as she had known it would. The doctor glanced from her stomach to her face in surprise. 'This scar,' he said quietly. 'How did you come by it?'

She had rehearsed what she would say and now the words came easily enough. 'I was involved in an accident some years ago when I was eighteen,' she said steadily. 'As a result of the damage done, I had to have a hysterectomy.'

'I'm sorry. That was most unfortunate.'

Most unfortunate. The worst thing that could happen to a young woman dismissed as most unfortunate. But then what else could he say? And she preferred the brisk matter-of-factness to pity anyway. The enforced intimacy with her fellow WAAFs had made her conscious of the silvery white scar over the last twenty-four hours in a way she hadn't been for years and she knew she was feeling a little raw. She had seen one or two of the girls glance her way in the bath hut and had felt like covering herself up then. But sooner or later people would notice. They didn't have to know what she had just told the doctor, though, merely that she'd had some kind of an operation.

'Yes, it was unfortunate but it's in the past,' she said, realising the doctor was expecting a reply. 'And with what's happening in the world now it doesn't seem so important any more.' That wasn't quite true but she didn't want to discuss it any further.

The doctor didn't pursue the matter, finishing the examination in silence apart from the odd instruction to the nurse who was helping him. Amy found she was trembling inside when she re-entered the waiting area. Although she had prepared herself for the question she'd known would arise during the examination she had never spoken about it before and it had upset her more than she'd expected.

'Are you all right?' Gertie was sitting with Nell and a couple of the other girls. 'You look a bit pale.'

'I'm fine.' Amy forced a lightness she didn't feel as she added, 'Frozen, but fine.'

The others nodded and there were mutterings about catching their death of cold, but Gertie kept her eyes on Amy for a while before turning away.

After the examinations were over, they filed into the cookhouse for a somewhat colourless meal of steamed fish roll followed by vanilla and semolina mould. Nell remarked that she couldn't tell which was which, even after she'd tasted them. Then they were marched outside and into a large hangar for their first drill, several of the girls nearly falling over themselves on the way to get a good look at a bunch of airmen who were strolling back from one of the distant runways.

'Eyes straight ahead.' The sergeant who was leading them didn't even bother to turn round, adding weight to the story that he had eyes in the back of his head. 'You'll be seeing them in the mess tonight no doubt.'

'Any you fancy?' Nell whispered in an aside to Amy and

Pamela as several of the men gave mock salutes, grinning. Gertie turned beetroot red.

'All of them.' Pamela gave a little wriggle of appreciation. 'Those uniforms are just so romantic, aren't they? I mean, let's face it. The Army and Navy can't compare with our boys.'

Amy let the other two talk on, falling back a little so she was walking with Gertie. The last thing she wanted was to get involved with a man again, and if ever she found herself longing for a pair of strong arms to hold her tight, she only had to touch the narrow line on her stomach for sanity to be restored. Anyway, who would want her now for anything more than a brief fling? And she couldn't envisage fooling around like lots of women her age did. Her marriage and the death of her child had seen to that. All the tears and anger and depression from that time had changed her irrevocably. If the war hadn't come along she would have continued to help Winnie build up the business and probably have accepted the partnership Winnie had kept trying to press on her. They'd had plans to expand and buy the building next door, but the war had put everything on hold.

The drill wasn't exactly a success. Everyone kept sailing off in different directions for one thing, causing the sergeant such frustration he threatened them with a ten-mile route march the next day if they didn't try harder.

'He's a bully,' Amy whispered to Gertie who had tears streaming down her face after being singled out twice in a row. 'If he stopped roaring and barking so much we'd understand him better.'

'Don't cry,' Nell added on Gertie's other side. 'Don't give him the satisfaction of seeing he's got to you.'

Amy exchanged a glance with Nell over Gertie's head. The last twenty-four hours had only confirmed her belief that Gertie was younger than she had let on.

Eventually they were allowed to slink back indoors, utterly frozen and starving hungry in spite of the stodgy food at lunchtime. There they learned that the sergeant – out of the goodness of his heart, as Pamela remarked bitterly – had arranged for them to receive buckets and brushes with which to clean the ablution blocks until dinner time.

Chapter 17

The following weeks passed in a blur of drills, lectures, kit inspections, gas-mask practices and a hundred and one other activities which were all part and parcel of WAAF life, but overall Amy's abiding memory of this time was sore feet. That and a strong sense of togetherness and friendship. When she would have stayed alone in the hut in her free time rather than mixing with the airmen, Gertie and the others wouldn't let her. And through their persistence she learned that many of the RAF boys had only recently left the protective shelter of home for the first time, and despite brave phrases and RAF jargon were very unsure of themselves. In fact most of them were little more than babies, she felt, and when she responded to the inevitable passes, ribaldry and invitations with a kind but firm smile and definite no, they appeared almost relieved to be let off the hook of swashbuckling bravado. The trouble was, more than one informed her gravely, they were associated with a force that had a reputation for danger, heroism and romance, and they felt they had to live up to it. But if she just wanted to be friends . . . She did, she'd inform each one gently, and then sit listening patiently as they relived the day's flying minute by minute.

She learned that flying was their first love however much they might like the opposite sex, and that they were where they were not because they were burning to go to war but burning to fly. But to a man they were ready to sacrifice their lives if it came to it. They both humbled her and restored her faith in the male of the species.

And then suddenly the women's passing-out parade was over and to hut twenty-three's pride not one of their number had given up and gone home. Now came the time they had all joined up for – their first posting to a real RAF camp. Gertie would have been bereft at the thought of being torn from the company of her new friends, but in the event both she and Amy were detailed to a station in Norwich; the rest of the girls were scattered at different camps all over the south of England.

'You'll keep in touch, won't you, lass?' Nell was busy stuffing her clothes and belongings into the brand new kitbag they had all been issued with, a tall, white, heavy tube of a thing which required its owner to be possessed of muscles like a wrestler's to have any chance of carrying it when it was full.

'Of course I will.' Amy shoved her tin hat into the top of her own bag and pulled the rope to secure it. Pamela had already exchanged addresses, as had all the girls, but they had all privately agreed that if, in the sweepstake of postings, it was possible for any two of them to stay together, it was better one of the duo was Gertie.

Amy glanced at her young friend. Because she had been

terrified she wouldn't be ready in time for the lorries which were giving the fledgling WAAFs a lift to the train station, Gertie had been up at the crack of dawn packing. She was standing by her bed now, one hand on her kitbag which was lying on top of the covers and her gas mask slung over one shoulder. She had admitted to them all one night that she was only just seventeen, having added more than a year to her age when she volunteered. She said she had joined up because some of her friends had. Amy didn't quite believe this. Although she had nothing concrete to go on she felt Gertie had enlisted to escape some domestic problem at home, but her friend clearly didn't want to talk about it.

Gertie caught her eye and smiled wanly. 'I managed to get everything in,' she said, 'but my jacket is going to be ever so creased.'

'So's mine but we'll iron them when we get to Norwich.' Gertie hadn't had a clue about how to iron her uniform when she had first arrived, but everyone had taken her under their wing and now she was as capable as the rest of them, if still without a shred of confidence. 'Right.' Amy took hold of the rope at the top of her kitbag, slung her gas mask over her shoulder and attempted to swing the bag onto the other shoulder. It landed on the floor with a dull thud just as the sound of impatient hooting outside told them they were keeping their lifts waiting. Everyone else had problems carrying their kitbags too, even Nell who was sturdily built and was fond of telling them all she was as strong as her brothers any day. Those of them who were light and slender, like Amy and Gertie and Pamela, didn't have a hope in heaven of ever lifting the things onto their backs.

The occupants of hut twenty-three made a somewhat

ignominious exit some minutes later, huffing and puffing and dragging their kitbags behind them. It didn't help morale when the RAF drivers threw the bags up into the back of the lorries as though they contained feathers.

Amy glanced round at the others in the lorry. They were all singing 'Hang out your washing on the Siegfried Line' with gusto. She could hardly believe she'd only known her friends for such a short while. It was strange because she'd seen plenty of goings-on in the café over the last years, they'd had all sorts to contend with at times, but Nell and the rest of them had awakened something in her which had lain dormant since she had left Sunderland. It would sound overly dramatic if voiced, but she felt as though they had brought her back to life, and the trainee pilots had played a part in this too.

When they all piled out of the lorry at the station, Amy found herself feeling as stricken as Gertie looked at the thought of saying goodbye to everyone. It helped a little that the others seemed to feel the same and there was a lot of sniffing and snuffling.

By the time the train steamed into Norwich station, Amy's equilibrium had reasserted itself. Not least because she felt a responsibility to chivvy Gertie along. They stood straightening their ties and smoothing their skirts, kitbags at their feet, as the train chugged off. A vicious icy wind made them hastily button their service greatcoats.

'I take it you're the two for the camp?' A young pilot officer had come up behind them and as they both swung round and saluted, Gertie stepped on Amy's toes which were still sore from two weeks of marching in new shoes. 'I had to come into town so I said I'd pick you up. Come on.' He whisked up their kitbags and led them out to a van, whistling cheerfully as he went.

The officer drove quickly and surely, keeping his eyes on the road as he filled them in about their new posting. Rows and rows of neat wooden huts seemed to stretch endlessly in front of their eyes as he drew to a halt. The airfield itself was someway from the rest of the camp to limit casualties in case of attack. As in most camps, the airwomen's accommodation, complete with its guardroom, was separated from the rest of the station and out of bounds to airmen.

After depositing them outside the WAAF CO's office, the pilot heaved the two kitbags out of the back of the van, wished them well, jumped back into the vehicle and disappeared off into the maze.

They stood there gazing after him like two little orphan Annies. 'No Nissen huts.' Amy's voice was bracing. 'Nell's sister said the wooden or concrete huts are miles better so we might not wake up with icicles on our noses here.'

Gertie nodded. The size of the camp overwhelmed her.

'Let's report in then.' Amy grasped her kitbag and hauled it to the door of the wooden building. This was it. She was about to be slotted into the great machine that made up the Royal Air Force's fight against the enemy and she just hoped she proved herself worthy when the chips were down.

By lights out that night Amy felt as though she had been in the camp days instead of hours. This was mainly due to the warm welcome she and Gertie had received from their fellow WAAFs. After the long rigmarole of initial camp procedure, they'd been shown to their sleeping quarters by a friendly administrative officer who had taken pity on their evident bewilderment. The officer had opened the hut door to find a number of girls cavorting about the room and jumping on the beds, shrieking like banshees.

On realising there was an officer present, everyone had stopped dead before hurrying to stand by their beds, one girl clutching what looked like a telegram in her hand and tears streaming down her face.

The officer had raised enquiring eyebrows at the girl, whose name was Isobel Turner, and she'd responded by gabbling, 'It's Philip, ma'am, my fiancé. He's wounded but safe. The Resistance got him out.'

The officer smiled widely. 'I told you not to give up hope, now didn't I? Well,' her glance scanned the rest of the girls, 'you'd better all carry on, hadn't you?' And with that she turned and left, closing the door behind her.

It turned out that Isobel's fiancé had been shot down over France some weeks before and they had been due to get married a few days ago. 'But that doesn't matter, nothing matters now I know he's all right,' Isobel beamed.

'I'm so glad for you.' Amy smiled at the tall lanky redhead and Isobel smiled back, and in that moment Amy knew she had found another friend. In fact she'd found a hut full, she reflected, glancing at the miniature portrait of her mother which she'd had copied from the original which was still in her bedroom at Winnie's. She turned off her torch and settled down for sleep in the darkness. After a while she was annoyed to find she was still awake; she just couldn't relax her mind, even knowing breakfast parade was at seven forty-five in the morning.

Their hut was much larger than the one at training camp; it held a total of twenty-four beds with a separate room tacked on the end for the NCO. Unfortunately the ablution huts were, once again, far away. Amy had been informed that the RAF chiefs deemed it unhealthy for them to be close to the WAAF sleeping quarters.

'The men's ones are much nearer them of course,' one of the girls had put in with mild resentment. 'But then that comes with us having to be in at eleven at night whereas they can stay out till twelve and us getting two-thirds of their pay and so on. I mean, they don't have our expenses, do they? It ought to be the other way round, if anything. We have to buy face powder and lipstick and cream and hair rollers—'

Someone had thrown a pillow at her at this point and she'd retired gracefully. Amy smiled at the memory but then her expression straightened at the thought of the next day. Possibly because she had mentioned running the café with Winnie on her application form, she had been told she would be assigned to the kitchens, her trade officially recorded as cook. She hadn't liked to point out that preparing and cooking meals for a small café wasn't quite the same as supplying the needs of hundreds of hungry airmen and airwomen. Gertie had been equally disconcerted to find she had been detailed as an equipment assistant. There was another girl in the hut working in equipment and she had scared Gertie to death when she'd told her she'd be working in huge premises, crowded with tall racks which were filled with a vast variety of goods, each with its own name and number which had to be recorded and recognised.

But they would both be fine, Amy reassured herself, bringing the blankets up round her ears and relishing the fact that this hut was a hundred times warmer than the ice-cold Nissen. There were lots of WAAFs around to help; the comradeship she'd already experienced in the few hours she had been here told her they wouldn't be left to struggle as newcomers. She hoped Nell and Pamela and the rest of hut twenty-three had been equally well received wherever they had finished up.

She would write to Nell and Pamela, she told herself drowsily as the emotion and physical exertion of the day kicked in and she felt her eyelids grow heavy. And perhaps Kitty too. Nell's broad northern dialect had made her think of Kitty more than once and she had to face the fact she should have let Kitty know where she was long before now. Charles was a different story.

She felt a spasm of the old turmoil and pain and turned over, burying her face in the pillow. She wouldn't think of Charles now but even that would have to be dealt with at some point. He wasn't a practising Catholic and she hadn't been in a church since she'd left the north-east, not a Catholic one anyway. She had slipped into a little Baptist church close to the café a few times and, in spite of the niggling feeling that she had committed a sin through attending a service in a non-Catholic church, she'd found peace there. She was able to pray again, but this time without the trappings of the religion she had been brought up in.

Would Charles agree to a divorce without any quibbling, or would he dig his heels in and make things difficult? She really had no idea how he'd react. But if she had to take Charles on and fight for her freedom, she would. She owed it to her baby.

The thought eased the agitation at what was to Amy a huge milestone for her future. She let her limbs and mind relax and in a few minutes she was asleep.

* * *

'Do you think you need to leave camp for training, Shawe?'

Amy stared back into the eyes of the tall plain woman in front of her. She knew what the corporal wanted her to say. As Amy had arrived at the camp, one of the WAAF cooks hadn't come back from a week's leave, having been severely injured when a bomb had fallen on her family's home, and the remaining cooks and kitchen orderlies were much over-worked.

'I think I'll be all right, Corporal,' she said. She wasn't at all sure she'd be all right but the rest of the team had prom-ised to teach her all the ins and outs of cooking for the camp dining rooms – one for the airmen and one for the airwomen – and the joint NAAFI where everyone congregated in the evenings. Amy had already heard stories of the all-ranks dances that were held regularly – admission sixpence, spirits a shilling and beer about fourpence – where the team would provide snacks and on special occasions a big buffet.

'Unfortunately it means a couple of us are serving,' Cassie, another WAAF, had explained. 'But we take it in turns to have a night off. And our station band is terrific, good as Roy Fox or Billy Cotton any day.'

The corporal now smiled approvingly at Amy; she had obviously given the right answer. 'That's the ticket,' she said. 'Get stuck in and learn on the job, that's better than any training school, in my opinion.'

'Course she hasn't dished up burned sausages and onions in the airmen's mess,' whispered Cassie as the corporal walked away. Cassie had been regaling Amy with some of her own blunders when she'd first come to the camp six months before. Amy wasn't sure if it was to encourage her or frighten her rigid. 'They all stood on the chairs banging their plates with their knives and singing "To Err is human, to forgive, divine".'

Amy giggled. She liked Cassie.

True to their word, the team of RAF and WAAF cooks and kitchen orderlies were patient, kind and reassuring over the next few days as Amy learned the ropes. The team worked well together, with plenty of good-natured ribaldry and flirting going on, but Cassie explained to Amy that it was an unwritten rule you didn't date someone you worked with closely. 'Too complicated.' She wrinkled her little button nose set in a pretty face under a mass of brown curly hair. 'And with all those lovely pilots to choose from, who'd pick a cook anyway?'

And then came the day when Amy was designated to be one of the cooks who stood and dished up the food in the airmen's mess out of the huge metal bowls that looked like pig's troughs. She had served in the WAAF's dining room before but not the RAF one which was three times as big, and she was nervous. Silly, she told herself, considering she had been married and lived with a man for two years, but she felt all fingers and thumbs.

Wrapped up in her white overall and with her hair tucked inside the white cap which resembled an inflated pancake, she manned an enormous tub of mashed potato and onion, but the unflattering garb merely drew attention to her beauty rather than hiding it. Amy was quite unaware of this and she kept her head down as much as she could, ladling out dollops of thick sticky potato on the plates thrust in front of her without raising her eyes. Until, that was, a voice said, 'Amy? Is it you?'

Other voices had spoken before this one and they had

been kind, friendly; passing the time of day while letting her know they liked what they saw, but only once or twice had she glanced up and then just to smile. Now as her eyes met those of the tall man staring at her as though transfixed, she said, 'Bruce?'

'It is you.' He slung his plate on the counter and reached out to take her hands, careless of the interested onlookers. 'I've been on leave but I'd heard there was a right cracker –' he stopped abruptly before continuing almost without a pause, 'a new WAAF in the kitchens. But for it to be you . . .'

'You . . . you're in the RAF?' It was a silly question in the circumstances.

He nodded and he didn't let go of her hands. 'Wireless mechanic,' he said briefly.

'I hate to interrupt such a touching reunion but he clearly isn't going to introduce me.'

Bruce was elbowed aside none too gently by the man who had been standing behind him. Bruce didn't seem put out, though; in fact he was smiling when he said, 'Amy, meet Pilot Officer Johnson.'

'Hey, any friend of yours is a friend of mine so cut the formality.'

Amy took her gaze from Bruce and turned to the other man, a polite smile forming on her lips. She felt something akin to an electric shock as she found her eyes held by ones of deepest green.

'The name's Nick.' Very white, even teeth flashed in a face that was tanned to a golden brown. 'And I'm *very* pleased to make your acquaintance, Miss Amy . . . ?'

'Shawe.' It took some effort to tear her gaze away. 'Amy Shawe.'

'Shawe? Don't tell me you two are related?'

It was Bruce who said, 'We're cousins,' and although his manner hadn't changed, Amy had seen the slight flash of puzzlement at her use of her maiden name.

The queue of people behind the two men were now making it plain they felt they'd been patient long enough, and when Bruce said, 'I'll see you in the NAAFI tonight, yes? You're going to the quiz?' Amy nodded. She hadn't been planning to go to the quiz between the RAF and the WAAF because it wasn't her turn to serve behind the counter and she felt she had a cold coming. She had thought she'd have a bath in peace for once with everyone at the NAAFI and then return to the hut for an early night with her hot water bottle and a mug of cocoa. But of course everything was different now.

'Big prizes on offer tonight.' The pilot officer was talking again, laughter in his voice. 'Two and six each in savings stamps.'

She was more in control of herself this time but still the handsome face under its shock of raven hair disturbed her. Because of this her voice was unusually cool when she said, 'I think that's a very decent prize,' but before he could say anything more, the pushing from behind became more pronounced and Bruce and his friend were forced to move on to the containers of stew and vegetables.

'Your cousin, eh?' Cassie was in charge of the next tub and her eyes followed Bruce and Nick as they went to sit down at a table some distance away. 'Pity he's just a wireless mechanic, he's quite dishy. You know who that pilot is, don't you? Nick Johnson?'

'Nick Johnson, I presume,' Amy said as drily as she could,

considering how shaken up she felt at the sudden encounter with the past. Bruce here, of all people. But then if it had to be anyone, she was glad it was Bruce. She hoped he wouldn't say anything about Charles, though, and did he know what had happened to make her leave Sunderland? Oh, she wished she could talk to him right now.

'No, I don't mean that, silly. What I meant is that he's the one all the WAAFs are madly in love with. He was in the Battle of Britain, you know, shot down umpteen Germans, according to the grapevine. A real hero, you know? And he's just so gorgeous, isn't he? But he's a real heartbreaker. Two or three dates and that's your lot with Nick. Mind, it doesn't put the girls off. It wouldn't put me off if he asked.'

Amy continued to dish up the potato as Cassie prattled on but she was only half listening. She should have said something to Bruce, tipped him the wink in some way not to mention to anyone she'd been married. Well, was *still* married technically. She didn't want to have to talk about it to anyone, answer questions, have people look at her strangely. It was one thing to lose your husband in the war, several of the WAAFs had joined up because of that very thing, feeling they wanted to get back at Hitler for the loss of their husbands, but quite another to be separated as she and Charles were. In spite of the fact that a good number of the WAAFs were carrying on with someone or other – a few of them, like Cassie, with more than one – she would still stick out like a sore thumb if the truth were known.

By the time they were back in the kitchens, a fatalistic calm had settled on her. She would go along to the quiz and cope with whatever presented itself, that was all she could do. And she'd already made the decision the night before to take up the threads of the past, so perhaps seeing Bruce was meant to be. And she was fond of Bruce; of all of them back home, he was the only one she could say she loved. He couldn't have been better to her if she had been his real sister. And now she'd seen him, now she knew he was here on camp, she found she was suddenly hungry for news about everyone. She hadn't expected that. She shook her head at her inconsistency and applied herself to the gigantic fruit crumble she was making.

When Amy, Gertie and several others from their hut walked into the NAAFI later that evening, it was packed with airmen and WAAFS and there wasn't a free table to be had. The noise was deafening and the beer looked to be flowing freely as everyone settled themselves for the quiz, deep-throated laughter erupting from a couple of the RAF tables now and again. There had been a bomber operation early that morning and two Spitfires had not made it back over the Channel; those who were mourning lost comrades were doing it in their own way and to hell with Hitler.

Someone jostled against Amy and a few drops of beer splashed onto her jacket. As a male voice said, 'Sorry,' she turned round and found herself once again held by deep, clear green eyes. As they looked at each other, she noticed white laughter lines radiating from the corners of his eyes but it wasn't only that which gave an impression of maturity. It was something in the way he held himself, in the set of his jaw. An arrogance. Without knowing why, Amy found herself bristling. She didn't like Pilot Officer Nick Johnson, she decided, however the rest of the WAAF contingent viewed him.

'Crowded tonight, isn't it?' He was talking easily and for a moment Amy wondered if he remembered her. Then he said, 'Bruce has been looking for you. Have you seen him?'

'No, no I haven't.'

'We're on a table across there if you want to join us.'

The white teeth flashed and she wondered if someone had told him he had the perfect smile. Then she chided herself for being bitchy. It wasn't like her but then her whole reaction to the individual in front of her wasn't like her. She wasn't one for taking an instant dislike to anybody.

'I'm with friends,' she said flatly.

'So? The more the merrier.'

'I don't think so, thank you.' She hadn't realised how tall he was earlier but he must have been at least six foot; he seemed to tower over her five foot six anyway. It was disconcerting.

Then she was taken aback when he bent his head and murmured, 'You don't like me very much, do you? Why is that?'

Out of the corner of her eye Amy could see Gertie and the others' interested glances, and she forced a cool smile as she said, 'Don't be ridiculous. I don't know you, so how could I dislike you?'

'I don't know. That's what I asked you.'

'Look, sir—'

'Oh, cut the sir drivel. We're off duty, forget rank.'

Amy drew in a long breath. He might be the most handsome man in the room but he was also the rudest.

She wasn't aware she was glaring until he said, laughter evident in his voice, 'You're even more beautiful when you're angry.'

'That's the oldest line in the book.'

'What book? I don't have a book. I've never needed one.' He grinned at her. 'That's the sort of thing you expect me to say, isn't it? I don't want to disappoint you.' He bent towards her again and added, 'You're ruining my Casanova reputation with that face, you know. You're supposed to be all dimpled sweetness.'

Suddenly she wanted to laugh. Biting her lip hard to prevent the glimmer of a smile escaping, she told herself she couldn't give him the slightest encouragement. 'Would you tell Bruce I'm over here?'

'Yes, ma'am.' He saluted with his free hand. 'Right away, ma'am.'

She eyed him severely. 'Thank you.'

'My pleasure.'

Immediately he'd begun to weave his way across the room, Gertie and Isobel were either side of her. 'I didn't know you knew Nick Johnson,' Isobel said as the three of them watched the tall figure.

'I don't, not really. He's a friend of my cousin and he was with him today in the airmen's mess. I didn't even know my cousin was on the camp.'

Isobel nodded. 'Well, just watch Nick,' she said darkly. 'He's a love-'em-and-leave-'em type and makes no apology for it either. Any girl who gets mixed up with him has to know the score and that's to expect nothing. Of course, most attachments on the station are only temporary, we all know that, but Nick's in a league of his own. He's very handsome though,' she added almost wistfully.

'What about Philip?' said Amy, smiling.

'Oh, he's twice as handsome.' Isobel giggled. She was due a forty-eight-hour leave the next day and was meeting her fiancé in the country hotel where they'd been due to spend their five-day honeymoon before returning to their respective stations. She had already confided to Amy and the others they didn't intend to get out of bed the whole time, having made sure room service was available.

When Bruce reached Amy's side he was smiling, his brown eyes telling her he was glad to see her, and Amy, touched by his obvious delight, reached up and kissed him on the cheek.

'Can we sit somewhere quieter for a bit and talk?' she asked him. 'You're not bothered about the quiz, are you?'

'No, I'm not bothered about the quiz,' he said softly. 'How about I get you a drink and we'll find a corner?' He turned to Gertie and Isobel, adding politely, 'What can I get you to drink, ladies?'

'Don't worry about us, we'll sort ourselves out.' Isobel was already dragging Gertie off after the others who had noticed some spare seats near the stage, next to a particularly rowdy RAF table.

Amy and Bruce ended up standing in the small entrance area from which the lavatories branched off on either side. At least they could hear themselves speak there.

Bruce stared at his cousin. Amy was thinner and more composed than he remembered. He had noticed it earlier in the mess. But then she had been through a packet whatever way you looked at it, he thought pityingly. He wondered what she had been doing the last few years since she had disappeared. He didn't blame her for that; everyone coped with grief in different ways and losing the baby must have devastated her. It had surprised him that she had left Charles, though, but Kitty had hinted all was not well even before the miscarriage but wouldn't say any more than that.

'Bruce . . .' Amy hesitated for a moment and then went on, 'Have you told anyone about . . . about Charles? That I'm married?'

'No.' They were looking into each other's eyes now, a straight look. 'When you said your name was Shawe I assumed you wanted it that way.'

'I do, yes.' Her voice had been eager and now she coloured a little. 'I'm not married except on paper.' And then she flapped her hand, adding, 'That sounds silly but you know what I mean.'

'Everyone was concerned about you when you disappeared.' His voice carried no reproach when he said, 'I think Kitty expected you to let her know where you were. She and my father went to see Charles, you know, just to make sure what he'd said was the truth. They spoke to the housekeeper and she confirmed you'd left of your own free will, that after what had happened you wanted to get away.'

The violet-blue gaze did not falter when she said very quietly, 'Did Charles tell Kitty he was responsible for my losing the baby? That he was drunk and trying to manhandle me, and that it wasn't the first time? Far from it.'

Bruce's face betrayed his shock, and when she reached out and touched his sleeve, saying, 'I'm sorry, I should have put it better than that,' he still couldn't speak for a moment or two.

'He said you fell.'

'I did fall, because of him. I was at the top of the stairs . . .' She swallowed, clearly forcing herself to say, 'Of course he wouldn't have wanted me to lose the baby. When he drank he turned into someone else, someone frightening.'

'Hell, Amy.' There was silence between them for a moment

and then he said, 'Why didn't you tell someone, for crying out loud? I know I'd moved away and so had Da, but you must have realised we'd have come and put the fear of God in him if you had let on?'

She bowed her head. 'At first it would have seemed like a betrayal somehow,' she said very quietly. 'Later, when I was pregnant, I thought he would change. But I did tell Kitty at Grandma's funeral that he was drinking too much. She . . . she didn't say anything to anyone then?'

'She just hinted all wasn't well between you but nothing specific.'

Amy nodded. 'Anyway, it's all water under the bridge now,' she said dismissively, finding she didn't want to talk about Charles any more. 'How are Kitty and Uncle Ronald? How are you? You're not married or anything, are you?'

Bruce grinned. Same old Amy. Changing the subject if she thought he was going to moan at her. But she *should* have called on him or his da. 'Kitty and Da are as happy as bugs in a rug,' he said, indulging her. 'Mam and the girls are still at Granda's. Kitty's mam and da died within a month of each other last year. I'm not married and there's no one special at the moment although the girls are queueing up, of course.' He raised mocking eyebrows and Amy smiled. 'And, oh aye, Perce is out.'

'He's out of prison? Is he in the Army or something?'

Bruce shook his head, finishing his beer in one swallow before he said, 'According to Da, he's up to his old tricks and knee deep in the black market, swaggering about and boasting he's swung the lead and avoided being called up by bribing some doctor who's on the fiddle. He started writing to Da when he was inside, and after he got out he went down to Manchester a few times to see them. They don't like it, in fact Kitty can't stand him. But he's still Da's son.'

'I thought Perce was all for your mam and Mr O'Leary?'

'He makes sure he keeps in with them an' all. Runs with the hare and hunts with the hound, does Perce.' Bruce didn't voice what he really thought at this point, namely that Perce's reconciliation with Ronald and Kitty was because of the beautiful woman in front of him. His da had told him on the quiet that every time Perce made an appearance he asked after Amy, and although they'd told him they had no idea of her whereabouts, he didn't give up. Bruce didn't like that. It worried him.

'I'm sorry about Mr and Mrs Price.'

Bruce became aware that Amy was waiting for him to speak and cleared his mind. 'Aye, it hit Kitty hard. It was some trouble with her stomach with Mrs Price, but according to the neighbours Kitty's da just gave up the will to go on once Mrs Price had gone. You wouldn't have thought it, would you, not with how Abe appeared on the outside.'

'I've long since lost faith with how folk appear on the outside.' And then, as though the words had brought them full circle, she flushed and said, 'Bruce, you won't say anything to anyone about what we discussed earlier?'

'About you being married?'

She nodded. 'I'm going to sort it out but not just yet.'

He stared at her but said nothing, wondering if she still had some feeling for Charles.

'I'm going to write to Kitty in the next day or two,' Amy told him, 'but after what you've said I'll ask her not to tell anyone, especially Perce. I'll tell them we've met up, that'll please them. Kitty always said you were the best of the bunch.'

Bruce smiled. 'Sensible woman.'

It was true, Amy thought, he was the best of the bunch. If only she had married someone like him, her life would have been so different, but of course he had never thought of her in that way. Suddenly she felt curious. 'I suppose you've had lots of girlfriends?' she said, realising afresh how good-looking he was.

'A few. A couple could have been serious but things never quite worked out. Perhaps I'm too picky.' He grinned again and she smiled back. Silly girls to let him get away, she thought, looking at him with new eyes.

The door to the main room opened and brought with it a gust of noise. Above the laughter and voices within, Nick called from the doorway, 'The women are whipping us in there, Bruce. Come on, we need reinforcements.' But his eyes were on Amy.

'In a minute. Get me another beer in if you want to be useful.' Bruce turned back to Amy as he spoke but she continued to look at Nick as the door closed. In response to her expression, he said, 'He doesn't mean anything, it's just his way.'

'He thinks he's God's gift to womankind.' Her voice was low but caustic.

Bruce stared at her for a moment. 'Like I said, it's just his way, he doesn't mean anything,' he said uncomfortably. 'Sometimes I think it's a defence for the way they throw themselves at him, and they do, you know. Shameless, some of them are. We rib him about it but secretly most of the blokes would give their right arm to be in his boots.'

Amy's voice was sharp when she said, 'Huh! Well, here's

one who wouldn't lower herself, and I dare say there are others, whatever he likes to think.'

'He's my friend, Amy.' His tone was reproachful. 'And he has been through the mill. It changes a bloke. Most of the pals he joined up with have long since copped it and he knows his luck can't last for ever. His two brothers were killed in the Battle of Britain and they were younger than him. How do you think that makes him feel?'

The door opened again and saved her having to reply. As two young WAAFs eyed Bruce on their way to the ladies' lavatory, Amy said, 'You go back in. I've got a headache and I could do with an early night.' Suddenly she felt all at odds with herself. But not with Bruce, never with Bruce. She held out her hand. 'Friends for fairs?'

He smiled, squeezing her fingers. 'Friends for fairs. Do you want me to walk you back to your hut?'

She shook her head. This funny feeling was all tied up with him; for the first time in her life she was seeing him as a man rather than her dear old Bruce and it was disconcerting. Forcing a teasing note into her voice, she said, 'You go back and help the great Nick Johnson. And I'm sorry I criticised him but I think he's very lucky to have you for a friend, if you want to know. I'm on duty in the men's mess tomorrow so no doubt I'll see you then. 'Night, Bruce.'

''Night, Amy.'

The WAAFs exited the ladies' as Amy walked off, the cheekiest saying brightly, 'Left you already, has she?'

'Looks like it.' Bruce grinned. 'But there's plenty more fish in the sea. Isn't that what they say?'

'Ooh, hark at him, and me with the surname of Kipper an' all!'

Chapter 18

Nick Johnson watched Bruce enter the room with the two WAAFs and all three were smiling broadly. His eyes went beyond them but when the door remained shut, the green gaze returned to Bruce who eventually reached the table. After a spot of banter with one or two of the other airmen, Bruce sat down beside him.

'How are we doing?' Bruce asked without any enthusiasm.

'Miserably,' Nick answered in the same tone, pushing a glass of beer towards Bruce and taking a pull at his own glass. Most of the airmen on their table were calling asides to the WAAFs sitting opposite, and under cover of the general chatter, he said, 'Where's your cousin run off to?'

'She's got a headache.'

'A headache?' Nick grinned, keeping his tone light as he asked the question he'd wanted to ask all evening. 'Isn't that more of a girlfriend's excuse? Sure you two aren't kissing cousins?'

Bruce looked him straight in the face. 'We were brought

up as brother and sister. Amy lost her parents early on and mine took her in. OK?'

'Fine, fine, don't take offence. I just wondered, that's all. She's a stunning-looking woman.'

'Yes, she is, but for the record she's not like plenty I could name. She's not into this "Eat, drink and be merry for tomorrow we die" frame of mind, Nick. You understand what I mean?'

Nick looked into his friend's tense face for a moment and then nodded slowly, and now there was no laughter in his voice when he said, 'I think so. You're warning me off, right?'

'I'm just saying she doesn't play around, it's not in her nature and if anyone, *anyone* spun her a line they'd have me to answer to.'

Nick shook his head slowly. 'Look, mate, I hate to mention it but your little lamb has landed smack in a den of wolves, and she's been noticed. Take it from me. And she's not a schoolgirl, Bruce. You've got to let her grow up sometime.'

'She is grown up.'

Something in Bruce's voice caused the green eyes to narrow. 'Meaning?'

'Meaning nothing.' Bruce swallowed half the glass of beer and wiped his mouth with the back of his hand. 'Don't get me wrong, Nick, Amy can take care of herself.'

'I don't doubt it.' Nick's voice was wry. 'I just wondered if you knew it. Believe me, she's all ice when she wants to be.'

'She hasn't fallen for the Johnson legendary charm then?'

'Not so you'd notice.'

'Shame.' Bruce's smile widened and then he ducked as Nick aimed a playful punch at his chin.

The two men didn't mention Amy again for the rest of the evening but she was on both their minds.

Amy wrote to Kitty the very next evening. She had spoken to Bruce again in the mess but briefly; he had been subdued and she knew why. Following the new tactic against the enemy which had been inaugurated at the beginning of the year, a number of their fighter pilots had escorted a Blenheim bomber unit over the Channel that morning. The simple aim was to force German fighters into the air in circumstances ostensibly favourable to the RAF, but although the theory was good, everyone on the station knew the practice was far from perfect. Until the boys were back safely, the camp was on edge and no amount of forced cheerfulness could hide it.

At the quiz the night before, Cassie had made a date with one of the young pilots she'd had her eye on for ages and she grew increasingly tense as the hours went by. At one point she seasoned the mutton stew with sugar instead of salt, but no one complained and it got eaten just the same. It was a great relief late in the afternoon when word came that every plane had returned to the airfield and there were no casualties.

Much to her annoyance, Amy had found herself thinking of Nick as she had gone about her work. It was only because he had irritated her so thoroughly, of course, that and the fact that her blood had run cold when Bruce had said Nick's luck couldn't last for ever. She wished he hadn't said that. If he'd been trying to make her feel bad, he had succeeded. Whatever she thought of Nick Johnson, she wouldn't wish for him to be hurt – she wouldn't wish for any of their lads to be hurt, she qualified firmly. And then she brought her mind back to the matter in hand and stared down at the paper in front of her. She'd already written to Winnie and Nell and Pamela; those letters had been easy. Kitty's wasn't.

'Dear Kitty, You're probably surprised to hear from me after all this time,' she read for the umpteenth time. She had got no further than that and the way she was going she never would.

She sighed, and then a little voice from the bed on her left reminded her she wasn't alone. 'Difficult letter?' Gertie asked tentatively.

All the other girls had either gone to the Black Swan, the cosy old pub where most of the airmen and airwomen socialised other than the NAAFI and where Cassie was meeting her pilot, or were rehearsing for the production the theatre company was putting on. Isobel and another WAAF were on forty-eight-hour leave.

'Sort of.' Amy tried not to show any impatience. Gertie was a good few years younger than herself and wasn't the type of person who ever wanted to be alone, but sometimes Amy longed for a little time to herself. It was hard to come by with so many women sharing the hut and all the duties of the station. She looked at Gertie now, saying, 'I thought you were going to write a couple of letters?' That was the excuse Gertie had made not to join the others when they had asked her.

Gertie shrugged and put down the book she had been reading. 'There's no one I want to write to.'

'What about your mother? Didn't she write to you the other day? She'll be expecting an answer soon.' To Amy's knowledge Gertie hadn't written home once during training camp or since they had been at Norwich. 'No doubt she's missing you,' she added encouragingly, though she wondered if this really was the case. There was something funny about Gertie's home, she was sure of it.

Gertie shrugged again, looking at her so strangely Amy didn't know whether to lower her head to her letter or go over and put her arm round the other girl. In the event she did neither, saying instead, 'Do you want to see a picture of my mam? She died when I was just a baby.'

'Did she?' Gertie slid off her bed and onto Amy's, perching at her side as Amy reached into the drawer of her locker and brought out the precious little portrait.

'Oh, she's lovely, Amy. Beautiful. And she looks ever so like you. What about your father? Did he bring you up by himself or did you have any brothers and sisters to help?'

'My father had already been killed in the First World War and I was an only child. An uncle took me in, Bruce's da. You know my cousin here? His da. So Bruce and I are like sister and brother. I didn't get on so well with the rest of my cousins though, or my aunt. She . . . she didn't like me.'

She didn't know why she was telling Gertie all this; she rarely spoke of personal matters.

Gertie said nothing, continuing to stare at the picture in her hand for so long that Amy assumed the conversation was at an end. Then Gertie said in a very low voice, 'My mother doesn't like me. Oh, she pretends she does, she's always going on about how nice it was to have a girl after five boys, but she doesn't, not really. Was your aunt like that?'

Amy stared at Gertie's bent head. The pain in her young friend's voice was upsetting. 'My aunt made it very plain to everyone she didn't like me,' she said quietly.

'That's better than pretending.'

'Gertie, I'm sure your mam does love you. It's just that some people have a job expressing their feelings.' She didn't know what else to say.

'She doesn't.' Gertie's head was still bowed. 'Oh, she loves my brothers, she can't do enough for them, but I've always known she doesn't like me. If ever my father or one of my brothers made a fuss of me she'd go all cold and huffy, and ten to one when we were alone she'd make some excuse to go for me. It got so it was better for me to try and stay out of their way because I got fed up with being knocked about. It's like she's jealous of me, of having another female in the house, but I can't help being a girl, can I?'

'Of course not.' Amy took Gertie's hand. 'What about your da? Can't he tell her to leave you alone?'

'She never does anything in front of him or the others. And once when I tried to tell him she changed it all round and made out I was lying and said all sorts of things. There was a terrible row and my dad said he was bitterly disappointed in me. I've never forgotten it. He . . . he said why couldn't I be more like the boys were with my mother? Why did I have to upset her all the time and be so awkward?' Gertie was crying now. 'And it's got much worse lately since I left school.'

Well, if Gertie was right and her mother was jealous of her, she could understand that, Amy thought, because Gertie was showing signs of developing into a very pretty young woman.

'So I joined up. I just went and did it and left a note. I knew my mother would persuade my dad not to do anything, she'd be too glad to get rid of me,' she added pathetically. 'It was my chance to escape everything, if you know what I mean.'

Amy nodded. 'I know what you mean,' she said quietly, giving Gertie a hug. 'I know all about escaping.'

'I thought so. I sort of felt there was something.'

Suddenly it was easy to begin talking. She told Gertie all of it, not leaving out a thing. It was the first time she had spoken of the death of her baby and the operation that had robbed her of ever being a mother, and she couldn't say she felt better afterwards. In fact she felt so worked up she didn't know how she felt. But Gertie cried for her and they hugged some more before Amy made them each a mug of cocoa and some toast. After this Gertie got undressed and climbed into her bed, falling asleep as soon as her head touched the pillow.

Amy picked up her pen. The words to Kitty flowed quite easily now. She asked Kitty's forgiveness for not writing before and said if Kitty wanted to write back she would love to hear from her. She mentioned she'd seen Bruce and asked her not to say anything to Perce.

Once it was finished, Amy breathed a sigh of relief. By the time the other girls began to dribble back to the hut, she was fast asleep in bed, curled up like a small animal under the blankets with her hot water bottle clutched to her stomach.

The next few weeks were hectic, but despite the often gloomy news bulletins and busy work day, Amy was conscious of feeling more at peace with herself than she had in a long time. She didn't understand why, and perhaps it didn't matter, but in facing up to what had happened by voicing it to

Gertie, something had settled deep inside. Her child would always be part of her, a secret sorrow held close to her heart, and she knew his loss and the certainty that no other babies would follow would always evoke a depth of emotion nothing else could, but she had to live with that. She couldn't do anything else if she wanted to make something of her future.

Since they'd had their heart-to-heart, Gertie seemed happier too. A side of her friend was emerging that showed Gertie to be bright and witty when she was with people she could relax with, and there were times when she positively sparkled. Bruce seemed to have taken Gertie under his wing a bit, Amy had noticed, and Gertie had certainly gained confidence from this and was no longer a shy wallflower at the NAAFI dances. Amy was glad for her, and it also meant she didn't feel wholly responsible for Gertie any more.

Cassie and her pilot were getting on like a house on fire which made for happy working relations; she walked about with a big grin on her face all day despite the constant ribbing she got from the RAF cooks. When she and Amy and sometimes June, another WAAF cook, took the sandwiches they prepared to the aircrews, along with their rations of chocolate, fruit and other items, Cassie always managed to grab a few moments with her pilot if he wasn't in the air. The three girls would sit for a few minutes on the grass watching the planes being overhauled and inevitably Cassie's man would stroll over, sometimes accompanied by other pilots. Amy didn't mind as long as they didn't include Nick. She saw him in the mess often, sometimes with Bruce or other friends, and again in the NAAFI in the evening, and it always disturbed her. Bruce was his normal friendly self, chatting with Gertie as much as her and pulling the younger girl's leg and teasing her, but Nick was more serious, often just sitting and staring at Amy with unfathomable green eyes. It was unnerving. Amy almost thought she preferred the womanising Casanova approach of the early days. And she still felt faintly unsettled about Bruce. Try as she might, she couldn't see him in the old way any more.

Kitty had written back a warm letter that made Amy glad she had contacted her. Nell and Pamela wrote too; it appeared Nell was training to be a fabric worker on a balloon squadron and Pamela was doing something so top secret she couldn't say what it was. Isobel married her Philip the first week of May, just as the weather changed and nightingales began to sing in the trees around the camp, and suddenly before they knew it the warm sunshine they'd all been longing for had arrived. This had less impact on Amy than most of the others because she was worried sick about Winnie.

The second week of May had seen a night raid on the capital that even Londoners, hardened by the horrors of nine months of the Blitz, were shaken by. In brilliant moonlight German planes had indiscriminately dropped hundreds of high-explosive bombs and incendiaries over the city, the Nazi High Command describing the ferocious attack as 'a reprisal for the methodical bombing of the residential quarters of German towns, including Berlin'.

The NAAFI had been silent when the newscaster had reported that historic London had been shattered and civilian casualties were high, and immediately Amy had written to Winnie, asking her friend to let her know she was safe. That had been on the morning of the eleventh of May. It was now the last day of the month and Amy had just received the news she had been dreading.

She stared down at the piece of paper in her hands, unable to believe she would never see Winnie's plump, bright-eyed face again. One of Winnie's sons had written informing Amy of his mother's death.

'Bad news?' Isobel noticed Amy's stricken face. Isobel's own eyes were pink-rimmed; her brother had been on HMS *Hood* which had been sunk by the *Bismarck* a week before, and he hadn't been among the handful of crew who had survived. The newspapers might have gloated that it was sweet revenge when the Royal Navy sank the German battleship three days later, but it hadn't comforted Isobel much.

'It's Winnie.' As Amy spoke, Gertie and a number of other girls who were nearby gathered round, sensing another tragedy in their midst. There had been far too many lately. 'She's gone.' She brushed back a wisp of hair from her brow, her hand shaking. 'The café, everything's gone.' All Winnie had laboured and sweated and strived for. The Germans had destroyed it all and taken her too. Her dear old Winnie. Their plans for the expansion of the business after the war and Winnie becoming more of a sleeping partner so she could spend time with her grandchidren wouldn't happen now, and Winnie had been so looking forward to it.

Amy went about her duties on automatic in the kitchens, and her state of mind wasn't helped when the camp grapevine reported A Flight had left at first light to join other squadrons in a mass fighter sweep escorting Stirlings to knock the hell out of the shipping in Brest.

Cassie's pilot, along with Nick Johnson, was in A Flight, and as was usually the case when there was no chance of seeing him hanging about the airfield, Cassie wasn't too enthusiastic about taking sandwiches to the airmen and airwomen manning their various posts there. June was in the sick bay with stomach cramps so Amy agreed to accompany the RAF driver, a cheery soul with a face as brown as tanned leather.

There were Spitfires dispersed around the airfield when they drove onto the fifty-foot-wide perimeter track, and as Amy's eyes took in their beautiful lines she remembered a recent conversation she'd heard in the NAAFI. Nick and an ex-Hurricane pilot had been arguing about the monoplanes' different attributes. She had been sitting with Bruce and Gertie and a couple of other airmen and had pretended not to listen, but out of the corner of her eye she had watched Nick's face as he'd spoken with passion about his machine.

'The Spitfire has all the speed and grace of a greyhound,' he insisted when the other pilot declared the Hurricane was more solidly built and reliable, 'and that's what you want when Jerry's on your tail, not a bulldog. She'll get you out of trouble and poke Jerry in the eye while she's doing it.'

She hoped his Spitfire was getting him out of trouble now. The thought popped into her head from nowhere and as though she had voiced it out loud she blushed, hastily jumping out of the van when it stopped outside the squadron commander's office. The ankle-deep grass in front of the buildings was bespeckled with myriads of tiny daisies and yellow buttercups, and in the distance she saw some members of B Flight stretched out on the warm green carpet with Monty, a springer spaniel who belonged to one of the flight lieutenants.

The airmen's yellow Mae West life-saving jackets shone brightly in the hot sunshine, and far in the distance the sound of a farm tractor added to the lazy scene. But the presence of the life-saving jackets meant the pilots were on a state of readiness and had to remain within a few yards of their machines.

Amy stood looking over at the somnolent group for a few moments before she opened the back of the van for the crate of food. One moment those young men could be lying dozing on the grass in the soft summer air, the birds twittering in the trees surrounding the airfield and bees buzzing in and out of the flowering white clover, the next they were called to action and all that that entailed. No wonder they played as hard as they fought. This made her think of Nick again and she felt a stab of self-reproach at her treatment of the tall, handsome pilot officer. She shrugged it away and got on with the job in hand.

She was on her way back to the van after dishing out all the food when Monty gave one sharp, piercing bark. The dog was well known for his ability to hear the sound of an approaching air engine well before his human friends did and could often be seen, according to Bruce, tail wagging and tongue lolling, scampering to greet his master on his return from an operation. But now the dog was rigid, tail straight out behind him and nose pointing upwards.

Amy turned, shading her eyes with her hand as she looked up into the blue sky, trying to see what Monty had heard. She hadn't expected A Flight to return so soon. It was the shouting from the airmen and then the sound of the warning siren that made her realise the dog had been trying to warn them that the approaching plane was not one of theirs.

She stood rooted to the spot right out in the open, distantly conscious of the pilots running to their planes, the dog barking, the RAF driver calling for her to get into the van and the siren going on and on. And then it was upon them, a lone raider zooming out of the blue, machine guns firing and passing by so close she could see the markings on the aircraft and the German pilot in the cockpit.

Clods of grass flew into the air as the bullets tore into the ground, and then the buildings were spattered as the aircraft made for its prime target, the stationary Spitfires. Quite what happened then wasn't clear to Amy, but instead of the aircraft swooping up into the sky it seemed to nose-dive straight into the ground almost on the perimeter of the airfield. There was an almighty crash; smoke and sheets of flame leaped into the air and enveloped the plane completely. Even from where she was standing she could feel the heat, and she watched as airfield personnel appeared from every direction and ran towards the blaze, the camp's rescue vehicles following.

It was obvious the heat was too great to get anywhere near the burning plane and that the pilot hadn't stood a chance, but it wasn't this that had brought Amy's heart into her mouth. It was the knowledge that the scene which had just unfolded in front of her could be happening elsewhere to *their* pilots, to Nick. It made her blood run cold.

And then Bruce was running towards her, shouting, 'Are you all right? Have you been hit?' and it jolted her out of her frozen state.

'I'm fine.' As he reached her she forced a shaky smile.

He took her into his arms, his voice rueful above her head as he said, 'Trust you to be in the thick of it,' but she could tell he had been shaken up by her near miss. She rested against him for a moment, the unsettling feeling coming over her again. He was so constant, so reliable, so good. There would be no hidden secrets with Bruce, no surprises. Life would be calm, peaceful. One halcyon day following another.

'There's no chance for the pilot, I presume,' she said.

'None, but don't feel too sorry for him. He missed you by inches.'

They both looked at the chewed-up grass at the side of her. 'I wasn't feeling sorry for him,' she said truthfully. 'Seeing it happen brought home how our pilots are facing the same sort of thing, I suppose.' She brushed a trembling hand across her face. It had all been so shocking.

Bruce nodded, taking her arm and beginning to lead her towards the van. 'The lucky ones get blown into eternity,' he said grimly. 'It's the poor blighters who end up maimed, burned or blinded that have it rough. You sure you don't want to come and have a cup of tea or something before you go back?' he added.

She opened her mouth to reply but the words never got voiced. Instead she came to an abrupt halt, her hand going over her mouth as she took in the bullet holes in the windscreen and the slumped man lying over the steering wheel.

She heard Bruce swear before he said, 'Stay here. Don't move.' As she watched him climb into the vehicle and check the inert figure she knew the driver was dead. When Bruce shook his head at her and jumped down from the van, she found she had to sit down on the grass.

'He called for me to get into the van,' she said faintly. 'If I could have moved, I would have.'

'But you didn't.' His voice was soft.

'No, I didn't. He has a wife and four bairns.' She stared up at him. 'His wife's due to have the fifth in two weeks' time. He was going home on leave the day before she was due. Regular as clockwork, he said she was, in having the babies. Never a day before or a day after the due date.'

The smell of the burning aircraft was acrid and Bruce's voice was even softer when he said, 'Come and have a cup of tea while I see about getting you back.' He pulled her to her feet, keeping a supporting arm round her waist as they walked away.

'I'm sorry for being such a weakling,' she said shakily.

'Don't be so daft. You're the last person that term applies to.'

She wasn't so sure about that. She glanced round to look at the van again. When Nick came back – she wouldn't allow herself to consider if – she wouldn't give him the cold shoulder any more. He probably hadn't cared one way or the other apart from feeling a little peeved, but nevertheless she would be the same with him as she was with everyone else. She didn't know why she had allowed him to catch her on the raw in the first place if she came to think about it, and she had been silly to keep up the antagonism. If nothing else, it gave him the impression she was bothered by him in some way, and of course she wasn't.

Incendiaries were exploding on the German plane now and she could hear Monty's excited barking as he ran hither and thither in the throng standing at a safe distance. It really was an inferno.

She drew in a deep breath in order to calm the racing of her heart. No one was black or white but made up of all shades of grey, and from what she'd seen of Nick over the last weeks he wasn't quite the Romeo she'd taken him for. She'd got things out of proportion, but as Winnie would say, pride makes a sparse meal, and perhaps it was time to eat a slice of humble pie. *Winnie.* Oh, Winnie, Winnie, Winnie.

She felt better once she had had a cup of tea. Bruce sat with her, talking about everything under the sun, and she knew he was doing it to take her mind off things.

It was as they were walking towards the lorry which was going to take her back to camp that Bruce said, 'I've been wanting to see you on the quiet, Amy. It's about Gertie.'

'Gertie?' She looked at him in surprise and he flushed slightly.

'Aye. We get on well, very well. She's a nice lass. I just wondered if she talks about me at all. You know.'

Amy was poleaxed. *Bruce and Gertie?* But why not Bruce and Gertie? she asked herself in the next moment. She stared at him, feeling as though she had had the ground taken from under her feet. 'Aye, yes, she does,' she said in the next moment, several little things Gertie had mentioned lately suddenly falling into place. She hadn't realised her friend liked Bruce in that way but now it was as if her eyes had been opened.

Bruce nodded. 'I just wondered,' he said, obviously trying to be casual. 'I wouldn't want to spoil a beautiful friendship by putting my foot in it and embarrassing her if she didn't feel the same way.'

'I think she likes you, Bruce,' said Amy, 'but you would have to ask her to be sure.'

He nodded. 'I intend to do that anyway but I guess I just wanted to see if I was on the right track. She's still quite young, after all.' Gertie had confided in him she was only seventeen.

'In some ways.' But in others Gertie's harsh treatment by her mother had made her grow up very quickly indeed.

They had reached the lorry now and as Bruce helped her

up into the seat beside the driver, Amy smiled down at him and said goodbye.

They would be perfect together, Bruce and Gertie, she thought as the lorry trundled its way back to the camp. And suddenly she found she was pleased for them. She hoped Gertie responded as Bruce wanted her to but that was between them. Whatever, something had been settled in her as Bruce had talked. Bruce wasn't for her and she wasn't for him, it had been madness to even consider such a notion. He was and would always be a big brother to her and that's the way it should be.

Chapter 19

When Nick walked into the NAAFI just after eight o'clock he admitted to feeling tired, bone tired. If it hadn't been for the attack on the airfield earlier that day he doubted he'd have made the effort to turn out tonight, but after Bruce had told him Amy had had a near escape, he needed to see her. Stupid. He acknowledged the self-admonition grimly. More than stupid, because she had made it clear by word and action a hundred times or more that she didn't give a damn about him. Unfortunately that didn't seem to make the slightest bit of difference to what more than one woman had told him they were sure he didn't possess – his heart.

He stood just inside the doorway and scanned the room. It was full of airmen and WAAFs and the atmosphere was almost partyish. Everyone had returned to base safe and sound although a couple of the Spitfires were shot up. A casual observer might be forgiven for thinking they'd all forgotten about the driver who'd been killed that day, but Nick knew he would have been toasted by more than one glass. It was part of the fight against Hitler that everyone kept their spirits up. He noticed Bruce and Gertie standing together but Amy wasn't with them. Damn it, perhaps she wasn't coming tonight.

Irritation rose hot and strong but his expression remained relaxed and easy; he rarely showed his feelings, he considered it a weakness. He saw Bruce raise his hand and answered in like before making his way to the two girls serving behind the counter who met him with wide smiles. He'd have a beer and then disappear; he'd had enough for one day and making conversation wasn't high on his agenda.

He took a long pull at the beer before turning from the counter and walking across the room again. He would drink the rest outside; it was a warm balmy night and after the hours in the cramped cockpit, the need to be out in the open was strong.

The air was still heavy with the scent of white clover and he walked a few yards and sat down on sun-warmed grass. He stretched out, his glass of beer beside him, and as always happened after a recent action, details which had passed unnoticed at the time came into clear focus. It had been a tumbling tangle of individual duels and jinking tail chases that day, every pilot dependent on his own skill and determination. Fighter versus fighter combat was always swift and savage, necessitating constant vigilance and instinctive reactions but today had been particularly hard. Or perhaps he was getting stale.

He put his hands behind his head and stared up into the sky, hazy with approaching twilight. If he was getting stale he'd better snap out of it damn quick or his next operation could be his last. Certainly on the flight home today, as his eyes watched the fuel gauge and he checked for damage, it had taken him a time to wind down. He had been conscious of rivulets of sweat soaking his shirt and running down his chest and arms but he'd felt detached somehow, tense and edgy. For the last couple of years it had been enough that he was still alive at the end of an action, that his will to conquer and survive had won through again, but lately it had been different and he didn't know why.

Who was he kidding? His eyes narrowed in self-deprecation. He knew exactly what was wrong with him.

He sat up and finished his beer in several swallows, staring into the distance. It was peaceful out here, he couldn't hear anything from the NAAFI and the quiet English evening was utterly divorced from the life-and-death struggle he'd just survived yet again. He had actually seen the face of that German pilot he'd shot down today and he'd barely looked old enough to wipe his own backside. The memory of the aircraft shrouded in flame and trailing a thick plume of smoke as it had turned in its death throes tightened his mouth, but he felt no real pity. It had been the enemy or him and that was the end of it.

'Nick? What are you doing out here all by yourself?'

He hadn't heard Amy approach and for a moment he just stared at her stupidly. Then he pulled himself together. He rose to his feet and smiled as he said, 'I could ask the same of you.'

'Me? Oh, I've just taken one of the girls back to our hut, she was feeling poorly. The others are all in there. Shall we join them?'

She was different. He stared at her, feeling he only had to say one wrong word and the old prickly Amy would be back.

Whether she read his mind he didn't know, but after a moment's silence, she gave a little grimace. 'Actually I was hoping I might see you by yourself.'

'You were?' He was probably dreaming this. Either that or she was setting him up for a monumental putdown.

'Aye, yes.'

The warm northern accent was part of her and always had the power to stir him. He wasn't smiling now but waiting quietly, eyebrows raised in silent enquiry.

'I . . . I haven't been very nice to you, I know that, and I wanted to say . . . well, sorry.'

'It's all right.' For crying out loud, he could do better than this, couldn't he? He tried to think of a casual throwaway line, something to bring a smile to her face and ease the embarrassment that was almost tangible between them, but his mind seemed to have gone blank. For once Nick Johnson of the glib tongue had nothing to say and wouldn't his pals just love it if they knew, he thought desperately.

'Yes, well, I just wanted you to know.'

She had actually turned away when he said, 'Amy? I heard about what happened today, and Bruce said something about you hearing bad news from home too. You must be feeling pretty shaken up.'

She nodded. 'It hasn't been the best of days but compared to what you and the others deal with all the time—'

'No, don't say that.' He cut her off abruptly. 'It doesn't make it any the less painful for you.'

Her eyes were unblinking as she looked at him and it seemed a long time before she said, 'I suppose not.'

'Look, do you want to go back in there?' And then in case she got the wrong idea he added quickly, 'I thought we could talk out here a bit, just talk. It's peaceful.' Peaceful! She was looking at him strangely, she probably thought he was stark staring mad or trying to make a pass at her. 'Of course if you want to go in, if they're waiting for you . . .' He was making a pig's ear of this.

'Yes. No. I mean . . .'

He watched her take a breath as his stomach turned right over. Why on earth had he said that? Why hadn't he simply escorted her inside? That way he would have at least got to sit with her for a while.

'No, I'm in no rush to go in but yes, they are expecting me. If you want to wait a minute I'll go and let them know I'm going for a walk. If you want to walk, that is?'

Walk? He wanted to run and shout and dance and sing. He smiled. 'Yes, I want to walk.'

When she came back out of the building she was a little flushed and he wondered what had been said inside. Should he have gone with her? He hadn't thought she'd wanted him to.

As she made her way towards him, she said, 'It's a lovely evening, isn't it? The war seems far away.'

'An eternity.'

'Evening is my favourite time of day, especially summer ones. Most folk like the morning best, a new day and all that, but I love the twilight and hearing the birds get ready for bed.'

He laughed out loud as she reached his side and they began to walk. 'You make it sound like they brush their teeth and have a bath.'

'Oh, they do. Well, not brush their teeth, of course, but haven't you noticed how often birds bathe and spruce themselves up? Winnie, my friend, always said they could teach some humans a thing or two about cleanliness.'

He knew from the way her voice had changed that this must be the woman Bruce had spoken of. 'I'm sorry about your friend,' he said softly. 'Do you want to talk about it?'

'I don't think I can.' Her voice wobbled a little and she kept her head down.

He had an overpowering urge to take her into his arms and comfort her. Not make love to her, not even kiss her, just comfort her. But she'd made it plain on a number of occasions she considered him the camp Don Juan, and he couldn't deny he'd sown his fair share of wild oats here. She would likely tell him it was the oldest line in the book if he said she was different, but it would be the truth. He thrust his hands deeper into his pockets. 'The shrinks would say it's best to talk but personally I can't say I agree with them. Not for some people anyway. I lost two brothers in the Battle of Britain and I had to deal with that by myself.'

'Were you close?'

He did not immediately reply; his eyes narrowed and he flexed his shoulders before he said, 'They were younger than me by four and six years, but yes, we were close. Being the older brother I suppose you could say they hero-worshipped me to some extent, and because I was in the RAF when the war started they wanted to be fighter pilots too. Spitfires, of course.' He gave a kind of twisted smile that wasn't a smile at all. 'I used to play the big man when I went home, you see, strut about in my uniform and all that.'

His voice was bitter and Amy blinked. She didn't know what to say. This was a side of him which was new to her.

'John was killed in the first week of the Battle of Britain.

He was twenty-four years old. David bought it when his air station, Biggin Hill, was razed to the ground. The courier despatched from Kenley to re-establish communication described the place as a slaughterhouse. Some big brother, eh?'

Amy stopped dead so he was forced to turn and face her. 'You don't blame yourself, do you?'

His face was grim as, staring back at her, he said, 'They wouldn't have gone in the RAF but for me.'

'But you can't say that, Nick.' And then she flapped her hand. 'Oh, I'm sorry, I'm being presumptuous, but if you wanted to be an airman and you're their brother it's probably in your blood, all three of you. And they sound like young men who would have wanted to do their bit regardless of you. Would they have sat at home twiddling their thumbs while Hitler marched?'

'Of course not.'

'So if it hadn't been the RAF it would have been one of the other services.'

'Amy –' He stopped abruptly. 'Look, I appreciate you're trying to be kind but it's something I've got to live with. OK?'

He felt guilty because he was alive and his brothers were dead. She knew it was a common feeling among men and women who had been involved in violent combat, the 'why was I spared?' self-condemnation, but she couldn't say that now. It would sound too patronising. Instead she nodded, trying to inject a note of lightness into what had become an emotionally loaded moment when she said, 'This probably just bears out your idea that the shrinks have got it wrong, doesn't it? About talking it out, I mean.'

'Probably.' And then he breathed deeply before he said, 'I've messed this up, haven't I.' It was a statement, not a question.

'This?'

'Us going for a walk together.'

She could hardly believe it but the blasé Nick Johnson was red with embarrassment. It was probably an inappropriate moment to acknowledge that she was fiercely attracted to this man and had been fighting the feeling almost from the first time they had met. 'Why do you think that?' she asked carefully. 'I feel privileged that you've talked about your brothers to me.'

The green eyes were rueful. 'Now you're being kind again.'

'No, truthful.' And then she smiled. 'But kind as well. I'll have you know I'm a kind person on the whole.' Was she flirting with him? she asked herself. But then everyone flirted all the time. It didn't mean anything, it was just part and parcel of service life. Besides, Nick was a confirmed ladies' man and the last person to take any banter seriously.

'Does your kindness extend to doing this again?'

'Walking with you? I don't see why not.' She hoped he had taken the hint that that was all he could expect.

'Thank you.' He spoke so seriously she wondered if he was making fun of her for a moment, but when she looked into his eyes she saw he was not. Her eyes moved to focus on his mouth. It was a nice shaped mouth, everything about Nick's face was nice. The word mocked her in its inadequacy.

The shadows were long in the grass now, dying streaks of sunshine making their surroundings almost beautiful. They continued to walk and talk for some time and Nick didn't even try to hold her hand. He told her about his boyhood in Kent and some of the high jinks he and his brothers had got up to, making her laugh, and Amy spoke a little of Bruce and the way it had been with her aunt and Eva. She did not mention Perce at all.

'So that was the reason you left the north and went to stay with your friend in London?' Nick asked. 'To get away from your aunt?'

'Partly.' She did not elaborate and he did not press her.

By the time he slowly walked her back to the airwomen's accommodation, Amy realised the Nick she had seen tonight was worlds away from the charming rogue she'd first met. She had almost been expecting to sense some secret side to him that wasn't very nice, she admitted to herself, but although his personality was more complex than she had first thought, Nick seemed to have no dark hidden side. Suddenly the night air smelled sweeter.

They stopped a short distance from the women's quarters to one side of the guardroom. Amy found herself wondering if he would try to kiss her. Instead he said, 'I've enjoyed tonight more than you will ever know.'

If she had replied truthfully she would have said she felt exactly the same. 'Bad day?' she prevaricated.

'Not particularly.' He grinned. 'But the usual round of snooker in a crowded NAAFI or going into town to get drunk only to avoid vomiting airmen in the squadron bus afterwards didn't appeal.'

'I've heard tales that that's not all you pilots do in town.' Immediately Amy said it she wished she hadn't. It implied she minded for a start, and secondly she didn't want to put him in the position of having to deny it.

If either of these things occurred to Nick he gave no sign

of it. 'Believe me, Amy,' he said very solemnly, 'you haven't lived till you've heard me sing "The Muffin Man" with a tankard full of ale balanced on my head.'

'Surprisingly, that's not high on my agenda for a good night out.'

'Pity. I can bob up and down while singing, if that makes any difference.'

'None,' said Amy, giggling.

'Then how about an olde worlde tea shop I know, run by two old dears who have grandsons in the RAF and therefore look after anyone in Air Force blue extremely well?'

'It's an improvement.'

'But is it a date?' Suddenly he was deadly serious.

There were probably a dozen reasons why she should say no. 'Yes, please,' she said, and then blushed scarlet when his whoop of triumph brought the corporal on duty in the guardroom hurrying out to see what all the fuss was about.

Later on, tucked up in her bed, Amy found herself dissecting the time with Nick bit by bit, sleep a million miles away. She liked him and he liked her, so what was wrong in indulging in a little light romance for a while? she asked herself. Nick knew she wasn't the type of girl to fall into bed with a man at the drop of a hat, she'd made that perfectly plain in the last weeks. She'd had loads of offers of dates from hopeful airmen, all of which she had refused, and Bruce had told her she'd acquired the nickname of the Untouchable among the men. In the nicest possible way, he'd been quick to reassure her when she'd said she didn't know if she liked that or not.

So Nick knew the score if he wanted to take her out now

and again. He knew she wasn't likely to finish the evening with more than a cuddle and a goodnight kiss. If he got fed up with that – and she didn't expect he wouldn't – then everything would just fizzle out. No harm done.

She turned over in bed, causing it to creak in protest. Everyone knew Nick wasn't into romance for the long term and that suited her just fine, but she would love to feel like a woman again, being spoiled, looked after, if only for a little while. There was nothing wrong with that, was there? No. There wasn't.

She turned over onto her stomach again, pulling her pillow over her head to dull the snores wafting about the room and went to sleep.

PART SEVEN

1942 Decisions

Chapter 20

'I don't mind, you know.' Kitty's smile was soft as she reached out and took Ronald's hand across the dirty breakfast dishes. 'I consider myself your wife and I am in everything that matters. What difference would a scrap of paper make to the way we feel?'

'It's not about that.'

'I know, I know, but as far as the folk round these parts are concerned I'm Mrs Shawe.'

'Aye, that's all very well but I want it legal and proper. There's the bairn to consider now, don't forget. I don't want him being born without a right to me name.'

'Ron, after this war there's going to be umpteen bairns who don't even know who their da is, let alone have a right to his name. And who says it's going to be a boy anyway? It might be a little lassie.'

'A lassie's all right with me, pet. As long as you and it are all right, I don't give a monkey's what it is.'

'Now don't start whittling again. I've told you I've never felt better and it's the truth.'

That was as maybe but he could have slapped that stupid midwife round the lugholes when she'd said Kitty was a bit old at forty-four to be having her first bairn. Thought herself the cat's whiskers, that one had, with her Government forms and the rest of it. 'Mrs Shawe is able to claim concentrated orange juice and cod liver oil from the Welfare Clinic, along with priority milk. Please make sure she drinks this all herself.' What had she expected? That he was going to snatch it out of Kitty's hands and guzzle it himself? He was worried sick about his lass and he wouldn't eat or drink until the bairn was born if it would help Kitty.

'Please, Ron.' Kitty squeezed his hand. 'Don't let that silly woman spoil us looking forward to having the bairn. The women in my family drop bairns like a hen laying eggs. I'm not worried.'

'No, you're right, love.' But he couldn't help worrying. And now here was May refusing yet again to consider a divorce and using language about Kitty he would never have thought she knew. And yet according to Bruce, May was as happy as Larry living back at her da's. He threw his wife's letter on the table. 'She's a bitter pill, is May. No wonder Eva and Harriet skedaddled into the Land Army when they got the chance.'

Kitty did not comment on this. If she was to give her true opinion, she thought Ronald's eldest girl in particular took after her mother in every way. Instead she said, pointing to the other letter Ronald had opened, 'Is that Perce's hand-writing? What does he want?'

'Asking if he can stay for a day or two at the end of the month.'

'Oh, Ron, not again. I wouldn't mind if he really wanted

to see you but he doesn't, not a bit of it. I'm sure he snoops about when we're in bed and you know what he's looking for. He's cottoned on we know where Amy is and now her and Charles aren't together he thinks he's in with a chance. What he'd do if he knew she was on the same base as Bruce I don't know. I . . . I don't like to say it because he's your son but he's not right in the head where Amy's concerned.'

Ronald heaved a sigh. He knew she was right. Twice he'd caught Perce looking through the bits of paper and letters and whatnot Kitty kept behind the wooden candlestick on the mantelpiece, and both times Perce had sworn blind he was after a box of matches. He hadn't been able to believe it at first when Bruce had put him in the picture about Perce being after Amy. Perce had never let on, at least not to him. Not that there was anything wrong in it as far as the law was concerned, they were only cousins after all, and perhaps if Perce had been up front about liking the lass he might not have felt it was . . . well, seedy. Aye, that was the word, seedy. Not that Perce would find anything in their house. Kitty made sure she got rid of Amy's letters once they'd read them and Bruce was always careful not to mention his cousin when he wrote.

'He tells me he'll have a side of bacon with him and some other bits and pieces.' He looked at Kitty hopefully. 'We could do with it, lass.'

'All got on the black market as you well know, and before you say I've accepted things from her upstairs knowing her son's on the fiddle, that's different. Mrs Ramshaw doesn't use what she gets us as a wedge in the door.'

'No, all right, lass, all right. I'll say that with the babbie being only a couple of months from coming I don't want you put about. There's barely room to swing a cat as it is.' Not that Perce would buy that. He knew Kitty didn't like him. Mind, with them only having the two rooms and scullery, it was true enough.

'Thanks, Ron.'

'Don't thank me, lass.' He stood up swiftly and pulled her up from the table with him, holding her as tightly as her protruding stomach would allow. 'It's me that should be thanking you every day of my life for taking me on. I know I'm no cop, love. A married man well over fifty and bringing you to two rooms in the worst part of Manchester.'

Kitty put a finger on his lips, her eyes full of love as she said, 'I've loved you all my life, Ron Shawe. I'd have gone to the ends of the earth to be with you. Don't you know that yet? But I never thought you'd look the side I was on.'

'So much time wasted.'

'But we have plenty in front of us, lad. This isn't going to be an only child, you know.' She grinned at him, her eyes sparkling.

Ronald bent his head and kissed her, taking his time about it. And when she snuggled deeper into him, her arms about his waist, he said, 'Remember how Father Fraser used to go on about heaven and hell when we were bairns, Kitty? Frightening us to death about the latter and maintaining we weren't likely to get in the former without his say-so? If he was here right now I'd tell him he could stick his bigoted idea of heaven. Just give me this for eternity and I'll be the most thankful man the Almighty lets through them pearly gates.'

She wriggled and pushed him with one shoulder. 'It's Saint Peter who mans the gates,' she said, 'and you shouldn't talk like that about a priest.'

'Not even that old goat?'

'Ron!'

'All right, all right.'

He was laughing so much she had to laugh with him, even as she said with as much reproach as she could muster for this man she loved with all her heart, 'It's bad luck to speak ill of the dead and him a priest too. And it was awful the way he died, all alone and no one finding him until his housekeeper came back from that week at her sister's. They reckon he must have lingered for days after that stroke, unable to move and lying in his own filth and all.'

'Aye, well, your mam and da took him with a pinch of salt, don't forget, but he all but ruled the roost when I was growing up. And he could have made things easier for our Bess if he'd wanted. Me da wouldn't have dared treat her like he did after Amy was born if he hadn't known he'd got Father Fraser's backing.'

'Well, he's gone now and that's that.'

It was a favourite saying of Kitty's when she wanted to end a conversation and again Ronald laughed, echoing, 'Aye, that's that,' just as the menacing wail of the siren began.

'Oh no, not now, not on a Sunday morning. We've had raids every night this week and now they're coming on a Sunday.'

'Sunday or not, we'd better get to the shelter.'

'Do we have to? It probably won't be anything much and I've got a lovely bit of brisket the butcher let me have which will need doing all morning. I was just going to put it on.'

'It'll wait.' He was already fetching her winter coat and hat. 'Come on, lass, look lively. It's bitter out so wrap up. I don't want you ill in bed with flu.'

After he had helped her on with her coat which strained at the seams when she had buttoned it up, he urged her towards the door. Kitty paused at the threshold, turning to face him and standing on tiptoe to kiss him hard on the lips. 'The last few years have been the happiest of my life,' she said softly, 'and now to have a bairn an' all. It's the icing on the cake.'

'Just shows there's life in the old dog yet.'

'That was never in dispute.'

'Believe me, lass, there was many a time I wondered afore we got together.'

'Well, you needn't have worried.'

As he hurried her out of the door into the hall beyond, the old lady who occupied the top part of the house came down the stairs, her sprightly step belying the fact she was well into her seventies. As the two women went ahead of him to the Anderson shelter which Mrs Ramshaw's son had insisted on digging out and installing for his mother, Ronald thought, She'll never know what she means to me, not really. It wasn't only in the generous giving of her body – it had been a revelation to him that a woman could give and receive such pleasure – but her total adoration of him that had made him feel like a man again. He wanted nothing more than to make her happy for the rest of his life.

They had just reached the Anderson shelter in the back-yard and got themselves settled in when the first dull explosions began, the anti-aircraft guns contributing to what was now a familiar sound.

'I'd just put me shin o' beef on,' Mrs Ramshaw said plaintively to Kitty. 'You put your dinner on yet?' And without waiting for an answer, 'I like to let me shin o' beef do for three or four hours, melts in the mouth then, it does.'

Ronald screwed his buttocks into his wooden chair and glanced at Kitty. She met his eyes and she was smiling. She was so good with Mrs Ramshaw but he had to admit the hours he'd spent in this shelter listening to the old woman rattle on about this and that without pausing for breath were a trial.

Another crunching explosion sounded and it was nearer this time. Good job he'd insisted they come to the shelter, looked like the blighters meant business this morning. 'You warm enough?' he said to Kitty, and although she nodded he was sure her teeth were chattering. It was cold enough to freeze the drips from your nose in here and with it only being the middle of March, there was no chance of it warming up for weeks. But would Mrs Ramshaw let him bring a paraffin stove down? Would she heck. Convinced they'd be burned alive if a bomb landed near enough to shake the shelter. Like he said to Kitty, if one was that close, likely the last thing they'd have to worry about was the damn paraffin stove.

He blew on his hands to warm them up but in the next moment he was on his feet holding Kitty close. The shuddering explosion had made both women scream and now Kitty clung to him, saying, 'That one was close, Ron, really close.'

'That means the worst of it is over. They'll be moving on to—'

He never got to finish the sentence because a thundering

roar took them both off their feet as their world erupted in shattered corrugated iron and dirt. Together they went down, his arms holding her tight and his body over hers and that of their unborn child.

Chapter 21

'Who needs some of this beetroot juice for tonight?'

'Me!' echoed from all corners of the hut and Amy smiled as she placed a jam jar half full of cooked beetroot juice on the table.

'Help yourselves then,' she said, 'and I've got some gravy browning for anyone who hasn't got any stockings.'

'You're an absolute angel,' Isobel enthused as she bounded across to her. 'It's *so* perfect having someone who works in the kitchens as a friend. Not that I don't like you for yourself,' she added hastily, 'but I ran out of lipstick and silk stockings ages ago.'

'Now the Yanks are in the war, folk are saying they'll bring plenty of stuff over,' said a tall blonde girl from the back of the room.

Isobel grimaced. 'My Philip's already laid down the law about the Yanks. He doesn't want me within six foot of one.'

'But they're our allies,' protested the other girl.

Isobel shrugged.

'Well, I haven't got a husband to tell me what to do,' the blonde said happily, 'and I intend to get closer than six foot.'

'Are you and Nick going to the dance?' Gertie asked as the others continued the discussion about the possible benefits of the arrival of the GIs. Over the last few months it had gradually become common knowledge that Amy and Pilot Officer Nick Johnson were seeing each other. No one had pressed Amy for details, not even on domestic nights which came round once a week, when all airwomen were forced to stay in and do domestic chores – something which was bitterly resented because the airmen escaped it. Amy had found she liked these nights, though, as did most of the girls. Secrets were whispered and confidences made and kept, and hut companions became real friends. By the time of the ritual toast and cocoa around ten thirty, everyone always agreed they didn't know why they made such a fuss about staying in anyway.

'Yes, we're going.'

'So are me and Bruce.'

Amy nodded. Bruce had asked Gertie out quite a few times now but he was still taking things very slowly because of the ten-year age difference between them. Amy could understand this, and she knew from the odd thing he'd said that the example of Charles rushing her had contributed to his wariness and that he wanted Gertie to be sure of her own mind, considering he was her first boyfriend. Nevertheless, Amy felt if ever there was a Jack for a Jill, it was those two.

'I don't suppose Cassie will be coming,' Gertie said now.

Amy shook her head. 'She's too cut up.' Cassie had married her pilot in December and lots of the WAAFs had got involved when they'd discovered the bride-to-be had no coupons for a new wedding outfit. Consequently Cassie had walked down the aisle in a beautiful silver-grey suit and a peplum and rose-coloured hat. Her blouse had been cut down from a silk tea-gown, which had also provided a saucy peek-a-boo bow for the hat. Everyone had been thrilled for her, as thrilled as they were horrified when a week ago Cassie's husband had been shot down over France.

'Poor Cassie.' Gertie shook her head. 'I don't know what I'd do if Bruce was a pilot.' And then she clapped her hand over her mouth, her voice rushed when she said, 'Oh, Amy, I'm so sorry, me and my big mouth. That was a stupid thing to say. I didn't mean anything.'

'It's all right.' Amy patted her arm. 'I wish Nick wasn't a pilot myself but then I don't suppose he would be Nick, flying's such a part of him.' She plumped down on her bed, her voice low as she said, 'I feel awful, Gertie, about Nick.'

Gertie sat down beside her. 'You still haven't told him about Charles?'

Amy shook her head.

'Don't you think you should?'

How did she answer that? The truthful reply would be to say she had never expected her relationship with Nick to go the way it had. Far from trying any coaxing or sweet-talk to get her into bed, he had played it absolutely straight down the middle from the word go. They'd had three dates before he had even kissed her goodnight. Since then their – what? friendship? love affair? liaison? – had progressed slowly but surely, though she felt as if Nick was handling her with kid gloves most of the time.

Amy looked into her friend's concerned face. 'I know I

should have told him in the beginning,' she said simply. 'Now I don't know how to.'

'Do you love him, Amy?'

She nodded. 'But I kept expecting he'd get tired of me and so there would be no need to say anything.'

Gertie stared into the lovely face in front of her. 'I don't think he's ever going to get tired of you,' she said.

'But what will he say? It's been months. I've virtually been living a lie, haven't I? And I've put Bruce in a difficult position, him being Nick's friend, and I know he's annoyed with me for not saying anything because he's told me so. It's a mess.'

There was a silence between them now and in the background the other members of the hut were squealing and carrying on as they stained their lips with the beetroot juice. Then Gertie said quietly, 'Tell him you didn't expect to fall for him, start with that.'

Amy blinked, bit on her lip and nodded. 'I'll tell him tonight. I've been thinking how to do it for weeks but I've just got to say it, haven't I?'

'It will be all right.' Now it was Gertie who patted her hand. 'Everyone knows he's crazy about you.'

Amy smiled weakly. Charles had supposedly been crazy about her and look how that had turned out. She was going to inform Nick that she was a married woman who had left her husband because his drunken violence had caused her to miscarry their child. As if that wasn't a big enough shock, she had to explain that the miscarriage had robbed her of having more babies in the future. Nick was a young man. He would want a family of his own one day when all this madness was over.

A light-hearted little romance. That was what she had expected this to be and it had been nice to be wanted again, to know someone was thinking about her at different moments of the day, to know she was just a bit special to him. To Nick. What she hadn't expected was to fall in love. But all that was no excuse for not coming clean about her past before now. It was just that she hadn't wanted him not to like her any more . . .

A big group of airmen and WAAFs were hitching a lift in two of the camp lorries into town that night for a dance the local Baptist church was putting on in its church hall. Bruce and one of the RAF pilots had drawn the short straws to drive the two lorries, which meant they couldn't get as merry as the others intended to do, not if they were going to negotiate the curves and bumps in the road on the way back in the blackout.

Nick was waiting by Bruce's lorry as Amy, Gertie, Isobel and some of the other girls made their way towards the RAF contingent. He looked clean and handsome in his uniform and more dashing than any man had a right to be, Amy thought, her eyes feasting on him as she raised her hand in answer to his wave. She wished they were going somewhere together, just the two of them, as they had the previous Sunday. That had been a wonderful day. They had hired cycles from a local shop and had a lovely time exploring the country lanes in the sharp cold March air. They had finished up at a little farm in the middle of nowhere where the farmer's wife had cooked them a delicious tea of sausages, steak, orange-yolked fresh eggs and fried bread for the princely sum of one shilling and fourpence each, all washed down with as much home-brewed cider as they could drink. Amy had arrived back at camp thoroughly replete and more than a little tiddly, clutching the huge bag of buttered cheese scones the farmer's wife had pressed on her as they were leaving. 'For some of your pals,' she'd said. 'I like to think some Greek wife fed my lad before he was killed. April last year it was, when Athens fell to the Germans. Twenty, my Arnold was, and he could have stayed home and helped his father on the farm but he wanted to be out there doing his bit for King and country.'

'You look sombre.' Nick put his arm round her, kissing her hard on the lips regardless of the others.

When she came up for air, she said, 'I was thinking about last Sunday and that poor farmer's wife. Her only son, Nick.'

He nodded, his expression changing as he added, 'But we're going dancing right now so you're not allowed to think of anything or anyone but me. Right?'

'Right.'

There was a great deal of singing and larking about on the way into town, but as Amy sat with Nick's arm about her shoulders, squeezed tight between him and Isobel, her heart wasn't in 'Boogie-Woogie Bugle Boy' or any of the other popular war songs being sung with such gusto. Would he understand how her deception had come about or would he distrust anything she claimed from now on? And she didn't expect he would want her for ever, not when he knew she couldn't give him children, but with life so uncertain, even tomorrow wasn't guaranteed so for ever seemed a million miles away. Oh, Nick, please don't hate me when I tell you. Her stomach turned over and she was glad of the din that prevented conversation because she couldn't have made small talk to save her life.

They all piled out of the lorries when they reached the car park adjacent to the church hall. Couples were already dancing to 'Tiger Rag' which the band was hammering out with more enthusiasm than expertise when they entered the hall. Down one side of the long room several tables were set with sandwiches and homemade cakes, along with a huge barrel of beer and plenty of bottles of homemade wine, cider, lemonade and other beverages.

Amy would have drawn Nick aside then and there but they were part of a group which included Bruce, Gertie, Isobel and others, and it would have appeared rude. Consequently they all sat down at one of the free tables at the end of the hall near the stage on which the band were playing, and there talk was impossible.

When Nick pulled her up to dance she didn't object, determining after a minute or two she would whisper for them to go outside where it was quieter. After months of procrastination, now she had made the decision to tell Nick everything she found she couldn't wait.

'You seem tense tonight.'

The music had changed just as they'd reached the couples dancing and now 'Blues in the Night' meant she was folded close into him. 'I am.' She smiled as she put her head back and looked up at him. 'I need to talk to you.'

'That sounds ominous.' Nick was smiling too but his green eyes held a questioning, slightly wary expression.

'Can we find somewhere quiet at the end of this number?'

'Why wait? I never want to be with other people if I can be alone with you,' murmured Nick.

Amy smiled at him, and then in the next instant her jaw slackened and her eyes widened in disbelief.

'Amy? What is it?' Nick's face showed his concern. 'What's the matter?'

Perce. What on earth was Perce doing here, at this dance? Had he come to find her? But that was silly, ridiculous, he didn't know she was here. And then as she watched the big heavy figure in a snappy suit make his way over to the table where Bruce was sitting, her heart began to beat in her ears so loudly it drowned out the music and Nick's urgent voice. She saw Perce bend down and say something to Bruce who had begun to rise when he noticed his brother's approach. Then Bruce seemed to fall back in his chair, shaking his head as Gertie, beside him, put her hand on his arm.

Amy wasn't dancing now. She was standing stock-still with Nick amidst the slowly moving couples all around them, and as Bruce searched the dance floor and then met her gaze, she knew. This was bad news. Something had happened. Something terrible, if it had brought Perce to find Bruce.

Their eyes locked and held, and then as Perce turned and looked to see where Bruce was staring, Amy's gaze moved to her elder cousin for one moment. The incredulous expression on Perce's face would have been laughable in any other circumstances.

She tore her gaze from the dark eyes across the room which even now had the power to make her tremble. 'It's Perce,' she muttered. 'Bruce's brother. There must be something wrong at home.'

She didn't look at Perce again as she made her way across the room but she knew he was staring at her the whole time. She could feel it. She reached the table with Nick at her side, his hand on her elbow. Immediately Bruce, his face ashen, said, 'I'm sorry, Amy. It's Kitty and Da.'

'No.' And yet she had sensed it the moment she had seen Perce. Somehow she had known it wasn't any of the others who had brought him to the camp. 'Are . . . are they . . .'

It was Perce who said, 'Their shelter was flattened. Funny thing is, if they'd stayed in the house they would have been all right. The blast only shattered the windows there. Still, better to go outright than be left like some poor blighters I know, that's what I always say.'

He was willing her to look at him. Through her shock and turmoil Amy was aware that although Perce was talking in a soft, suitably sombre voice, it was a façade. He was angry she was here with Bruce, angry she had been dancing with Nick. All the years since she'd seen him last hadn't changed a thing. She forced herself to meet his gaze now, determined he wouldn't see how he frightened her still. 'They died instantly?'

'Oh aye, no doubt about it.' He moistened his thick bottom lip with his tongue. 'I've been looking for you,' he added after an infinitesimal pause.

He was trying to intimidate her like in the old days. As the knowledge hit, she heard Bruce stand up and say, 'Well, you've found her so that's saved you some time, hasn't it?' The harsh tone of his voice was enough to cause Nick's eyes to narrow and everyone to look first at her and then at the two brothers.

'You're on the same camp.' Perce was speaking as much to himself as Bruce. 'Cosy, eh?' he said in a different tone of voice. 'Very cosy. And I suppose Da was in on this.'

'I don't know what you're talking about.' Bruce's voice was more controlled now. 'Amy happened to be posted to the same camp as me a few months ago. End of story.'

'End of story?' Perce turned to face Amy and Nick, his

gaze moving to Nick's arm round her waist. 'Oh, I see, like that, is it? You've had your nose pushed out by one of these flash so-an'-sos. By, she never aims low, does our Amy. Likes 'em from the top of the pile. I saw your husband the other day if you're interested,' he added as his gaze focused on Amy's white face. 'Still drinking himself to death because you ran out on him.'

'Shut your mouth.' Bruce's voice was a growl.

Amy felt Nick's arm fall from her waist. Ignoring the others she said, 'I can explain. Nick, this isn't what it seems.'

'You're *married*?'

Before she could answer him, Perce said, 'Forgot to tell you that little fact, did she? Oh aye, she's married all right. Gave all of us the eye for years before selling herself to the highest bidder. Fancy rich widower, our Amy snared, and then when she got fed up with playing the loving wife she high-tailed it to the lights of London. She—'

Bruce launched himself at his brother. His hands gripped Perce's throat as the two of them overbalanced and sprawled among the couples dancing. Several women screamed and men shouted, a couple of them endeavouring to separate the brothers. They rolled about the floor, Perce aiming blows at Bruce's head in an effort to break the stranglehold.

'This is disgraceful, disgraceful.'

'Never would have seen such things at a church dance before this dreadful war.'

'Of course, there are all types in uniform these days and half of them haven't got the breeding.'

Amy was vaguely aware of the comments from a table to their right where a party of matronly women and their spouses were sitting, but she was staring at Nick, clutching him to stop him walking away from her. 'It isn't like he said, I swear it. You have to listen to me. You must let me explain.'

Nick's eyes were as clear and hard as glass when he said, 'I asked if you were married.'

'No, not really, only on paper. I left him years ago and there were good reasons, believe me.'

'Why should I?'

'What?'

'Why should I believe you now when you've been lying to me for months?'

'I haven't. I never said I wasn't married.' She was doing this all wrong. 'Please, come outside, Nick. I swear I was going to tell you all about my past tonight even before Perce came.'

He allowed her to pull him through the now mostly silent crowd. Perce and Bruce had been dragged apart and when Perce recovered enough to scream insults of the most base kind, more men joined the group holding him and Bruce apart.

The band had stopped playing initially, but now some wit amongst them struck up 'Two Lovely Black Eyes' as Amy and Nick exited the building, a gust of laughter reaching their ears in the moment before the door swung shut.

'How old is he?' Nick turned to face her in the windy darkness, his face granite hard. 'Your widower?'

'How old?' She stared at him in confusion. 'What's that got to do with it?'

'Didn't he die quick enough for you, was that it?'

In contrast to Nick's white face, Amy's was flaming. She stepped back a pace from him. 'Charles isn't old.'

'Charles? Is that his name? Good old aristocratic ring to it, I'll give you that. And so if Charles wasn't on the verge of popping his clogs when you married him, what happened? Didn't he give you free rein with the filthy lucre? Was that it?'

'Stop this.' She felt she was going to be sick.

'And Bruce was in on the joke as well, was he? Well, at least I know where I stand with him. With friends like him, who needs enemies?'

Her face was now as devoid of colour as his but in spite of the terrible things he was saying she found she couldn't defend herself as vehemently as she would have liked. She deserved this, a little voice in the back of her head was saying. She had been the world's biggest fool and she was reaping what she'd sown.

'Do they all know?' Nick swung his hand towards the village hall. 'Your pals? Have they all been tittering while they watched the great Nick Johnson make a blasted fool of himself?'

'Please don't be like this.'

'How do you expect me to be?' His voice sounded level now and very cold. 'Should I make some quip and say it doesn't matter to save my face? Well, it does matter. It matters like hell and right at this moment I want to put my hands round your lying little throat like Bruce did to his brother in there and squeeze until there's no breath left in your body.'

'Do it then.' She didn't flinch. 'But let me explain first.'

He stared at her, his face working, and for a moment she thought he was going to let her have her say but then with a muttered, 'Oh, to hell with you,' he stalked off into the night.

Chapter 22

His mother had always said he was prone to cut off his nose to spite his face, and by golly he'd proved her right last night. As the ground crew strapped Nick into the cockpit of his Spitfire, his mind was replaying the conversation with Amy for the hundredth time. Why hadn't he listened to what she wanted to say instead of walking off? At least that way he would know all the facts instead of being left in this limbo.

The cockpit smell – a mixture of fine mineral oil, high-grade fuel and something indefinable – assailed his nostrils but the normal buzz it gave him was absent. He was too strung up.

He went through the pre-flight routine automatically, then taxied out and turned the aircraft into the wind. After coughing loudly his Spitfire blew a short stream of pearly-white smoke into the air, roared into life and began to skim over the ground. The familiar procedure focused his mind but once airborne and slotted into formation, thoughts of Amy returned.

He had been beginning to regret his handling of the situation which had erupted with such suddenness even before Bruce had had a word with him this morning and told him that there were reasons, terrible reasons, for Amy's actions. He had to listen to her, Bruce had insisted. He'd regret it for the rest of his life if he didn't. And now Bruce was up before the CO for the fight last night and might not be able to tell Amy he'd agreed to talk.

A break in the radio silence alerted him to the fact he needed to jiggle the control column to adjust his position in the formation, and after that he concentrated on the very physical business of flying the aircraft. They were out on a bombing raid against a power station and as they neared the target the sky suddenly became full of German planes, 109s coming from seemingly every direction. On sighting the enemy, his heart began to thump, his nerves tightening and every sense honed to the matter in hand, the crisis of the evening before put on the back burner.

'Don't let's give them any more target practice than necessary, gentlemen.' The squadron leader's voice was dry as it came through the headphones in the helmet, but even as he spoke, Nick saw a Spitfire going down in flames to the left of him. One glance and then he concentrated on the intense flak the formation was coming under. Now the whole sky was filled with dirty brown puffs as the battle heightened, but this didn't faze him. In fact he felt better now the real business of fighting Jerry was under way. Waiting for their appearance was the worst bit. As a Me109 came for him, he went into a steep climbing turn, pushing the throttle forward for maximum boost as he did so. It was a manoeuvre he had done a hundred times in the past but this time he saw sparks on one wingtip and pieces flying off. The aircraft shuddered with the impact of the collision with the German plane, and now as he tried to turn starboard and gain height, the rudder pedals didn't respond and the Spitfire dived earthwards.

Years of training meant he didn't have to think about what to do next. He yanked the canopy release mechanism and the hood whipped away. He baled out, pulling the D ring on his parachute. There was a heart-stopping slight delay before the parachute deployed and then he was floating away from the battle above and into a layer of cloud, below which the enemy-occupied countryside of France stretched.

Amy stared at Bruce. As soon as she had seen him walk into the airmen's mess and look straight to where she was serving heaps of mashed potato and onion, she had feared the worst. He'd searched her out earlier, his face bearing evidence of the fight with Perce and his manner short as he'd told her he had a message from Nick that he wanted to talk to her. Relief had made her knees sag. Now she was ramrod straight as her cousin made his way to the counter.

'It's Nick, isn't it?' she said as he reached her.

'Several of the planes were shot down, his was one of them.' And then as if realising his tone was too abrupt, he added, 'I'm sorry, Amy. One of the pilots thinks he managed to bale out so there is hope he's OK.'

She nodded, continuing to slap dollops of potato on plates. Nick had been shot down. Nick had been shot down. The refrain beat in her head before she said, 'Thank you for letting me know. Will you tell me if there's any news?'

'Of course.'

She watched him walk away and out of the door, his

stiffness telling her he was still angry with her. When he'd come to see her first thing, he had told her that he had explained to Nick that there were extenuating circumstances which had made it hard for her to think about the past, much less talk about it. 'I also told him that my brother has never been all the ticket where you're concerned,' he had added grimly, 'and his version of things is a pack of lies.' He hadn't wanted her thanks when she'd tried to express them, informing her abruptly that the situation they found themselves in had been preventable all along and that he did not appreciate being put in an impossible position with a man whom he counted as a friend.

Amy brushed a wisp of hair from her brow, leaving a trail of mashed potato in its wake. The next moment it was gently wiped away by Cassie who had been privy to the recent exchange. 'Don't worry, Nick'll be all right. I feel it in my bones.' Cassie squeezed her arm reassuringly. 'And Bruce will come round, you know he thinks the world of you.'

Amy tried to smile but it was wobbly. 'Thanks, Cassie, but I've made such a mess of things. I don't know what I'll do if that pilot was wrong and Nick didn't bale out.' Even the thought of him being taken as a prisoner of war was terrifying, but to consider anything else . . .

'You would cope, same as we all do,' Cassie said soberly, before adding, 'But you're a dark horse, I'll give you that. All this time and never letting on you were married.' The news had gone round the camp like wildfire and the general consensus of opinion was that Nick had been treated very badly. If he didn't come back, Cassie felt Amy was going to find life somewhat rough.

'We had separated long before the war started and I didn't

think of myself as married when I joined up.' Even to Amy's own ears it sounded weak, as it had done when she'd said the same thing to Isobel and the others the night before. Only Gertie had been wholly in her corner, staunchly stating that in her opinion folk were far too quick to condemn without knowing the facts.

The rest of the afternoon dragged by and when at six o'clock a message came to say Amy was wanted in the CO's office, she knew what it was about. She was going to be hauled over the coals for lying about her marital status when she joined up and maybe for being instrumental in causing the rumpus at the village hall too. But she didn't care what they said or did to her. Not with Kitty and her uncle gone and Nick maybe captured or worse.

Amy was aware of the CO's secretary's keen glance when she presented herself in the outer office but she kept her face blank. She gave her name and waited while the secretary buzzed through on the intercom. Before Amy knocked on the CO's door and opened it, she took a deep breath, and she was glad of this when she saw who was sitting on the other side of the desk to the CO.

'Hello, Amy.' Charles's voice was quiet and he looked immaculate as he got to his feet with the courtesy which was an integral part of him.

She didn't answer him. She dragged her gaze from the man who had first stirred her girlish passion and looked straight at the CO as she gave her name, standing to attention.

'Your husband,' the CO stressed the second word slightly, 'has requested to see you in private. I have certain duties to attend to and will be back in twenty minutes.'

'Yes, ma'am. Thank you, ma'am.'

The CO nodded grimly and swept out of the room.

'Come and sit down.' Charles gestured at a chair.

She remained standing exactly where she was. 'I don't wish to sit down.'

He wetted his lips and swallowed before saying, 'This will be easier if we can behave in a civil fashion, Amy.'

She supposed it would but she was fighting so many feelings she didn't know which one was uppermost. When she had contemplated seeing Charles Callendar again she'd always imagined she would feel the same hatred that had carried her through the years after the miscarriage, but disturbingly the emotion that seemed to dominate was a kind of amazed pity. No one would believe the man standing in front of her with such haunted eyes was only twelve years older than she was. He looked at least fifty-five and that was being kind.

'Please sit down,' he said again, but when she complied, he didn't sit down himself. He rested both hands on the end of the table and bowed his head. 'Perce came to see me first thing this morning.'

She should have expected he would but her mind had been so focused on Nick she hadn't given Perce a thought. Bruce had mentioned that a couple of the more burly airmen at the dance had frogmarched Perce to the train station and seen him on his way, so she had assumed he had gone back to Sunderland. She hadn't thought further than that.

When she didn't speak, Charles raised his head. 'Sorting through what he said, and I tell you now I didn't believe half of it, I gathered you have a friend here at the station. A man friend.'

She nodded. She felt odd, numb.

'Is . . . is it serious? I mean, are you both—'

'We're in love,' she interrupted sharply. She couldn't stand this, not with Nick missing.

'I see.' He closed his eyes for a moment and then turned and sat down, resting the side of his face in his hand which obscured his expression when he said, 'I had always hoped . . . But of course I understand. I behaved abominably. I did think about trying to find you but . . .'

She stared at his bent head. 'Are you still drinking?' she asked baldly. His lack of reply was all the confirmation she needed — that and his haggard looks. 'Why?'

'Why?' He rose from the chair and walked across the room to the window and stood looking out for a moment or two before he spoke again. 'Because I can't stop.' He swung round and looked at her. 'It's a disease, a drug, worse than any opium den because it creeps up on you so gradually. Everyone has a drink, it's part of social life, after all. We had watered-down wine as soon as our parents considered us old enough to join them at the dinner table.'

'Your brother is not a drunk.'

She meant to shock him with her choice of words but if she did he gave no sign of it when he wearily agreed, 'No, he isn't. But neither is he weak or foolish.'

'You all but ruined my life.'

'I know.'

'And you killed our baby.'

'Amy —' He broke off, moderating his voice when he said, 'Please don't. I . . . I don't expect you to forgive me and I can't forgive myself for what happened that night. It seems monstrously unfair that you've had to bear the consequences of that fall and always will.'

'Yes, it does,' she agreed steadily, her hands twisted tightly in her lap.

'I've never stopped loving you.'

'And I've never stopped loving our son. I never even got to hold him before they took him away.'

'Amy . . .' As he made a move towards her she jumped to her feet, her hands out in front of her, palms facing him.

'Don't, Charles. Look, I can't do this now, not right now.'

'You think I'm some kind of monster.'

'No.' She looked at him sadly. 'Just weak, but that's worse.'

'You want a divorce.'

It was a statement not a question.

'Yes, I do.'

'The business went downhill fast after you left and I sold it before it became a liability. My brother invested the money for me and it's done very well, possibly because I haven't been involved in the decisions,' he added with a touch of bitterness. 'Anyway, what I'm saying is that your half will amount to a considerable—'

'I don't want your money.'

'Don't be silly, you're my wife. You're entitled to—'

Again she cut him off, her face flushed. 'I don't want anything except my freedom. I've managed perfectly well over the last years without your money.'

'Amy, I can never give back what the surgeon took away but at least let me make some reparation. I've been drowning in guilt and shame for years.'

She gulped in her throat. She wanted to hate him. She felt she was letting her baby down by not hating the person who had caused his death, but now, with Charles standing in front of her, a broken man, she couldn't. 'I can't discuss this now,' she said. There was a torrent of tears inside her, but whether they were for her baby or Kitty and Ronald or Nick or even Charles she didn't know.

'No, of course not. I'm sorry about Kitty and your uncle.'

She let him think that was what she had meant and accepted his condolences with a stiff little bob of her head.

'But we have to talk, Amy. You do see that.'

She nodded again.

'When?'

'I've got a forty-eight-hour leave this weekend,' she said tensely. 'I'll come to the house on Saturday. You do still live in Ryhope?'

'Yes, I do. It's my link with you.'

She let that pass. 'But let me make it perfectly clear that I don't want anything from you, Charles. Not a penny.'

'All right.' He thrust his hands deep into his pockets, his face working. 'But just come. Please.'

Charles remained standing exactly where he was for some moments after Amy had left the room, his thoughts in turmoil. He had always known she would be a beautiful woman when fully matured, he told himself, but the last few years had turned her into more than that. There was a presence about her, a dignity, and it was natural. It was so like her to refuse the money. The sight of her had twisted his heart until he'd found it hard to breathe normally. He sat down abruptly.

She hated him. Whatever she said, she hated him. And he deserved it. But to think of her with another man, *loving* another man. He put his hand over his eyes. He was still sitting like that when the CO returned a few minutes later.

Chapter 23

'*Amy!* Hey, wait. I've news!' Bruce leaped out of the van he'd driven far too fast from the airfield just in time to prevent her boarding the bus to the train station on Saturday morning. He ran over to her, careless of the fact that he'd left the van in the middle of the road. 'He's all right, Nick's all right. He landed in an orchard and as luck would have it, the farmer's daughter's in the Resistance and took him straight to a safe house.'

'Oh, Bruce.' They were both oblivious to the bus drawing away. Amy clutched hold of his hands. 'When's he coming home?'

'Can't say. They're talking about getting him out via Spain but that's all I know and even that's hush-hush. Someone did me a big favour by telling me that much.'

Amy nodded, her eyes shining. Still holding tight to his hands, she said, 'I'm sorry I've made things difficult between you and Nick, Bruce. I've been so selfish, I should never have asked you to keep such a thing from him.'

'I don't really understand why you were so adamant he mustn't know. The fact that you were separated from Charles and had no intention of going back to him would have been enough for Nick if you'd told him you were married. He's a man of the world, not some idealistic schoolboy who couldn't have coped with the truth.'

She removed her hands from his and dropped her head. 'That was only part of the truth, though.'

'Part of it?'

'Nick wants children, doesn't he? It's natural, most men do.'

'Yes, I suppose he does. He's said the odd thing about him keeping the Johnson name going now his brothers have gone, that sort of thing, when we've talked about surviving the war. Why?'

'I can't give him babies.' Her voice rose with nerves. 'I can't get pregnant again, ever. When I had the miscarriage something went wrong due to the fall and they had to take everything away.'

Silence followed and when Amy raised her eyes to Bruce's face, she saw he was staring at her with a stunned expression.

'Oh, Amy,' he said softly. 'Amy, pet. So that was why you felt you had to get right away; it wasn't only the miscarriage. Does Charles know?'

She nodded wordlessly.

'I'm so sorry, lass.' He reached out and drew her to him, putting his arms round her as she laid her head against his chest.

'I thought the thing with Nick would fizzle out,' she whispered. 'He's got a reputation for playing the field. I never expected he would want to get serious.'

She didn't know her own worth, she never had, thought Bruce. It was probably all to do with the circumstances of her birth and upbringing, compounded by Charles's treatment after they were married. Right at this moment Bruce wanted to throttle Charles Callendar.

'You thought Nick wouldn't want you any more if he knew it all?' he asked softly.

'Why would he?' she said bleakly. 'He doesn't have to forgo being a father, he could take his pick of women and have children. And I suppose I felt that I couldn't tell him half of it, it was either all or nothing. And so I chose nothing. Which was wrong and unfair. For him, for you. I . . . I was just so happy and I didn't want him to look at me differently, to see me as damaged goods.'

'Stop that talk.' His face was stern as he looked at her. 'I know Nick. That thought wouldn't enter his mind. He loves you and you love him. That's all that's important. He would want to take away your hurt and disappointment, to make up for what you've lost. That's how I feel and I'm just your big brother.'

'But it wouldn't be fair to ask him to give up so much even if he loves me enough to do it.'

'Do you trust him as well as love him, Amy?'

She nodded.

'Then it'll be all right. You have to tell him it all when he gets back.'

She nodded. 'I will tell him. I don't expect anything from him but I'll tell him. And regardless of how things work out with Nick, I intend to set the wheels in motion about the divorce. I should have done it a long time ago but I've buried my head in the sand, I suppose.'

Bruce smiled. 'It's a very pretty head. Now climb in the van and I'll drop you at the train station.'

They talked of Kitty and Ronald on the way to the station, of how happy Ronald had been for the last few years. Amy knew Bruce had thought the world of his da and it was some comfort to him to know he'd died a happy and fulfilled man. Bruce insisted on accompanying Amy into the station, and after she'd shown the stationmaster her free travel warrant he came onto the platform with her. As the train departed she hung out of the window calling, 'Thanks, Bruce. And ask Gertie to be your lass properly. She loves you and you love her and time's too precious to waste.' She lost sight of him as the train gathered speed, billows of smoke from the engine hiding him from view. But at least she and Bruce were friends for fairs again. That was one good thing to come out of this horrible tangled mess. Probably the only good thing.

Amy reached the house just after one o'clock in the afternoon. She had been glad to leave the train, having been stuck in a carriage with two formidable ladies who for half the journey had bemoaned the fact the Government had banned the baking of white bread, before going on to the disgraceful lack of good clothing material available since the war. Considering both women were dressed to the nines in fur coats and hats, the restrictions seemed barely to have touched their lives.

Amy took a taxi from Central Station, deciding she couldn't stand a prolonged tram journey. Now she was here in Sunderland she wanted to get the visit over as quickly as possible and return to the air base. If she wasn't in time for the last train, she would book into a hotel overnight, but she didn't really want to remain in the town if she could help it.

Large craters and blitzed buildings bore evidence to the fact that the Luftwaffe had been busy in the north-east, but Ryhope was dozing in bitterly cold March sunshine when the taxi drove up the drive of the home she had left a hundred years before – or that was what it felt like. After she had paid the driver and the taxi had disappeared, she stood on the drive for some moments. She had been utterly bereft when she had last seen this place, she thought, glancing round at the neat hedges and recently dug flowerbeds. Were they planted with vegetables in accordance with the Government's urging, or a profusion of flowers as had been the case when she had lived here? And then she shook her head at her capriciousness. Why was she thinking of vegetables and flowers at a moment like this? she asked herself. She was going doo-lally.

Her heart beating so hard she felt it would jump out of her chest, she made her way to the front door and, ignoring the bell, brought the brass knocker down twice on the wood. And then she jumped back, her glove smothering what would have been a startled cry when the door was immediately flung open. 'You made me jump.' She looked at Charles accusingly.

'I was in the hall.' He stood to one side, waving her into the house. 'I've been in the hall since eleven o'clock waiting for you to come. Pathetic, isn't it?'

She didn't answer this. She could smell the stale whisky on his breath and knew he had been drinking the night before. 'I want a divorce, Charles. I'm here to discuss a divorce and nothing else.'

'I know.' He rubbed his hand over his mouth. 'Come into the drawing room and sit down while I fetch the coffee tray. I have a daily now, Mrs Riley, she works from eight to midday and prepares my evening meal. She got the tray ready before she left today. There's a sponge cake but I'm afraid it's made with dried egg. She would have—'

'Charles, please.' The tone of her voice stopped his gabbling. Amy took a deep breath. 'I don't want coffee, thank you. I want us to sit down and talk.'

He stared at her and then blurted, 'Give me another chance.'

'What?'

'I'm begging you, Amy. Give me another chance. I've been in hell since you left me. The number of times I've thought of ending it all but I haven't even got the courage for that. I'll do anything you want, I swear it, but just come back to me.'

She took a step backwards at the same time as the air raid sirens in the town began their ominous whine, but neither of them commented on the warning. 'There's no question of that, Charles. I thought you knew that.'

'It's because of him, isn't it? This pilot Perce said you were with.'

Charles was ill. Whether it was the drink or something else Amy didn't know, but she could see he was ill. 'If I had never met Nick I'd still be asking you for a divorce.'

Her calmness deflated him. He nodded, his voice more controlled when he said, 'I had to ask. Just in case . . . But of course. I understand. After what happened, how could you ever forgive me?'

She knew he wanted her to say that she had forgiven him.

The plea was there in his eyes. But she couldn't. They stared at each other, the familiar smell of the drawing room — a mixture of beeswax and leather chairs and thick carpet — bringing a host of memories to Amy's mind. Painful memories. Memories she could have done without.

She opened her mouth to suggest they got started on the details of the divorce when they heard what sounded like an aircraft rapidly losing height with a terrible whining, screaming noise. As the sound became ear-deafening, she was aware of Charles throwing himself over her and then the room exploding around them. And then . . . nothing.

She became aware of sounds first. Clinking and voices but muffled and far away, and then the sound of a child laughing but this was cut off abruptly, as though someone had put a hand over its mouth. She wanted to open her eyes but it was too much effort and so she remained quite still, just listening.

When she next surfaced she sensed things were different. It was quiet for one thing, and whereas before a kind of orange light had beaten against her closed eyelids, now a restful darkness covered them. She felt tired, very tired, but not so tired she couldn't open her eyes in spite of the ache in her head and the pain all over her body.

Slowly she turned her head on the pillow and immediately there was a movement and then Nick was bending over her, his voice soft as he said, 'You're awake, that's good. Everything's all right, darling, and I'm here. Don't worry about a thing.'

She wanted to ask if he was real or if she was imagining him, because he was in France, wasn't he? And he had to come home through Spain. But she mustn't tell anyone about that because it was secret. This wasn't Spain. Where was she? She would ask him. But instead she closed her eyes again and went to sleep.

The next time she opened her eyes she found her mind was clearer. The room was still shaded in darkness but when she turned her head and looked at the man slumped in the chair at the side of the bed she knew Nick was real. She watched him sleeping and as she did so she became aware of the drips and wires all around her. She was in hospital? Why was she in hospital? And then she remembered. She had been with Charles and there was a bomb. Was it a bomb? There had been a noise anyway. Oh, her head hurt. She screwed up her eyes against the pain and when she opened them again Nick's green gaze was just above her. 'You're safe, darling,' he murmured. 'Can you hear me?'

'Yes,' she whispered back.

'I love you, my sweet. Forgive me for being such a fool. Bruce has told me everything. Everything. And it makes no difference. I want to marry you just as soon as you're free. There can never be anyone but you for me, I knew that as soon as I saw you. It was as sudden as that.'

She wanted to tell him she loved him too but she couldn't keep her eyes open a moment longer.

The clatter of a trolley and a cheerful voice saying, 'Are we ready to wake up yet, Miss Shawe?' brought Amy's eyes open to a room filled with bright sunlight. 'That's right.' The nurse was middle-aged and brisk. 'Just thought you might like to freshen up and then we'll see if you can manage a cup of tea. No, no.' As Amy went to try and sit up, the nurse was at her side, pressing her gently into the bed. 'You lie still for now, dear. Don't want to rush things, do we? Nurse Burns and I will do all the work and then once you're comfortable we'll see about sitting you up.'

Amy glanced about her and saw the drips had gone. She vaguely recalled a nurse talking to her in the night and then a bit of coming and going, and now she said, 'Nick? Has he gone?'

'Your young man? Oh, hours since, once he knew you were all right. He'll be back tonight at visiting time and Matron says you can be moved to a main ward, so that's nice, isn't it?'

'How long have I been here?'

'A good few days, dear, but the doctor will explain everything shortly.'

Amy let them wash her without protest, she felt too exhausted to mind. When they had finished and the bed was changed and she was in a clean nightie, the two nurses plumped up the pillows and then carefully eased her into a semi-sitting position. She felt giddy and sick for a few moments and this, more than anything, brought home how ill she was. She wanted to ask lots of questions but after having a few sips of the tea she went to sleep again.

The doctor turned out to be a middle-aged man with one of the kindest faces Amy had seen. He was already seated by the bed when he woke her up by gently touching her shoulder, and when she opened her eyes he said quietly, 'It's nice to see you back in the land of the living. Mr Callendar was pleased when we told him the news.'

'Charles? Is he all right?'

The doctor didn't answer this directly. What he did say was, 'You have been very poorly since you were admitted ten days ago but that's to be expected. Can you remember anything of what happened?'

'A loud noise.' Why hadn't he answered her question about Charles?

'The loud noise was a German plane which unfortunately took Mr Callendar's roof off when it chose to crash in his garden. I understand pieces of wreckage, maps and equipment were spread over most of Ryhope, along with a number of bombs which happily failed to detonate. The bomber crew did not survive the crash.'

Amy stared at him. 'I was only supposed to be on a forty-eight-hour leave.'

The doctor smiled. 'I think your CO will appreciate you haven't gone AWOL, Miss Shawe.'

'What's wrong with me?'

'The main problem as far as we have been concerned was severe concussion, but you also have a broken leg, fractured ribs and bruising and lacerations.'

'And Charles?'

'Mr Callendar's injuries are more critical. There is no easy way to dress this up, I'm afraid. His back has been crushed. Having said that, he has actually been lucid since he was brought into the infirmary. He . . .' The doctor gave a polite cough and appeared slightly embarrassed. 'He has informed me of your circumstances and that you have been separated for some years.'

'Yes, we have.' She was feeling very tired, she couldn't believe how tired.

The doctor must have realised this because he stood up. His voice low, he said, 'Rest now. You must resign yourself to getting plenty of rest over the next weeks. We'll talk again later.'

'Can I see Charles?' Amy roused herself to ask.

'At some point, of course.'

'Today?'

'Miss Shawe, I don't think you realise how serious your condition has been. It really wouldn't do to rush things at this stage.'

She was becoming increasingly agitated inside as she fought the exhaustion blanketing her body and mind enough to say, 'I want to see him, *please*. I have to see him. He . . . he saved me. He threw himself over me just before the crash happened.'

'Now, now, don't distress yourself.'

'Please, I have to see him.' She had to make things right. Charles wasn't a bad man, just a weak one, and they had loved each other once, before it had all gone so terribly wrong. She couldn't let him lie there thinking she hadn't forgiven him. What if he died before she could tell him?

The doctor shook his head. 'This is most irregular and not what I would advise, but perhaps if you are well enough we'll see about wheeling you into his ward for just a moment or two. We shall be moving you onto a main ward later today, perhaps a slight detour then wouldn't be out of the question. Now, do rest, Miss Shawe.'

Amy was asleep before he had walked out of the door.

It felt very strange to think she had lost ten days of her life through the concussion, and she still felt so groggy she knew she had to submit to being confined to bed, with all the embarrassing procedures that involved. Later that day, though, when the doctor himself wheeled her into Charles's small side ward which held four occupants, Amy knew she had got off lightly. A severe-looking sister was sitting at a table near the door, and the curtains were drawn round two of the beds. The patients in the other two – one of whom was Charles – had the appearance of corpses.

Charles had his eyes closed but when Dr Shelton said, 'I have a visitor to see you, Mr Callendar,' in an over-hearty voice, the transparent eyelids rose and there was immediate recognition in the dark eyes.

'Hello, Charles.' As the doctor positioned the wheelchair at the head of the bed, Amy reached out and took one of the thin, limp hands lying on the white coverlet. 'I'm being moved to a big ward and I asked if I could see you en route,' she said awkwardly, aware of the doctor behind her. 'How are you feeling?'

'Better.' It was a hoarse whisper. 'Now I know you are going to be all right.'

She had thought he looked ill ten days ago but now he was truly nothing but skin and bone. Something stirred in her, and to combat the sudden pricking of tears, she said brightly, 'You're going to be all right too, I'm sure of it.'

There was a glimmer of a smile. 'My determined Amy. I dare not be anything else now, dare I?'

'Absolutely.'

He shut his eyes again and she could see the sweat on his brow and knew he must be in a great deal of pain, but she had to say it. She leaned forward, squeezing the motionless fingers in hers as she said, 'Thank you for what you did at the house. I wouldn't be here but for you.'

His eyes opened again. 'Nonsense,' he muttered faintly.

'It's true. One of the nurses told me the reporter who described what happened said just that in his article in the *Echo*.'

'What does he know?' Again the colourless lips tried to smile.

'I mean it, Charles. You saved me.'

At this his head moved agitatedly on the pillow and Amy felt the doctor stir behind her. 'Never can make up for what I did,' Charles said, 'but want you to go on. You're young and so beautiful, want you to be happy . . .'

His breathing was coming with great effort now and the doctor's voice was soothing when he said, 'Your visitor will be back soon, Mr Callendar, but for now Sister is going to give you a little injection to make you feel better.' And Amy found herself whisked out of the room with a swiftness that brooked no argument.

Out in the corridor, the doctor said quietly, 'It was time for his medication, Miss Shawe. Please don't distress yourself.'

Amy brushed the tears from her cheeks. 'Is he going to get better?'

Dr Shelton sighed. 'This can wait until you are feeling a little more like yourself.'

'Please, I want to know.'

'He is paralysed in the lower half of his body and this will not change. Certain internal complications have put a strain on his heart but we're hoping that time will ease this. Unfortunately Mr Callendar was not a well man before this incident occurred. I gather from his own doctor that his liver has been under stress for many years and that he doesn't eat properly or look after himself. His doctor told him only a short while ago that he would be lucky to see another birthday unless he altered his way of life.'

Amy stared at him. 'I see,' she whispered.

'So you will appreciate we are battling against the odds.

Having said that, I am frequently surprised by how men and women rally if they have the will to live. I have seen patients slip away who really have very little wrong with them, and others, like Mr Callendar, go on for years if the life force is strong. It really does depend on the individual human spirit.'

She stared into the lined face. 'And if he feels he has nothing to live for?'

'Ah . . .' He shook his head and shrugged.

By the time she was placed in the tightly made bed in the seemingly endless ward full of other tightly made beds, Amy was too exhausted to eat or drink. She was aware of the curtains being pulled round her bed and the sister's voice saying, 'No visitors for Miss Shawe this evening, Nurse. I really can't understand why she wasn't brought straight to the ward,' in a tone which proclaimed deep irritation. Then Amy knew no more until the next morning.

She awoke some time before the rest of the ward stirred, lying in the semi-darkness listening to the snores and snorts from the other patients and the low murmur from several nurses sitting at the table in the middle of the room. Someone had pulled back the curtains from around her bed at some point, but after carefully raising her head from the pillow and glancing round once, she remained as though asleep. She needed to think.

Dr Shelton came to see her after breakfast and this time he was accompanied by an entourage which included the dour-faced matron. He seemed different in front of his junior doctors, detailing her injuries as though she was a bug under a microscope.

Amy remained quiet and still until the little group was

about to move on, then she said, 'Doctor? How is my husband?'

She saw him blink in surprise. Aware of her situation and, no doubt, of Nick's vigil by her bed, he clearly hadn't expected her to claim Charles as her husband so openly.

'Mr Callendar is as well as can be expected.'

'Will I be able to see him today?'

'Miss Shawe—'

'Mrs Callendar,' she interrupted the doctor firmly. 'My name is Mrs Callendar.'

She saw him glance at the matron who remained deadpan. He cleared his throat. 'Mrs Callendar, I don't think that is wise. You are very weak and Mr Callendar sleeps most of the time; he is under heavy medication.'

'He will want to see me.'

'Be that as it may—'

'He needs to see me. You said yourself he needs to have the will to fight. I can give him that.' Even this short conversation was tiring her but she was determined not to let it show.

The doctor glanced at the matron again and now the good lady seemed to take pity on him. She moved closer to Amy's bed, her voice totally at odds with her forbidding appearance as she said softly, 'Mr Callendar was distressed for some time after your visit yesterday, I'm afraid. In view of that it would be best to leave things until he is a little stronger.'

'He won't get stronger if we leave things.' Amy could see the group round Dr Shelton looking askance; clearly one didn't usually argue with Matron. 'I need to tell him he has to get well, that the house doesn't matter. We . . . we can find another house.' There, she had said it. The enormity of

384

what she was going to do, what she was going to *give up*, made her voice tremble. 'If I don't tell him, he won't fight, Matron. I know it.'

It was the matron who now glanced at the doctor, and in answer to her silent enquiry, he said, 'I leave things of this nature to you, Matron. Do as you think best.' And he moved on down the ward with what looked like relief on his face.

'We'll talk about this in a few minutes, Miss – Mrs Callendar,' the matron said briskly, 'once the doctor's rounds have finished.'

'Thank you.' She couldn't fight the swimming sensation in her head any longer. It came and went but just at the moment it was overpowering. As the matron bustled after the team of doctors, Amy was glad to lie back against the pillows and shut her eyes.

It was after lunch before Amy was wheeled into Charles's small ward which she had learned was a room reserved for patients who needed priority care. It was just the same as before, even to the curtains being pulled round the two beds opposite him. The nurse parked the wheelchair next to the bed and murmured, 'I'll be back in ten minutes, all right? Sister says not a second longer.' Her eyes darted towards the person sitting rigidly at her post just inside the door. Amy nodded and the nurse disappeared.

'Charles?' She could detect no movement in the body lying so white and still under the coverlet and for a moment she felt a sense of panic. Then his eyelids fluttered and slowly opened. She was conscious of two drips on the other side of the bed, one holding blood and the other a clear liquid. She hadn't noticed these the day before and for a moment it threw her. 'How are you feeling?' she heard herself say inanely.

It seemed to take enormous effort for him to mumble, 'Like a house fell on me,' but she took the humour as a good sign.

She grinned at him, determined not to show how close she was to weeping. Following the line she had taken with the doctor, she said, 'Looks as though we'll have to find a new place once we're out of here but perhaps that's not a bad thing. New start and all that.'

He stared at her and for a moment she thought he hadn't understood. Then he shut his eyes, his voice a whisper when he said, 'No. I wouldn't let you do that.'

'Do what?'

'Sacrifice yourself.'

'It's not like that,' she said huskily. 'You're my husband, till death do us part and in sickness and in health. Remember?'

'You want a divorce.'

'Not any more.'

He was becoming agitated again. Amy hoped old eagle-eyes by the door couldn't see.

'Amy, listen to me.' He had to breathe in and out a good few times before he could go on. 'You are someone very special, I knew that from day one but like the weak fool I am I destroyed everything between us. I failed you. I . . . I failed our child. I have no right to live and still less to expect anything of you. I detest myself.'

'Don't, Charles.'

'You don't have to be sorry for me and I would never let you throw away your life for the second time. Just promise me you'll be happy, that's enough.'

386

'I want us to get back together.' She stared at him, willing him to believe her.

He was breathing hard but his voice was calm when he said, 'I don't, not any more. I want a divorce.'

Suddenly she found herself glaring at him. 'For years I hated you,' she said angrily, 'and it ate me up inside. Then when I saw you again I realised I pitied you more than anything but still it hurt. Then that day at the house when you tried to protect me, I knew the old Charles, the Charles I fell in love with was still there deep inside. I . . . I don't love you like I did, I can't pretend, but we've been through so much. We have our son, the knowledge that he existed, that he was real, and no one else can share that. While we're alive, he is too. Oh, I can't explain what I feel but I don't think he's gone for ever, I think we'll see him again one day. And we're his parents, it's not right for us to forget that or him.'

'I have never forgotten him,' Charles whispered, his face ravaged. He hadn't forgotten either of his baby sons.

'Nor have I.' Amy reached out and clasped his hand. 'And you didn't mean for it to happen, it was an accident. I do know that.' It pained her that the look on his face was that of a child, disbelieving even as it was apparent how much he wanted to believe. He wasn't sure she meant what she was saying. Would she have felt like this if he hadn't been so badly injured? She didn't think so, she admitted honestly. What she did know was that at some point over the last days pity and compassion had swilled her mind clean and now she was doing what she felt compelled to do.

Charles stared at her. She had taken him utterly aback but he wanted to believe her more than he'd ever wanted anything in his life. 'And him?' He found he didn't want to bring the man Perce had seen her with, the pilot chap, into the equation but he had to. He had to know. 'You love him, don't you?'

She looked at him and he read the answer in her face even before she whispered, 'Yes, I love him but it's over.' Or it would be very shortly.

He should ask her if this chap had left her or whether she had left him. If she had finished with him because she was going to come back to him out of pity or whatever it was. He should ask but he was too frightened of the answer because he wanted her back, on any terms, and he couldn't keep up the effort of being noble. Not with heaven within his grasp. Before she had walked in here all he had wanted was to die; he couldn't believe his body could hurt this much without his heart giving out. Now, looking at her, he wanted to see another dawn. 'You're sure it's over?'

She nodded. 'You sleep now.'

He moved his head slightly, tried to say something but began to cry instead. Silent tears which took the last remnants of his pride.

'Don't. Don't, Charles.' He felt the touch of her lips on his brow and then heard the sister stand up and walk over to them. 'It will be all right, I promise.'

'And I promise no more drink.' He clutched her hand. 'Whatever happens, no more.'

'All right, all right. Rest now.'

Her voice was soothing and he felt she didn't believe him but he would make her believe him, he told himself. She moved away and the sister bent over him with a syringe. He heard her say, 'One more minute, Mrs Callendar,' after she had injected him and then Amy's face was there again.

'She . . . she said Mrs Callendar,' he whispered.

'Well, that's my name, isn't it?' She smiled at him.

The drug was already taking effect and he knew he wouldn't know anything more for a while in a few moments. He drew on all his remaining strength to say, 'I mean it, Amy. If I get out of here I won't touch a drop.'

'You'll get out of here,' she said quietly. 'I promise.'

Nick was smiling when he came onto Amy's ward that evening. She watched him as he approached her bed. He looked big and confident and handsome, and she would have given the world for everything to be as he thought it was. But instead she was going to pull the rug out from under his feet and hurt him badly, and she didn't know how she was going to get through the next few minutes.

In the event it was even worse than she had expected.

He gathered her into his arms as he reached the bed, careless of the other patients in the ward and the nursing staff. He held her tight, murmuring how much he loved her and how she had scared him to death, how he wouldn't have wanted to go on if anything had happened to her.

For a few seconds she rested against him, wondering how she would find the strength to go through with what she had decided to do. But she had no choice really, not deep down inside. She would never know a moment's peace for the rest of her life if she walked away from Charles right now. Winnie had been a great one for saying that a person couldn't escape their destiny and that life was all mapped out from when the first breath was taken. They'd argued about it often but perhaps Winnie had been right after all.

'All the time I was in France and making my way back to England I thought of you,' Nick whispered against her hair. 'You were the prize I was coming home for. I knew I'd make it. Whatever it was you had to tell me, however bad it was, I knew we wouldn't be parted somehow. I didn't even change my clothes when I got to the base and learned what had happened to you. And when I got here and they said you'd been out of it for over a week, I prayed for the first time in years. Crazy, eh? You rail against God and blame Him for all the grief in the world and then as soon as something really matters again, He's the first call.'

'Nick, please, we have to talk.'

Her stiffness finally got through to him and he straightened. His green eyes were narrowed and faintly puzzled. He kept hold of her hand as he sat down on the chair at the head of the bed. 'OK, we'll talk,' he said, his tone indulgent. 'But just remember what I said to you the other day. I don't care about anything except us being together. If you want children in the future we'll adopt: if you don't, that's fine by me. I just want you as my wife.'

'This isn't about me, not in that way.' She didn't know how she was going to tell him. Oh God, let me be doing the right thing. 'It's Charles, my . . . my husband.'

His expression didn't change but she felt his hand jerk slightly as it held her fingers.

'He's badly hurt, paralysed.'

'I know.'

She just had to say it. 'I can't leave him now, not now.'

He didn't let go of her hand but he leaned back in the chair, his body distancing itself. 'When then?'

'I'm going back to him, Nick. I have to.'

'The hell you do,' he said very softly.

'He needs me. He'll give up if he has nothing to live for.'

'That's not your problem or mine.'

'It's not yours, no, but we're man and wife. We made vows—'

'Don't give me that.' Now he did remove his hand from hers, his voice low but intense. 'This is emotional blackmail, can't you see that? He's using the tricks he tried in the past. Bruce told me how you stayed with him, believing things would work out, giving him a second and third and umpteenth chance, but a leopard doesn't change its spots, Amy. You've cut the man off for years, you wanted a divorce, you wanted *me*. That's the truth of it. All this is just woolly thinking because of what's happened.'

'He isn't using emotional blackmail, just the opposite.' She took a deep breath. 'It was me who decided to go back to him, he didn't expect it.'

'No? He just managed to look suitably pathetic.'

'Nick, I don't expect you to understand. I don't really understand myself. I just know I couldn't live with myself if I don't do this. We wouldn't be happy, it would blight everything.'

'Do you love him?'

'You know I don't.'

'Do you love *me*?'

'Nick, *please*. Just accept I've made up my mind. You . . . you'll meet—'

'Don't say it.' His tone changed swiftly. He said under his breath and with some fury, 'Don't you dare say I'll meet someone else as though it's that simple. Damn it all, Amy.' He leaned forward again, taking her hands in a grip that was bruising. 'I love you. I shall spend the rest of my life loving you. How can you put him before me? Whatever he's feeling can't be as bad as the hell you're consigning me to.'

'I'm sorry, I am.'

'You're going to send me away?' Disbelief warred with recognition that she meant what she said. Their eyes held for long moments, his full of incredulous, impotent fury and hers swimming with tears. 'Then you never really loved me,' he said heavily, rising to his feet and looking down at her with a coldness she'd never seen before.

She made no protest, she said nothing at all. In that moment she felt she had died inside.

He turned and walked away down the ward, pausing at the doors for just a moment before pushing them open and stepping through without looking back.

Chapter 24

Nick arrived back at the base early the next morning, just after his squadron had returned to their sleeping quarters after a night mission. On entering his hut he was met by a barrage of friendly insults by the airmen within, but his terse rejoinders warned them all was not well and within moments the talk died down. When Bruce made his way over to his friend, Nick filled him in on what had happened, his voice clipped.

'And you accepted that?' Bruce was astounded. 'Are you mad, man? Charles will be a millstone round her neck all his life, whereas you two—'

'There is no us two.' When Bruce went to say more, Nick said, 'Leave it. It's finished. She's made up her mind. She insists he didn't try the bleeding hearts routine and I believe her. Amy is doing what she wants to do.'

'Aw, that's not fair. She's doing what she feels she has to do and that's different. But she's wrong. Paralysed or not, Charles won't change.'

'I told her that and it makes no difference. Now, forget it. What's been happening while I've been gone?'

Bruce stared at his friend and he was deeply troubled. If Nick was right, and there was no reason to doubt him, and Amy had made up her mind to take care of Charles, no one would be able to persuade her otherwise. He had loved her all his life and he knew how stubborn she could be. But she was making a terrible mistake. A mistake which wouldn't only ruin her life but that of the man standing in front of him now.

'It's all right.' Nick touched Bruce's arm briefly. 'It wasn't meant to be, that's all. Just another wartime romance hitting the dust.'

He didn't mean it. Bruce remained silent and embarrassed; he did not know what to say.

'So, like I said, what's been happening?' Nick said again.

Bruce shrugged. 'You've heard we hit the Ruhr valley pretty hard a couple of nights ago? There's talk of a new bombing campaign now this Sir Arthur Harris has taken over. The lads are already calling him Bomber Harris after he said he means to knock the hell out of Jerry.'

Nick nodded. 'Suits me.'

'Oh, and Gertie and I have decided to make a go of it, seriously, you know?' It wasn't the best moment to say it, not with Nick raw about Amy, but Bruce knew Nick well enough to know his friend wouldn't appreciate any pussyfooting about.

Nick nodded. 'I thought it was on the cards. Marriage in the air, is it?'

'We'll just see how things go for now.'

He didn't expand on this and Nick wasn't sufficiently

interested to pursue it, not that he would have got anywhere if he had.

Early that afternoon, Nick and his fellow pilots emerged from the briefing which was sending them on a raid escorting bombers to industrial plants near Béthune. They had been told the RAF had begun a round-the-clock offensive against German arms factories, German-controlled industries in France and German gun emplacements in the Calais area. Hundreds of tons of incendiaries and high explosives would rain down on the targets, overwhelming the German fire-fighters and Luftwaffe. 'This is a new strategy, gentlemen, and it will be unrelenting.' The CO had glanced round the room, knowing some of the men had been up most of the night and had had only three or four hours' sleep. 'It is going to be busy out there so keep your wits about you.'

Keep your wits about you. As Nick went through the normal pre-flight procedure, the words of the CO stayed with him. Marie Petit, the French farmer's daughter, had said the same thing to him the afternoon she had led him through St Omer's broad cobbled square surrounded by cafés and a hotel full of Germans. The walk had been necessary to reach his guide to the escape route, but it had been risky. When Marie had decided a German soldier sitting outside one of the cafés was looking at them a little oddly, she had reached up and kissed him full on the mouth, ruffling his hair after-wards and calling him a naughty boy. He could taste her now, warm and plump and mellow, like good French wine. Not that he had prolonged the kiss. His mind had been too full of Amy.

He pressed the starter button and felt and heard his engine

roar into life. He taxied swiftly out behind the leading aircraft and then he was tearing down the runway and into the air.

Once in battle formation, he relaxed. He'd been wondering how he'd feel the first time up in the air after the crash, but in the event it was just another day's flying. Far better to be up here where he had to concentrate than on the ground where there was time to think. A voice broke the radio silence and announced that lack of oil pressure was sending him home, but there were more than enough Spitfires escorting the bombers. Soon there was just the sky above and the sea below, the mass of aircraft like winged insects intent on reaching a choice feeding ground.

At first the Luftwaffe appeared like a batch of enemy insects in the top half of his bulletproof windscreen, but things soon changed. It wasn't long before the sky was criss-crossed with streams of white tracer from shells converging on aircraft and the fight was on to destroy before he was destroyed. The sudden bang and then the gaping hole in his starboard wing came as a shock.

'Not again.' He said the words out loud, not quite believing he was going to lose another aircraft so soon after the first when he had come through the rest of the war without a scratch. But then, as the gas tank behind the engine blew up and the cockpit became a blazing inferno, disbelief turned to agonised terror. He was burning and there was nothing he could do about it except try to bale out, but his grilled hands wouldn't obey him. He felt the skin of his face on fire but through the searing pain some instinct kept his charcoaled fingers groping for the release pin securing the restraining harness. Just when he thought it was all over, he was out of the cockpit and tumbling in cool air, over and over.

He had to pull the ripcord. He would die if he didn't pull the ripcord, and contrary to how he had felt during the last twenty-four hours, he suddenly found he didn't want to die. The trouble was his hands were lumps of raw meat and wouldn't obey the message his brain was sending them. Three times he tried to pull the chromium ring and on the third attempt there was a jerk and then the silken canopy mushroomed, whole and unburned, above him. He had never seen such a beautiful sight.

The brief euphoria vanished when the shock of his injuries combined with the cold air at twelve thousand feet above sea level took hold. His violent shivering turned his body into a dangerous pendulum, and the smell of his burned flesh made him nauseous.

He must have passed out because when he hit the water he went right under the surface before he came to, emerging to find himself tangled in the parachute and in danger of being dragged down to Davy Jones's locker. Spluttering and splashing and cursing, he fought with the release mechanism. Once free, he inflated his Mae West as they had been drilled to do in training.

With the life jacket keeping him afloat, he lost consciousness again. The next thing that registered was acute pain, made ten times worse on his face by the sea salt drying on raw flesh.

The book of rules stated he must float about until rescued, he thought with dark humour. It said nothing about leaving a trail of blood and bits of burned skin in the water, nor of how precisely the rescue would take place before he died of his injuries. The only good thing was that the icy water was numbing the pain in his hands slowly but surely.

How long he was in the sea before the big old trawler steamed by he had no idea. Life had been reduced to one bob of the waves after another and the monotone in his head which told him he had to stay alive. His eyes were so swollen he couldn't even be sure it was a ship until he heard voices calling to him.

As he was lifted aboard by the amazingly gentle, grizzled fishermen he thought of the stories he'd heard where people's lives flash before them in times of life and death. He hadn't experienced that. Nor had he thought of anything or anyone whilst in the water; staying alive had consumed every moment. Did that mean he was going to make it? He was in a bad way, he could tell from the men's faces he looked as bad as he felt, but he could stand anything if he didn't lose his eyesight. He'd always had a horror of going blind.

He knew he was passing in and out of consciousness, but the warmth of the ship and the thick blankets which had been tucked round him brought back the feeling in his hands and he welcomed the times when he knew nothing. He was vaguely aware of reaching a harbour, of being transported onto the quay, of questions being asked by a quiet voice and then an ambulance ride after an injection which only took the edge off the unbearable pain. And then there was the hospital and a clean white bed, and this time the injection took the pain somewhere far away. A doctor explained he had to be operated on immediately but such was his exhaustion he could barely reply.

And then came the surgeon and the anaesthetist and other blurred figures and he realised he was in an operating theatre. Just before he was given the anaesthetic, he remembered Bunny Taylor, a Spitfire pilot who had been in the Battle of

Britain with him and who had been badly burned. He had driven to Sussex with several other pilots to see Bunny in hospital. The place had housed apparitions who had featured in his nightmares for weeks, and it was common knowledge Bunny's marriage had folded because his wife had been revolted by him.

He was one of them now. The hypodermic syringe pierced the vein in the hollow of his elbow joint. Thank God Amy would never be called upon to pretend the sight of him didn't make her feel squeamish.

PART EIGHT

1950 The Road Back

Chapter 25

'The funeral was well attended.' Edward, Charles's brother, patted Amy's arm as he spoke.

She forced herself to smile. 'Yes, it was. Charles had lots of friends hereabouts.'

'He was extremely happy the last eight years, you know. He told me so on more than one occasion. In fact, strange though it might sound when one considers his infirmity, I think he was the happiest he'd been in the whole of his life. All thanks to you, m'dear.'

'Thank you, Edward.'

'I mean it. It can't have been easy for you.'

No, it hadn't been easy but not really for the reasons Edward probably imagined. Amy knew people pitied her, a young wife tied to a paraplegic with constant major health problems. Problems which meant any breaks away from home were out of the question. But it hadn't been the hard work involved in caring for Charles that she had minded so much. He'd been so grateful for one thing, pathetically so. And the gruelling routine had actually been a blessing in a strange kind of way; it had helped to numb the pain that was with her day and night, the pain of losing Nick. Never a day went by that she didn't wonder where he was, who he was with, what might have been.

She had realised very early on she would go mad if she didn't get out of the home she shared with Charles for a few hours each day. Her discharge from the WAAFs had come through some weeks after she and Charles had been injured, once the doctors had realised complications with her broken leg had meant it was going to take some months to mend properly. But as soon as she was able, she had arranged the employment of a part-time nurse in the afternoons and taken up voluntary war work in a munitions factory canteen. Later, when the war had ended, she had given her time to the local children's home. The few hours' break from the house and the company of ordinary healthy people had been a life-saver and Amy knew it. It was a panacea against those moments when she found herself resenting the position she was in, and then the guilt that followed.

It had been her dream to adopt several children who had been orphaned by the war but Charles's doctors had advised against this. They had been worried their frail patient could not cope mentally or physically with the stress and noise which went hand in hand with having children living in the house. Amy could see their reasoning. Charles's heart never really recovered from the accident and the injuries he had sustained meant he was in almost constant pain, but it had been hard to come to terms with at first.

All in all, though, the years between 1942 and 1950 had

run smoothly in the Callendar household and Amy had seen to it that her husband's environment was a peaceful and happy one.

Although she thought of Nick all the time, she had only spoken of him once to Bruce during the last eight years, and that had been in the very early days when Bruce and Gertie had visited her in hospital while her leg was mending. She had asked her cousin then to tell her if Nick was killed and Bruce had promised he would. Even after Bruce and Gertie were married just after the war finished, she resisted the temptation to attend the wedding in case he was there, using Charles as an excuse not to travel down to Sheffield where Bruce and Gertie had settled. To talk about him or try to see him would have been a betrayal of Charles, that was the way she felt, besides which the words he had spoken as he had left her had seared her mind like a branding iron. He thought she didn't love him, when in fact she loved him so much it was a physical ache in her chest at times. In her good moments, when she was feeling strong, she told herself it was probably all for the best he thought this way. It would have freed him to carry on with life, meet someone, settle down and have a family. In her bad times these same thoughts tortured her and she had to confess she wanted him to love her for ever, selfish though that was, and to know that she loved him.

Amy glanced across at Bruce and Gertie who were chatting to Betsy and Ruth and their husbands. The twins, along with Bruce and Eva, were the only members of Amy's family to survive the war, but Eva had gone off to America after marrying a GI and no one had heard from her since. May and her parents, Harriet and little Milly had been killed in

May 1943 during what turned out to be the last bombing raid on Sunderland. A parachute mine had devastated their house when Harriet was home on leave from the Land Army; the twins had been in Sunderland infirmary with scarlet fever and so had escaped the carnage.

Perce had met a different end. According to the *Echo*, he had been killed by a hit-and-run car in the blackout one night. There had been whispers that one of the ne'er-do-wells Perce associated with had decided Perce was cheating him and had taken his revenge. No one was brought to task for the crime, however, and the incident soon faded from people's minds.

Amy had been ashamed to confess to herself that she'd felt deep relief at Perce's death. Since living in the town again she had felt menaced by her cousin's proximity, and as she confided in Gertie one day shortly before Perce's accident, strange things kept happening, strange, frightening things. A window smashed by persons unknown, a dark silhouette standing in the garden one night when she had gone to shut the curtains, the bell rung in the early hours but no one at the door, foul rubbish including a dead rat tipped in the front garden and, more scary than anything else, the odd phone call when all she could hear was heavy breathing. These had all stopped when Perce had died.

Gertie slipped over to Amy now, her swollen stomach bearing evidence that her third child was expected soon. She put her arm through Amy's, saying, 'Bear up, kiddo. It's nearly over.'

Amy nodded. 'It's such a lovely day. I keep thinking he would have been looking out over the garden and watching the birds.' When they had bought the small detached bungalow on the outskirts of Bishopwearmouth, Amy had immediately had the two double bedrooms knocked into one large room. It bordered the garden and by doubling its size enabled their room to be both bedroom and sitting room. Charles's bed had been positioned by the large French doors Amy had had installed, which gave her husband a wonderful view of the bungalow's extensive grounds. If the weather was clement the doors had always been open, but even on the coldest days Charles had been able to look out at the goings-on of the birds he loved.

'How are you feeling really?' Gertie asked with the privilege of an old friend. Although they only saw each other a few times a year, the two were still close and talked on the telephone often.

'Odd, I suppose.' Amy looked out through the bungalow's large window to where quite a few of the assembled guests were standing talking and drinking in the warm June sunshine. 'All of a sudden I've got time on my hands after having every minute of the last years accounted for. I keep thinking Charles's medication is due or that I've got to turn him; oh, a hundred things.'

Bruce had joined them as Amy had been speaking and now he said, 'That's perfectly natural and it will fade in a little while as you pick up a different sort of life.' He was privately of the opinion that due to Charles's complete dependence on his wife, Amy had taken the role of a mother without realising it, which would increase her sense of loss now. There was no doubt she'd felt tender affection and compassion for Charles, and Charles had worshipped the ground she walked on. Bruce hadn't expected Charles to keep to his promise to lay off the drink but even if he had longed for one he hadn't mentioned it and had remained sober. Bruce had had the unworthy thought at first that Charles might try and bribe the nurse or persuade a friend to bring a bottle in but Charles had proved him wrong, and Bruce was very glad of it.

He looked into the face of the cousin he loved and admired. She was still beautiful, outstandingly so, but she looked every one of her thirty-four years. The sorrow she rarely spoke of, that of her inability to have a child of her own, combined with the hard physical work of latter years had given her beauty a very mature air. There were more than a few flecks of silver vying with the golden tints in the still thick, rich brown hair, and even when she was smiling the deep blue eyes carried a wealth of sadness.

'Have you any plans?' he asked. 'What you're going to do with yourself now?'

Amy shrugged. 'There's all the clearing out to do. Charles's medication would fill a small room all by itself. And I might take a short holiday in a few weeks. Pamela's offered me the use of their villa in Margate anytime I want it.'

'Who's taking my name in vain?' Pamela appeared at Amy's shoulder, her arm tucked through that of a tall, white-haired man. She had married the RAF CO from the base she had been stationed at during the war four years ago, and the two appeared blissfully happy. Her husband had a country estate as well as the villa in Margate but the two were rarely at either residence, preferring to spend most of their time travelling round Europe. Her husband was almost double Pamela's age but it didn't appear to concern either of them. Sadly, Nell hadn't been so lucky. The plucky northern lass had been killed when a Stirling had crashed on take-off at the airfield she'd been assigned to, landing in a hangar where Nell and some other WAAFs had been working. Nell had been trying to drag one of her friends clear when the bombload had exploded.

With Pamela's arrival the group talked of inconsequentials until Amy left them to circulate among the friends and family who had come back to the bungalow after the funeral. In the six days since Charles had died in her arms, she had kept busy organising the service and then this reception, putting on a spread which belied the fact England was still firmly in the grip of food rationing. She had cleaned and baked, weeded the garden and cut the lawns until everything was pristine and gleaming, but now it would soon be over and she would be left on her own.

Even as she stood talking to the priest who had taken the service, her mind was moving on a different plain altogether. What would Father Collins say if she told him she had longed for this day lots of times over the last years? Not for Charles to be dead, no, not that, but for her to be able to have some freedom. Freedom to go for a walk if she felt like it, to have a bath without keeping one ear cocked for Charles's bell, to sleep all night without having to set the alarm every two hours to turn Charles in his bed, just . . . freedom. From care, from responsibility, from worry. She had been ashamed of herself for thinking this way but every so often the feeling had risen up in her.

But now? Now she dreaded everyone going and panic was making her heart beat a tattoo under the calm exterior she was presenting to the world. Which was silly, ridiculous. Sooner or later she had to face the fact that Nick was some-where in the world living, loving, laughing without her. She couldn't use the punishing regime she'd inflicted on herself for the last years to duck reality any more.

'. . . in heaven.'

'I'm sorry?' She stared into the young earnest face of Father Collins. She hadn't heard a word he had said.

'I said it must be a great comfort to you to know that Charles is now receiving his reward in heaven for the pain and discomfort he bore so bravely on this mortal plain.'

'Yes, of course.' He was nice, Father Collins, but she could no more confide in him than fly to the moon.

'What do you intend to do now?'

Why was everyone asking her what she intended to do? How could she answer that? Charles hadn't been gone two minutes. And then she forced the irritation down to the place where she had kept other unacceptable emotions for the last eight years and smiled at the young priest. 'I'm not sure.'

'Of course, of course. Early days, early days.'

Early days. Yes, it was early days but then again eight years had passed. 'Excuse me, Father.' She left him without another word and made her way back to Bruce and Gertie who were now standing apart from the rest of the crowd. 'I need to ask you.' She was looking straight into Bruce's face and she saw something which led her to believe he had been waiting for this. 'I need to ask you about Nick. How he is. Where he is. If he's happy.'

Bruce glanced at Gertie. Just a fleeting glance but enough to cause Amy to say, 'He isn't . . .'

'No, no, he's alive and kicking.'

Then he was with someone. Ecstatically happy. Married with a quiverful of little Johnsons. She swallowed hard. 'I suppose he's married.'

'No, he isn't married. There's been one or two long-term relationships but he's never . . . No, he isn't married.'

'Happily living in sin, knowing Nick.' The flippancy didn't fool any of them.

'He's not with anyone at the moment, Amy.'

Then what had made Bruce look at Gertie like that? Amy abandoned the last of her pride. 'He doesn't want you to talk about him to me. Is that it?'

Bruce hesitated. The brief millisecond was aeons long. 'Not for the reason you are probably thinking.'

There could only be one reason. And she deserved it. She knew she deserved it and she had no right to think it could be any different. It wasn't until this moment that she realised how the possibility of seeing Nick again, of there being some slight chance for them had sustained her through the last eight years. Embarrassment, humiliation and a consuming sense of pain made her voice clipped when she said, 'It's all right, Bruce. I won't mention him again. Let's forget it, shall we, and—'

'He was burned, Amy. Horribly burned. Disfigured.'

She stared at him, hearing the words, conscious of the people milling about in the background and Gertie's troubled face, but unable to take it in straightaway. After some moments she managed to whisper, 'When?'

'Just after you'd split. Well, the next day actually. He was eventually put under the care of Mr McIndoe. You've heard of him?'

'No.'

'He's the best consultant plastic surgeon in the world, let alone the Royal Air Force. He did great things, Nick's still able to use his hands to some extent.'

She felt the world begin to spin and it was only Gertie's quick thinking that provided the chair for her to sink into. And it was Gertie who said, 'He didn't want you to feel sorry for him, Amy. Like you felt for Charles, I suppose. He said you had made your choice and he didn't want it complicated by him. He swore Bruce to secrecy, me too, and although we didn't agree with him we couldn't do anything else. You know Nick, he's fiercely proud and independent.'

On my darling. My love. Disfigured. Burned. And I didn't know. All this time and I didn't know.

'He's not too bad now, Amy. Well, not really. But you know Nick. Always full of confidence and self-assurance.'

No doubt Gertie thought she was helping but she was making it worse. The Nick she'd known wasn't like that at all. He'd been as vulnerable as the next man. As Charles. *Had she made the wrong decision?* Amy physically squirmed in her chair. Because of some misguided sense of right and wrong, had she made the wrong decision?

She must have spoken out loud although she wasn't aware of it because Gertie said softly, 'I don't think so, dear. Nick's a survivor, you know that, but Charles wasn't made that way. You gave him eight years of happiness in a life that had known very little, and you did what you thought was right, regardless of what you really wanted. I don't think you can say that was wrong.'

'Where . . . where is he?'

There was a pause and then Bruce said, 'He works for the British Aircraft Corporation selling airliners. He loves it.'

'Does he ever ask after me?'

'Every time we speak.'

Nick. Oh, Nick. 'I have to talk to him. No, I have to go

412

and see him.' It was the only way Nick would believe his injuries didn't matter a jot, if she proved it to him, face to face.

'He won't agree to that, Amy.' Bruce was clearly finding this difficult. 'He abhors pity.'

'Pity?' Amy glared at the man who, next to Nick, meant more to her than anyone else on earth. 'Who said anything about pity? I'm not a child, Bruce. I know what people with bad burns can look like. There's Joy Garfield up the road, she had her face taken off by a doodlebug. And then George Benson—'

'OK, OK.' Bruce held up his hands in surrender. 'It's just that I know he wants you to remember him as he was.'

'And then we continue living the next forty or fifty years apart? Oh, I'm not saying he'll want me after all this time.' Amy stared at Bruce and Gertie, her eyes swimming with tears. 'But it'll be up to him. All I can do is go to him and say I'm his if he wants me. I have always been his, that's never changed for me.'

A large fat lady with a black squashed tomato of a hat waddled up and spoke a few words of condolence to Amy. Amy had no idea who the woman was. Probably the wife of one of Charles's old business colleagues.

When the lady had gone, Bruce said, 'All right, Amy. It will probably be the end of a beautiful friendship when Nick finds out I've given you his address, but all right.'

'Thank you.' Amy smiled her relief. 'You do see I have to try, don't you?'

Bruce's grin included both women and it was rueful. 'You being you, I do see that.'

'And it must be a surprise.'

'Shouldn't that be phrased shock?'

'Shock, surprise, whatever.' Amy looked steadily at them both. 'He must not know I'm coming. If I don't give him the chance to refuse to see me it's a fait accompli.'

'Now she's talking French at me . . .'

Chapter 26

Bruce called Amy the day after the funeral to say he had found out Nick was out of the country on business for a couple of weeks and his secretary couldn't be specific as to when he was expected back. But he'd ring and let her know when he had news. OK?

It wasn't really OK but after a maudlin hour or two Amy pulled herself together. She wasn't going to sit and twiddle her thumbs, she had masses to do and she had better get on with it. She hadn't slept a wink the night before and at some time during the tossing and turning and making herself endless cups of tea, she had decided to sell the bungalow forthwith. A stage of her life had definitely ended and she needed to slam the door on it.

A couple of days after Charles passed away, his solicitor had called to see her. Mr Callendar had asked him to do this at the appropriate time, he informed her gravely, and he had promised he would. He needed to tell her that as well as the bungalow and the car she'd purchased some years before, after learning to drive, there was a tidy sum in the bank. He wouldn't want her to run away with the idea she was a rich woman, but there was certainly enough for her to live frugally for the rest of her life.

Amy thought back to this conversation now and she knew there was no way she could spend her days going to the bridge club and having little rides in the car and growing old with a couple of cats for company. Whatever happened with Nick. If things worked out between them, and she hardly dared hope they would, then her future would be with him. If not, then she would find a job working with children, perhaps even as a live-in matron at a children's home or something. Whatever, she would *live*.

The next few days saw Amy sorting through a mountain of paperwork, a little of which it was necessary to keep but most of which she burned. Then came clothes. Charles's things she gave away. Most of her own she packed, apart from a few items for daily wear. Charles's books and personal mementoes and such she put into two large crates which she sent to Edward; she kept nothing for herself. She had her memories both good and bad, and they were the only things she wanted to take with her into the future.

Amy found herself staring intently at the miniature of her mother often during this time which was one of tears and sadness as well as burning hope for the future. The original had been lost along with everything else when the German plane had destroyed the house in Ryhope. Bess's calm lovely face was the one permanent, unchanging anchor in a world that had gone topsy-turvy again, and Amy slept with it by her bed each night.

The first people who came to look at the bungalow fel

in love with it immediately and offered the full price without prevarication, expressing an interest in most of the furniture when Amy said it was also for sale. They were a young couple, a sweet, unworldly pair who were due to get married at the end of the summer. Amy liked them very much and when the young woman went into raptures over the number of birds in the garden, she knew they were the right ones for the place.

Bruce rang one night in the middle of July to say Nick was back, just as Amy was ironing the curtains she had washed that morning. Every curtain in the bungalow had been taken down and laundered, every carpet cleaned, every rug beaten to within an inch of its life, every work surface scrubbed and every item of furniture polished to gleaming perfection. The physical exertion had helped to keep her mind off the possible outcome of seeing Nick, at least in the daylight hours. The nights were a different kettle of fish; the gremlins came out in full force then. But in all her whirling doubts and fears, one thing remained constant. She had to try.

'He's just clinched quite a big deal apparently,' Bruce said, 'so he's taking a couple of days off to relax at home.' Home was a cottage in Sussex, according to Bruce, and this had surprised Amy. She had imagined Nick would have settled for an impersonal bachelor flat, something of that nature. 'Look, Amy, are you sure you've thought this through?'

'Positive.'

'No doubts?'

About going to see Nick? Not one. About the outcome? Myriad. 'Bruce, this is something I have to do however it turns out.'

There was a short pause. 'You've got to prepare yourself

for the fact he has changed, and I'm not talking about the burns now. There's an edge to him somehow, a cynicism, a "I don't care what the hell you're thinking" attitude that goes more than skin deep. It's not that he has any trouble attracting the opposite sex –' Bruce stopped abruptly, then said sheepishly, 'Sorry, but he doesn't, so it's not that. It's not bravado.'

'That's good,' Amy said quietly. 'At least if he listens to me and gives me a chance I shall know it's not because I'm any port in a storm.'

'No, there is that. Look, Gertie and I have been talking. Do you want us to come with you?'

'And have Gertie drop the baby on his doorstep? Somehow I don't think that would help matters much.'

'I couldn't leave her with the bairn so close.'

'I wouldn't want you to. I shall be perfectly all right, I promise.' And then her voice softened. 'But thank you, both of you, for all your support and concern.' Her voice became brisk as she added, 'Now I'm going to say goodnight so I can pack an overnight case and be away first thing. It's a long drive but with your directions I'm sure I shan't get lost.'

'Ring me at work if you do and I'll try to put you right. You've got my number, haven't you?'

'Yes, I've got your work number, Bruce.' She loved him dearly but she wished he wouldn't worry so. 'Now concentrate on Gertie and the baby. Tell her I'm praying for a little lassie this time.' They already had two boys and Gertie had confided in her some weeks ago that she would love a girl.

'I'll do that. Bye, Amy.'

'Bye, Bruce.'

Contrary to what she had said she remained sitting for a long time, her thoughts in the past. And it wasn't only Nick she was thinking of. She had loved Charles at the beginning, albeit a romantic, girlish love, and she had loved him at the end but in a different way entirely. But what she felt for Nick was so far removed from any of this as to be incomparable. If he didn't want her she would never marry anyone else, she knew that.

During the war she had known lots of women who had had more than one man, many more in some cases. Even here in Sunderland it was common knowledge that this woman and that had had 'friends' visiting them when their husbands were away fighting, and more than a few marriages hadn't survived when the husband had come home. Because of the war, divorce wasn't the scandal it once had been, even in the Church. Times were changing fast. And here was she at the age of thirty-four having only ever slept with one man, and the last time being well over a decade ago.

She stood up at last and wandered into the kitchen. She made herself a cup of tea which she drank staring out of the window into the darkening twilight.

She had thought her life had ended when she lost her baby and the chance ever to be a mother. It wasn't really until Nick had come to see her in the hospital and whispered they could adopt that she had ever considered the idea. Since that time it had been with her always, even though it hadn't been possible when Charles was alive. But if Nick still wanted her she would forgo adoption if he had changed his mind about it and consider herself well blessed nonetheless.

But she was jumping the gun here. She finished the tea and washed the cup and saucer before walking through to her bedroom. Enough thinking. It only wound her up until her thoughts spiralled and she found herself going round in circles. Tomorrow would determine the rest of her life sure enough, but however things turned out she wasn't going to crumble. She wouldn't let herself.

Surprisingly she slept well, but when she awoke it was with the very clear picture of a sweet little face in her mind. She had always been grateful that as time had gone on she had never forgotten the tiniest detail of that one brief glimpse of her son. She only had to close her eyes to see him and this she did often. But last night it had been different. Last night she had dreamed of him, and instead of the nurse whisking him away he had smiled and reached out to her and she had held him close to her breast. She had sat down in a big old rocking chair and cradled him in her arms, gently rocking him to sleep, and as she had looked down at the tiny sleeping face she had known – in the manner of dreams – that he was the first of her children and that there would be others. She'd woken up with her face wet with tears and it had taken some time to pull herself together, but strangely a sense of peace had descended that hadn't been there the day before.

It stayed with her as she got ready to leave, put her overnight case in the car and locked the bungalow door. It stayed with her throughout the long journey which, in spite of her brave words to Bruce, she had been nervous about. She stopped at lunchtime, eating the sandwiches and drinking the flask of coffee she had brought with her before starting on her way again. She got lost once on the outskirts of Peterborough but she didn't panic, merely stopped at the nearest garage and asked directions for East Sussex. After a slight detour she was soon back to following Bruce's detailed instructions again.

The long summer twilight was beginning when she reached the perimeter of the South Downs. She drove another mile or two and then stopped the car next to a drystone wall, where she got out to stretch her legs. She had just passed Ratton village so she knew she was close to the spot where she had to turn off the road and onto an unmade lane. Several hundred yards on, Nick's cottage was set all by itself in what Bruce had described as a field. She breathed in the warm air scented with sun-ripened grasses and wild flowers, staring over the wall at the fat cattle idly chewing the cud in the distance. The only sound was the low drone of fat bumble-bees in the flowers at the base of the wall; everything else was quiet and still.

She didn't know what the dream the night before meant or whether it meant nothing at all and was simply a dream. But whatever, it had been wonderful to hold her baby and feel him in her arms, to be happy. Just to be his mam.

'Thank You.' She looked up into a sky which threatened a storm after the heat of the day, knowing she wasn't saying thank you to Father Fraser's God of fire and brimstone, nor yet Father Collins's who was altogether more reasonable. In fact she didn't think God was Catholic at all. He was . . . God. It was man who tried to put Him in the little boxes of creed and denomination. 'Thank You,' she said again, wiped her eyes and got back into the car.

There was a man stripped to the waist scything the thigh-length grass in what was indeed a field. Amy had parked the car where Bruce had told her to, crossed over the lane and opened the big three-bar farm gate secured to the gatepost with string. After carefully making sure the gate was fastened again she began to walk along the narrow track which had been trampled in the meadow.

The man had his back towards her but even from a distance of some hundred yards or so she could tell it wasn't Nick. This man was twice the breadth Nick had been when they last met; powerful muscles rippled under the nut-brown skin as he worked. And he must be an older man, much older, if the grey hair was anything to go by. Probably an odd-job man or gardener Nick employed, she thought as she wound her way up the slight incline towards the large sprawling cottage some distance away. Not that there looked as though much gardening had been done here for some time.

The man was whistling as he worked and intent on the task in front of him, the long curved blade of the scythe making short work of the gently waving grass. As she neared him she could hear the soft swish of the murderously sharp cutting tool, and thinking to warn him of her approach so he didn't jump and thereby do himself harm, she called, 'Hello there. I wonder if you know whether Nick Johnson is at home.'

The big figure froze, half bent, and then slowly straightened, and even before he turned to face her she knew. She braced herself for what she might see, determined not to react, and then she was staring into the green eyes, those beautiful green eyes. For a moment they were all she saw, the knobbly scars and grafted flesh beneath the thick shock of what once had been raven-black hair barely registering. 'Hello, Nick,' she said quietly.

He didn't answer her immediately; he stood quite still with the scythe now held loosely in his maimed hands as he watched her close the few yards between them. It was only when she was standing right in front of him and so close she could see there were no lashes to his eyelids that he said, 'Amy.' His voice was without expression.

He hadn't forgiven her. He didn't want her. The tight feeling in her chest made it difficult to speak but to her surprise her voice sounded quite normal when she managed to say, 'I hope you don't mind me coming to see you. I felt . . . Well, there are things to say.'

She had forgotten the painstakingly worded speech she had perfected over the last days, and faced with his continuing immobility she began to stammer. 'I know . . . I know it has been a long time and I should . . . should have written first or phoned, Bruce told me that. He . . . he gave me your address but please don't blame him, I made it difficult for him to refuse.'

'Why have you come?'

She was trembling from head to foot. He seemed so indifferent. She had prepared herself for anger or bitterness or even the biting sarcasm Nick did so well. In the past his tongue had had the cutting edge of a whip when someone displeased him. But this lack of emotion was something else. Perhaps he was embarrassed. Maybe he had someone waiting for him in the cottage above the field.

She drew on all her strength and said, 'Charles died a little while ago.'

He blinked but said nothing.

'I . . . I was thinking about what you said the last time we saw each other, that I had never loved you.' And then she knew she just had to say it or she would turn and run. 'You were wrong, I just wanted you to know that, that's all. Every day of the last eight years I have thought of you, every day.

I love you, I've never stopped loving you and I never could. I did what I did because I had to, not because I wanted to. There is a difference. I don't expect you to understand that but, if nothing else, believe that I loved you, that I still love you. That's all I wanted to say. I . . . I felt you had the right to know.' She lowered her head and stared at the cut grass, the rich smell wafting on the faint summer breeze. Her stomach was turning over and over.

She was just about to turn away when he said, 'Did Bruce tell you about me? About the accident?'

She nodded, raising her head and looking at him. 'At first he wouldn't, but when . . .' She stopped, her face burning, not knowing how to put it. She dropped her gaze again.

'What?'

'When I thought you had forbidden him to speak of you to me because you hated me, he told me.' She stopped again. Nick had made a sound deep in his throat and she lifted her gaze and looked into his eyes. They were as green as emeralds, green and clear and possessed of a drawing power that made you forget the damaged face. No, no, not forget it, that wasn't right, she told herself dazedly. The beautiful eyes gave the marred patchy skin something that was almost magnetic to the beholder. She could well understand how women still flocked to his door. He had something now he had never had when he was just handsome.

'How could you think I hated you?' he said huskily, his voice dropping so low she could scarcely hear him.

'Because I deserve your hate,' she whispered.

'Never.'

He had still made no move towards her and now she closed her eyes, knowing in the next moment she would fling herself at him and disgrace herself if she didn't shut him out from sight. The next move had to come from him and she still wasn't sure how he felt.

'And what do you think? Now you've seen me?' When she opened her eyes and then her mouth to reply, he silenced her with an upraised hand. 'I still take longer than a four-year-old child to dress myself and do up shoelaces. Could you stand to see me fumbling around or would it drive you mad with irritation or . . . pity?'

One little word, but it could separate them for all time. Charles had accepted and even been grateful for a love that had self-sacrifice linked to it. Nick would find it an abomination.

Her heart was racing. She had to make him *see*. And then the words were there. 'You are an original, Nick Johnson. You always were,' she said softly, a small smile playing about her mouth. 'I started off by being annoyed at your arrogance and pig-headedness and falling in love with you didn't change that. You can be selfish and insufferable and you never doubt that you're right, even when it's *proved* you're wrong. Life with you will never be calm and harmonious, I know that. But you are also tender and gentle and noble and vulnerable and a hundred other things besides, which I'm not going to tell you because you're already big-headed enough as it is. I can't promise you won't irritate me because when you're being mulish about something you're the most irritating man in the world. What I can promise is that the emotion of pity is a non-starter. It doesn't apply where you are concerned.'

He turned his head away from her for a moment, looking up into a sky from which the first fat raindrops were beginning to fall. Then he pulled her roughly into his arms, kissing her hard and long, his mouth only lifting from hers to mutter, 'Hold me tighter, tighter, Amy.'

And she held him tighter. She held him as though she would never let him go, hardly able to accept the miracle that had happened. She had dreamt of this, in her wildest dreams she had dreamt he would kiss her like this and she was glad the flames had spared the warm firm lips that had thrilled her in the past.

It was a long time before they slowly walked up the meadow to the cottage and the rain had all but stopped. They were both soaked to the skin but neither commented on it. Some weak rays of late evening sunshine were daring to poke through the clouds, and in the distance a faint rainbow stretched across the sky. A blackbird was singing in the hedgerow at the bottom of the field, the pure notes winging their way on the rain-washed air.

'You'll marry me soon and defy convention?' he asked softly. 'We've a lot of time to make up for, you and I.'

She thought of the raised eyebrows and gossip. The war might have changed things but not so much that a young widow marrying again within just a few weeks of her husband's death wouldn't attract some condemnation. And she didn't care a fig. 'Yes,' she said. 'Tomorrow if you like.'

'You shameless hussy.' He pulled her into him, his voice suddenly deadly serious when he said, 'I never stopped loving you, not even in the early days when I was so filled with anger and resentment that you had chosen him over me.' As she went to speak he put his finger on her lips. 'That was the way I saw it then,' he said softly. 'In stark black and white. It took this,' he touched his face, 'to start me thinking in shades of grey.'

'Oh, Nick.' She stared up at him, her blue eyes misty with love as she gently traced a path round Mr McIndoe's handiwork. 'Was it awful?' she whispered brokenly.

Nick thought of the thirty-one operations he had endured on his hands and face, of the sheer unadulterated torture as McIndoe had stripped the thick scaly scar tissue off his distorted webbed hands from knuckles to wrist before he could even start the skin grafts that would give him back the use of his fingers. The pain had been so bad at times he had found it hard to believe that such things could be, and only the fact that he was in a hospital where there were men worse off than him had kept him going. Agony and self-pity, hatred and revenge had been constant bedfellows, the last two emotions directed against the Germans. It had been his determination that they weren't going to win and leave him a burned cripple that had made him work towards getting fit enough to be passed for flying duties by the RAF Medical Board twenty months after the accident, despite being told by all and sundry it was highly unlikely. But he had done it. He had spent the last months of the war up in the air again. Ironic that it was easier to fly a plane than make a decent knot in his tie or do up his own shoelaces.

'Pretty awful,' he said now to Amy, kissing the tip of her nose. 'I'll tell you all about it one day.'

'You promise?'

He nodded. 'But not now,' he said quietly, his mouth falling on hers. For now it was enough that they had survived the war, that they were alive and together and a blackbird was singing on a lovely summer's evening in a free England. What better start to the future could there be than that?

EPILOGUE

Nick was not greedy. He only kept Amy all to himself for a few months but then it was he who broached the matter he knew was so dear to her heart, and together they started the adoption process.

The four children between the ages of five and nine who came to live at the cottage from children's homes were all war casualties. Two had been abandoned by single mothers when they were born, and the other two had been orphaned by Hitler's bombs. They came to their new parents one at a time over a period of nearly two years, and all four had problems. The physical injuries were easier to deal with than the emotional hurt, but Amy was waiting to lavish the care, reassurance, tenderness and most of all the love each one so badly needed. With Nick's help, a solid foundation was established in each child's life and the nightmares and fears began to fade.

As the years went by and the four grew into healthy and confident adults, more children were added to the family in the cottage. Foster children this time. More sad and sometimes defiant little faces that spoke of things children should never be called upon to bear but whose healing was slow but sure in the love they received.

Life was not always a bowl of cherries but it was family life, rich and varied and full of ups and downs.

The precious miniature of Bess had pride of place in the middle of the big wooden mantelpiece in the sitting room of the cottage, but it was to a little arbour in what was once the meadow – which had long since been landscaped into a garden-cum-adventure playground – that Amy was most often drawn. She always went there when she needed to find a sense of peace and direction for some problem or other.

The arbour had been built on the spot where she and Nick had embraced that first summer's evening so long ago when she had come back to him, and there was a small plaque mounted on the back of the wooden seat inside it.

It read:

In memory of my beautiful son.
Until the day I hold you in my arms, I hold you in my heart.

Your loving Mam

Always I'll Remember

Rita Bradshaw

Abigail Vickers is over the moon when she meets and falls in love with James Benson, who feels just the same way. Even the jealousy of her embittered mother, Nora, can't spoil Abby's happiness.

It's 1939, though, and at the declaration of war James decides to enlist. Nine months later, after the first bombs have fallen on Sunderland, news arrives which will break Abby's heart. Devastated, she joins the Land Army with her dear friend Winnie. Together with Rowena, a new chum, they're sent to a Yorkshire farm, where life for all three girls takes astonishing twists.

With Abby out of the picture, Nora seizes an opportunity to hurt her daughter in the most callous way. When the cruel truth comes to light, Abby needs all her strength to make the right choices and be true to those who need her most. Whether lasting happiness is hers to find, only time will tell . . .

Acclaim for Rita Bradshaw's novels:

'Romantic sagas don't come better than those penned by popular author Rita Bradshaw . . . A gritty tale with a soft centre, this is a beguiling story of love, betrayal and hope' *Lancashire Evening Post*

'Catherine Cookson fans will enjoy discovering a new author who writes in a similar vein' *Home and Family*

'All published writers have skill and creativity, but a few have more. It's called magic. I'm beginning to believe Bradshaw has it!' *Historical Novels Review*

0 7553 0623 6

headline

Candles in the Storm

Rita Bradshaw

A fierce storm is raging when Daisy Appleby is born into a fishing family, in a village north of Sunderland, in 1884. When her mother dies from the fever a few years later, it falls to Daisy to run the household and care for her family. Life's hard: the sea barely yields a living, and then there's always the anxious wait for the menfolk to return . . .

In the storm that takes her father and two brothers, Daisy risks her life to save a handsome young stranger from certain death. Although William Fraser is captivated by his spirited, beautiful rescuer, his rich and arrogant family despise Daisy. A tangled web of lies tears the couple apart, and Daisy must overcome tragedy before she can find her destiny . . .

Acclaim for Rita Bradshaw's novels:

'If you like gritty, rags-to-riches Northern sagas, you'll enjoy this' *Family Circle*

'Catherine Cookson fans will enjoy discovering a new author who writes in a similar vein' *Home and Family*

'Rita Bradsaw has perfected the art of pulling at heartstrings, taking the emotions to fresh highs and lows as she weaves her tale' *Sunderland Echo*

0 7472 6709 X

headline